HOLYOKE

The Belle Skinner Legacy

Cover Photograph by Terry Ashe
Book Design and Layout by Don Brunelle

 This is a work of actual history and fiction. Individual characters portrayed in this book are fictional, except for those who are named as real persons by historical accounts. Any resemblance to actual persons in this book is entirely coincidental. Any opinions expressed or implied are those of the author and do not reflect those of any real persons mentioned in this book who are living or dead.

Library of Congress Cataloging Information
Holyoke - The Belle Skinner Legacy
Published by
The Flats Press, P.O. Box 189, South Hadley, Massachusetts 01075
First Printing – November 2005
Printed in The United States of America by
Marcus Printing Company, Holyoke, Massachusetts

ISBN 0-9776196-0-5

HOLYOKE
The Belle Skinner Legacy

A historical novel that centers on the life of an extraordinary turn of the century woman amid the fall of a historic city, forewarning the decline of a great country

Jack Dunn

The Flats Press
P.O. Box 189, South Hadley, Massachusetts 01075

DEDICATION

For those people, including my parents, who built the City of Holyoke with the sweat of their brows, the kindness of their hearts and the strength of their faiths, making a better world for us all.

ABOUT THE AUTHOR

Jack Dunn is a native of Holyoke, Massachusetts, where he returned to live to write this book. He has previously written two books, THE DIARY OF GENERAL WILLIAM GOFFE, and THE VATICAN BOYS, as well as a screenplay, THE ANGEL OF HADLEY, that was based upon his first novel. An international businessman with a worldwide reputation for designing and selling medical electronic systems, Jack Dunn has written many magazine articles, both fictional and non-fictional, that have been published in the United States, Ireland and Great Britain. Several of his medical articles have also been translated into Chinese, and have been published in China.

His investigative novel, THE VATICAN BOYS published in 1997, detailed the circumstances surrounding the death of Roberto Calvi, the banker who was a central figure in a $790 million bank fraud scandal in Italy that involved members of the Masonic Lodge, also known as Propaganda 2 or P2, with ties to international crime syndicates. In 1892, the banker's body was found hanging from Blackfriars Bridge over the Thames River in the heart of London's financial district. Initially, the cause of death was listed as a suicide. THE VATICAN BOYS was a book posing questions regarding the real cause of death and the banker's relationship with the Opus Dei organization of the Catholic Church. The case was re-opened by Interpol and Scotland Yard in 2001. Since that time, two people have been convicted for the murder of the banker, and several have been indicted in crimes relating to it and other bank scandals, ones that not only involve the Vatican Bank, but several other large banks in several countries of Europe.

PHOTO BY TERRY ASHE

ACKNOWLEDGEMENTS

When I discovered that the last credible book about Holyoke was written many decades ago, I decided that it was time to take a closer look at the city's remarkable past, for several reasons. In doing so, I relied heavily upon two books to document the numerous important events that took place in Holyoke's past. HISTORY OF HOLYOKE MASSACHUSETTS by Anna U. Scanlon in 1939 was extremely informative, as was Wyatt Harper's book, written in 1948, THE STORY OF HOLYOKE. The book by Craig P. Della Penna, IMAGES OF AMERICA, HOLYOKE, with its wonderful old pictures and descriptions of Holyoke's historic buildings and landmarks was also helpful in documenting Holyoke's past.

As is the case of most books, this one could not have been produced without the help of many talented people. Professionally, I have many people to thank for helping me with this book. The first person I wish to recognize is another native of Holyoke, Ann Maggs, the singer and actress who plays Belle Skinner in performances at Wistariahurst. Most important to me is the archivist, Ann, who meticulously recorded and copied many of the letters, journals, newspaper articles and other relevant correspondences of Belle Skinner and the entire Skinner family. She shared with me all of this documentation and asked for nothing in return. In connection with this, I give my sincere thanks to all of the members of the Skinner, Kilborne, Warner and Hubbard families who have donated letters, journals, pictures, other materials and personal belongings to the City of Holyoke and the Wistariahurst Museum for the purpose of documenting Holyoke history. My good friend, Terry Ashe, a nationally famous photographer has won many awards for his remarkable pictures. The photograph for the cover that he took shows his keen eye and strong appreciation of beauty. Terry took the picture of City Hall while hanging off the roof of the building across the street from it. Only someone from Holyoke, with vivid memories of his life here growing up with us, would take such a risk to capture a timeless moment for everyone. I thank him and his lovely wife Sarah for helping me. Another friend from Holyoke, Don Brunelle designed the wonderful front and back covers for the book. As usual, with his creations, the artwork is stunning. His careful coloring and positioning of the images are a tribute to his remarkable skills. In addition, Don designed and produced the layout and made the final corrections for the book. This was not an easy task. The City of Holyoke has benefited greatly from his meticulous work and his involvement in this project. He and his wife, Jean, have been wonderful to me and I appreciate everything they have done. The Marcus family especially Ben Marcus and his daughter, Susan Goldsmith, could not have been more helpful to me and to everyone in Holyoke to make this book a memory for the city. They are a tribute to the community values that I write about in this book – the ones that make Holyoke great.

One of my editors, Kitty Axelson-Berry was very helpful with the formation of the first drafts of the book. In addition to this, she went with me to the village of Hattonchâtel to help me accurately document what Belle Skinner had done there. I am thankful to her for what she did. Bob Stock helped coordinate the final editing of the book for me. Debbie Babbitt did a wonderful job in editing the final versions of the book. Her gift is her ability to change the right words and sentences to make the book flow more smoothly. Her fine work is much appreciated. And I can't thank Sue Gallup enough for her outstanding job of proofreading the finished book before it went to press.

When I began this project, I first went to Yale University to the school's Collection of Musical Instruments where the Belle Skinner Collection is. The curators were most helpful in showing me what Belle had found. In addition, the staff and volunteers at the Wistariahurst Museum proved to be a wealth of information about the history of the Skinner family and the famous building where the family lived. Those at the Holyoke Public Library, especially Sarah Campbell, the curator of the Holyoke History Room and Archives, were all very informative and generous with their time and knowledge. The pictures provided by the library are wonderful additions to this book.

Personally, I am indebted to many whom I love. First, my daughter Kimberly; I began writing when she was a baby. I dedicated my first book to her twenty years ago. Like that work, this one is for her as is everything I write. It is what I leave behind that I know has the most value for her to remember me by. After my daughter, my family of origin is foremost in my thoughts. My parents, James and Eileen were the two most wonderful people I have ever met. They were perfect examples for us all of love, respect and a strong faith in God. These things, they learned in Holyoke. My brothers, Jim (his wife Judy), Frank (his wife Joanne) and Tom are strong – like their father. My brother Billy who died when he was three – is a life-long inspiration. My sisters Maryanne (her husband Ron), and Eileen are kind and loving – like their mother. My uncles, aunts, nephews and nieces, in-laws, cousins and my many other relatives who are members of the 'clan,' dead and alive are respectfully acknowledged as being very important to me. Families tie cities together, countries too. My cousin, Marty Dunn has been a tremendous help to me, and is as important as anyone else in the production of this book. Without his help this book would not have been finished. I thank Kathy Dunn for her unbending support and her continual involvement and dedication to the many worthy causes within Holyoke for which she volunteers.

In that one of Holyoke's greatest attributes is the humor of its many inhabitants, I feel compelled to interject a little here. Marty's father, John Dunn, my namesake told me that if I didn't pay tribute to his enormous achievements in the winning of the Second World War, and the building of our great city that he would come back to haunt me. So, I hereby bow to his wishes, not wanting to hear ringing objects in my sleep someday. There is only one "Beezer" in the world; he is a gift to us, as is his wife, Florence.

Dr. Sam Pizzi is one of the rocks that I have built my life on. His wife, Alberta gives him the strength to show many of us our way when the storms of life are howling, and we are blown off course for a time. They are both perfect examples of the morally courageous people I write about in this book. Dr. Peter DaSilva has been another wonderful friend to me. He and his wife, Janet, are a loving, respected couple. I appreciate them beyond words. Gary Ensor and his wife, Terry, are remembered fondly.

I would be remiss in not paying respect to those who were influential in motivating me to write this book. Like Holyoke, I see America as being in trouble, not just from the terrorists, who legitimately threaten us, but those who are more devious, those in our government who undermine us by not respecting what is right for everyone as directed by our sacred constitution. It's about legitimate power and the abuse of it. What is the truth and what are the lies? I gratefully acknowledge the thoughts of those who speak intelligently about these things, in helping me write this book. The courage to speak the truth is what will help us change things. Considering this, I have no trouble paying respect to anyone who charges a beach or fights in a desert in a war zone. Like the heroes of the past that landed on the beaches of France, I respectfully pay homage to our brave soldiers who have been, and are sent into what our leaders call "harm's way." I see little "harm" being done to the politicians who make the decisions to send our sons and daughters into battle. Part of the reason I wrote this book is to pay tribute to those brave people in the war zones fighting under questionable circumstances.

But, Holyoke and America are not just about courage, truth, family and doing the right thing for everyone. They are about responsibility, especially when times are tough, and the hurricanes are hitting us everywhere. Who can we trust to tell us what is real, and who is out just for their own interests? It's time we all took a good look at who "they" are, and where they are taking us.

I could go on and on for pages, acknowledging lists of people from Holyoke and elsewhere who are important to me, those responsible for making Holyoke and America such an interesting place to write about. But, I think I'll let the pages that follow say the rest. Suffice it to say that everyone who I know, knew of, read, saw or heard about from Holyoke has contributed in some manner to the creation of this book. Without all of you, there would be no story.

AUTHOR'S NOTE

Belle Skinner, 1866–1928. It came as no surprise to me that one of the champions of women's suffrage was from Holyoke, since so many talented people have grown up there. What is interesting about Belle Skinner is that she completed most of her accomplishments before she could even vote.

In life, driven by experiences, circumstances and luck, one can create or destroy. Nothing stands still. This principle is called momentum (or movement). Once in motion, a body remains in motion, unless acted upon by an outside force to produce a change. Usually applied to physics, this law applies brilliantly to the human condition.

Belle Skinner was an outside force. By using the power of her wisdom and energy, she changed the direction of many things. However, she has never been given adequate credit for the effect she has had on the Women's Movement in America or for that matter the world.

PROLOGUE

Holyoke is a warning. It is an omen of what will happen in the United States if the moral, spiritual, social and governmental declines continue unfettered without reversal.

The following excerpt from Honor Holyoke, The 75th Anniversary, 1873–1948 is applicable not only to Holyoke, but our great country, The United States of America.

"So, we come down to the present day in our brief chronicle of the great story of Holyoke. In perspective we may see the good and the bad, the profit and the loss, the mistakes and the all-wise decisions. Looking backward we review a long period of agriculture beginnings upon which was superimposed a fast-moving industrial civilization. Climactic moments appear in the daring triumph of mid-century skill that encompassed the harnessing of the great river, to the overnight instrumentation of the industrial revolution, the building of a city. Crowning achievements have been the raising living standards through the rapid production of industrial wealth, the successful upward struggle of people who pinned their faith on the ideal of America, the resolution of economic stresses and religious intolerance in the light of a kindlier day, the development of a culture that is truly Holyoke's own, the growth of a genuine love of community that comes from the belonging to a city that is worthy of the best."

When we read this, we should bear in mind that it was written by a resident of the community in 1948, when Holyoke was thriving and vibrant. Because the city's economy and the quality of life provided were inspiring, its people were full of excitement. Holyoke rode this wave for another twenty-five years, until the late 1960s, when a terrible downslide began. It ultimately brought the city to where it is now: a shell of what it once was. What cost billions of dollars, hundreds of thousands of lives and more than a hundred years to build, was destroyed in less than forty years. A city that should have been preserved as a historical monument, documenting America's heroic past, is instead a neglected national treasure.

INTRODUCTION

The first page of advertisements in books like HONOR HOLYOKE, THE 75TH ANNIVERSARY, 1873–1948, (printed by Doyle Printing Company of Holyoke, Massachusetts, in 1948) is routinely reserved for the most respected businesses in the city. In this book, it is largely taken up by a description of the founder of the Skinner companies:

"The Hundredth Anniversary of William Skinner & Sons marks the beginning of the second century in textile progress, paralleling the greatest period of Industrial development in our country's history. In the course of a century, the name of Skinner has traveled far and wide. The man who started all this was born in London in 1824. He worked a few years in an English Dye Plant before coming to the United States, a boy of 19. He formed the company of Warner and Skinner, but soon withdrew to establish his own mill on the banks of Mill River in Williamsburg, Massachusetts. Five miles up the Mill River an earth dam held a large reservoir of water for the citizens of Williamsburg. One spring morning the dam burst and the cry of flood rang down the valley. Although 200 people died in the flood, it might have been much worse had not the watchman at the reservoir and the driver of a milk wagon spread the alarm. On hearing their cries William Skinner ran through his mill, warning his employees to take to the hills. He himself was the last to leave the doomed building that was wasted away at his very heels as he fled for high ground. William Skinner saved all of his employees but the business was gone. Two things only remained, his private home and the reputation of Skinner products. Skinner moved his house to Holyoke, Massachusetts, built his new mill and resumed production of his quality products. His two sons, William and Joseph Allen, joined him in the business which became known as William Skinner and Sons."

By the time William Skinner died in 1902, he was one of the richest, most successful businessmen in America. He left his fortune to his family.

PREFACE

Holyoke is a city in Western Massachusetts, in the United States of America, with a remarkable history dating back to before the American Revolution. In 1620, Massasoit, the Native American Chief of the Wampanoag, governed most of Massachusetts and Rhode Island. He signed the earliest recorded treaty in New England with Governor John Arver. The treaty established peace among the Indians and the Pilgrims. That treaty, as well as the good relations between the Indians and the settlers, was to last for over forty years. In 1621, the Pilgrims invited Massasoit and some of his people to the first Thanksgiving Day held in the colonies. His eldest son, Wamsutta, became the Sachem (or Chief) in 1661, when his father died; and Wamsutta honored the treaties. In 1662, his second son, Metacomet, (known as King Phillip by the settlers) succeeded his brother as Chief of the tribe. He honored the treaties until early 1675, when he led an uprising against the settlers with a confederation of tribes (Wampanoag, Metacomet and Norwottuck), in a conflict now known as King Phillip's War. He had been provoked when his territories were encroached upon. It was a brief conflict. By the summer of 1676, King Phillip and his Indians had been defeated by the colonists in several major battles. The last ones were fought in and around Hadley. Phillip was killed in August of that year. At the same time, the Agawam Indians had stopped attacking the settlers in the Springfield area. Along the Connecticut River, just north of Springfield, there began a small settlement in the valley. It was called the Third Parish.

Like Springfield, the Third Parish was relatively flat with slight dips and turns, and grand views in most directions. To its west rose a series of tall hills. To its north rose an unusual range that extended in an east–west direction; unlike most other ranges in the East, which extend north–south. It was breathtakingly beautiful.

The John Riley family was the first immigrant family to settle and build there in 1729. Before long the Third Parish had donned the new name, Ireland Parish. It was not just the Riley family's heritage that brought about this name change, but the shared heritage of an influx of settlers that had arrived at this time. The Irish newcomers established the first fortress in Holyoke, around 1730, on what was once called Country Road, now Northampton Street. Not long after building the fort, the settlement's farmers began to work the nearby soil on that same road, not far from today's Cherry Street.

More than one hundred years later, in 1850, Holyoke was established as a town. It was named after Captain Elizur Holyoke, an explorer who had first arrived in the 1630s. Holyoke was officially incorporated as a city of the Commonwealth of Massachusetts in 1873 and soon after had its first mayor, W.B.C. Pearsons. He was followed by Mayor H.P. Crafts. By the time the third mayor, William Whiting, won the keys to the city, Holyoke was fast becoming a frontrunner in this country's Industrial Revolution. Under Mayor Whiting's leadership, aided by the efforts of prosperous local businessmen, the city became world famous for its incredible paper and textile production capacities.

By the turn of the 20th century the Paper City, as it was called, was not only one of the most prosperous urban centers in the United States, it was also unique in other ways. Holyoke was the first planned industrial community in the nation to utilize a system of dams and canals for generating and transferring power to its mills. Energy generated by the use of flowing water from a dam that at the time of its construction on the Connecticut River, was the largest in the world; and a multi-level canal system, unlike any other anywhere, put Holyoke thirty years ahead of the rest of the world with its innovations.

Holyoke's factories and mills produced paper, silk, wire and many other fine products. Its companies were heavily invested in, being well respected by New York and Boston investors, the nation's moneymen at the time. Businessmen from all over the world came to Holyoke to buy and sell goods. When all the mills were running at full capacity, Holyoke produced a greater variety of industrial products in a year than any other city in the world.

In the early 1900s Holyoke was a vigorous city, gleaming in the midst of an incredible growth phase. This was due mainly to the efforts of talented people who were unified in making their city and lives productive and meaningful. Without a doubt, by the 1940s, Holyoke was one of the most affluent cities in America. It was a peaceful place for those who had fought in the war to return to at the end of World War II, a symbol of hope for a seCuré future. Those who came back were not disappointed. In its greatness, the city produced hundreds of thousands of successful people, *The Children of Holyoke*, who now are scattered all over the world, sharing the values learned from the great men and women who built the city and those who came here to live.

The decay and collapse of Holyoke began in the late 1960s. Some saw it before others and got out. Others, being proud (or maybe just loyal), took longer to leave, and some remained. When operations were moved to places where labor was cheaper and power and supplies were more accessible, the City of Holyoke began to decline with the closing of a number of its larger mills. One after another, the businesses left when labor and utilities became more expensive. Workers were no longer spending their money from earnings paid by the mills; retail stores downtown were affected and began to close up or move out.

Within a few short years most of the higher-class stores had relocated to a shopping mall on the outskirts of the city, where it was newer and safer. When the mills and businesses closed, the blocks of tenement apartments that once housed the workers became vacant. There were hundreds of them. Not wanting to lose rents, corrupt landlords and their politicians sought out other ways to keep their investments alive; they found that they could successfully solicit the federal and state governments to bring in tenants from outside the country for their apartments.

It was around this time that the illegal drug industry also invaded Holyoke. It came from New York and Colombia and began to locate its dealers in the lower wards of the city in these once vacant apartments. Holyoke became a mecca for drug peddlers. Drugs and poverty are a bad combination. These two factors produced a complete social and economic collapse in Holyoke. Promising the would-be immigrants a better life, the landlords and drug dealers used and abused them once they arrived here. In doing so, they began a process that contributed significantly to the decay of the entire community. The landlords bled the welfare systems for their own gain, and reinvested little in the community (money that would have benefited everyone). They were a stark contrast to the founders of Holyoke who would never have put up with illegal drugs and did not neglect to invest in the community. What can be said about the drug dealers' effect on Holyoke? They are the real terrorists, destroying most of the cities in America, invading our country from the inside. It is a crime.

Because of these corruptions, Holyoke has been enduring a slow agonizing death. The drugs and violence, accompanied by citizen apathy and the city government's inability to deal with the overwhelming problems, have contributed to the social and economic decay of the city. It's what happens when the wrong people take control and place their own interests above what is best for everyone. Today, many of the wonderful buildings constructed during the city's boom era are gone, boarded up or burned down. In comparison to the time of its financial greatness, Holyoke is a disaster economically. Socially it is struggling, trying to breathe. Most of what was memorable in the city is gone, except for those few museums, historical societies and organizations whose members are trying desperately to keep the memories of Holyoke alive. A once lovely and proud city sits sadly in a valley at the bottom of the still beautiful mountains that surround it, crying out hopelessly to return to its honorable past.

One more page needs to be read from the Honor Holyoke 75th Anniversary book to show how quickly things can change if the people in a city, or a country, don't protect what is of value. It is the First Prize Essay in a contest run by the city of Holyoke, written by Robert Gibbons in 1948:

> *"Our Heritage is a challenge to us. It is a challenge to carry forward all the hopes and ideals our fathers foresaw; a challenge to keep unblemished our natural inheritances, our glorious mountains and the picturesque river, to keep them ever beautiful. It is indeed a challenge to keep our city a prosperous one, a city that will continue to grow, a city with a name in the world, a challenge to keep alive her culture, to keep her high educational opportunities and her churches, always structures of beauty and inspiration. It is truly a challenge to keep Holyoke a healthy city with breathing space for all, good living conditions, good working conditions, good hospitals, and excellent playgrounds. A challenge to keep her a city in which men can differ politically and religiously and still live peacefully. Ours is a beautiful heritage, one that it is a privilege to live up to, and a heritage so high and so noble that our children's children, even as we, will be proud to accept it."*

I wonder what Mr. Gibbons would write if he could see Holyoke today? But I guess we need to know where we have been in order to see where we can go.

Photo Courtesy of the Holyoke Public Library

"There are only three cities in the world, Holyoke, Paris and New York." – Belle Skinner

ONE

New Haven Connecticut • December 13, 2004

With the 2004 presidential elections over and George Bush re-elected to a second term, Maggie O'Reilly was feeling depressed as she walked out the front doors of the Duncan Hotel on Chapel Street in New Haven. How could Bush have been "re-elected?" Had the elections been rigged or did voters actually want him to be president? Would the world survive another four years of him? It would take only five or ten minutes to get to the church, so she had plenty of time. Carefully looking up and down the street before crossing to the other side, Maggie thought idly how much she hated being late to Mass.

At the corner, she turned onto a side street that lead to College Street and then headed left along the New Haven Green, passing the First Methodist Church. She could see the large pillars of Woolsey Hall up ahead. This meant she was only a few blocks away. As the cold air was biting at her, she quickened her pace, looking forward to the comforting warmth of the church.

It was hard to stop thinking about her personal situation: how things seemed to change so fast. She had left her job as a Boston Globe news reporter a year ago to work for the presidential campaign of U.S. Senator John Kerry from Massachusetts. She had been a personal aide to the senator, a high level player in his entourage since almost the beginning of the campaign. The excitement she had felt, expecting a new beginning in America, had ended abruptly with the Republican machinery defeating the Democrats. How they had managed it, she still didn't know. It was hard to understand how people made such bad choices, she thought. In fact, she didn't even believe that the elections were valid. Reinforcing her position, she remembered that Kerry had been the clear winner in voter exit polls. Again, she wondered why the Democrats had not contested the election. There were some serious questions about the legitimacy of the last two presidential elections, when Bush had been "elected" and then "re-elected." Whether or not the elections had been fixed or the number of votes fabricated, the Republicans had squeaked to victory in key states. They had used computer hardware and software of dubious reliability; and relied on talk-radio and television to increase the level of voter fear and hate, mostly of outsiders and homosexuals. To Maggie, it didn't seem that gay rights should be a main issue for voters.

Those in John Kerry's camp, who anticipated that the Republicans would be this organized and devious, lost out to others who could not see the mind control that Bush's people were employing to get people to believe that they were in imminent danger from terrorists and others. Moreover, what irritated her most was the Republicans' use of God's name in the last stages of the election. They had used God: to get elected, to get their mandate to kill, to gain more power and control and to accumulate more personal wealth. Maggie was still wondering when God had become so heavily involved in the election, and why the Bush people thought they were his chosen representatives on earth, when they were murdering innocent people for oil. Thinking about it made her cringe.

Maggie knew it was over now. Now that Kerry had lost, she had to evaluate her own future. She had to move on, like it or not. She'd do the best she could. Starting here, in New Haven, with her son, she needed to make up for some lost time.

She was still hoping that something dramatic would happen to make everyone realize how dangerous these people in Washington were. They kept saying: "A new day is rising in America, a new time." This was on their newscasts, from the television stations they owned. It was sickening to listen to the lies. It was even worse to think that they were announcing a terrible "new day:" the Apocalypse, Armageddon, and the End Times too many of them looked forward to. Even without the Apocalypse, one way or another, America was in a lot of trouble. Without knowing it, they were going to get what they had chosen. The country had been duped.

Maggie realized that she was one of the lucky ones. Being an only child and a trust fund baby—her father died when she was in her twenties—opened up options for her. Taking a year or two off from work was not an issue. Others didn't have this luxury. Most of those working on Kerry's campaign needed to get the system fixed. They needed to stop the new moneymen from stealing from them and diverting their money to the ultra-wealthy, and to war. They had children to feed. With the spiral of effects, from companies cutting jobs and prices soaring, they had no savings left.

As she reached Grove Street, Maggie tried to change from her negative rumination on dirty politics. She took a right, thinking about more pleasurable things like her son, and stopped for a second. Maggie leaned against a building to shield her face from the wind and get her bearings. The cold of the day was almost disorienting.

"Politics is not the only emotionally satisfying thing in life. At least we won the World Series," Maggie said, laughing to herself. Win a baseball game and lose the country. Thinking about the Red Sox's seventh game, Maggie wondered how something as silly as "the curse of the Bambino" finally ending, could make her so happy.

Two students passed Maggie and she overheard them talking loudly. They were glad their exams were over. It brought back memories of Maggie's college days. She remembered her time at Boston University when, after an exam, she had met Bill, the man she would marry. And now their son, Tom, had the same exam pressures. It caused her to flinch just thinking about it. He'll be done later this afternoon, she thought. Then, if I can find the restaurant he likes, where he wants to have pizza, somewhere around the School of Music, I'll buy him a beer and we can talk about his test. Tom always did this to her. He would make her look for a place that she didn't know how to get to. She wanted to take him to a nice restaurant, like the one at the hotel. He wanted to go to the place where all the kids hung out. But, he would never let her spend a lot of money on him. He was thoughtful in that way. Ever since Bill died, five years ago, Tom had tried to make things easier for her. She smiled, thinking of how she loved him for that. He was a good kid.

Maggie started thinking about Bill, missing him terribly, and then stopped. Her counselor had warned her not to wallow in thoughts of Bill being gone. She tried to think about the church that she was going to. Its tower was now visible as she looked farther down the street. If she focused on it, the architecture, the dark stonework, the thoughts might go away, but they didn't. Bill was gone and she hated that fact. She couldn't stand feeling the loneliness. Maggie forced herself again to think of other things. She considered the many forms of intellectual and physical stimulation she could employ to free her mind of negative thinking. Music and art were the two that excited her the most. At this point, sex was not an option. Her mind was racing, trying to rid itself of the memories of her husband. The church would comfort her. It would stop her from dwelling on what she had lost. Church was her salvation.

The stone structure was directly across the street. At Saint Mary's, Maggie would try to lift her spirits. God would help her. She read the sign, "The Property of the Dominican Friars," and remembered how she and Tom had come there during his orientation weekend. Maggie couldn't remember who had taught her about spiritual things, or when she decided she needed God in her life to feel whole. She couldn't pinpoint the exact moment when she had decided to start practicing her religion again, to attend Mass, to pray. Was it because of the foundation laid by the nuns in Catholic grade school? Perhaps that had finally taken hold, she thought. It could have been after Bill died, when she was distraught and felt helpless; a kind priest had come to help ease her pain.

Now, Maggie was a devout Catholic who went to church at least three times a week. She had neglected her religious devotions during the months of the campaign. Staying busy, she didn't have an opportunity to even dwell on the past. Nowadays, with plenty of time on her hands, the memories of Bill flooded her head. It was time to reevaluate her priorities, and get back to what worked. Maggie's faith gave her something to hold onto. Maggie's faith worked. Last night she'd dreamt about Bill. Remembering her dream, she knew today would be tough. She'd need her faith to get her through.

Maggie would try to be inconspicuous, but it was impossible. Walking into the church, she was conscious of being noticed. Tall, almost six feet without shoes, Maggie moved with the grace of a ballet dancer. Years of dance and a short-lived Broadway career had molded her body's every movement. She even looked graceful walking on concrete and stone. What's more, Maggie was always impeccably dressed. Now, carefully folding her olive-colored London Fog overcoat, she entered a side pew. She tried unsuccessfully to be quiet.

Her long blond hair settled down around Maggie's shoulders, as she knelt to pray. Turning her head, the sun streamed through the stained glass windows above, and she shielded her blue-green eyes from the sun. Athletic and beautiful, Maggie was one of those good looking people others wondered about: Why was she so lucky? Maggie didn't think this way about herself; being beautiful wasn't always a plus. For the most part, Maggie didn't even feel attractive. She was a little shy, and even more so, since Bill had died. Though she was comfortable being forty-three, she was not at ease being by herself. Maggie was often sad, and her therapist told her that she was understandably grieving. Since leaving the campaign trail, getting through each day was becoming a chore. The two things that kept Maggie going were her son, who was doing so well, and her faith in God. Looking up to the light, she thanked God for both.

There was an African-American nun in a light blue dress two rows behind Maggie. The nun was crying tears of sorrow and she caught Maggie's attention. She turned her focus back to the marble altar where the priest was beginning to say Mass. But, she couldn't help but wonder why the nun was crying? Maggie's thoughts returned to the good things left in her life, and she was grateful for several moments. Just then, as always, sorrow, bitterness and dismay, the emotions she feared most, re-asserted themselves.

"At least half of us aren't mindless," she said aloud, thinking about the huge number of people who had voted for her candidate. We're going to have to suffer along with those who voted for President Bush, not that I believe so many actually did, she thought. And even so, it was hardly the 'mandate' the Republican party claimed it was. It's like giving Jack the Ripper a knife. Realizing she was just working herself into a tizzy, she tried to focus on the holy man in the front of the chapel. She needed to bring peace into her life through Jesus Christ. For some reason, the black nun in back of her singled her out, handed her a pamphlet, and returned to her pew, crying again. It was "Conditions for a Just War," published by the United States Catholic Conference, Inc. in 1994, that the nun had handed to Maggie. On the front cover was a photograph of a soldier and the words, "The fifth commandment forbids the intentional destruction of human life." Then it outlined the acceptable conditions for taking life. Maggie realized the nun had been crying over the dead children. Why hadn't John Kerry used this kind of public relations in his campaign? The election was deeply upsetting to humanitarians all over the world. The conditions were not being met and innocent people were being killed. Why weren't they searching out alternative solutions of more intelligent and just ways to fight international terrorism? Opening the brochure, Maggie read:

> *"The strict conditions for legitimate defense by military force require rigorous consideration. The gravity of such a decision makes it subject to rigorous conditions of moral legitimacy. At one and the same time:*

- *The damage inflicted by the aggressor on the nation or community of nations must be lasting, grave and certain*
- *All other means of putting an end to it must have been shown to be impractical or ineffective*
- *There must be serious prospects of success*
- *The use of arms must not produce evils and disorders graver than the evil to be eliminated. The power of modern means of destruction weighs very heavily in evaluating this condition."*

Knowing that George Bush and his administrators had never, and would never in the future, consider adhering to any of these conditions, Maggie nearly burst out in tears too. She suspected that Bush and company did not actually have the ability to understand complex matters. Her tears, suppressed, turned into near-hysterical laughter, a breach of etiquette that didn't matter to her. Those who were in power should be ashamed and embarrassed they had used God's name in vain.

TWO

Holy Mass lasted only forty minutes, but Maggie stayed longer, wanting to pray by herself. She thought about the last few years. Nothing was the same without Bill who had not only been her partner, but her best friend. They shared everything, had a terrific son, a good life and then bang; he had a stroke and was gone. Maggie was alone with their son. It had not been easy for her. She missed Bill more each day.

Working at the Globe and then for Kerry had been useful diversions. Maggie would not admit it openly, but she was struggling to keep herself together. The investigative reporting had worked for a while, but something had been missing from the politics. What it came down to was that the Democrats were cowards and the Republicans were delusional. Maggie thought a new approach was necessary to change the system. Government definitely needed a good cleaning out. She would start with the Supreme Court, whose members were supposed to protect the Constitution, but did not. Perhaps she should organize her own citizens' meeting involving a wider variety of people, and she would give it teeth and demand change. It might be time to remove politicians from defining politics.

All of these thoughts ran through Maggie's head, as she looked at Jesus on the cross, above the altar. She wondered if He had been at all interested in politics. Concluding that He had not been, Maggie realized it was past one o'clock, the time she had planned to leave. She had reflected enough on events and situations that she had no control over; praying wouldn't change politics. Maggie decided to concentrate on things in her own life that she could have an effect on.

Maggie strolled down Hillhouse Avenue, knowing she had a few hours to kill before meeting her son for dinner. A red stone building with six small pillars in front momentarily caught her attention, or perhaps it was the strong wind that had suddenly blown her in the direction of its entrance. Whatever the case, the sign on the door interested her: "Yale

University, Collection of Musical Instruments."

Hoping to warm up, use the restroom and perhaps see an interesting exhibit, Maggie went into the Museum. She immediately noticed a woman with short brown hair and blue-green eyes in an office, standing near the desk of an older gentleman with a reddish beard.

"May we help you?" the woman said courteously.

"I'm here visiting my son and saw your sign," Maggie responded. "Do you have a bathroom I could use?" She whispered the words.

"Sure, it's down the hall," the woman answered, pointing.

A few minutes later Maggie returned to the office. "Are you interested in our collection?" the man asked. "Would you like to see it?"

"Yes, I guess." Maggie was hesitant, but it was cold outside and she had some time on her hands.

"Forgive us, my dear," said the older gentleman. "My name is Richard Roberts. I am the director of music here, and this is my wife, Susan, the curator of the collection." He smiled at Maggie in a friendly way, noting her elegance.

"Maggie, Maggie O'Reilly." She stumbled on her name as she momentarily lost her balance. Maggie had tripped on something, a stone block used to keep the door open in the summer.

Sorry about that," Richard apologized. "That damn thing is always getting in the way." It was apparent he was irritated with his own negligence.

"I'm fine." Maggie said reassuringly.

"Do you mind, Richard, if I give Maggie a tour?" Susan asked her husband.

"No, don't be silly. We can finish all this up later," Richard answered.

"Why don't you start upstairs?" he suggested, continuing to observe Maggie, thinking she looked familiar. Perhaps she was a model or actress.

"This way then," Susan said, as she motioned to the stairway nearby.

The two walked up the stairs, making small talk. Their conversation was mostly about Maggie's son, how he enjoyed his political science program, loved Yale and his professors. Yes, Maggie had noticed that all of the students were nervous because it was exam week. And no, neither Maggie nor any members of her family had gone to school here. When they reached the top of the stairs, the idle chatter ceased as a painting caught Maggie's attention. There, before her, was a woman in a red dress.

"Why do they always look so serious in old portraits?" Maggie asked the curator.

Susan looked back down the stairs, making sure her husband couldn't hear her. "Her dog died," she answered, showing her sense of humor.

"Excuse me." Maggie was caught off guard by Susan's unexpected good humor.

The curator suppressed her laughter at first, and then unexpectedly let it out. Susan appeared to be more relaxed than she'd been in eons. Enjoying the moment, she led Maggie into a spacious room. Recovering, Susan said apologetically, "I'm sorry, I couldn't resist. I'll not do it again."

"That's really OK," Maggie said, immediately sympathizing with the curator. "Who was she?" Maggie asked, referring to the portrait they had passed.

"Belle Skinner," Susan responded, matter-of-factly.

"And who was Belle Skinner?" Maggie felt an immediate camaraderie with Susan, and hoped she wasn't one of your straight-laced museum curators. They had already spoken casually about personal things, and Maggie found herself eager for more conversation.

"Probably one of the most interesting ladies of the last century, Maggie. She had one of the finest collections of musical instruments in the world. It is on loan to Yale."

Maggie saw spinets, pianos and harpsichords, about fifteen of them in all. "What makes them so special?" It was a reasonable question.

"Their age of course," replied Susan brightly, "the condition of the pieces and the fact that not many like them exist. They are all one of a kind." She was more focused now. Maggie could see that Susan was proud of the collection. "Belle Skinner was a member of the William Skinner Family of Holyoke, Massachusetts," Susan continued. "They were silk and satin merchants. The man who founded the company, her father, was William Skinner. He had come to the United States from London. Not much is known about him before he arrived, apart from the fact that he had worked for an English dye plant. Once in the U.S., he formed a company in Williamsburg, Massachusetts, with another man. William Skinner soon withdrew to establish his own mill—later, it became mills—on the banks of the Mill River in Williamsburg." She paused and then went on.

"Mill River was not a big river, but five miles up from Williamsburg an earth dam and reservoir had been built. It held back water for the citizens of the town to use and release for their mills. One spring morning in 1874, with the snow melting and a downpour of rain, the dam burst. Most of Williamsburg, including Mr. Skinner's Unquomonk Mills, was totally destroyed by the raging water. In addition to the buildings that were washed away, about two hundred people lost their lives.

After the tragedy, Mr. Skinner was enticed by a man named James Newton, a builder who represented himself and the Holyoke Water Power Company, to come to Holyoke and build a new mill. Newton offered him a parcel of land, rent-free for five years, for a mill or mills, and property to build a house on that amounted to a city block, all for one dollar.

Taking advantage of the opportunity, William Skinner moved his wife, Sarah Elizabeth Allen, his children and what was left of his business, to Holyoke. In addition, he moved what was left of their house in Williamsburg, one section at a time, on rafts and ox-drawn carts. The house was set up on property delineated by Hampshire, Beech, Cabot and Pine Streets. The Skinner home was called Wistariahurst, after the hanging vines that his wife loved and planted there. The vines even did well," Susan smiled. "They established themselves within a few years, and were an impressive adornment when they flowered in the spring. The house, by the way, still exists. It has been restored, and is now a museum owned by the City of Holyoke.

William Skinner's first mill in Holyoke was completed and began operations in 1874. When his two sons, William and Joseph Allen, joined him in the business two years later, it became known as William Skinner and Sons. By 1902, the company was generating revenues of $6.5 million. They had expanded its operations all over the world. The family operated their business in Holyoke for eighty seven years. Their main sales office was on Broadway in New York City, and other smaller offices were all over the United States. By the time they sold their business to The Indian Head Mills Company in 1961, the Skinners were known all over the world, and their family was incredibly wealthy." Susan paused. Seeing Maggie's interest, Susan continued with enthusiasm, pleased to have such a willing audience. "The little girl in the painting with Belle is her younger sister, Katherine, and the other girl is her older sister, Elizabeth. The two boys were William and Joseph. William was the oldest of the children in the family, and Joseph was born third after Elizabeth." Susan chuckled, thinking of how serious the portrait looked. She finished her historical account, and glanced back at the painting, reflecting on the fact that Maggie was the first person to comment on the Skinner's demeanor.

"How do you know all of this?" Maggie asked, impressed by the conciseness of her account.

"They pay me a lot of money to know this," Susan responded. Encouraged, she picked up where she had left off. "The history of the family is important, but their incredible generosity is even more impressive. What Belle left to us is priceless. Come here. Look at the quality of this instrument." Susan motioned for Maggie to follow. "Some pieces in the room are from the Belle Skinner Collection, and some are gifts from other benefactors."

In the center of the room was a small musical instrument that looked quite delicate. Susan began her descriptions knowing she had captured Maggie's attention. Pointing to her left, at a Spinet, she said, "That one was once owned by Marie Antoinette. Turning Maggie's attention to the one in front of them, she said, "This is an Ottavina Spinet, made by Pascal Taskin in Paris, in 1778. The case and lid are varnished with an ivory background, and the interior of the lid and name board are delicately painted. There is a rose painted on the soundboard with the maker's initials. Look, but don't touch." Susan was reciting her memorized descriptions. "They both are part of the Belle Skinner Collection."

Maggie was impressed. Putting it into perspective, she said, "So, around the time we were fighting the revolutionary war, this was made in Europe."

"Precisely," Susan answered.

"Follow me." Susan continued, purposely directing Maggie away from the piece de resistance for now. "This is a virginal."

Maggie interrupted her. "A what?"

"A virginal, which is like a harpsichord. It was made in London, in 1666, by Adam Leversidge. The mechanisms are the same, but the case is designed differently. The case and concave lid are oak. The interior and soundboard are painted. And, the inside case is decorated with embossed gilded paper. This instrument is also part of the Belle Skinner Collection."

"And this?" Maggie asked, moving ahead of Susan. Maggie was looking at the painting on an instrument. She recognized it as being Flemish. "What is this little jewel?"

"A double virginal."

"You've got to be kidding, a double?"

"Made by Hans Ruckers in Antwerp, in 1591."

"What is this worth?" It was the same question everyone asked.

"It's priceless," Susan replied. As a matter of fact, when this semester is over, I plan on bringing in some of my own equipment to document its age and condition more accurately. Once I'm through, it will be even more priceless than it is now! Does that make sense, more priceless?"

Maggie was captivated by what she saw. These items gave her a sense of timelessness. They were so painstakingly wrought hundreds of years ago, and so carefully preserved ever since. It was compelling to imagine them being played by people whose lives were so different from hers, yet so much the same.

"The painting on the interior of the lid shows the contest between Apollo and Marsyas," Susan continued. It was the kind of painting you'd only see in well-established art museums, a dark background, contrasted by a wonderful panoply of lighter shades for the subjects in the foreground. "Only eight have survived. Belle Skinner found this one." Susan, realizing how overpowering some objects of art can be, directed Maggie's attention away from the double virginal to other, less commanding pieces in the room.

After about an hour of viewing harpsichords, spinets, guitars, a violoncello, lute, oboe and other musical instruments, Susan invited Maggie to have a cup of tea. Drained from walking around the museum and seeing the instruments, Maggie accepted the invitation without hesitation.

"How could anyone have so much?" Maggie talked, as Susan poured the tea.

"From what I understand, this is only a bit of their collection, the tip of the iceberg. The Skinners actually donated other objects of art, money and buildings to many different institutions all over the world. They were an incredibly wealthy family, and very generous." Susan sat down, smiling happily; she could tell she had found a like-minded woman.

"It's hard to imagine someone giving up so much." Maggie said, humbled by the Skinner family's generosity.

"It depends on how each person values what they have. What is its significance in their lives?" Susan had thought about this topic a lot. "It depends on what's important to them. Some people are never satisfied. They want to get more and more. They are greedy in their pursuit of money. The Skinners were not at all like that. They loved people, and wanted to share with the world what they'd found and loved."

Maggie was impressed. This woman, this curator, was not afraid to speak her mind. Susan was direct, and what she voiced was truthful. Maggie was reminded of why she had joined John Kerry's campaign; trying to put a stop to the conspiracy of greed, she had done what she could.

"Tell me about Belle Skinner, Susan. What was she like?" Maggie was captivated by the history that surrounded her. She was engrossed, and couldn't wait to hear more. God had given her this gift, in being here, in this museum.

After a lengthy discourse and the discussion that ensued about Belle Skinner, the two parted company at the front door. "Good luck, Maggie. Please tell your son to stop by. I'd be happy to show him around."

Dazzled, Maggie walked down College Street. Something had just happened that she couldn't explain. It was as if a switch had gone off, and it felt good. There was a surge of energy she had not experienced since the election results had been announced. Maggie heard the cell phone ring in her purse, and quickened her pace. Tom was probably checking in with her, because she was late. So, Maggie would find the restaurant quickly, they'd have pizza and beer, and the long anticipated mother–son time together, before she'd return home in the morning. Just beyond the School of Music and around the corner, Maggie saw the sign for the restaurant. As she crossed the street to meet her son, she could not stop thinking about what she had just been in the midst of. The instruments had been so beautiful, she thought to herself, and what was up with the etymology of that one, the virginal. Maggie couldn't help but chuckle.

THREE

Maggie slept later than usual the following morning. It was Thursday, nearing the end of a long week. Last night, she and Tom had stayed at the Naples until 11:30, eating, drinking moderately and talking. It had been a long while since they had spent that kind of time together. Maggie explained what it was like to travel with a man running for President, and what she had learned along the way. She apologized profusely for not being able to connect with him more frequently last year, but she had been trying to make a statement. They ended the evening with Tom walking Maggie back to the hotel, and she gave him one of her tender, loving hugs. Because Tom had a final the next day in the afternoon, they were unable to meet for breakfast the next day. So, being a good mother, Maggie encouraged him in the right direction. "Study, study, and do good, honey. Learn everything you can. We're going to need you kids to help change things. This little battle is not over by a long shot. The election was only a lesson to us that we have to try harder. Soon everything is going to be different. Believe it, and it can happen." He hugged her back. As he turned to walk away, Maggie could see the tears in his eyes. He always cried, when he left his mother. "I'll see you this weekend at the house, Tom," Maggie reminded him, reassuringly. "We'll have lots of time to catch up during the holidays," Maggie shouted after him, as he reached the swinging doors of the hotel. Hearing this, Tom turned and blew her a kiss. He loved his mother.

An hour after Maggie had finally gotten out of bed, drinking her room service coffee, she remembered her dream from the night before. It had startled her awake. This one was not about Bill. The dream had not been frightening or upsetting. It had been exciting. Maggie had seen the picture from the landing of the Museum. There, in her subconscious mind, was Belle Skinner.

After checking out two hours later, Maggie found herself sitting in the parking garage. There she was, just a block away from the hotel, looking at a map. Putting the car in gear, she pulled up to the Indian gentleman at the booth, and paid her ticket. "Which way to 95 North?" Maggie asked, double-checking her directions.

Counting money and not looking at her, he responded mindlessly, "Take a right out of the garage, and then a left at the second light. You'll see the signs." He must have said the same thing 20 times a day. With accurate directions, Maggie steered her Silver V60 Volvo left at the second light. She stayed in the middle lane, seeing the red, blue and white signs for Routes 91 and 95 North to her right. Within five minutes, she was heading out of New Haven on Route 95 North. The Interstate would take her up past Boston to Salem, where they lived. It was a straight shot from New Haven to their town.

Minutes later Maggie drove to the junction where Routes 95 and 91 converge. She began to change lanes, first looking in the rear view mirror, to make sure it was safe. Just as she was about to go to 95 North, something happened that caused her to change her mind. It was an impulse. Quickly, Maggie turned the wheel back to the left, moving the car too abruptly into the passing lane. Hearing a horn, Maggie's attention was jolted back to the highway, where she had almost hit the car that was trying to pass her. Maggie realized she had been daydreaming. For some strange reason, at the last minute, she had decided to take Route 91 instead. Maggie drove the car cautiously now, to settle down. Having no idea why she had changed routes, she continued on. Then it came to her: Route 91 North would take her up to Holyoke. That was where she wanted to go. Passing through Hartford forty minutes later, she remembered how problematic that part of the highway was. The signs were awkward, the lanes confusing, and sometimes the traffic out of the city was backed up for miles. Maggie hated it when she had an assignment in Hartford, especially if she couldn't get out of the city till dark. Since it was mid-afternoon, Maggie fortunately sailed through the Connecticut city, and in thirty minutes passed through Springfield, Massachusetts.

Maggie hadn't been in this part of the state in years. Immediately, she noticed the big, silver, ball shaped building to her left. She knew it was the Basketball Hall of Fame from the pictures she had seen. Maggie remembered the men in the sports room arguing about where basketball had actually started. One man would always say, "It wasn't just volleyball that started in Holyoke, basketball began there too, at the old YMCA.

James Naismith put up his first fruit basket there, in the old gym."

Another would say, "It was in Springfield." They always made a five-dollar wager, and it never got paid. Neither man could prove the other one wrong. Maggie could ask Tom about it when he got home this weekend for semester break, then she would know for sure. Perhaps he'd want to come here and check it out.

Not far up the road, Maggie saw the signs overhead, Routes 91 North and 391 North. The sign on the right, Route 391, directed her to Holyoke. In five minutes, she had reached the end of the highway, and took a right there, on High Street. Being on empty, Maggie stopped at the first gas station she could find, which was right off the exit. As she got out of her car, she saw two Puerto Rican boys walking about thirty feet away from her. Seeing them, Maggie asked, "Do you know where the Wistariahurst Museum is?"

Without wasting a second, one of the young men replied, "Why don't you 'hurst' this, bitch?" thrusting out his groan in a lewd manner, and then giving his friend a high five. Maggie turned toward the Mart in the gas station, ignoring this disgusting gesture. Having been a reporter for a newspaper in a big city, she was used to this type of bad behavior; still it never failed to shock her. Maggie knew it was best to just ignore it, and be thankful to God that her son had better manners.

Maggie approached the young woman, with the pierced nose ring, behind the counter. "I want to fill it. Could you tell me where the Wistariahurst Museum is?" Maggie asked the young woman the same question she had asked the boys outside.

"Cash or Credit," she retorted, not answering the question.

"Credit and I would like a coffee too. Please put a large one on the card," Maggie used her politeness to be disarming. She walked over to the coffee bar, and poured herself a cup. Returning to the register, she asked the girl the same question again.

"I have no idea where isteria is, lady," barking out the words. The girl obviously had not paid much attention to the name of the museum.

Deciding she didn't want to deal with this fresh little girl any more, Maggie changed her charge to cash. "Just make it twenty dollars, plus the coffee." Maggie shot the young woman a disdainful look. Despite her desire to be a good Catholic, Maggie couldn't help but return the girl's disrespectful attitude.

Pumping her gas, Maggie began to look around. It was almost five o'clock and getting dark. The two boys from before were nowhere to be found. Maggie felt the little hairs on the back of her neck stand up. This was her warning to be cautious; she knew she felt threatened. After the last of the pennies of gas were pumped into her tank, Maggie pulled out the nozzle and screwed on the gas cap. Getting into the car, she put her coffee into the holder on the dash and locked the doors.

Maggie turned right onto the one-way street, and stopped at the red light of the first intersection. The sign there read, "High Street." Accustomed to streets with this kind of name being at the center of town, she drove straight ahead, once the light turned green. Proceeding slowly, she immediately noticed the terrible condition of the buildings around her, some of which were boarded up. There were others that were just vacant with broken windows. Maggie felt like she was in Roxbury. The city seemed to be abandoned; no one was walking around. Though the centers of most cities are slow at around this time, this one was dismal.

A bit further down High Street, there was a newer looking building that was lit up dimly. Reading the sign, Maggie could see that it was the headquarters for the city's fire department. She pulled into a parking space in front of the building, locked her car, walked to the front door and rang the bell. A young man in a blue uniform answered, "Hi, can I help you?" He opened the door for her to enter.

"I'm looking for the Wistariahurst Museum," she told him.

"It's up on the corner of Beech and Cabot." Being a fireman, it was part of his job to know how to get around town.

"How do I get there?" she asked.

"The next street down is Hampshire," he pointed. "Take a left and go up the hill six streets, to Beech Street. Take a right and you're there. It will be on your right. It takes up the whole city block. You can't miss it." He was polite.

"Thanks." She began to leave, not wanting to take up more of his time.

Following her out, he said, "It's closed during the week, you know. It's only open on the weekends and Mondays."

Turning to him, she asked, "What time will it open on Saturday?"

"One o'clock, I think."

"The library, then, is it open on Thursday nights?" Wanting to go there too, it would have to be first, instead.

"Yes, until 8:30." He was trying to remember if this was accurate, and wondered why a beautiful, older woman, like Maggie, was in downtown Holyoke. She, in turn, felt like a mother to him. Tired from the week, and this long, drawn out search for the museum, Maggie grew restless with his monosyllabic answers. She waved her hand in impatient circles, so that he would pick up the pace. Taking the hint, he refocused. "The library is one street up, two blocks over. But this is a one-way street, so you have to go three streets up to Essex Street. Turn left, and then take another left on Maple. It's right there in the middle of the square. There is a big green and white sign, in English and Spanish. The street sign on Essex isn't there anymore, so you have to be careful not to miss it. Angry residents have torn down most of the street markers."

"Thank you." Maggie smiled and exhaled loudly.

"One more thing, Ma'am," he said. "Be careful around here. I was serious about some angry residents. Holyoke can be a rough place, and it's not safe at night." Heeding his warning, Maggie locked the doors of her car after she got in. She pulled out of the parking space and waved appreciatively to the fireman, heading toward the library.

It was very dark on Maple Street, but the library sign was lit and so was the walkway. As she approached the library, Maggie was wondering where she would stay that night. Perhaps there was a better section of the city, with a decent hotel. Standing at the bottom of the entrance steps, she turned to make certain she had set the car alarm. Maggie's car looked conspicuous, parked in front of the library. The blip noise assured her that the alarm was set. She felt a bit more secure after hearing it, but not a lot.

Looking around at the more impressive buildings across the street, Maggie's eyes couldn't help notice a beautiful stone church on the next corner up. As she started to scrutinize the other buildings surrounding the library, Maggie noticed something odd again. They all appeared to be empty, not occupied. There were no lights on inside or outside the church, apartments or the offices on all of the streets that she could see. And, there was still no one walking anywhere, coming or going. Maggie felt like she was in a ghost town.

Walking into the front foyer of the library, Maggie was approached by an old man with white hair and very thick glasses. "May I help you?" He was very formal.

"Yes, I'm looking for information on the city's history. Do you have any recent reference books or guides?" Maggie knew the questions to ask. If she wanted to know about Belle Skinner, there had to be some mention of her in the city's historical records. In addition, if Maggie wanted to learn as much as she could about Belle Skinner, she would have to know about the city Belle lived in.

The old man turned slowly, and walked behind a counter. Coming back towards Maggie, she observed that he was holding only three history books and one picture book. As he handed them to her, she asked, "What's this?"

"That's it," he answered curtly.

"What do you mean, that's it?" Maggie was confused. "That's all you have, three books and some pictures? Are you trying to tell me that these are the only books that have been written on the history of Holyoke?" She was flabbergasted.

"Yep, only three books in 50 or so years. There are some older ones up in the Holyoke Room, not too many though. But, that's closed. You'll have to come back tomorrow, if you want to look upstairs." The old man did not appear to think that any of this was odd. Maggie did not know quite what to say, which was highly unusual for her. She took the books and headed towards one of the reading rooms. He called out after her, "You can't take them out, and please be careful. They're the only copies we have."

Surprised by the librarians concerns, Maggie walked back to address him, "Let me get this straight," she was dumbfounded. "You have only three books, and a picture book of the history of Holyoke? And, you have only one copy of each book in the main library of the city?" This was absurd.

He gave Maggie a seemingly cold look over the top of his glasses, and didn't respond. He'd had enough of her. His look said it all.

Realizing the futility of the situation, Maggie turned back toward the reading room, and shook her head. Finding a comfortable, leather, wing back chair, she took off her coat and sat down. Still reeling from the state of affairs, Maggie focused on the covers of the books she had been given. To start, she chose the one on the top. It had been written by Wyatt Harper. Because it was the only book without loose pages falling out, she would read this one first. Maggie put the other books to the side and settled in to peruse her selection. Remembering the library closed at 8:30, she checked her watch, not wanting to lose track of time. Her first forty-five minutes in Holyoke had been troubling enough, and now she looked around to see that the old man and she were the only ones in the library. Perhaps what people had said about the city was true. It could be a dangerous place.

FOUR

Maggie wasn't exactly sure how she had gotten to the Holyoke Mall, but she was glad to be there. She was happy to be in a place where there were people and activity. Leaving the library with a guard hadn't left Maggie with a great feeling; seeing her car still parked in the street, not stripped, did. Maggie hadn't learned much about anything from what she'd read there, but she'd only skimmed the books. There was not enough time to do anything else. Maggie had a rudimentary understanding of the city, but nothing like what she wanted to have. At least she had found a hotel at the mall, and for that she was grateful. The first question Maggie asked the desk clerk at the Holiday Inn was, "Is my car still going to be in the parking lot when I get up tomorrow?"

The young black man assured Maggie, "You are in the good part of Holyoke Ma'am, everything will be fine. We have security policemen check the parking lots every hour. It's not like downtown here." Only half believing him, Maggie checked in, and went directly to her room. She was exhausted from the whole ordeal. At this point, Maggie figured she would take her shower in the morning and go right to bed. The only thing on her mind was getting some sleep. Before Maggie dozed off, she made sure the door was double locked.

The telephone rang at 8:00 A.M., according to the instructions Maggie had left with the front desk the night before. She picked up the receiver and mumbling, thanked the person on the other end. Rolling back over, she lay there looking up at the ceiling, solely thinking about what she had learned so far. There was not a lot of information about the Skinner family in the books she had read last night at the library. One brief description of the family only connected them to the silk business. Maggie photocopied what she thought was pertinent from the books. It was mostly just vague Holyoke history. Maggie decided to go back down to the library. Maybe there was an older book in the upstairs room the old man had mentioned that would give her more information. Besides, it was sunny out, and she was sure it was safer in the daytime.

Maggie had realized that her decision to come to Holyoke was prompted by Susan, the curator at Yale. Susan had aroused Maggie's curiosity, and now she wanted to learn as much as she could about Belle. Perhaps the books in the Holyoke Room would give her more answers. After the library, Maggie planned to go up the hill to Wistariahurst. She was confident there would be a lot more information there. But, Maggie had plenty of time for that; she remembered that it didn't open till tomorrow. She had the whole day to spend at the library, to learn about Holyoke.

The director of the Holyoke Room was very helpful. Realizing Maggie's genuine interest in the city's past, the librarian took out some of the older history books, and let Maggie photocopy them and take all the notes she needed. She spent most of the day doing this, and was drained by the time she left the library at 4 o'clock. While heading back to the hotel, Maggie thought she might do some shopping and get something to eat, for a change of pace. Christmas was coming up quickly, and she was way behind in her gift buying. So, Maggie went to the busy, modern Holyoke Mall, and spent her night and a lot of money there.

The next morning, Maggie resisted the temptation to go back to the library. There were a few loose ends in her mind that she wanted to tie up, but Maggie thought it was best to save her energy for Wistariahurst. So, she lazed around her room until checkout time, reading the notes and looking at the pictures she had taken the day before.

At exactly one o'clock, Maggie parked her car on Beech Street, across the street from the entrance to Wistariahurst. The restored home of the Skinner family was right in the middle of a neglected neighborhood, in the rundown old city. It looked terribly out of place. Clean and well taken care of, it was recently painted, crème colored with white trim and a gray slate roof. It was as Susan had described it: the buildings took up a whole city block. It looked like it had been built in sections.

As Maggie looked at the entrance directly across from her, she noticed that the door was wide open. Maggie crossed the street carefully. An elderly woman with white hair was standing in the doorway looking out, as if she was waiting for someone to arrive. Maggie thought the woman was there to show her in. Behind this woman, a younger woman was talking to some people, beginning to give a tour of the estate. Maggie listened to her opening description.

Wistariahurst COURTESY OF THE HOLYOKE PUBLIC LIBRARY

"In 1959, Belle's sister, Katherine Skinner Kilborne, and her heirs, donated this property to the City of Holyoke."

"That's an interesting driveway," Maggie said to the older woman, as she walked passed her. Maggie had proceeded into the foyer of the mansion, trying to listen to the tour guide. Paying little attention to Maggie, the frazzled, older woman kept looking out toward the courtyard.

"Did you see the dinosaur prints in the rocks?" she asked Maggie.

Maggie had not. "No," she answered politely.

"They were brought down here from the mountain when the house was moved. Mount Tom is full of them." The older woman began shuffling back toward Maggie, who was trying to decide what to do. "I'm sorry my dear," the old woman apologized to her. "It's just that Santa is coming. There's a party for the children in the Music Room, and he should be here any minute." She smiled.

"I hope I'm not interrupting anything." Maggie was concerned.

"No, no. Not at all, my dear. But, the children come first. It's like the old days, when the Skinners had the Christmas parties for the city's children. It's a reenactment." Maggie could tell that she was proud of what they were doing. Just then, another older woman, wearing an old fashioned dress, came walking to the reception desk where they were standing.

"Is he here yet?" she asked the woman at the doorway.

"No. Any minute though," the woman in the doorway responded.

"And, who are you?" the woman in the old fashioned dress asked Maggie.

"Just a visitor." Maggie answered, not sure the museum was still open to her.

"You'll have to wait until the party begins before we can show you around," the woman said.

"No problem," Maggie answered.

"Why don't you wait in the sitting room. It's down the hall, to the left of the chandelier. We will come get you when everything settles down." The woman was cordial.

Walking through the hall where the large glass chandelier hung in the middle, Maggie turned left and went into the sitting room, as the woman had told her to. It was a small reading room, and Maggie was surprised to find a third elderly woman sitting in a chair, looking out the window. Hearing Maggie come in, the woman turned and warmly said, "Hello."

"Hi," Maggie responded, noticing that the woman had to be eighty or ninety years old. She had bright eyes and white hair and looked quite elegant in her beautiful Victorian dress.

"Do you have children? Are you here for the party?" the old woman asked.

"*No*. I mean, *yes*. Well, what I mean is, *yes* I do have a child, but, *no* I am not here for the party. I didn't know anything about it. Besides, my son is 20 years old, too old for children's Christmas parties." Maggie smiled at the woman, sensing genuine warmth from her.

"No one is too old for a children's Christmas party, dear. I'm here, aren't I?" The pleasant woman smiled back. Knowing she was right, Maggie said nothing, and waited for the woman to go on. "Then why are you here?"

"I came for a tour. I'm just a visitor," Maggie informed the woman, repeating what she had told the others.

"Well then, why don't we have one." The woman turned sideways, and struggled to get up. Maggie noticed that she was limping and in pain, as she walked with great effort to sit in a chair that was closer to Maggie. Pausing for a moment, the woman turned to Maggie and pointed to the chair next to her for Maggie to sit. Maggie was alarmed, noticing the woman's labored breathing. The elderly woman spoke up, seeing Maggie's concern, "I'm fine dear, just a little short-winded." As she recovered, she continued sharing, "It's hell to get old, you know." Maggie sat quietly as she observed the woman's breathing slowly improve.

"Are you all right?" Maggie finally broke her silence.

"I'm fine. They tell me I shouldn't have an operation to fix the hip, to use a wheelchair all the time. But, I'll walk till I fall down. Never give up, that was my mother's motto."

"She must have been a very strong woman," Maggie said, being polite.

"Are you from Holyoke?" the older woman asked.

"No, I'm from Salem," Maggie told her.

"From where the witches are?" The woman was surprised.

"Yes." Maggie was used to the question, and found it best to be brief with her reply.

"Ever see any of them?" She was trying to be funny.

"Not yet. Although, a few of my neighbors look very suspicious." Maggie had picked up on the older woman's sense of humor and before long the two of them were laughing together. Though they were generations apart, one older and one middle aged, they were enjoying each other's company, sitting in the room where Belle used to sit. Interrupting their laughter, commotion broke out in the front of the house. The two detected the familiar calling out of Santa Claus.

They heard, "Ho! Ho! Ho!" and then the children began to scream and the party began.

"Do you feel it?" she asked Maggie.

"What?" Maggie was uncertain what the older woman meant.

"In your stomach, the excitement my dear, isn't it contagious? That's what Christmas is all about. It's like when you were a child. Don't you just love it?"

"Yes." Maggie did. When Bill was alive, it was their favorite time of year.

"That's why you are never too old, because part of us is always a child." The older woman decided to begin the tour, and Maggie was eager to hear about the Skinner family. The older woman stood and walked back over to the window where Maggie had first seen her. She gazed out the window and spoke now with more emotion. "Holyoke wasn't always this way you know. It was once a beautiful place. I remember being just a girl, walking down High Street on Thursday nights, that's where the boys were." She shot Maggie a cute smile. "Or going to the movies at the Victory Theatre on Saturday afternoons, and the trips to Mountain Park to ride the Carousel. Once in a great while, we would get to go to the Canoe Club on the river. Holyoke was wonderful back then, an exciting city to be living in. We all had so much fun." The woman sighed. "It was like we lived in Camelot." Maggie could tell that the older woman's mind had returned to the good old days.

Maggie's mind went there too. "Tell me about it."

"Well, now I won't date myself." The woman paused, "What did you say your name was, dear?" The older woman was being polite, knowing Maggie had never given her name.

"I'm sorry. My name is Maggie, Maggie O'Reilly."

Nodding her head, the older woman said, "I'm Katherine."

Knowing each other's names, Katherine continued, "When the men came back from the war, there was a lot to do. God knows how we all suffered during that war, we missed them so. Many of them didn't come back, but those that did built up the city to what it had been before the war. You know, it wasn't just the success of the factories and mills, my dear, although their prosperity was what made the rest of the city run. There was magic here then, and many opportunities. The emotional atmosphere was different also. We wanted less, appreciated more. Don't forget, we were depression babies. We knew what it was like to go without a meal. So, when there was food on the table, we were thankful to those that put it there. And money, yes, there was a lot of that in Holyoke, but it wasn't our God. It came because we did things right. It was the result of our efforts, not our reason to live. We just wanted to be happy, to make others happy." Katherine paused. "Downtown was where most everyone worked, in the mills, the shops and in the stores. We sold what was made here in the city. Some girls, like me, worked in the mills. I worked for my father, in his office. Others worked in the stores, or in the other factories. There were hundreds of businesses here then." Katherine's eyes were transfixed, transported back in time, seeing it all again.

"It was different after the boys returned, though. During the war we were alone. Only the older men were left here. They didn't go to war. So, we were accustomed to making our own good times, while the young men were away. When they came back, everything changed. There were dances and concerts at the Valley Arena. The promoters brought in most of the big bands to play for us. And walk, how we walked! When we weren't walking, we rode the streetcars all over town, to the different parks and playgrounds. They were clean and kept tidy. There were ten different activities to do on any given day, including work days. There was none of this watching television nonsense. We were too busy doing things, living our lives." Katherine paused and changed gears, gaining enthusiasm. "City business, like our private lives, was thriving on good will. Walking down any of the streets in downtown, you couldn't find an empty store. The shopkeepers knew most of us by name, and we all had accounts with their stores. We did our business in the city, and helped each other's businesses be successful. There were department stores to shop in, stores run by people who lived in Holyoke, Steigers, McAuslin and Wakelins, Grants, Childs, Gallups. I could go on and on. I can still remember in Gallups, the way they put the money into the tubes to get it to the office. The air would push or pull the tubes between the floors. It was some type of vacuum system. And there was this wonderful little pharmacy on Maple Street. It had one of those old-fashioned soda fountains in it, where they made the best ice cream sodas. I can still taste the chocolate in my mouth."

Maggie stopped her, "What was it called?" inquiring eagerly.

"I can't recall dear, Irish though. Anyway, I clearly remember the names of the important lawyers, the bankers, the investment people who kept the money flowing and the city ledgers profitable. The politicians were honorable and respected. The city's leaders kept them that way, honest. The lines were drawn very clearly, and no one crossed them in Holyoke, or there was hell to pay. We didn't make the laws up as we went along. They were already there. It was wonderful, dear. People came from all over to see the prosperity that was here. Holyoke was named a model city by those who came to visit. It was because we did things so well, by working hard *together*, for *all* of our dreams." Katherine was vehement. "We had ethics and cared about each other. And, we loved and took care of our beautiful city." She paused to take a breath, her passion was obvious. "On any given night, you could walk on any street downtown, and see a hundred people you knew. The street lamps were always lit brightly, and the policemen patrolled the city on foot, ensuring our safety. There was little trouble back then. No one questioned their authority, they respected their power. The men had enough fighting overseas, and didn't want any trouble here. Back then, Holyoke wasn't like the rest of the country today, with all the violence. We wanted to live our lives in peace. We all had families, and sent our children to the finest schools. We worshipped together at the churches, where the priests, rabbis and ministers taught us about God, and what was right and wrong, by their books and their examples. We kept things simple. We focused our energies on our families and on our community. We made it a nice place to live for everyone. And we succeeded, because there were people like the Skinners to help us, to show us the way. They gave back what they made, and in doing so made life better for everyone who lived here in Holyoke. None of us would have these memories without the generosity of those who were more fortunate. Of course, that is the way of the world, my dear. It's what separates places like Holyoke in the 1950s, from Holyoke in 2004."

Maggie could see that Katherine was becoming heartbroken, thinking about how the city and its people had changed. In order to give Katherine a moment to regroup, Maggie asked her a question. "What keeps you here? If it bothers you so much to see the decay, why don't you leave, like the others?"

Katherine looked intently at Maggie and said, "Respect!" Only one word. It put everything into perspective very quickly.

The two women were interrupted by someone standing at the door. It was the curator of the museum, Candice Michaelson. She directed her words to the older woman, "It's time for you to give the children their gifts, Miss Kilborne."

"Yes, of course. Candice, this is Maggie. She has come to visit us." Katherine began to get up slowly, and the curator was by her side, knowing Katherine would need help. Candice held her by the arm.

"Won't you join us with the children, my dear?" Katherine asked Maggie. Maggie nodded her head, accepting the kind invitation. She followed the other two ladies into the Music Room where the party was underway.

Maggie was taken aback when they walked through the Conservatory, next to the Music Room. The curator told Mrs. Kilborne how nice it was that she could be here and said, "I'm sure your aunts would be proud of you." Maggie became slightly embarrassed, realizing she had been talking to a member of the Skinner family without knowing it, for the last half hour. When they reached the head table where the gifts were, Mrs. Kilborne was seated there in the very middle, the place designated for the most important person in the room. Standing in the corner, Maggie couldn't help but pay attention to Katherine. Maggie admired the way Katherine treated the children. It was so touching.

Motioning for the curator to come to her, Mrs. Kilborne whispered something into her ear. The children in the room were noisy and excited, all trying to get close to Santa Claus, to sit on his lap and tell him what they wanted for Christmas. The curator walked through the line of children and came over to Maggie. She thought the curator might ask her to leave, because she was not an invited guest. This was not the case. The curator smiled as she finally broke through the line, and she gently touched Maggie on her shoulder. "Miss Kilborne wants to know if you would be kind enough to join her, and help her hand out the presents to the children?" Candice entreated. Looking at her in amazement, Maggie understood a little better now what it was that the wonderful older lady named Katherine had said to her: no one needed an invitation. Here, everyone was welcome, and they all were the same.

After the party, Maggie helped Candice escort Katherine out to the car that was waiting for her, to take her back home. As she watched the car drive away, Maggie thought about what a sweet lady Katherine was. Sitting and listening to Katherine was like being with Maggie's own mother. There were no airs about her; Katherine called it like it was. She was full of love and kindness. Maggie couldn't remember meeting anyone like her in a long time. Most definitely, no one Maggie had met on the campaign trail was genuine like Katherine. Maggie wondered why? And they were trying to be elected to represent us.

Once everything had settled down, and most of the children had left, Maggie was given an abbreviated tour of the mansion by one of the staff members. She apologized for being so brief, but they had to close in an hour, so she was limited. Her name was Alice, and she tried her best to fit everything in with the time they had left. Reading from a manual, she intoned:

"The Skinner family moved to Holyoke after a flood in the Mill River had destroyed their mills and most of the homes there in 1874. Some of the rooms of this house, that were not lost, were from the original home in Williamsburg, being hauled down here in sections. Much of the house you see today reflects the taste and style of Belle Skinner. Belle's father died in 1902, and her mother died in 1908. Mrs. Skinner's will stipulated that the house be left to her unmarried children, William and Belle. Belle made changes to the house in many ways, which made it completely different from the one she grew up in. Belle was an active and imaginative woman, and this home reflects her personality and social standing.

She graduated from Vassar College in 1887 with a major in French and a minor in Music. She traveled the world, and was influenced by what she saw. While the house was very Victorian in style when she grew up here, Belle slowly changed the house to embrace the revival style architecture of the Beaux Arts movement. The movement started in France and was filled with the architecture of the classical era. Belle was influenced by it and other styles of the period, including Colonial Revival. This style was a movement, an attempt to celebrate Colonial America's pre-industrial agrarian past, a more simpler and homogeneous time. Attempting to do this, Belle collected antiques, reproductions, and emulated fashions from the Federal and Georgian periods." The young woman was finished with her introduction. They started looking around the mansion in reverse, not from the front end, but from the back of the house. They began with the Music Room, since they had been there already for the party. It was unique to say the least. Seeing it was one thing, taking it all in and learning about it was something else.

Starting again, the cultured Spanish girl said, "In 1907, Belle developed an interest in collecting rare musical instruments. The ones she collected included violins, harpsichords and spinets. They were beautifully ornamented and in working order, totaling over 80 pieces. Belle had this room made to display her collection. It was finished in 1914. The room reflects the Italian Renaissance Revival style. Most of the surfaces are made of plaster-type composite materials, finished to look like marble. Some parts are real marble, including the fireplaces and the column pedestals. The room was constructed by Italian workers who were brought in from Italy to build it, so that the music would reverberate off the walls, floors and ceilings. Belle was the one who thought to do that!" There were twenty marble pillars in the room, two fireplaces in the center, and a small cubical at the end with a large window in it that overlooked the gardens outside. On the top of the cubicle was a small sitting area, like a tiny balcony.

"What's that?" Maggie asked her, pointing.

"The Musicians Gallery, for the director or conductor. It's accessible by a stairwell."

The next room was the Conservatory, also called the Breakfast Room. It was very bright, in contrast to the windowless Music Room, with seven sections of windows that extended from near the ceiling down to the heating radiators and flower boxes. The plants looked healthy and quite well cared for. Maggie's guide liked this room. You could tell by her enthusiasm in describing it. "The Breakfast Room was also added in 1914. The room has a cork floor, a fine detailed stained glass peacock set in the window. There were more. Only one peacock survives. Most likely it was fashioned by Louis Comfort Tiffany Company in New York. The Skinners made a lot of purchases from this company, including the famous *View From Oyster Bay Window*, depicting the Wistariahurst vines that bloom in May." She produced a picture of the leaded glass piece she was describing, and showed it to Maggie. "Come this way please," she instructed.

The Dining Room was next, and was almost as dark as the Music Room, mostly because of the color of the wood. "This was one of the original rooms brought down from Skinnerville by Mr. Skinner," Alice told her. "This room was enlarged and redecorated by Belle in the early 1900s. Entertaining was important to the Skinners. As leaders in their church and other social institutions, socializing played an important role in their relationships with other Holyokers. It was also important for business. Their social life and business world were entwined, just like the vines that covered their house. The walls were decorated with silk damask fabric and the room was expanded. Attached to the Dining Room is the Butler's Pantry. The small room separates the Dining Room from the Kitchen, which is behind it. Inside the door, on the right hand side, you can see the call system. Members of the family, or their guests, used it to contact the maids to serve them." She opened the door for Maggie to see in.

Walking back through the Dining Room, Maggie thought that it was a formal room, and much different looking than the other two rooms, because it was older. It had a glass chandelier hanging over a large dining table in the middle of the room that was surrounded by high back chairs. The walls were covered with family pictures.

When they reached the Great Hall where the other bright, large chandelier was hanging, Alice looked again at her manual. "The Great Hall was the last addition to the home by Belle Skinner in 1927. The addition of the two rooms changed the entrance of the house from Pine Street to Cabot and Beech Streets. At the time it was constructed, many of Holyoke's wealthier residents were moving up the hill to the Northampton Street area. Belle's nephew, William, had a home there. By shifting the focus of the house to the new and better neighborhoods, Belle may have wanted to make the house more suitable for her contemporaries." Alice stopped. Looking to Maggie, Alice asked her if she had any questions. She did not. Alice continued, "William and Belle loved to entertain in this room, because it was so spacious and could accommodate a large number of people."

Looking around, Maggie could see what she was talking about. The entrance Maggie had initially come through was in this room. Once you entered the house through it, you were in one of two large rooms. There were several fireplaces in the rooms, and the floors were made of wood and were finished. Besides the openness of the Great Hall, there were large pictures of each member of the Skinner family hanging on the walls. They stood out. Once Alice had finished up there, she asked Maggie what she would like to see next. They had only a little time left before the museum closed, and Alice couldn't show Maggie everything today.

"I would like to see the upstairs quickly, if that's OK?" Maggie asked.

"Fine, follow me. But we'll have to make it quick." The young lady was very well mannered.

As she began walking up the elaborate winding wood staircase that extended from the first to the second floors, Alice continued with her informative presentation. "Notice as we climb the stairs the wrought iron peonies that are entwined with the wood of the staircase. Each flower opens up a little more until we reach the top. The last one is in full bloom." Picking up the pace, the women went into the bedroom that was on the Cabot Street side of the house, the one Belle slept in. It was a plain room, not ostentatious. The most remarkable things about the room were the bathroom that was attached to it, and the moon bed that was brought here from Belle's apartment on East Street in New York City. The room was elegant in its simplicity.

"This was originally Belle's mother's bedroom. Soon after her mother's death, Belle hired the Casper Ranger Construction Company of Holyoke to install a new hardwood floor, update the bathroom, and otherwise improve the appearance of the room. Belle used this as her bedroom for 20 years. The photos on the wall portray Bell's taste in decorating. She chose early American pieces, and wallpaper depicting a mill scene and a shepherdess. Belle's taste reflects her interest and nostalgia for earlier times. Preserving and protecting early Americana, and reviving the styles and buildings of their Anglo ancestors, was seen as a civic and patriotic duty by those who lived here. They were preserving a link to a time that was seen as more stable and desirable. Belle eventually gave the room up for her nephew Stewart and his wife, Barbara, to use. At the time that Belle restored the room, sanitary conditions were an important consideration. The transmission of disease was being linked to unclean habits. The cold water flats of the downtown districts of Holyoke were a perfect example of this. Not having hot water in them, germs created diseases that spread wildly to the people living there. This house had indoor plumbing and hot water, and the Skinners were conscious of the importance of cleanliness. Through the bathroom is an adjoining room, which was used as a nursery for Stewart and Barbara's baby, Belle Skinner Kilborne. The medicine cabinets in the bathroom are of interest. A wide range of beauty products were the rage in America when Belle redid this room. Respectable women were now sporting makeup, and the bathroom was becoming important for preparing oneself for public presentation. The light bulbs in the rooms do not have shades, because they were a new innovation, and it did not occur to people to hide them. In fact the bulb itself was considered to be interesting and exciting." Alice was helpful in explaining everything she could to Maggie

Moving Maggie quickly to the next room, Alice launched into another description, "This room was originally used as a bedroom, but now exhibits furniture from the Skinner Coffee House, which was opened by Belle and Katherine in 1902 as a memorial to their father. Noticing the

View of "The Flats" Courtesy of the Holyoke Public Library

number of services for men in the city, such as the YMCA and other fraternal clubs, Belle and Katherine focused their attentions on providing services for women and girls. The Coffee House was a place for working women to gather, socialize, relax and much more. The Coffee House provided for the physical and emotional needs of the women and children, including subsidized meals, clothing, medical services, bathing facilities, child care and emergency housing. Recreation and education, including playing the piano, newspapers, classes in English, child rearing, theatre and dance, cosmetics, elocution, the importance of cleanliness in preventing diseases, and lectures on many other subjects were arranged at no cost for the women and girls in the area. In her will, Belle left the Coffee House $100,000 as an endowment for operations to continue."

The women saw a few more bedrooms upstairs, including one in the servants' quarters that was impressive, because it showed the respectful way the Skinners treated those who worked for them. The young lady then made her apologies to Maggie. Looking at her watch, Alice told her that their time was up. Perhaps on another day, they could walk the halls again, and Alice could show Maggie what they had missed. Maggie thanked her for her time and left; having received an abbreviated tour didn't matter. Maggie was able to glean what she had wanted, and actually got more out of her visit than she had anticipated.

Maggie remembered that Katherine had asked her to do one more thing before leaving the city. "Go and look at the architecture of the buildings here, dear. See the height of the towers. These were the peaks we reached for." Respecting her wishes, Maggie did what Katherine asked. Before she left the city, Maggie drove around looking at the heights and spires of the buildings. Observing them, Maggie understood the prominence Holyoke had risen to.

Driving back to Salem, Maggie tried to picture what the buildings must have looked like to Katherine when she was a young girl. Though Maggie desired to put herself back in time with all her heart, she could not get the images of a run-down Holyoke out of her head. Looking at their condition now, it was impossible to see what Katherine had described.

As she arrived in Salem four hours later, Maggie noticed the colorful Christmas lights that decorated the town common and the houses that surrounded it. She saw a group of Christmas carolers singing at a house down the street from hers. Gazing at this picturesque scene, Maggie couldn't help but compare it to what she had just left only hours ago in Holyoke. She had thought a lot about her tour of the once bustling city. While it was true there were wonderful old buildings and houses everywhere, much was missing, especially for Christmas. The Holyoke of today was not festive, not engaging or inviting at all. It was dirty, and it didn't appear that many holiday activities were planned or taking place anywhere in the city. There were only a handful of string lights decorating the downtown area. Even the Christmas tree in front of the huge, old, stone city hall was set crooked in its base. There seemed to have been little effort made by anyone to decorate the city. It left the impression that no one cared to celebrate the coming of Christ. None of the city's public buildings had candles in their windows, and there were no colorful wreaths to be seen anywhere. The old light posts, replications of the old gas lamps that used to brighten the streets, were not even lit. The difference between Salem and Holyoke was profound. Salem was festive. Holyoke looked like it was on a death watch. It wasn't celebrating anyone's birthday. Maggie wondered what Katherine's Holyoke was like during Christmas. When Katherine and the rest of her friends celebrated the holidays and the holy day together as a community, Maggie was sure everyone felt happy and secure.

Downtown Holyoke at Christmas – 1930s COURTESY OF HARRY CRAVEN

Maggie attempted again to go back in time, imagining everything looking so differently than the dark city she had just left behind. She desperately desired to envision "the great old city" that had been seen through the eyes of the remarkable woman she had met at Wistariahurst. Now, Maggie wanted to see it at its best. She began by visualizing the hustle and bustle of the busy city; the old trolleys were transporting everyone across town, and the throngs of people were walking everywhere. The whole city was alive with music and cheer, as Salem was today. For one brief moment, Maggie did see the City of Holyoke as it must have been long ago. But, as quickly as the vision came, it vanished, replaced by the overpowering images of what still is, the empty buildings and darkness. Walking along the sidewalk to her own front door, Maggie looked back to the bright lights of Salem and the festivities continuing into the night, and shook her head. How neglected Holyoke had become, how terrible it really was, if a city could have feelings, this one would be sad.

FIVE

Maggie awoke the next morning to the sound of her son in the bathroom. Tom had been at the house before she arrived. That evening, some of his high school friends had come over to visit and stayed late. They were having a few beers together, which was fine with Maggie. She had excused herself at midnight to go to bed, and let the kids be by themselves to catch up on each other's lives, with one caveat. "No one drives. You all walk home." Maggie was adamant and not to be messed with. They never disobeyed Mrs. O'Reilly. She had quite a reputation in town.

"Morning," Tom said, as Maggie walked into the kitchen.

"Hi, honey. Did you make coffee?" Knowing he had already, because she could smell it. Maggie held out her cup. This was their ritual. Tom knew his mother didn't function well in the morning without at least two cups of coffee. He had been doing this for her since Bill's death. Looking at her son, Maggie could not help noticing how much he resembled his father. Tom was very handsome with blonde hair and green eyes, just like his dad. When the girls in the village spoke about Tom, they would use the word, *hot*. Maggie knew that her son was good looking, but to her his sweet disposition was paramount.

"When did you get to bed?" Maggie asked, sipping her coffee.

"Around three," Tom replied, nonchalantly.

"Any plans for today?" she inquired.

"I thought I would take you shopping," he smiled, and kissed his mother on the forehead.

"Where?" Maggie was excited. Tom knew how difficult the holidays were for her.

"Anyplace you'd like. But, let's not go to the mall. It will be crazy there. Would you like to take a ride into Boston? Just like we used to, it will be fun," he stopped himself from continuing. Tom realized he was talking about things the three of them used to do together. "Sorry Mom. I didn't think," he hugged her, feeling awful. Maggie was crying. Tom found it hard not to talk about his father. Tom was adjusting better to his Dad's death than Maggie was. Mature for his age, Tom had gone to a counselor who helped him understand his feelings. He wasn't angry now, like he had been at first, but he knew his mother was still unsettled about it. She came unhinged easily. Maggie thought about her husband. It wasn't fair that he was dead. It just wasn't the same for either of them without Bill, she thought.

Maggie was still thinking about Bill hours later. Trying to distract herself, she curled up on the couch in the family room, and listened to music. Tom had decided to get some exercise in, and had called one of his friends to go jogging. Knowing they would most likely go out somewhere after he'd finished, Maggie decided to take some time to look at what she had copied at the library in Holyoke. Spread out in front of her, all over the floor, were papers. There were photocopies of pages from books, notes, pictures, newspaper articles and more. It was everything she had collected since she started her little investigation about Belle Skinner and Holyoke.

Maggie tried to organize the mess in front of her. One of her shortcomings was keeping things in order. She never had a problem with remembering things, but she could easily confuse one piece of paper with another. Maggie also had a habit of accumulating excessive amounts of information. She knew she needed to remedy this as well. Maggie had the tendency to pick up everything written that might be even the slightest bit informative, everything. She was a reporter, and someone had told her to do this, and she took that literally, to the limit. Maggie had once done a story about the new Ted Williams tunnel in Boston, which was going to replace the Callahan tunnel. In researching it, she found herself interviewing everyone involved in its construction and funding. By the time she was finished with her interviews, Maggie had a very large box full of notes. She had accumulated so much material, she would need to write a book to get it all in. Though the thought had crossed her mind, Maggie was not up for writing a long story. Thinking about the incredible monies involved, and the characters she had met there, it certainly was a good plot to build on. Something had to be done, so Maggie wrote a short piece on how the agents of the federal government were investigating the use of money that had been collected in taxes by the state to build the tunnel. Finishing it without making many conclusions, Maggie was glad to be done with it. Too much was being covered up to make much sense out of what was going on in Boston. Even the feds were having a hard time getting to the bottom of it. Once they figured out one thing, something else surfaced, and they were back at the drawing board again. Maggie had decided to drop it, and let them be the ones frustrated with the "Big Dig" fiasco.

This particular puzzle about the Skinners was going to be easier for her to unravel, she thought. Maggie kept telling herself that. She had been careful to leave everything in well positioned piles on the back seat of her car. Knowing her propensity for disorganization and accruing masses of information, Maggie was staying ahead of the game, or so she thought. She had not realized till now, just how much useless information she had collected. There was the New Haven pile from Yale, with all of the information from Saint Mary's Church and the School of Music museum; the Holyoke pile, with the papers from the downstairs library and the Holyoke Room; the pile of notes she had taken at the Wistariahurst Museum; and the books she had bought at the mall, from the Images of America series, with old pictures of Holyoke in it. There was also a postcard collection series, somewhere. All Maggie had to do was organize the piles, and read the books. At least that's what she kept telling herself. Then I should have a pretty good idea what it is I am actually doing. Maggie kept reassuring herself that she was heading somewhere with this.

Three hours later, Maggie awoke to a door closing. Her son and his friend had come back from their run, and were in the kitchen. She had given up trying to make sense of the mess she had created, and opted to taken a nap. Maggie figured it would help get rid of the headache she had gotten from reading too much. She knew the boys would be hungry, as usual, so she got up to fix them something to eat. Confident tomorrow would be a better day to try and make some sense of it all, Maggie stepped over the mess, and went into the kitchen where the boys were.

Maggie spent Christmas week at home with her son. Happy just to be together, the two did some local shopping, and talked a lot. Maggie and Tom even discussed how they were coping with the loss of Bill. Talking about the good times all of them had seemed to ease the pain. The subject of Holyoke was on her mind, though. Maggie thought that she might be using it to divert her attention from those things that made her unhappy.

The following day was a down day for them both, a reading day.

Maggie had made a deal with Tom about presents. Instead of buying her a gift, she had asked him to help her with some of the Holyoke research. Tom agreed to help his mom, seeing her dilemma. Maggie was trying to make sense of all the papers she had accumulated. He would put them in some type of order, and evaluate the portion of material that she felt would be hard for her to understand. In the end, Tom knew everything would come together, it always did, but he had no idea how his mom got from point A to Z. Being highly organized himself, especially compared to her, it was easy for him to see the progression of her collections. And he knew his mother's habits, by the time the two had finished sorting through the papers, they had everything in its proper place.

"Thank you." Being funny, Maggie held out her hand for Tom to shake. He walked off to his room with a stack of papers to continue to sort, leaving her to comb through the rest of the collection.

Knowing she had to know something about Holyoke first if she was going to understand the Skinners, Maggie thought she'd spend Christmas week piecing together a brief history of the city. This was where she shined. Maggie could take a hodgepodge of information, deconstruct it, and understand it in ways few could. She could also come up with a story line to make it interesting. By Christmas Eve, Maggie wanted to have finished her personal account of the history of Holyoke. To a point, she thought; it didn't have to be perfect, and it was a self-imposed deadline. It would not only be enjoyable, but a useful distraction from the depressing thoughts of this holiday season. Taking her first set of notes, Maggie began the slow process of piecing it all together.

Holyoke's pre-historic times were somewhat accounted for by dozens of dinosaur tracks and fossils found in the Smith's Ferry district of the city. Skipping 190 million years to the 16th century, the area (now the Pioneer Valley) was known as home to several Indian tribes: the Nonotucks, near the area that is now Northampton; the Woronocos, near today's Westfield; and the Agawams, near Springfield. Most of the villages were located in the higher hills, near the area's rivers, rather than the flatlands. It is clear that the Great Rapids, the largest river, the Quannitukut (now the Connecticut) was a dependable resource for all of them.

The Quannitukut, which means "long river," in several different Indian languages, extended from the mountain lakes of today's New Hampshire, near the Canadian border, to what is now the Long Island Sound in New Haven, Connecticut. Along the way, it runs between the mountains of Mount Tom and Mount Holyoke, and formed a boundary between the Algonquian coastal Indians and the Iroquois, or Mohawks, to the west. There were numerous trails running from the coast through the area and north, to what is now Canada. Ancient Indian graves have been found throughout Holyoke and along the Connecticut River, in Depot Hill, Mosher Track, and Springdale; several were unearthed during the construction of city parks, including Canonchet Park in 1890.

There is strong evidence of explorer-settlers in the area, including William Pynchon and Captain Elizur Holyoke, who arrived around 1633, anxious to engage local Indians in the beaver trade. A parlay between an Indian sachem (chief), Whaquinnicut, and Massachusetts Governor John Winthrop in 1633, encouraged the settlement of the Springfield region. A preliminary survey of the valley by one of Pynchon's men, Joseph Parsons, led to the establishment of several beaver trading sites. One of these sites was between two mountains separated by the river, a section later to be known as Holyoke.

Captain Elizur Holyoke and Rowland Thomas came up the Connecticut Valley and named the westerly mountain, Mt. Thomas, and the easterly one, Mt. Holyoke. Captain Holyoke settled and became the third magistrate of the Springfield territory; only to die February 5, 1676, while commanding troops in King Phillips War. There is no record of his burial place, although his wife, Mary, is buried in Peabody's Cemetery in Springfield, with an elaborate tombstone marking her grave.

Upon his death, Elizur's son, Captain Samuel Holyoke, took over his command. He did not live long, however, and died the following autumn at the age of twenty-eight, fighting in the Indian wars. Another of Elizur's sons was John Holyoke, whose name appears as the recorder on the record of a deed in 1660, two years before the formation of Hampshire County, which included the present counties of Hampden, Franklin, Hampshire, and Berkshire, comprising all of Western Massachusetts, stretching from the banks of the Connecticut River to the area near the Hudson River. One of John Holyoke's descendants, Reverend Edward Holyoke of Marblehead, became president of Harvard College in 1737. A Dr. Frank Holyoke, descendant of Elizur, arrived as late as 1870.

The first-known settler to buy land in the Holyoke area was John Riley, who purchased sixteen acres from the legislature in 1684. His land lies north of the present boundary between West Springfield and Holyoke, partly along what was called Riley's Brook. It is unlikely, however, that he ever settled there.

By 1696, thirty-two families had settled along the west bank of the Connecticut River in the territory of Springfield. This territory started at the southern boundary of Northampton, and extended (with the exception of Smith's Ferry) to Holyoke, West Springfield and Agawam. The Third Parish (also known as North Parish and Ireland Parish) of Springfield, now Holyoke was first settled around 1730 by John Riley, and Captain John Miller, who was a patriot of the early Indian wars. By 1745, six families were living in Ireland Parish, mostly in the area of Northampton Street. Bela Parsons settled here and lived in the Mount Tom Reservation in 1770, not far from where a hotel named the Eyrie House was to be built, almost a century later. Constructed in 1861, on Mount Tom's northern peak, the building was destroyed by a fire in 1900.

In 1795, Benjamin Ball bought a large tract of land from the legislature in what is now the Elmwood section of Holyoke. At the time it was called "Baptist Village," and indeed, a Baptist church was built there. Another church, the "Lord's Barn," would soon be built nearby. Two other early settlers were Captain Luke Day and Samuel Ely, both of whom took part in Daniel Shay's Rebellion, where the local people rose up against the politicians in Boston after the Revolutionary War. New immigrants came to Ireland Parish every year. Churches were erected and homes were built. Most of the residents were engaged in agriculture, but soon within this same section the following were constructed: a sawmill, a gristmill, a tannery, cement works, a textile mill, a tavern and a distillery.

Two ferries crossed the river, one south at Springdale and one north at Smith's Ferry. Just below the Holyoke Falls, at the site of today's South Hadley Bridge (the Old Holyoke Bridge), there was also what was called a swing ferry. The ferries were a marvel of ingenuity. A stone wharf topped by a tall pole was built mid-river. A long wire was strung to the pole and attached to the boat, which was then able to make use of the swift currents and be carried safely across by them.

Near the north ferry was the shad house. Shad fishing, using seines, was a lucrative practice at that time, and the villagers used the shed to store and sell the catch. Farmers and peddlers would come from twenty miles away to purchase shad every spring, and families would store the salted-down fish in barrels for use throughout the year.

Most of Holyoke's early growth was in what is now the Elmwood section, the area known as Baptist Village, and along the road from Springfield to Northampton, now called Northampton Street. Below Calvary Cemetery, in what is now Whiting Farms, was the farm of Enoch Ely. On the upper corner of Beech and Northampton Streets was the farm of Benjamin Ball. He also owned the land now comprising the Beech Street Parks. William Whiting had his farm on land in the present Smith's Ferry district, (then the property of Northampton), just below the Holyoke line. The old Fairfield Homestead, formerly the Morgan home, was in front of the Whiting residence on Northampton Street and Lexington Avenue.

Northwest of the bridge over the Boston and Maine Railroad tracks, where Main Street and the Flats district connect, was the farm of Samuel Ely, in the area known as Depot Hill. Most of what is now known as the Flats was his. His farmhouse was on the present site of the Holy Rosary Church. He sold some of his buildings in 1867 to a Mr. Bowers and a Mr. Moser. There are three streets in this district that bear each of their names respectively. The section south of the City Hall was a great pasture; there were no buildings south of Dwight Street, except those on Northampton Street. South of Dwight Street there were sand banks, shrubs and scattered trees. The section where the Depot was located, on Main Street, was mostly meadowlands; where High and Dwight Streets converge there was a stretch of bog bordered by a small lake. In the Springdale district, there was a farm owned mostly by Mr. Jed Day who had a landing there, where boats docked to transfer freight from riverboats to teams of oxen and horses, that would take goods to the upper districts and to Northampton. The old burying grounds were across from Enoch Ely's farm on Whiting Hill, and on Rock Valley Road. Some graves are still there.

There was a section known as Money Hole Hill in Holyoke. A notable story of the early days was that of the manufacturing of counterfeit money. A gang of experts came up from Chicopee, and made bogus silver coins in Money Hole Hill at the bend in the river, just above the dam site. They were finally caught, and the leader was condemned to have his ears cropped for punishment. The hill retained the name to commemorate the incident.

Crafts Tavern, formerly the property of a man named Abner Miller, and purchased by Chester Crafts in 1832, was operated by Mr. Crafts until his death in 1871. It was famous throughout the north and south districts, and was located on Northampton Street. It was moved not far from there, and renovated by the D.A.R. when Holyoke celebrated its 50th anniversary. Directly across from the Crafts Tavern, one of the district schools was built to educate the children.

Almost all of the first families who came to Ireland Parish were involved in agriculture. They were simple farmers. Many of their farms were on what is now called Northampton Street. Besides the Ball family there were the Whiting, Miller, Fairfield, Morgan and Enoch Ely families there. Samuel Ely owned most of what is now called the Flats, the area where the Boston and Maine Railroad would later lay their tracts.

The principal development in the area during the next fifty years was the construction of a large number of houses and farms between Springfield and Northampton on the road that is now Route 5, and the building of a dam. In addition to this, there was the building of more churches, district schools, and the beginnings of land acquisitions in other sections of the area that is now called Holyoke.

There were no railroads in Ireland Parish during these years. All freight hauling was done by teams of oxen and by river crafts. Hartford was the closest trading town, so all goods and products in Holyoke came from, and went there.

Produce and manufactured goods were carried down the river in sloops, scows and barges. Getting things to Hartford was easy, because of the currents. Receiving anything from Hartford was another story. The currents were dangerous, and there were other obstacles. Once reaching South Hadley Falls, the boats could go no further. There was a drop in the river of about 60 feet there. So a canal, the first in the country, was built. For a toll, powerful teams of horses and yokes of oxen towed the boats back up the two and one half miles of the river to the other side of the falls.

In 1827, a small wing dam was built to divert the currents for the boat canal, and at the same time furnish power for a mill constructed by the Hadley Falls Company, owned by John, Stephen and Warren Chapin and Alfred Smith, who were granted a charter by the Massachusetts Legislature to do this. (Many of these rights were passed on to the second Hadley Falls Company who eventually sold out to the Holyoke Water Power Company.) This was the beginning of Holyoke's involvement in the Industrial Revolution. The beginning of what made Holyoke great.

By 1846, Boston mill owners with holdings in Lowell and Lawrence, and a handful of New York investors, recognizing the huge potential of the Hadley Falls, set out to buy 1,100 acres of land in Holyoke on which to build a dam and cotton mills. Most of the land was owned by local families, and the rest by the Hadley Falls Company. In addition, a new company started by Thomas Perkins, George Lyman and Edmund Dwight had already been authorized to build a dam, locks and canals in the Connecticut River for the development of a waterpower system.

With great efforts, an entrepreneur with many achievements in business, George Ewing, knowing the success of the Lowell and Lawrence mills, began to negotiate the necessary agreements with all parties. The project was beset with problems. Some of the landowners in the area of the dam site were reluctant to sell out to the "cotton lords" as the old school democrat, Samuel Ely called them. Cotton was king in Massachusetts at this time like it never was in the south. Greed set in, and those owning the other land parcels raised their prices, and the Boston investors backed out.

Being enterprising and persistent, the agent for the new, New York investors, the same George Ewing, overcame the obstacles, and by 1847 had bought 1000 acres in the name of the Fairbanks Co. for $119,000. But, the New York investors did not go ahead with the project. They sold out their interests to those from Boston who negotiated with the owners of the Hadley Falls Company to pay them an agreed upon price, with permission for them to take stock, valued at $100,000 in a new water company, to be formed.

The Boston Financiers controlled over twenty cotton manufacturing companies in New England. Outstanding among them were George W. Lyman, Edmund Dwight, Samuel Cabot, William Appleton and Ignatius Sergeant. Those in the Fairbanks Co. were Lyman, Dwight, Cabot and Sergeant, with the treasurer being James K. Mills. Mr. Ewing was paid $20,000 for his services, and named as superintendent of the dam project that began in 1847. Because of disagreements with the investors about the wages they were paying his workers, Ewing never finished what he started. Another engineer, C.P. Rising, took his place.

There was a "planned community" Ewing and the investors envisioned that came to be called "New City." It was the creation of the second Hadley Falls Company that was formed on April 28, 1848. Notwithstanding other setbacks, like a cholera epidemic, the first dam was completed on November 4, 1848. It cost around $75,000 when finished, using the efforts of 1300 men a day. When fully constructed, built with timbers, the dam was over 1000 feet long and 30 feet high. The whole of the structure was bolted together to the bedrock of the river bottom. It was a masterpiece of construction to behold. Looking like the engineering marvel it was, the new company dam was allowed to settle itself for a night before the builders tested it. A grand party was held that evening to celebrate the completion of what was being called "the greatest achievement in America in the last decade," by newspapers all over the world. The celebration was held at the company offices close to the dam, and the owners, engineers and workers partied all night.

The following morning, with great interest, because of its potential, both economically and from an engineering standpoint, the gates of the dam were closed, the water of the Great Rapids was allowed to rise slowly, and thousands of people waited in eager expectation to see the marvel of the century begin its work. Then the unthinkable happened. The dam began to spring a small leak, and then another. The stone bulkhead at the west side of the dam began to weaken. At three o'clock that afternoon, the unimaginable happened. The dam collapsed, and the tons of river water it had briefly held, flowed uncontrollably into the valley below. It was a disaster.

The hopes and dreams of the men that planned the enterprise were "not totally shattered," as one observer put it. Early the following spring, the construction of another dam was started. Learning from their previous mistakes, the engineers avoided further failures. The second dam was finished on October 21, 1849. The structure cost more than $150,000 this time. But now, when they released the water, it held. There were no parties this time, though the project was finally a huge success. There was only one slight problem in the following years. In 1868, small leaks were detected, and an apron was put in place to remedy the situation. The second dam would remain standing, without too many other leaks, until a permanent stone dam replaced it in 1900.

The implementation of the mission to construct the "First Planned City in America," according to the developer's master plan was taken one step at a time. By the time they finished the project, the investors intended to build fifty-four cotton mills, and construct a series of canals throughout the city. They intended to use the energy created by the dam to provide hydroelectric power for the mills. Using the canals, they could sell property rights to investors. By the standards of the time, this multimillion dollar project was an enormous undertaking that captured worldwide attention. But, there was a storm brewing, and it finally hit the city, just as it did all over America. It was called a depression. With the economic depression of the 1850s, growth slowed and building stopped in Holyoke, just like everywhere else. After building only a handful of mills in Holyoke, feeling the awful effects of the Panic of 1857, the Hadley Falls Company declared bankruptcy in 1859. Not giving up on the "New City," Alfred Smith bought out the investors of The Hadley Falls Company in 1859 for $325,000. He incorporated a company called, The Holyoke Water Power Company, with himself as its President.

Amused by all of this wheeling and dealing, Maggie finally looked up from all her notes. She was getting another one of those headaches from reading. It was becoming a problem lately, to read like she used to without this happening. Just then Tom walked into the room, and put down four pages of typed paper on his mother's desk. "You can scan these in now, they're all in order. Merry Christmas, Mom. Now I don't have to go buy you a sweater." He smiled and kissed her, knowing he would anyway.

Looking up at him, Maggie asked, "What did you find out?" she kissed Tom back.

"Technology. Innovation. Creativity," answering her, intentionally separating the words.

Appreciating how smart Tom was, Maggie valued his ability to understand things she could not. She looked at him with a grin on her face, knowing he was going to tell her how they did it. "Do you think you could elaborate a little?" Maggie loved it when Tom did this to her. He enjoyed being cute when he knew something she did not.

"These folks in Holyoke were way ahead of their time. They found a way to produce low cost energy before the rest of the world even imagined it. The dam and the canals were a brilliant concept in the production and transmission of power. But Mom, they didn't only conceive the idea, they actually produced it. Waterpower exists wherever there is a drop in the level of water. There is a drop in the level of the Connecticut River between the upstream rapids and the Holyoke dam. It says in these papers that a fall like this occurs for about a mile and a half in the valley between Mt. Holyoke and Mt. Tom. This is what made the building of the Holyoke dam possible." Tom paused, looking at his mother intently. "Do you understand what they built and how it worked?"

"Explain it to me," she said graciously.

"Unlike the greedy oil barons of today, who monopolize energy for immoral profits, stealing from us common folk, the people who built the water power system in Holyoke created cheap power. This was how they got the investors who built the factories to come to Holyoke. Instead of gouging the mill owners, the Hadley Falls Company that became the Holyoke Water Power Company sold them energy at a fair rate, and in doing so brought in other businesses by showing the potentials and successes of the first mills that located there. Success breeds success. By using the example of the first paper and textile mills that used their power, showing how profitable they were, the company was able to entice more business into the city and sell more power to many other customers."

Maggie could tell that Tom was impressed with the intelligence of the architects of the booming infrastructure. As he continued, Maggie was proud to see him using his apperception as she had taught him, considering how all the parts related to each other. She agreed with his deductions.

"The energy company used their ability and capacity to create, not destroy. Like I said, they had a jump on the rest of the country with their efficacy. They could have been greedy, monopolizing and overcharging the people, as you can clearly see happening now with oil, but they were smarter. They wanted to build a city that would last a long time, where everyone shared and succeeded. Like building blocks, their concepts were a sturdy foundation for others to build on. And it worked, people flocked to Holyoke to take advantage of the inexpensive new power system to build their businesses." He paused.

"Where's the copy you made of that poster, the one from the Holyoke Water Power Company?" Tom asked. "You know, where they're advertising for customers, from the picture book?" Tom was motioning for his mom to find it. After a moment of shuffling through papers, Maggie extricated it from a pile, and held it out for him to take. As Tom turned it toward her, the message of the ad was clear: The poster was three feet high and two feet wide. It read, "The Holyoke Water Power Company" on the top, and then advertised its offerings, "Cheap and Reliable Power – Lots for Stores, Tenements and Residence Purposes, The Greatest Improved Water Power in the World." Holding it up he said "This certainly would catch people's attention" as he gave it back, and sat down next to her on the couch. "Well, it worked. Just like the canal system they built. The canals were the key to the whole thing, Mom. It's how they transferred the power generated from the river water to the plants, and provided the factories with the water they needed for running their buildings and manufacturing. You see, the idea of using the water to generate energy is not a new one, it's ancient. But because of a variety of factors, Holyoke was one of a few places in the country where a system like this could actually be built. The water above the dam they constructed is what is called 'potential energy.' It is useless unless it is turned into active, usable energy. It works something like this."

Tom leaned against one of the cushions, knowing it would take a little while for him to explain to his mother the ingenious way those in Holyoke had used the river water to produce hydroelectric energy. Then he did what his mother loved. He said only one word to begin, to get her interested. "Vision," he smiled, knowing she appreciated his mind.

"What do you mean?" she asked.

"Well it's one thing for something to be there, and it's another for someone to *see* that it's there. The potential of the river, the dam and everything associated with the power project had to be visualized by someone before it could exist. Can you imagine the intellect of whoever it was that actually thought this whole system up and then built it? It was in the 1850s, Mother! Christ, they were still riding horses in Holyoke back then!"

As he continued, Maggie raised her eyebrows, communicating to Tom her displeasure with him using the Lord's name in vain. Tom sustained

The Holyoke Dam Courtesy of the Holyoke Public Library

his enthusiasm as he explained the depth of understanding the men from Holyoke had of mechanics, physics and natural laws, everything necessary to produce the waterpower system.

"There's a section, in the HISTORY OF HOLYOKE MASSACHUSETTS book, you photocopied, written by Anna Scanlon, published in 1939, where a man named F.W. Murphy explains it in layman's terms." Quoting the man's descriptions, Tom continued, "'Water power exists whenever there is a drop in the level of the water. There is a drop of about 60 feet in the level of the river between the rapids and the dam and this made possible the building of the Holyoke dams. There is a similar drop in level from the 1st level canal to the river and this made the canals possible. Water power is created by the running of the water through gates on the canal bank into the mill race where it turns a water wheel as it falls into a lower level canal.'" Tom stopped and looked at Maggie, "This is the simple version. Understand it so far?"

Nodding her head, yes, Maggie's brow was furrowed. Tom knew to go into more detail.

"Mr. Murphy wrote: 'The drop in the level of the riverbed is our most valuable natural resource. To it we owe our industrial development, and because of it of it we were able to build a dam to hold back water which, at will, we can drop about 60 feet through the mill races of our factories to turn the water wheels and put into motion the heavy machinery of our factories. Our development as a city and our leadership in paper making would have been impossible without the canals which permit us to use over and over again the water held back by the dam. The building of the canals was made possible by the natural slope of the hills of the city and the river which curved conveniently around the lower wards of the city and assumed a position almost parallel to the canals.'"

Tom paused for a moment, thinking about everything he had memorized, and then went on giving his explanations one step at a time to help his mother organize her own ideas. "He goes on to evaluate why the canals were necessary to power the mills, 'Water power is used by running the water through gates on the canal bank into the mill where it turns the water wheel as it falls into the lower canal. Canal water is used in Holyoke for three purposes: turning water wheels; in the process of manufacture; to generate electricity by turning turbine generators of electricity. Paper production also requires great supplies of water not only to run the tremendously large machinery, but also in the washers and beaters and on the paper machines. If the development of Holyoke's water power were taking place today, (1939) as opposed to the second half of the 1800s, instead of an expensive canal system which brought the water directly to the mills for power, we might possibly develop enormous plants for generating electricity at or near the dam. Then the water power, changed to electric power, could be brought to the mills by means of electric wires and any water necessary for manufacturing purposes would be brought through pipe lines.'" Tom looked at his mother and said, "But in the 1800s this was not an option. There were no wires. So, they visualized, and then actually created a different way to transmit the energy, a canal system."

Continuing his quoting from the history book, Tom said, "'On the Holyoke end of the dam there is a red brick building called the Gate House. Here are located the head gates through which the water flows from behind the dam and out into a short stretch of canal which can be called the canal feed being the upper end of the first level canal. The first level canal branches off to the right (south) and the canal feed flows along a few hundred feet, until it passes under the Holyoke Water Power Electric Station and turns hydro-electric generators as it drops into the sec-

The Gatehouse (Upper Left) at the Dam Courtesy of the Holyoke Public Library

ond level canal. Meanwhile, the first level canal flows south, just below Front, Railroad, Bond and Commercial streets sending water to the second level canal through the mill races of the Whiting, Prentiss Wire, Beebe & Holbrook, Wauregan, Skinner, American Thread, Alpaca I, Crocker McElwain, City of Holyoke Electric Light Station, Dickenson, Parsons, Linden and Alpaca II: furnishing power to all those mills and then winding up at a dead end adjacent to one of the Alpaca buildings just before it reaches Jackson Street. If we take the start of the second level canal at the over flow at the Holyoke Water Power hydro-electric plant where the first level ends, it goes both to the right and left, extending south along Race Street where it receives the water coming under the mills from the first level canals and finally overflows over a falls where Canal Street meets Main Street just north of the entrance to Falco field. In the other direction the second level canal flows from the hydro-electric station along Canal Street beyond the Street Railway office by the main plant of the Holyoke Water Power Company until it finally overflows at a falls at the other end of the third level canal.'"

"Could you slow it down a little, dear?" Maggie asked, evermore impressed with his analytical capability. Tom simply smiled back, knowing how complicated the design and building of the dam and canals actually was.

"OK, the mechanics of the whole power system are unbelievable, Mom. You get the point though, right? The water was used over and over again to power the factories." Tom was enjoying this.

"I get the idea," his mother said.

Simplifying it for her as best he could, Tom again quoted the man who explained it all so well in the book, "'By building three parallel canals, the second 20 feet below the first and the third 12-1/2 lower than the second, we are able to have water rush from the first (highest) level canal through the mill gates, along the mill races where it turns the water wheels and turbine generators and then out through the arched portholes in the mill's foundation walls into the second level canal on the next lower level. The same water goes through mill races and water wheels in flowing from the second to the third (lowest) level canal and the same process is repeated again with the water in the third level passing through the mill races under the mills into the river which is still at a lower level. With a minor modification in the second and third level canals this is how the Holyoke system works.' Impressive, huh?" he asked his mother. Tom

First Level Canal Courtesy of the Holyoke Public Library

Second Level Canal Courtesy of the Holyoke Public Library

Third Level Canal Courtesy of the Holyoke Public Library

continued, "It's like the Mayans, if one looks at their foresight in the construction of the Mayan calendar. Someone had to *see* it before they could draw it. If one looks at Holyoke, one can see the same vision in the design and construction of the city's dam and canal system." After he made the comparison, Tom laid back on the couch. He was starting to sound like the book he had been quoting.

Tom began to better explain the mechanics of the dam and canal system to his mother. Summarizing Holyoke's dam and canal marvel for Maggie, he paraphrased the explanations of Mr. F.W. Murphy once more, reinforcing them with some of his own. "Think of it as a miniature model, Mom. Try and picture this water power system as a model on a table in front of you. If you *see* it in your mind it's easier to understand what they did."

Watching Maggie close her eyes to visualize his explanation, Tom continued, "The development of Holyoke's waterpower system depended on a number of factors, including a drop in the level of the water, an ongoing supply of it that was provided by mountain streams and lake water flowing into the Connecticut River. The elementary principle of waterpower requires water at a high level flowing to a lower level. It did. The dam was built to control the flow of water it held above into the canals that were at lower levels, and the speed of the flow of the river water was controlled by the amounts of water released through the dam by its flow controls. The running water entered the mills through the millraces, and it propelled the contrivances that were created to move the mechanisms of the machines, like the water wheel on a long shaft; the water striking the blades turns the wheel, which in turn rotates the shafts that permits the running of other machinery, by a means of belts and gears, to run the larger machines. In its brilliance, it's simple." Tom paused, making sure his mother understood what he was saying. Maggie nodded her head for him to proceed. Tom now emphasized certain key phrases to bring home his point.

"This was the theory that began it all, that made it all possible. Once they decided this, the Holyoke engineers made it all work, by building it. The *vision* was that they could construct a series of canals to use the water of the river released from the dam to create reliable, almost unlimited supplies of energy. But, the water had to be there in sufficient amounts in the first place, and was, thanks to nature. There also had to be a drop in height from one point to another to begin with, which, thank God there was. Otherwise the whole concept would not have been possible. The building of the canals was made feasible by the height of the river, and the natural slopes of the hills of Holyoke. By building three parallel canals, one below the other, the water would rush from the highest level, through the mill gates, along the millraces where it turned the water wheels to generate power from the rotation of the wheels, and electricity by turning turbine generators. Then it flowed out arched portholes in the mills' foundation walls into the next canal on the next lower level. Everything had to be constructed, *pitched* in the right direction to keep the water constantly *flowing downwards*. In theory the same water could go through millraces and water wheels in flowing from the second to the third lowest level canal, and then the same process would be repeated again with the water in the third level canal, passing through millraces under the mills into the river which was still, at a lower level. These theories were actually put into practice in Holyoke! This was what was conceived of, built, and ran the hundreds of factories of the famous first 'Planned City in America.' Building it, and having everything work together properly was more spectacular than putting all of the stone blocks of the Egyptian pyramids in place, and then standing back to watch them settle in as one solid structure."

Opening her eyes, Maggie said, "I'm proud of you, but not just for this." It was not easy to drag this complicated information out of the menagerie of papers she had given him. Maggie greatly admired her son's capacity to make simple, what was complex. His father had taught him to do things like this. When Maggie pictured in her mind what Tom was describing to her, she could actually see it operating.

Maggie wanted to regurgitate the information, confirming she had understood it and extrapolating where she could. "So, Mother Nature has to provide almost perfect conditions, the river water in seemingly inexhaustible supplies, flowing in the right direction with a significant drop in the river bed at just the right places." Maggie smiled, knowing she had gotten it right.

"*Yes*," Tom answered Maggie, smiling back at her.

"Then they had to build what was at the time the largest dam in the world by hand. With the world watching, because nothing like this had been attempted before," Maggie added, now grinning. "This was needed to start up everything," Maggie paused, "to harness the water that would provide the power they needed to run everything in the city."

"That's right." Tom gave her a look of encouragement, to continue.

"Once they built it and it stayed up, they had to devise methods of regulating the flows of water to produce the energy in adequate amounts to run everything in the city." Maggie was speeding along now.

"Correct," Tom interjected.

"The contours of the City of Holyoke had to be the way they were so that the three levels of canals could be built in such a fashion that the water flowed constantly downwards back towards the river, after supplying power to the hundreds of factories that were built on them in exact locations to allow all of this to happen." Maggie had remembered points from her own research.

"*Yes.*" Tom was impressed.

"The canals were built on three levels, one below the other, and hundreds of factories were constructed along them, all utilizing the energy produced by the dam and canal system to operate their buildings and machines."

"*Yes,*" Tom said, urging her on.

"The millraces to these factories had to be made exact so the water would flow in. Once it did, it had to be powerful enough to turn the power generators and the water wheels that in turn moved the belts and gears to power the thousands and thousands of different machines that must have been in the mills, those that were on all of the floors, in the hundreds of factories, built along the canals of Holyoke."

"That's right," he said, proudly.

"Once this happened, the water had to flow out properly through portholes cut meticulously in the factories' foundations so that the water could pass onto the next factory on the canal, and then the next. After it powered all the mills on that level canal, it flowed down into the next level canal to the factories that were there, and did the same thing. They used the same water to provide power to all the machines, in all the factories, on all three different canals."

"Go on." Tom knew his mom had the whole picture now.

"Once the water raced through all of the canals, and powered all of the factories on all three levels, it went back into the river which, just by chance, was at a lower level than all three of the canals and the factories."

"And?" he prompted Maggie.

"None of this existed before someone could *see* the natural potentials that were there, and then envisioned the utilization of these potentials by building a power and transfer system that was unique to say the least, in that nothing like it had ever been constructed before, anywhere in the world." As she finished saying the words, Maggie began pondering the caliber of intellect it would take to dream this up.

"That about sums it up, Mom. A clean, inexpensive, almost inexhaustible supply of energy, possible because the inventive developers of Holyoke put the whole puzzle together. They saw that the natural components necessary for the system to work were there, and then they had the imagination, and the courage to take the risks to build it, by hand, one wheel barrel, one shovel at a time." Tom couldn't let it go, till he reminded Maggie with a few final statements on the significance of what was done in Holyoke. "Remember, what gave Holyoke the one-up on the rest of the world was the fact that they were the creators, the innovators of this type of water power system. They were the first people in the world to build a city using water to produce energy in this manner, and built a huge industrial complex that required a massive work force to operate. Hundreds of thousands of jobs were created in Holyoke, because of the low cost of power. Not the reverse, like now, where power is expensive and the companies go overseas to find cheap labor, ruining the lives of many American families. Because those in Holyoke did things the right way, they had an incredible advantage over the rest of the world for decades, and in the process built a healthy, prosperous community for everyone to live in."

Putting it all in perspective for his mother, Tom summarized his thoughts on why those in Holyoke were able to do all of this, with one word, "Destiny."

Maggie looked at him lovingly, understanding exactly what he meant. For all of this to come together, at one specific time and place was incredible. It was as if someone had put all the pieces there at just the right time for them to figure it all out. "How did the power companies actually make money selling such cheap energy?" She entreated him, confident he'd figured that out as well.

Tom was prepared for this question also, knowing so well his mom's need to know this kind of information. "By not gouging their customers, they increased demand by bringing in new ones, investors to build their factories and businesses in the city. Once these people made money, they built more factories, and hired more workers. The word spread quickly in the investment world, and many more entrepreneurs came to Holyoke to make their money. It was all part of the Holyoke equation: success produces more success, but *only* if everyone shares that success. This was the real idea behind the whole 'Planned City' concept. Everyone had to be benefiting for it to work, including the power company."

"What else?" Maggie knew there was more.

Looking at his mother, he said, smiling, "Once they finished paying for their initial investments everything they took in was pure profit except for maintenance. They paid for the dam, the canals and everything associated with the construction and running of it very quickly, because of the numbers of factories they brought in to use their power. As the demand for their power grew, they just let out a little more water. It was brilliant, and for a time, acceptable, because everyone benefited from their creation." He just shook his head, admiring how incredibly resourceful they had been to think of this. "Fortunes were made in Holyoke because of this foresight. These men were geniuses, Mother, not street hustlers like the people running big business today."

Changing the subject, he said, "Hey, I'm still in the exam mode, Mom. This was fun. It sure beats the hell out of trying to understand why the three branches of the federal government aren't functioning like they were designed to by our Founding Fathers, those other honorable, amazing intellectuals. Why have their checks and balances failed?" he asked rhetorically. "At least when the Holyoke boys finished their project it all came together. It still works, I think. That's a tribute to them." Tom was awed by the achievements of the designers and contractors who built the dam, canal and factory system in Holyoke.

Seeing that it was six o'clock, Tom asked his Mother a more serious question. "When's dinner? I'm starving. All this talk about work is making me hungry!"

SIX

The next morning, Maggie picked up where she left off the day before in her studies of the Holyoke experience. The one that happened a hundred years ago, that as her son had accurately put it, "made fortunes for a lot of people." Bringing herself and her computer back up to speed, Maggie collected her thoughts by reading what she had already typed.

By 1860, the closest trading town to Hadley, Northampton, Holyoke, West Springfield, Springfield and a few other settlements in the Connecticut Valley was Hartford, Connecticut. Trading was done by boat, using the waters of the Connecticut River to transfer supplies to the settlers. Most of them relied upon hunting, fishing and agriculture to survive. But that was about to change.

Men from Boston and New York were coming to the area in droves, looking for investments, low risk manufacturing opportunities, based upon the successes of plants in Lowell and Lawrence. Not anticipating it, something happened, something that would change the face of the valley forever. It happened in Holyoke.

Holyoke wasn't just a part of the Industrial Revolution, it was a jewel of the Industrial Revolution. Prior to the completion of the dam, there were only a handful of factories in Holyoke, nothing much to speak of, only a few mills producing some materials.

The Hadley Falls Company had up to this time built only three small mills, including what they called Factory No 1. When the dam neared completion, they set out to build more, a blacksmith shop, a machine shop and an office building. The first water wheel for generating power was installed in the No. 1 mill in 1850. During the next decade, nothing much was developed. Ventures were planned, but there was not a significant amount of activity or investment.

But, by the end of the 1850s everything changed.

In 1859, after the Holyoke Water Power Company bought out the Hadley Falls Company, the national economy, stimulated by the Civil

War, increased the demand for manufactured goods. Holyoke grew rapidly.

Taking advantage of the low cost energy offered by the new power company, a number of industries built factories along the canals, and began to produce high-quality papers, threads, silks, cottons, wools and other products.

These mills needed laborers. Poor people, hearing about these jobs, came to the city to get work. They came from all over the world: Irish, French–Canadian, German, Polish, Jews and other immigrants came to Holyoke to work. The city population rose from 4,600 in 1855 to 35,600 in 1890 when industrial growth peaked.

The Parsons Paper Mill, started by Joseph Clark Parsons, was Holyoke's first large paper mill. The name, Edward P. Bagg III is associated with the Parsons family ever since the founding of the company. They built a factory on the canals in 1853. Parsons was associated with several other Holyoke paper mills, the Farr Alpaca that produced wools, and he was an incorporator of several banks, including the Third National bank in Springfield, the Hadley Falls Bank and the Holyoke Savings Bank.

In 1854, two small cotton mills were taken over by the Lyman Mills. The Holyoke Paper Company opened in 1857. The Whiting Paper Company came shortly afterwards, around 1865, and the Riverside Paper Company in 1866. The Franklin mill opened also in 1866. By the end of the century, there were over fifteen other paper mills in the city. This was one of the reasons that Holyoke was referred to as the "Paper City of the World."

Besides the paper companies, the canals were lined with factories that produced textiles, wire, threads, rubber, wools, machine parts and all sorts of other manufactured products. A coal company opened, the William Whiting Coal Company, to distribute coal and wood to people living in the city. A newspaper began to circulate its publications of the city news. It was called the Hampden Freeman, and was succeeded by the Transcript, owned by the Dwight family.

Huge buildings were built to accommodate all the businesses. Among the most prominent was the Gothic style City Hall, a structure that resembled the enormous buildings of London that could be seen from all over the city. Across the street from that was another important building. The Delaney's totally marble building, standing on High and Dwight streets, was constructed entirely by John Delaney, from top to bottom,

Delaney's Building On High & Dwight Courtesy of the Holyoke Public Library

inside and out, out of marble that he had hauled in from Vermont.

In 1869, the Holyoke and Westfield Railroad was built, linking the towns of Holyoke and Westfield. In Westfield, it connected to the New Haven Railroad Canal line and the Boston and Albany Railroad. The railroad was mostly a freight carrier railroad.

Because of the incredible successes of the business community, Holyoke's residential districts developed. Block, or tenement housing was the most popular in Holyoke, with hundreds of buildings put up, most in the lower and middle wards of the city.

The finer houses were built further up the hills: in the Churchill, Oakdale and Ingleside sections; and the Dwight, Lincoln and Northampton Street areas of Holyoke. The large homes and mansions were constructed with fine woods, supplied by the lumber mill, opened by Joseph Curtis Lewis. He opened a lumberyard in 1871, just above the dam.

Land speculators came from Manchester, New Hampshire, and bought large tracks of land in what is now the Highlands section of the city. This area became a wealthier section of town, and many of the wonderful Victorian homes, built during Holyoke's glory days, are still there.

The Kenilworth Castle was built by the owner of the Albion Paper Company, a Mr. E.C. Taft, at the bottom of Mount Tom. Looking like it belonged in the mountains of Austria, the reproduction of a European castle was world famous.

In the last part of the century, the city's fortunes continued to be affected by the national economy. It went up and down. But, by the 1880s, Holyoke had become a boomtown, both in industrial growth and in other commercial enterprises.

The busy downtown district on Main Street became known as Depot Square. The Square was close to the railroad freight yards, and the passenger train station where the Boston and Maine, New Haven, and Connecticut River Railroads loaded and unloaded their freight, as well as dropped off and took on their passengers each day. Depot Square was the focal point of business activity in Holyoke for decades, until other

Holyoke's Kenilworth Castle COURTESY OF THE HOLYOKE PUBLIC LIBRARY

Depot Square COURTESY OF THE HOLYOKE PUBLIC LIBRARY

businesses and public offices opened on High and Maple Streets. Then that section became the focal point of Holyoke's business. The Depot was a bustling center of activity, with trolleys coming and going, horse drawn carts carrying people and materials over the cobblestone streets, from and to the mills, to the living areas, and to the sections where the churches and parks were. Two construction companies, the P.J. Kennedy Company and the Daniel O'Connell Company, were doing a great deal of the new building in the city.

In Depot Square there were banks, a French bakery, a Jewish meat market, a German sausage shop, an Irish grocery, furniture shops, small hotels, many restaurants and of course, there were the bars. There was also a brothel opened by Carrie Pratt on Lower Westfield Road.

Maggie smiled. "They would never have stayed, if there were no bars or prostitutes."

There was great entertainment in Holyoke in the form of theatres. The Majestic and Bijou were two of the famous Holyoke movie houses. The others were the Victory and the Strand.

Many churches of all denominations were constructed, and Sundays everyone went to church dressed in their finest clothes. Religion was an important factor in the growth of the city. The oldest churches in the city are the First Baptist Church on Northampton Street, the First and Second Congregational Churches and Saint Jerome's Catholic Church. All of these churches built schools.

The city library was constructed in 1870 with land given by the Parsons family, and money donated from many people, including William Skinner, William Whiting and J. P. Morgan, the world famous financier.

Public and parochial schools were also built during these years. The old Gamwell Academy that was put up by the settlers on Homestead Road had been torn down, and there was a need for more up-to-date public schools. This produced many new schools all over the city, for all grades, from first grade through high school. Fire stations were put up, and a central police station was constructed.

Doctors and nurses came, and hospitals were erected to tend to the sick. Sister Mary of Providence, from Quebec, came here. She took care of the orphans, and established many child welfare programs. Her nuns opened clinics to take care of the sick, and eventually a hospital. Other sisters followed who taught in the schools, and took care of the poor. Rabbis, ministers and priests tended to the souls.

A lot of pharmacies opened their doors to dispense medicines. The chemists brought in, mixed and dispensed what the people needed to treat the diseases that infected the city. Most of the remedies were made from plant extracts, opium and morphine substances. At one time there were nineteen independent drug stores in the city.

William Whiting became friendly with William McKinley when the President came to Mount Holyoke College, the elite girls' college opened in 1837 in South Hadley, that the Skinner family helped support. McKinley came to attend the graduation of his niece there. William Whiting's son, William F. Whiting Jr., became a confidant of President Calvin Coolidge, and was the successor of Herbert Hoover as Secretary of Commerce for the United States government.

A large hotel called the Holyoke House was constructed by E.M. Belden, and opened in 1865. It is said to have rivaled the best that were available in Boston. Only the elite who visited Holyoke could afford to stay there.

On March 25, 1878 the famous Opera House of Holyoke opened to a thrilled, packed audience. Built by the Whiting family, it became a landmark of the city for decades. Some of the greatest American actors and actresses of all time came to perform there. They stayed in the beautiful

Windsor Hotel that was also built by the Whiting family. Sarah Bernhardt, George M. Cohan, and Al Jolson were just a few notable names who performed at the Opera House.

Holyoke became a mecca for investment and employment. Businessmen and women from all over the world flocked to the city hearing about the incredible opportunities. The Japanese came to sell the Skinners the silk filaments from the silkworm cocoons they needed to make their silk products. Germans came looking for turbine parts and wire products. The French came looking for the fine wools and threads. Everyone came to buy paper, or sell the rags to make it.

The Holyoke Street Railroad was running trains in and out of Depot Square by the 1870s to connect Main Street with only some of the upper town sections. Not wanting to develop their operations further, they sold the business to William Stiles Loomis in the 1880s. He electrified the trains, and expanded the distances the trains traveled to other areas, including sections he had bought in Elmwood. He also bought up most of Mount Tom, and soon the trolley routes included the mountain area.

Holyoke's Opera House COURTESY OF THE HOLYOKE PUBLIC LIBRARY

Looking North Towards Mt. Tom Courtesy of Harry Craven

By 1894, he had connected all of his properties to the lines, and in addition had built an amusement park called Mountain Park at the base of Mt. Tom. The rides at the park were some of the finest in the country, with a remarkable carousel. It was housed in a large circular building in the center of the park, right where the trolleys dropped the people off to ride the rides.

In 1896, Mr. Loomis built the Mt. Tom Railroad, and a year later, with considerable efforts, he constructed the first Summit House on the top of Mt. Tom. Patrons of the hotel would take HSR trains from downtown to the trolley passenger discharge building at Mountain Park. Arriving there, they would then go to the lower station house at the park and board a train of the Mt. Tom Railroad that would take them to the upper station, and the Summit House at the top. The construction of the cable cars, and the way they operated was unusual. They used a system of counterweights, one car countering the weight of the other, to safely bring the guests the one mile to and from the top and bottom of the mountain. At the time, it was the only system like it in the country. The mountain hotel is said to have been one of loveliest resorts in the world. When it was operating at full scale, kings and queens came to stay there.

While miners were looking for gold in the west of the country, those in Holyoke manufactured silks, fabrics and other materials, and built the machinery that made it. It has been said, that at the turn of the century, Holyoke's industrialists and businessmen were some of the wealthiest

Dwight Street Around 1910 COURTESY OF HARRY CRAVEN

people in the world. The Skinner Mills alone sold $6.5 million of their products a year by 1902, and they were still growing. Considering the size of the city, there were more millionaires in Holyoke, per capita, than any other city in the United States. By today's standards, they were all very, very rich.

Turning the pages of her notebook, the data Maggie had collected moved her and Holyoke into the 20th century. Maggie forged ahead, reading her notes, and looking at the copies she had made of the history of Holyoke. As she continued reading, Maggie suspected Holyoke would have a dark side.

By the early 1890s, another depression hit America. The city felt its pains for decades. Even though business growth continued at a feverish pace in Holyoke, with the construction of buildings, tenements, churches and homes, not everyone was prospering. For some strange reason, the people of the city, more than the owners of the mills, began to be dramatically effected by the economic crunch caused by the depression. It seemed to have something to do with the distribution of wealth, and the quality of the living conditions for those who lived around, and worked in, some of the mills of the city. Their money became less valuable; they had to pay higher prices for everything. It began when the clocks ticked the world into the 20th century.

In 1902, the City of Holyoke took over the operations of the Holyoke Water Power Company by popular vote, voted on by the men who voted at the polls. The people thought the government could do a better job of running the power company than private business.

Wondering if this had been a good idea, to let municipal government run a private enterprise, Maggie turned only a few more pages, thinking she had read enough for now. "It usually creates conflicts of interest," she said the words aloud to herself. Contemplating, Maggie thought the taking over of the power company by the city was similar to what is happening now, a hundred years later, except in reverse with private enterprise taking over the national government. She knew that it was not a good idea to mingle the private economics of a city, or country, with the government, or vice versa. It never worked out in the people's best interest. Corruption always sets in. It's inevitable, and prices go up. Suddenly, she felt tired. Maggie had been working for hours.

Looking at her notes and the input on her computer one final time, Maggie was satisfied. She had reached a point where she was content to stop for a while. There is always tomorrow, she thought, plenty of time to try and understand more of what had happened in Holyoke. Knowing the mall would be crowded if she waited much longer, Maggie headed out to finish her last minute Christmas shopping. Buying a few Christmas presents for her son was more important. Holyoke would have to wait.

SEVEN

Maggie and her son had a wonderful Christmas together. They visited friends and relatives on a whim on Christmas Eve. Then, arm in arm, they went to the town common to listen to the carols being sung. There were hundreds of people at the common. Then, Maggie and Tom went to midnight Mass together. Once that was over, they went home to get some rest and wait for the morning to open presents. Santa had not come yet.

Maggie remembered looking around the crowd at the concert, wondering if Holyoke was having a similar affair. She thought not. She recalled Katherine telling her about how the city had been lit up brightly in the old days, and how festive Holyoke was then, when they all gathered in front of the City Hall to celebrate Christ's birthday. Maggie suspected that not one person was standing in front of the City Hall this Christmas Eve. It would be a pity if she was right.

The day after Christmas, Maggie began to study more of the history of the city of Holyoke, and to type into her computer her version of what had taken place there a century ago.

In 1890, Holyoke had a population of 36,600 people, by 1917, that figure had risen to 62,210 people. Commercial investments, by this time, were staggering. Mills and factories were everywhere. The canal section of the city was lined with mills.

Like New York, Holyoke became a melting pot for many immigrants. Irish, Scottish, Polish, German, Russian, Jews and other immigrants all arrived looking for a better way of life for their children and grandchildren, than what they'd left behind. It has been said that a sign was erected, not far from the Statue of Liberty and Ellis Island that read, "Holyoke—200 miles," with an arrow that pointed north.

During these years, the factories that were so vital to the growth of the city prospered and multiplied. Building upon their successes, many investors funded new factories, and the number of mill buildings grew dramatically. World demand for products made in Holyoke soared. There was plenty of work, fair wages, decent housing and a reasonably healthy community. For thirty years, investments in Holyoke flowed like the river water over the dam that powered the city. It seemed as if the huge profits would never stop, just like the endless flow of water from Canada.

Life in Holyoke was not without its troubles and tragedies, which were not all economic. The first Summit House that sat atop Mt. Tom burned down in 1900. It was a terrible loss to the community, and William Stiles Loomis built a second Summit House in 1901, to replace it. The second Summit House was even more beautiful, and profitable, than its predecessor. With its grand dining room and fabulous guest rooms, it was one of the most respected, elegant resorts in the world.

Moving her research from the highest point in Holyoke, Mount Tom, to the lowest, the tenements in the areas of the canals, Maggie pondered the conditions of the workers in the city, those who could not afford to stay in the grand hotel. In 1910, even though working conditions in the mills were good, Holyoke had the third highest populated tenements of

Whiting Coal Company & The Skinner Mills Courtesy of Harry Craven

any city in the United States. In these cold-water flats, diseases like cholera, tuberculosis, and typhoid surfaced. In addition, the air along the canals was choked with chemical-laden smoke from the mills' chimneys seven days a week, twenty-four hours a day. The effects of air pollution, lack of sanitation and hot water, and overcrowding contributed to rampant ill health among the workers and chronic conditions that would not become evident for years.

During the first ten years of the 20th century, there were several epidemics in the city. Many lives were lost. Every family was affected, both rich and poor. In some ways these disasters brought the families of Holyoke closer together. In other ways, it separated them.

These and a variety of other factors began to affect the level of investment made in Holyoke's industry. There was the development of alternate forms of energy that offered competitive cities a chance to attract the new businesses. In some ways, it was cheaper for the factory owners to locate any new plants in other parts of the country, closer to their customers, or to the timber, in the case of many paper companies. Overcharging for services by the railroad companies was a huge problem, and the Holyoke Gas and Electric Company, now owned by the City of Holyoke, went up on its rates. What had been Holyoke's strength, its energy, was now Holyoke's weakness. Those who controlled the gas and electric companies began to be called the Power Barons. Maggie knew that everyone loses when energy moguls suck too much out of the economy.

In addition to all the tragedies, illnesses and economic hardships, a number of dramatic events and lifestyle changes occurred in the early part of the 20th century that would change Holyoke and America forever. First, the Federal Income Tax Law passed in 1913, subsequently World War I began, and then, the Prohibition Act was passed, giving birth to the Roaring Twenties. The final blow was the Stock Market Crash of 1929. This produced the Great Depression of the 1930s. While each of these factors in its own way produced terrors for everyone living in the nation, all of these elements in combination, completely changed Holyoke. Most of the people who lived in the city during the Great Depression saw the other side of Camelot. In many ways, this was the beginning of the downfall of Holyoke, the demise of a great city.

Maggie abruptly lifted her fingers off the keypad, and leaned her head back against the chair. Now knowing Holyoke's stellar past, she couldn't help but wonder about its journey to become the city she now knew. Realizing this would be a whole new chapter for Holyoke, albeit not a good one, Maggie decided it was time to take a break. A little more coffee was needed, if Maggie was to have any hopes of reading all of this, let alone processing it. She could feel her mind beginning to wander, and knew caffeine would help her concentrate. So, Maggie got up from her computer, went to the kitchen, and made a fresh pot of coffee.

Maggie jolted her mind and body back into focus with two cups of coffee. She felt better. Back at the computer again, she scrolled to the last paragraph. Maggie had to refresh her mind. Ah, *yes*, the demise of Holyoke.

The 16th Amendment to the Constitution, the Income Tax Act of 1913 made people begin to think differently about how to run their businesses and where to invest their money. If businessmen were going to have to pay a tax on their profits, it made no sense to openly invest it. So, big business, in forming corporations, began to be the norm, and companies began to look for ways to hide their money by moving it around and taking deductions. It was hard to hide the large sums of money made in the factories of Holyoke. So, considering the alternatives, the owners began to shelter it, or invest elsewhere, sometimes out of the country. Unfortunately, those who worked for them didn't have the same options.

Enough said, Maggie thought.

Getting on to the First World War, Maggie remembered from history classes that it was the assassination of Archduke Franz Ferdinand, the heir apparent to Austria's Emperor Franz Josef, and his wife Sophia, Duchess of Hohenberg, by the Bosnian Serb, Garvilo Princip that started it all off.

Maggie went online, and seeing the Google pop-up, she once again appreciated what the Internet had done for research. A mere ten years earlier, she would have had to go through the library's history stacks to get facts. Now, a search by name resulted in a chronology of events for World War I. The war began after the Royals were shot and killed on June 28, 1914. By August 1, various hostilities had been declared, sides had been drawn, and military forces were moving into place. Austria-Hungary had declared war on Serbia, which allied with Russia and declared war on Germany. Germany declared war on France, entered neutral Luxembourg, and occupied neutral Belgium. Within three weeks of the assassinations of the Archduke and Duchess of Austria, Great Britain entered the war. Large Big Bertha canons began firing, and within a year most of the world was embroiled in the conflict that would ultimately be called the Great War. Although the United States didn't enter the fray until 1917, a considerable amount of financial aid, munitions, and other supplies began being shipped out of U.S. harbors to England and France, within weeks of the start of fighting.

In Holyoke, business prospered. The conflict in Europe created a need for Holyoke's products, especially wool for uniforms and socks. Skinner silks were used in the manufacturing of the first silk parachutes. Prentiss mills' iron, steel, non-ferrous wires, and filaments were purchased for lightbulbs. Paper companies thrived on the volumes of writing paper needed for the constant communication all around the world.

On a negative note, the war was bad for Holyoke because many of the men from the city were called upon to go and fight in the war. Without these men to work in the factories, it became hard for the owners to keep up with production. There were only two options. They had to decrease production, or use the women and children of Holyoke to make up the difference. Overworking the women in the city and child labor became a problem for some of the poorly run mills. Unable to keep up with the production for the orders that they had, the mill owners looked to their contacts in the South of the United States for help. The first wave of black workers came to Holyoke shortly after the war began.

Woodrow Wilson obtained a Declaration of War from the Congress in 1917. It was a provision of the Constitution that the Congressmen perform this duty. When they did, America was officially in the war until the end. So, all of the able-bodied men were called upon to serve their country. By the time the war finally ended, when the treaty of Versailles was signed on June 28th, 1919, a lot of money had been made in Holyoke. In the process, many lives had been lost, and the whole society felt the devastating effects of the terrible conflict that was anything but great.

Many Holyoke soldiers didn't come back home from Europe. Because of this, their families were destroyed. When the lucky ones who did survive returned home, they were never the same. They came back to a city that didn't look quite like it had when they left. There had been a transformation in the city, as well as in them. Some of the changes were not so good.

The tight little community they had known wasn't there anymore.

Maggie detected there was light at the end of the tunnel, though perhaps a very small one. "And it was probably powered by some of those Prentiss wire filaments made in Holyoke," Maggie said the words out loud. "Just trying to brighten things up. Ha! Ha! No pun intended." Maggie thought she might need another break, but decided to forgo it.

Forging on, Maggie started to read aloud, "The 18th Amendment to the Constitution was passed in 1919. Prohibition was here. Looking back, everyone wonders why. It just allowed the wrong people to take over the distribution of alcohol, and make large sums of money doing it." And, it also made for a great deal of violence and crime that wasn't there before, Maggie knew.

Maggie continued on in silence. The year 1920 began a new decade in America, one that is still talked about when discussing the good old carefree days, if that kind of time really exists. The illegal gin flowed all day, and everyone partied and danced all night. Some danced so much, they couldn't get to work the next day. Then, they didn't have a job.

Because of the ban on booze, the States each entered into a new phase of their social history, one filled with money, anything goes attitudes, corrupt politicians and gangsters. The whole moral atmosphere in the country changed. There were those who enjoyed the new subcultures, while others wanted to keep the moral values taught to them by their forefathers.

"So it goes in New York, it goes in Holyoke," someone had once said. But, that was not the case now. The big cities, like New York, Boston and Chicago were where the action was. That's where the criminals ran the gambling, the booze, and kept the "girls" busy. In comparison, for the most part, Holyoke remained civilized and moral. The residents of the city had invested too much in their community to allow this type of activity. You could take a train to New York, if you wanted to party with the high rollers.

That's not to say that Carrie Pratt's house on the hill wasn't busy every night in Holyoke. Or, that the illegal bars weren't busy, they were. More than one prominent citizen was arrested when the police raided Carrie's brothel, or the newer ones, run by Mother Rice and Pruddie Williams. Many more were let out the back door of the police station, drunk, and told to go home.

But, unlike the larger cities, where the real serious corruption was going on, Holyoke inhabitants were struggling hard to hang on to what they had worked for and their livelihoods. They continued to make their living honestly by going to work every day. And, they were God fearing people. They didn't want to commit sin. So, they kept their activities low key.

For Holyoke, relying on its factories, and not on people's weakness to make money, the roar of the twenties made very little sound in the city. It did hurt its economy by taking money out of circulation that could have been invested in building factories, instead of buying those things that were illegal. When a lot of the country's money is diverted into buying illegal alcohol by vice organizations, those elements of society that are controlled by crime syndicates, legitimate businesses suffer. Not to mention the drain they create on the social systems.

When organized crime wanted to expand the reach of its vices, they came to Holyoke. They knew that was where the money was, and they wanted it. The thugs, the unsavory ones, the transients, the loafers, and the con men all began to find their way into the city. When they arrived, they took money from those who had earned it honestly. It was hard keeping the corruption out, because of the many trains coming into the stations from so many places every day, with so many people on them that no one knew. Depot Square on Main Street, never quite looked the same again.

Maggie sat back, and thought about the movies she had seen about the 20s and 30s in America. In "The Godfather, " the head of the Mafia, played by Marlon Brando, had the most impact on her. His power grew out of the depression. He made everyone fear him. Maggie's mind did a quick comparison between the moral character of the founders of Holyoke, and the man everyone was terrified of in the movie. It was like comparing God and the Devil.

Looking back at her computer screen, Maggie realized she was getting further along with things. Her fingers pushed the keys as she pressed on to wrap up the last part of her story. "Well, one of the last parts," she said aloud, as she mused about her research into the components of Holyoke's decay.

Maggie read the first line of an article written by a New York Times editor, "They started pulling the money out earlier, but in late October in 1929 crooked stockbrokers having greatly overvalued a large number of stocks, sold them at high prices, removing huge sums of money from the market. Then, it crashed." Maggie knew that the results of their actions produced the worst economic and social depression in America's history. It lasted for over 10 years.

Greed, unbridled, destroys everything it touches. It's like a poisoned river flowing into its tributaries. That's why it is one of the seven deadly sins. Greed makes things die. Maggie remembered who told her this. It was her father. It was the reason he quit his company. He could see the greed begin there, and he wouldn't be a part of it.

For Holyoke, the devastation was felt with the unemployment the crash created for thousands of workers in the city's factories. Without work, these people could not buy food for their families, pay mortgages or rents, and heat their homes. Many could not survive.

By the 1930s Holyoke's industrial base was mostly divided between two industries, textiles and paper. So, one would think there was some type of balance so that the whole city would not go under. Such was not the case. When one industry is affected, every industry is affected. Holyoke business was hurt badly by the stock market crash. With orders cancelled, business lost, cost of materials up, production by the mills was curtailed, or halted. Workers were sent home and the powerful smoke rising above the factories' chimneys became noticeably less each day. The production of goods was down, the money was drying up, and the city of Camelot was ill.

Then the unthinkable happened in Holyoke. As the businesses began to fail, bankruptcies began to occur, and the great mills along the canals began to shut down. The city waded through the marsh of desperation with the hope that the State or Federal Government would find a way to save their city from total collapse. Maggie read from her notes, "The cruel aspect of the creeping depression was the total diminishing purchasing power, everywhere. No one had any money."

Thinking of the recent crash on Wall Street with the stocks of the late 1990s, Maggie began to see similar patterns. "They did it again," she said, thinking about the stock manipulations, how some stocks were worthless now.

Returning to her notes, Maggie read, "By 1932, The Bureau of Labor Statistics of the United States Labor Department estimated that there were 20,000,000 unemployed people in America. People who had been gainfully employed before were now out of work. The final numbers could be as high as 30,000,000."

"Jesus Christ," taking the Lord's name in vain, Maggie broke her own rule. "No wonder Holyoke died. Those poor, poor people." As Maggie began to visualize workers and their families, she was reminded of "Schindler's List," the movie directed by Steven Spielberg. She could see the Jews in the camps, and how they were lined up, tortured and then gassed. How immoral that was. Maggie couldn't help but compare that to the corruption of those in power that caused this suffering of the depression. After corrupt stockbrokers and company executives stole the money, the regular folk had to stand in bread lines. Knowing their children were starving to death, the factory workers who built Holyoke began to beg for food. It was one of America's worst moments.

Then, Maggie thought about those wonderful people she had read about, who ran the Farr Alpaca in Holyoke. They tried to do things differently, to make the American dream come true for everyone. She remembered they had a plan. Sorting through her piles, she pulled out the description of the company they ran. Maggie wanted to read about how they tried to prevent things like this from ever happening. Holyoke wasn't just way ahead of its time in ideas relating to dams and canals. It had new ideas about producing just about everything. There were powerful thinkers who came to the city with marvelous ideas they wanted to try. The books call them the Utopians.

What most people don't know was that one of the greatest socioeconomic experiments conducted in the 20th century was done in Holyoke. The plan was a noble test envisioned by two radical thinkers who brought their concepts to Holyoke, and made them a reality in the form of a company. There was a powerful element of Christianity in their theme. Maggie turned the pages of her notebook to the description of the company. She had written it all down, because she was so impressed by what they actually did accomplish.

The owners of the company, Herbert M. Farr and Joseph Metcalf moved Mr. Farr's small factory from the small town of Hespeler, Ontario Canada, to Holyoke in 1874. Once relocated, they renamed it, the Farr Alpaca Company. The company produced 750 different kinds of cloths, and was a highly profitable venture during the time it operated in the city.

Farr Alpaca Company COURTESY OF THE HOLYOKE PUBLIC LIBRARY

But, profits were not the only concern of the owners.

Most of the theories associated with the running of the Farr Alpaca Company, which were far in advance of the times, were those formulated by Joseph Metcalf. They were concerned mostly with socio-economic relations between the company and its employees. His philosophy was that one who contributed capital to an industry, and the one who contributed labor and effort to the same enterprise, both had a financial interest in the earnings, and besides being paid, the workers should benefit from their investment.

Such a noble philosophy was radical thinking in his time, but Metcalf put his theories into practical operation with such success that his workers wrote him a letter on January 27, 1915. "The employees of this company believe this is one of the most important steps which has ever been taken in this country to resolve the problem of relations between capital and labor."

Metcalf's plan embodied the belief that a man who contributed a hundred dollars in labor aided the firm to the same extent as one who put in a hundred dollars in capital, and so was *entitled* to a dividend at the same rate. The second generation of Farr Alpaca managers applied similar principals to the new situations that changing times brought about. The conditions of the workplace were monitored, and the ideas of the workers were considered when making decisions. The company established a dispensary with a physician, nurses and a dentist. A thoroughly equipped hospital was maintained so that any employee in need of care would have it.

The arrangements between the company and the employees exceeded in completeness that of any other industrial plant in the United States. When the mills were separated on different streets, two hospitals were provided to give services. A visiting nurse to call on employees sick in their homes was added to the benefits not long after. Treatments were not just confined to emergencies. The prevention of sickness was a high priority for Farr Alpaca. In fighting one of the city's major problems, tuberculosis, the causes of the disease was addressed.

Socially, the employees had a meeting place capable of seating 2,000 people, and entertainment was brought in constantly. A variety of sports teams were formed and a large playing field was built for the employees to play their games on. It has been written, "The Farr Alpaca has done more for the city of Holyoke than any other firm in America in many ways. Its wage rate is the highest in the world. Its general treatment of its help has been exceptionally good and its interest in the welfare of its thousands of employees is one of the best in the world." The altruism shown in the company created by Herbert Farr and Joseph Metcalf paid off in dividends, economically and socially.

All during the 1920s, the company had accumulated a surplus of millions of dollars, and had made many streets in the city rich from the products it manufactured. The worthy industrialists of Holyoke, like Farr, Metcalf and the Skinners, were the engines that pulled everything along. But the merchants, the banks, and the other businesses in the center of the city were the trains. Working together, they kept Holyoke on its tracks.

The Farr Alpaca Company reinvested much of their profits into programs and bonuses for their employees. Not only were they the first to provide other healthcare benefits, but tuberculosis was not the problem it had been in the city because the company arrived. In addition, outbreaks of other infectious diseases were prevented by forcing the city to have landlords clean up tenements where their workers lived. But, like most revolutionary ideas that benefited the workers, the social experiment put into practice by the two benevolent men with good hearts, failed with the depression that was caused by the greed of dishonest men. Farr Alpaca was a casualty of the corruption. It closed its doors in 1933, and a good part of Holyoke died with it.

Maggie wondered why the power barons, gangs, crime lords and thieves of Wall Street always won. What had occurred in the 1990s, just a decade earlier was the second or third time around for these people in America. It's as if they are still kicking the Farr Alpaca Company over and over again. Maggie wondered why people let them get away with it. She was feeling sick just thinking about it.

Looking away from the computer, Maggie realized time had gotten away from her. She needed to go to the store and pick up some food. Tom would be coming home for dinner soon, and she promised him something special tonight. He was leaving in the morning for the Caribbean on a vacation with some friends from Yale.

Maggie was grateful after what she had just read. She could buy the food unlike those poor people who had to stand out in the cold in the bread lines. They were proud and courageous people who fought in the First World War to preserve freedom and democracy, and they had built the City of Holyoke.

EIGHT

Maggie had spent the day after Christmas piecing together her information on Holyoke's history. She finished with a fairly accurate account of the historical events of the city. As she printed it out, she was happy that she had been able to make some sense out of all the information she had compiled, even if it was only for her benefit.

It was now Monday, and she was sitting in her car parked at curbside just outside the Air Jamaica Airlines Terminal at Logan Airport. Tom's flight was leaving in an hour, and she was giving him final instructions as he kissed her goodbye and retrieved his one suitcase from the trunk.

"No smoking dope. That Jamaican stuff is all over the place down there. They'll start at you as soon as you leave the airport in Montego Bay." Maggie was being a responsible mother. She knew about this kind of thing from working at the "GLOBE." "I'm serious Tommy, they line it. You don't know what you're smoking. "

"Ok, Mom. I know. I told you I don't smoke weed. Lighten up!" He waved to her one last time as he headed into the building to meet his friends.

Maggie believed him, but she still had to say it. The last thing in the world she wanted was to get a call from him that he was sick, that far away from home, or in a jail in the Caribbean.

Now making plans for herself, Maggie recalled a conversation she had had with Candice Michaelson, the day before on the phone. The curator had told her that "*Yes*" she could see some of the Skinner family papers that were at the museum, and "*No*" she would not be there. Candice had a meeting out of town.

"But, I'll leave word for someone to let you in. Tracey Lynch, my assistant will show you what we let people see." The curator was very specific. Some of the family papers were not to be viewed by the public. They had their rules, Candice told her.

The drive back to Holyoke from Boston seemed faster than when

Maggie came from there to Salem. Maybe it was because she took the Mass Turnpike West this time, and it was just a shorter distance than going through Hartford on Route 84 to 91 north. Looking at the neat package next to her that was her history of the city, Maggie was content with what she had put together. But, this wasn't her main objective. She was much more interested in Belle Skinner. Maggie wanted to know what made her tick and why she did the generous things she did in her life. What made her the forceful personality she was, according to everyone's descriptions so far? Maggie decided that she wasn't going to leave Holyoke until she knew the answers to everything.

Purposefully, Maggie arrived in Holyoke when it was daytime and still light out. Driving through the old part of the city, she was again amazed at what she saw. It was awful to see such neglect, she thought, wondering why someone wasn't doing something about it. Hearing the sounds of a fire truck behind her Maggie pulled over to the side of the road to let it pass. Once it did, she saw the smoke coming from a building in the distance. Someone at the newspaper had once told her that fires were commonplace in Holyoke. He had joked, "It's their urban renewal program."

Pulling into the same spot she had the last time she was parked on Beech Street, Maggie noticed the overhanging porte-cochere outside the mansion where the cars usually parked. Seeing no cars in the driveway, she gathered up her things and went to the back door where Candice had told her to go in. It was the service entrance to the museum, and the door was open just as the curator said it would be. Looking at her watch and seeing it was a little past noon, Maggie thought she was just a little early. She told Candice she would get there by 1:00 P.M.

"I'll wait in the reception area for her," Maggie said to herself, as she walked through the dining area. "Maybe she's getting lunch." Passing by the spiral staircase, and looking at the pictures of the Skinners hanging on the walls, Maggie heard a noise upstairs. Assuming it was Tracey Lynch, Maggie headed up the stairs.

Entering one of the rooms next to the bedrooms, Maggie was surprised to find a man sitting at a conference table. He was leafing through the pages of a book, and had papers surrounding him. He was handsome, looked to be in his early fifties, with light gray hair and blue green eyes. Maggie noticed his eyes, because their color was so bright. He was dressed neatly with casual pants and a turtleneck sweater.

"Hi," he said, seeing her walk in.

"I'm sorry. I though you were Tracey Lynch." Maggie felt like she was intruding.

"Do I look like her?" he smiled.

"No, No. I'm sorry to disturb you." It was not like Maggie to be so apologetic.

"Tracey went out. She said someone might be coming in to look at the Skinners' papers." The man was disarming, noticing how beautiful Maggie was and his tone relaxed her.

"That would be me," Maggie smiled.

Getting up, he walked over to her. "I'm John Merrick, and no I don't work here. I'm a visitor just like you are."

"Candice didn't mention there would be someone else here." Maggie sat in the chair next to where John had been sitting. Putting all of her things on the table in front of her, she was careful not to move the papers he was looking through. He then sat back down next to her.

"Are you a historian?" she asked him.

"No, a writer. I came to Holyoke, *perhaps* to write a book." He was uncertain and conspicuously emphasized the word *"perhaps."*

"About what?" Maggie asked him.

Pausing before he answered, Maggie could see him choosing what he would say very carefully. *"Reality."*

Maggie immediately thought of her son, and how he would answer with only one word. She thought it must be a man thing. Still confused, Maggie pressed him to explain, "I don't understand what that means exactly."

John was enthralled by Maggie's beauty, and found himself uncharacteristically willing to share his thoughts. "I grew up here in Holyoke, back in the 1960s and 70s. I left because I felt there was more to the world than what was here. I traveled and saw a lot of it. When it was time to settle down, I did for a while. But, getting restless, I worked on the road for a while, here in the States and abroad. I managed a few different companies. I design and sell things, medical electronic devices."

"I thought you said you were a writer?" Maggie was puzzled.

"Writing books never pays the bills." He frowned and then smiled.

Maggie thought he was cute. "What do you mean, you're writing about reality? Can you elaborate on that?" she smiled back.

"It's not what's going on out there." John moved his head to one side, motioning to show her he meant what was outside the window. "Whatever it is that they're selling." He was referring to what had gone on this year. John was a bit disappointed in what the nation thought was real.

Wondering if John had all his screws, Maggie asked him a question that she felt would reveal his level of competence. "What does Candice think about what you're doing?"

"She is the one who asked me to come back home and look at this. We went to high school together, she's an old friend. I played baseball with her husband." John's eyes looked down at the papers on the desk; he was intuitive and aware of Maggie's tactic to figure him out.

"Does your *'reality'* include the Skinners?" Maggie was direct.

"It includes everything that *means* something, those things in life that are genuine." He stopped, got up, and walked over to a window. Watching the cold winds blow snow over the dead flowers in the gardens outside, he asked her, "Why are you here?"

"An interested spectator." Maggie was shrewd, and wasn't going to let him turn the tables on her. Being a reporter, she never allowed this. It was a skill she learned.

He was impressed with her wit and quickness. "OK. You win. I left Holyoke because I thought it couldn't give me the opportunities I needed to make myself *'successful,'* whatever that means now. When I grew up here, Holyoke's final glory days were coming to an end. We all had fun. But, we all knew it was time to get out. The writing was on the wall, not just the graffiti written on the walls down on High Street, but everywhere. Everyone could see the city begin to disintegrate. There were business failures, the city government was not effective in revitalizing the neighborhoods, and the federal money sent in here was being, shall we say, misappropriated. We, the children of those who were the last great generation of Holyoke, knew it was time to get out while we could. So we did."

"A lot of American cities went through the same turmoils." Maggie was being charitable.

Knowing this, John said something that took Maggie completely by surprise. "The Puerto Ricans didn't ruin Holyoke, you know."

Again, being confused by what he was saying, Maggie waited for him to explain, thinking he would. She had no idea how this was related to the Skinner family.

Seeing Maggie's expression, he did continue. "I'm sorry, I forgot. You're not a child of the city. Well, back in the 60s and 70s, Holyoke began a meltdown. The Holyoke we all grew up in began to look more like a ghetto than the reasonably pleasant place it had been when we were kids." He paused to see her reaction. Seeing none, he went on. "Every trip back home was painful for all of us. It just kept getting worse and worse. Most of us were working in different areas of the country, and had good lives. When we came back to see our parents, we couldn't believe what *they* had done to our city. Wanting to make excuses for what was happening, many people blamed the migration of the Puerto Rican population into the city as the cause for the decay. Racial violence in the schools became a serious problem. They had to have police in the schools for years. And, the downtown districts where they lived were filled with drugs. It was unsafe to go down there. I can remember one visit back, when a few of my buddies and me went to a bar on Hampden Street that we used to frequent when we lived here. There was a group of gang members in the bar. It was not long before a fight broke out. It was normal to feel this way, to express this resentment for those people who you were told destroyed what you loved. They thought we were white bigots. They didn't like us much either."

"You used the word normal?" she questioned him, being her inquisitive self again.

"It is not normal to dislike people you don't know, just because someone tells you to." He had thought a lot about this.

Understanding him, Maggie delved a little deeper. "What changed your mind?"

"Part of the reason I came back here was to get that answer. I guess I started trying to look at things from their perspective. Believe me, I'm not making excuses for the bad ones, or the drug dealers who came here, and are still here. There is a bad group in the city. But the majority of the Puerto Ricans who are here are good people; looking for the same things those people in 1900 were looking for, a better life for themselves and their kids. Let me tell you what I found out. Then, you might understand a little better why I am questioning what *'they'* call reality here, and everywhere else in America."

He stopped and came back to sit next to her. Noticing her beautiful eyes, he went on. "Those who first came here from Puerto Rico originally came from two towns, Comerio and Salinas. The next group came mostly from Mayanguez, Villalba, Veya Boya and Yabucoa. This was the first wave of Hispanic migration to Holyoke, about thirty or so years ago. The major occupation of the families was agriculture. Most of the immigrants came from the highlands of the island, those areas that are undeveloped and isolated. They raised sugar cane and tobacco there. Father Bonneville, an apostolic missionary came here to Holyoke to study the immigration years ago. He documented this as being the beginning of the Spanish migration. Now what in God's name do people who are farmers come to Holyoke for?" He was not asking Maggie the question. He was emphasizing a point. "It's not like we have fields growing on High Street!"

Seeing that Maggie had no idea what he was talking about, John went on. "For welfare." He had answered his own question. "That's what they told us, and keep telling us. It's an easy way for them to get us to be biased against the Hispanic population. It's like our ruling class trying to blame the middle class, or the poor for ruining America, when their hunger for money and power is doing it. Divide and conquer, it's an old trick." Maggie could see how serious John was about all this. He was not amused in the least.

"Who are 'they'?" Maggie asked him.

"The slum lords, the city was, and is full of them." John was just beginning to make his point. Becoming slightly agitated, thinking about what they were doing, he continued, "When the factories began to close in the 1960s, and business here began to weaken, everyone began to leave. Like I said, people saw it coming. But, when everyone did, there was the little problem of hundreds of tenement buildings, and many low income housing projects being vacated. The owners of these apartments and dumps needed someone to move in. They needed federal and state monies to make up for monies they were losing in rents. They didn't want to let the migration out of Holyoke affect or depreciate their assets. They didn't want to lose their investments. So, they went to Puerto Rico, made a few quick deals with some shady political people there, and the problems suddenly went away. The landlords flew in planeloads of families, and put them all on welfare programs." He stopped again, looking for a reaction from Maggie, but there was none. She was just listening to him. Her face was a blank slate, like when she was interviewing someone.

John went on, "I believe the phrase is 'to victimize.' They abused thousands and thousands of families by telling them that there were opportunities here that were not here at all. When the families arrived, the landlords signed them up for the welfare programs. By doing this, they started a process. The cycle of one generation after another of poor people who were forced to live lives according to the bent rules made by these crooked landlords and politicians. Of course, this *affected* Holyoke. It brought turmoil to the city. Not in the way it was diseased when the cholera or the tuberculosis was here. But the human plagues, those diseases that people create, the drugs, the violence, the social and physical decay of the people and the city. These infections are just as deadly." John looked at her, wanting her to say something.

"What happened next?" was Maggie's response.

"They squeezed out the last drops of blood from Holyoke, using the Puerto Rican people, and the state and federal programs to do it. Like I said, the Puerto Ricans were victims of our own corrupt society. They were not the disease, not the plague itself." John looked at Maggie to see what her impression was of all this.

Letting down her guard, Maggie remarked, "This same thing has happened in all of the big cities, with lots of ethnic groups being victimized like this. I saw the same abuses in Boston when I worked there. Hell, we did stories on it."

"I know," John said. "It's everywhere now. But, the real serious problems arise for these people in the second and third generations, when their children become conditioned to welfare and poverty. They are being pushed into holes they can't get out of. It's not fair. Instead of educating them by showing them how to get to the upper levels, these guys are repressing them by keeping them in their apartments, to collect the rents. The city's founders would roll over in their graves if they saw their city being used like this, by these landlords." John was on a roll.

"When these people are forced to live lives like this, to be subjected to this type of humiliation, they look elsewhere for their highs, their satisfaction, and they get angry. I don't blame them. I would too. Once this happens, they do desperate things. By the time the 1980s and 1990s rolled around many 'enterprising' young men had networked with New York and Columbia, and set up a very profitable business selling drugs here." John was telling Maggie what she already knew. The fact that Holyoke was a major drug distribution center on the east coast was not a surprise to her.

"The drug issue is very complex now. It's a national problem, one that needs federal attention. The city and the state can't stop it by themselves.

Too much money is involved, too many payoffs, too much violence. Christ, it's a war now, one were losing. Putting that aside for a moment, the harm done to the Puerto Rican community by these landlords is ongoing. Now they're running 'new' programs. These poor people and their children are still the victims of their contrivances. It needs to stop." John was emphasizing that the repression and drug abuse issues needed to be separated.

Maggie thought John was starting to sound like a preacher. Wanting to get to why she had come here Maggie asked, "What does all of this have to do with the Skinners?"

John could not be swayed and stayed committed to what he had been talking about. "A lot. It's hard to get someone to fix a problem, when they are the problem. The landlords and their *lackeys* will never change the welfare systems by giving the people lower rents, or higher payments, or education packages to get to Harvard." John was emphatic and Maggie got the point.

"Just like the bankers who crashed our markets, and won't give us our money back. They keep the Puerto Ricans and those other poor people they lured here subordinated by low welfare payments. And now the middle class of America is being impoverished, drained by high prices. It's the same people who are doing this to all of us, the moneychangers they call them. In Holyoke, the politicians subsidize the falling down buildings of the landlords at the poor people's expense; in America they subsidize the crashing economy at everyone's expense."

Maggie was amazed at how similar John's thinking was to hers, but she didn't let on. He just looked at her, wondering what she was thinking. Eventually she put her unanswered question about the Skinners aside for a moment, and agreed with John. Maggie was remembering the discussions she had on the campaign trail with a few very intelligent economists about the Robber Barons; those who could ruin entire economies by manipulating values. They would take control of a lot of healthy companies; entice investors to put money in by showing inflated profits, sell stocks when they went high, making huge amounts of monies and then walk, leaving the companies with no value. She knew that the recent stock market upheaval was a perfect example of how this could be done, and how eventually, it affected the whole economy. To compensate for lost revenues in the stock market, the commodities companies like the oil and drug companies would just raise their prices to make up for any shortfalls.

It was a scam.

Maggie made the time out sign with her hands. "Too heavy, and much too early in the morning. I need something a little lighter, John. Can you please get back to the Skinners?" Maggie was interested in his thoughts, but wanted to take one step at a time, a little slower. She appreciated what he was saying, but that was not why she was here. "As a matter of fact, how about some coffee?" She thought it was in order.

"Sorry, but you did ask," John responded. Trying not to be offensive, he made a final comparison for her. "In the past, it would be like buying Mr. Skinner's mills, running them for years, and taking out large profits by selling the silks at high prices, reinvesting nothing into the company to maintain and expand operations, and then selling the company off leaving the workers without jobs, and the community without a valuable asset to pay taxes to support the city." John realized he was combining things, but they were related. "In the old days, the mill owners and the other honorable people like them would never have allowed things like this to contaminate their city. When William Skinner and the other strong people of the community ran the city, nothing like this happened. They cared too much for what was just and righteous, to let things like this occur. Everyone's morals were different back then. *Reality* was different." John had finally made his point.

Changing the subject, Maggie asked, "What are you going to write your book about?"

"Who said I was going to write a book?" John answered back, noticing again how appealing Maggie was. "I said I was contemplating it." John smiled, letting her know he was just trying to make a point. Maggie was thinking he probably didn't need that coffee after all. He seemed stimulated enough.

Giving him the benefit of the doubt, she said, "Well, I just assumed you were. Forgive me. I'm being presumptuous. I shouldn't be." Maggie was sincere, and did not want to offend him. John seemed like a nice guy, even if he was a little fiery. It was also nice to hear someone call it like he saw it. Most people were running the other way, hiding. Or, spending most of their time and energy surviving, because of the troubles John's landlords and other money gluttons were creating.

"Let's just say the option is open to discussion." His calmed down demeanor set her at ease. "I was actually working on a novel down at our family's house on the Cape. It wasn't coming together for me. When I came home for Thanksgiving, Candice asked me to take a look at all of this Skinner stuff. That's all. Nothing may come of this." He was being honest, even though he had found some things that intrigued him.

"Can I see some of the documents?" Maggie was polite. She wanted to see what John looking at.

"Be my guest. I'll get us a cup of coffee from Candice's office." He got up to leave the room, just as Tracey came in downstairs.

"Black please, no sugar," Maggie answered, noticing his strong athletic build. As her eyes followed him going towards the stairs, she thought back to the inception of all this: being blown by the wind into the building at Yale. Maggie knew there were accidents, and opportunities. Looking down at the Skinners' papers now, wondering what was in them; Maggie thought how inexplicably things happened, all for a reason. For her, here, after bumping into closed doors, others were opening.

NINE

Once Tracey took off her long wool coat, warmed up and helped John pour three cups of coffee, she went with him into the room where Maggie was. Not being tall, only five foot five, and not blonde, she was a redhead, Tracey was a complete contrast to Maggie. What was even more noticeable about her was a loud, but pleasant attitude. Tracey was adorable, still looking cold, all bundled up in more than one sweater.

"Hi, I'm Tracey Lynch," she said as she handed Maggie her coffee.

"I'm Maggie O'Reilly," she took the cup, smiling.

"Ah, another Irishwoman. I see you already met our friend John." The assistant curator closed the door to the room. "It's too cold out there. God, I wish we could go south for the winter. Don't you hate the winter Maggie? Or are you one of those ski people who like to freeze their 'you know what' off." She didn't quite finish her statement, but Maggie got the message.

"Be nice Tracey," John kidded her. "I was filling Maggie in on the local news of Holyoke." He was being entertaining.

Rolling her eyes, Tracey commented, "Don't believe everything he says, Maggie. Sometimes he tends to sound like the novels he writes in his spare time. How many is it now John, three?" Not waiting for a response, she went on. "But, we put up with him anyway, most of the time." She was being her humorous self. "We're trying to cure him of his bachelor ways, though. Since he graduated from Springfield College, he hasn't even come close to marrying anyone. John's been single too long. He's not normal," Tracey smiled.

"Don't start," John said. He remembered very well how he had been engaged to Cathy after college, but they called it off.

"He needs to find a nice woman and settle down. He'll come around when the right one comes along. Sometimes he does listen to us." Tracey continued, looking at John and recalling the crush she had on him in high school.

"That's a good thing, isn't it," Maggie answered her, noticing again the clear blueness of John's eyes.

Looking at Maggie, Tracey went on. "Well, what exactly is it that you're looking for?" Tracey was referring to the Skinners' papers.

Pausing only briefly, Maggie answered, "The last time I was here, I didn't get to see many of the rooms. I wonder if you could show me the house, as you know it. Then, I'll have a better idea of what really interests me." Maggie decided to take things in order this time.

"No problem. Where would you like to start?" Tracey got up and opened the door, shooting John a cute, mischievous look that told him to behave.

John just shook his head, knowing what Tracey was doing. "You be good or I'll call your husband to come and get you." John had no problem keeping up with her banter.

Ignoring him, she turned back to Maggie who was smiling, enjoying the harmless banter.

"I think I would like to see the Library." It's always interesting to see what people read. It tells you a lot about them." Maggie began to follow her out, looking back at John as if to say goodbye.

"I'll most likely be here when you get back from your tour. Maybe we can finish our talk."

"I'd like that," Maggie responded. She felt a twitch in her stomach, but wasn't sure what that meant. Walking down the hall, Tracey began to describe the treasures that were everywhere in the second floor corridor of the house. Along the way, Tracey filled her in on John, saying that he was a nice guy, just a little eccentric like most writers. Maggie tried hard to focus on Tracey's first set of descriptions, about Wistariahurst, but she was too preoccupied on her other evaluations, the ones of the handsome man she just met, who wanted to explain reality to her.

After the two women had left the room, John thought about his life. Someone once told him he was a Renaissance man. Doing many things, he excelled at everything he tried. Lately, John had been questioning the choices he had made, and found himself trying to prove something. His careers had never made him feel fulfilled. What John had done for work excited him for a time, but it provided only short-term satisfaction. John knew he never had the genuine stability he desired in his life. He never had a wife or children. With John's last love, he thought he was close. They had made plans together, and had a good time just being with each other. Then life pulled the rug out from underneath him. Thinking about it made him long for something that would make him happy. Stopping himself, John went back to reading the papers in front of him.

"Wistariahurst was bequeathed to William and Belle in their mother's will." Tracey was explaining the history of the mansion to Maggie. "Belle made most of the decisions concerning improvements and management of the house," Tracey said. At the staircase she turned and asked, "Do you want to know about the construction of the building and its history? Is that important?"

"Yes, please."

"All right," she said, moving down the hall to Belle's bedroom.

"Alice already gave me a brief tour of this room," Maggie said.

"Well, allow me to elaborate on the subject," Tracey said. "Belle brought the moon bed from New York. As you can see, the room is plain, not overdone. Belle used this room until a little problem arose in the family. Her sister Katherine had married a man named Robert Stewart Kilborne on April 4, 1904. In the years that followed, they had three children, Stewart, Betsy and Billy. Belle's nephew Stewart was her favorite. She made no bones about it. While he was attending Yale in 1925, he fell in love with a wonderful girl named Barbara Briggs. Stewart wanted to marry her but the policy of Yale forbid undergraduates to be married. His father was against the marriage, wanting Stewart to finish his education first. Rather than wait, Stewart and Barbara eloped. Stewart was expelled from Yale, and the couple went to live in New York, with the support of Belle. The addition was put on in 1927, the year before Belle died; she had this room expanded for the couple to live in. Not agreeing with Yale's puritanical rules, Belle helped them to get settled. Apparently, it worked, because Stewart became president of the family business in the 1940s. She was like that. Belle helped everyone, and if she didn't agree with the established norms of what was acceptable, 'protocol,' she just went her own way. Not just in this circumstance, but with everything she did, all through her life. That is why Belle was who she was, and why Belle made such a difference in the world." After they had walked around the room and gone into the bathroom where Tracey reiterated Alice's descriptions of the fixtures, they walked out into the hallway with Tracey still talking.

"Most of the bedrooms upstairs have been restored. This one was originally used as a bedroom, but now exhibits furniture from the Skinner Coffee House." Tracey showed her in. "The Coffee House was opened in 1902 by Belle and Katherine as a tribute to their father, to provide a place where working women and girls could gather to socialize and relax. It was just one of the things that Belle involved herself in to help people." Looking around the room, Maggie thought how nice it was that they did this for the girls.

After inspecting many of the objects in the room, and looking at the picture of what the Coffee House looked like, Tracey suggested they go downstairs. "Follow me, and I will show you the rooms down there. Did Alice take you through all of them?" she asked Maggie.

"No, only some," Maggie answered her.

"Tell me if I'm being repetitive," Tracey said, as they walked down the staircase to the first floor.

Walking on the first floor, Tracey began to talk about the main section of the house, and what had been done there. "The staircase we are on is a French Beaux Arts design. It leads down to a main room that is the Great Hall that was part of the original home from Williamsburg. The wonderful parquet floors, mahogany wood beamed ceilings and elaborate woodwork are all made from the finest woods and materials available at the time the home was constructed. You know, of course, that parts of the house were moved down from 'Skinnerville'?" Tracey wasn't sure what Maggie had been told.

"What's Skinnerville?" Maggie asked.

"It's what people called Williamsburg, when the Skinners lived there," Tracey answered. "What do you know about them?"

"Some things. Not a lot, actually." Maggie thought it best to let Tracey tell her everything she knew. Remembering most of Alice's descriptions, and Susan's at Yale, Maggie had a fairly good idea about the history, but she was sure there was more.

Tracey began in the Great Hall. "They call these rooms the Great Hall, because it's where everyone gathered when they had large parties. The pictures you see hanging around us are those of the Skinners, both families. You know that William B. Skinner had two families?"

"No, I wasn't aware of that." Maggie began to look at the names and dates under the portraits. They had walked to the Cabot Street side of the mansion where the New Entrance was built.

"The man who started all this was born in London in 1824. William B. Skinner was a boy of 19 when he came to the United States. He had some skills having apprenticed under his father in the silk business in England. When he came here, he found a job in 1843 in Northampton at one of the small silk mills that was operating there. In 1849, he married Nancy Edwards Warner Skinner who was born in 1825, and they had two children, Eleanor 'Nellie' Warner Skinner Warner who was born in 1850, and died in 1929, and Nancy 'Nina' Warner Skinner Clark who was born in 1852, and died in 1922. His first wife died in 1854. He bought a run down mill in Williamsburg in 1857, and began to operate his own business. By 1858, he had constructed a three-story mill, and was quite prosperous."

Tracey showed her the portraits of two women on the Cabot Street side of the house. The first was Eleanor Warner Skinner Warner, and near it was Elizabeth Skinner Hubbard Allen. In a second large room of the wing, also hung with portraits, Tracey began to explain the subjects. "William had married again in 1856. His second wife, Sarah Elizabeth Allen Skinner, was born in 1834, and died in 1908. He and Sarah had eight children: William Corbett Skinner, 1857–1947; Elizabeth 'Libby' Skinner, 1859–1927; Joseph Allen Skinner, 1862–1946; Louise Skinner, who died in infancy; Ruth Isabel 'Belle' Skinner, 1866–1928; Mary Louise Skinner, who also died in infancy; Mary Emma 'Little May' Skinner, 1868–1872; and Katherine Skinner Kilborne, 1873–1968.

"How awful," Maggie said, thinking of all the children that died. "First his wife dies, then his children by his second wife. Mr. Skinner had his share of troubles, didn't he?" Maggie was right on target, saying what a strong person he must have been to survive all of this. His wife was too.

"The family was living in Williamsburg when the flood came in 1874, the one that destroyed his mills and the town. The house was just completed when the waters washed some of it away. Besides losing his wife and children, he then lost a lot of what he had built up. Thank God not one of his children were killed when the flood hit." Tracey stopped. "Did Alice tell you any of this?" she asked Maggie, wondering what Alice did explain to her.

"She was in a hurry, understandably. The museum had to close for the day. I'm sure she told me about some of it, but I can't quite remember what." Maggie wasn't sure what Alice was supposed to have told her, and she didn't want to get Alice in trouble.

"No problem. We'll just do it all again." Concentrating back on those who lived here, Tracey went on. "This Great Hall and the new entrance were added onto Wistariahurst in 1927. The rooms are the last additions made to the house during Belle's lifetime. The fashioning of these rooms moved the entrance of the house from Pine Street to Cabot Street. Belle thought the name sounded more proper. She moved the two stone lions that are mounted on the wall outside on Cabot Street to guard the way in. These restorations were completed the year before her death. You can see that there are paintings of William, his wife Sarah and their children in the Great Hall." Pointing down the hallway she said, "The rooms on the Pine Street side of the house are from the original estate, one being the Library."

Next she moved Maggie into the Dining Room. "This is another room that was moved down from the original estate in Williamsburg. It's where the family gathered each night for dinner, and where the famous dinner parties of the Skinners were held. They called it the Oak Room and it's part of the original house that was moved here. The Dining Room was redecorated in 1910. Belle thought that considering their social standing, it needed to be bigger and more formal. She covered all of the walls with a silk damask fabric that was terribly expensive. On the buffet are some pictures showing the room when it was set for guests. As you can see, it had to have been a wonderful experience to attend any of these dinners."

Maggie looked at the black and white photos, while Tracey continued with her presentation. "The kitchen is adjacent to this room and is separated by the butler's pantry." Taking Maggie's arm Tracey directed her towards the other rooms she had already seen. Tracey began to describe the Conservatory and the Music Room.

"I've seen these rooms before. It's where the Christmas party was." Maggie smiled, remembering Katherine.

"I was away and couldn't attend. Candice told me that Mrs. Kilborne took a liking to you." Tracey smiled. "She said you reminded her of someone."

"She's a wonderful person," Maggie said earnestly.

Saying nothing more about the relatives of the Skinners, and understanding that the rooms had already been explained to Maggie, Tracey began to walk her towards the Library, pausing briefly to look out a window. "On the cement pad stood a corkscrew pedestal-based sundial that Belle purchased in France in 1911. It was moved here from the corner of the perennial garden in 1928. The Conservatory was another part of her redesign of the mansion from 1913 through 1914. She thought the house needed light and wanted to let in as much as possible. So she built this." The two were standing on the cork floor of the Conservatory looking out the Pine Street side of the house that overlooked the gardens. "They also used this as a Breakfast Room."

Pointing, Tracey went on, "In the summer we have the yards looking splendid, just like Belle did. She was quite fond of her flower gardens. In 1909, she hired Wadley and Smythe of New York City to plan and plant a formal perennial garden. Each planting was marked carefully." She continued telling Maggie about Belle's love of beautiful things. "Not satisfied, and wanting to make the gardens even more elegant, Belle hired Herbert Kellaway from Boston to design a rose garden, and put in a watering system as part of his project. The rose gardens contained a wide variety of species, including a climbing rose arbor. It has been said that Belle had a rose brought in from every country in Europe. Belle worked in the gardens herself to improve the yards' appearance, and brought in more and more flowers each year. In 1916, a Japanese Tea House was brought in from New York that Belle had bought from a dealer and assembled at the end of the roses. It was surrounded by an Asian influenced garden. Then she added a fountain, a koi pool, cedar trees, a mulberry tree and statuary. Can you just imagine how beautiful the yards must have been when she was finished?" Tracey had seen pictures of what it had looked like, and knew how incredible it was."

Still looking out, Tracey amused Maggie by telling her one of Belle's pleasures. "She had a pony."

"She had a what?" Maggie didn't believe what she had just heard.

"A pony, his name was Relief. Belle loved to give the children rides out on the lawn. When he died, he was buried properly behind the Carriage House with the other family horses. They were even respectful of their animals." Tracey smiled, thinking how kind Belle must have been to have done things like this. "She wanted to make her world beautiful by filling it with lovely things and making everyone happy." It was obvious to Maggie that Belle Skinner appreciated all aspects of life. "Not just for herself, Belle wanted everyone to feel the warmth of what she had brought here." Tracey continued, "She was proud of what she did here, but she didn't do all of this for herself alone. She wanted to make Holyoke beautiful by bringing to it those things she collected."

Moving back through the corridors, Tracey took Maggie to the Parlor, passing by the Leather Room where Belle used to like to read. "They call it the Leather Room because the walls are covered with leather. It was originally her father's bedroom, but after he died the children turned it into a study. This room was a part of the house that was moved." Tracey was brief in her accounts of the study, wanting to get to her favorite room.

"William and Belle thought that they should have a place to show their friends and business associates art work, paintings and other purchases they had made on their trips around the world. This room is called the Parlor or the Quirk Gallery. It was originally two adjoining rooms. When Belle's parents were in charge of the house the room was very dark with drapes covering the windows, and it was cluttered with furniture. Around 1907, Belle remodeled it, hiring contractors to make it into one room with a Classic Revival style in mind, placing Doric columns where the dividing wall had been. She brightened up the space with light wallpaper, and filled it with French provincial furniture, and American colonial and federal antiques. The statue in front of you is Flora, the goddess of flowers and spice, carved by C.F. Summers in 1895. Notice how it turns on its base, so that you can view it from all sides. Initially Belle used this room to display her collection of antique instruments, until the collection grew too large for the room. The portion of the ceiling with paintings is part of a decorative scheme dating from the 1890s, but covered with white canvas by Belle during the 1907 remodeling. It is typical of a style used by the wealthy influenced by European designs. Presently we use this room for exhibits, because it is so large and well lighted."

Maggie liked the feel of the room. It was obviously created to impress. She thought Belle wanted her guests to be surrounded by objects that reflected her cultured tastes and wealth. They walked out into the hall.

The two women finally were just outside the room Maggie wanted to see first. It had just taken them a little time to get there. Tracey had wanted Maggie to appreciate what Belle had done in the other rooms first. Tracey had her reasons.

Pointing to her right, Tracey said, "This is the site of the original front entry when the house was moved. The Pine Street porch outside was maintained as a sitting area. It has been said that their father, William spent many nights sitting out on the piazza, as they called it, smelling the perfumes of the flowers, and appreciating his life." Tracey was describing what she had seen in the in family pictures.

"It really is unique," Maggie said.

"This is the Library. It is where the books you wanted to see are, although much of the family's book collection has been removed." Tracey did not elaborate. "The original floor pattern is covered with bookcases. The paneling is reminiscent of Georgian paneling, but on a grander scale. The fireplace was replaced in 1927, when Belle remodeled the room. It was, at one time, two separate rooms, the original hall and Library. They used it as a family room. When William Skinner was alive, he gathered his family in this room, and read them passages from Shakespeare and the Bible, believing these to be important in their education."

Glancing over to the mantle clock, Tracey saw the time and asked Maggie for an indulgence, being a little flighty again. "I have to make a phone call, Maggie. Why don't you look around and read anything you would like. There are also pictures in this room you might want to look at. I'll leave you to yourself for an hour or so and then come back. When I do, we can discuss anything you have questions about." Tracey was getting nervous, thinking about the call she had to make. She always got like this when she had to talk to someone about her children, and one of them had been sick for three days now. The test results should be back today Tracey thought, hoping it was nothing serious. Being highly motivated, very confident and perhaps a bit manipulative, Tracey could deal with most anything with ease, except her children being ill.

"Thanks. Take your time, I'll be fine," Maggie said, deciding that she liked Tracey. She was vivacious and intelligent. As Maggie began looking through the books on the shelves, trying to get an idea of what interested the family, she came upon *A History of France*, the first book that caught her attention. Maggie picked another out, not being interested in that, this one from the middle section. It was George Orwell's *Animal Farm*. Belle had died in 1928, the Museum booklets had said, almost twenty years before *Animal Farm*'s publication, but Maggie was certain Belle would have wanted to read this allegory. It was about a group of animals, who take over a farm in an attempt to create a paradise of justice and equality, but a totalitarian state emerges instead. In it, Orwell describes the atrocities of Stalinist Russia, and what can happen when people lose control of their government. Picking up another, Maggie continued to read more.

It seemed like only a few minutes went by when she looked back up to the gilded clock. Maggie saw that she had been reading the second novel for almost an hour. Not being able to put it down, she kept turning the pages to find out more. It was another that she had read in college, but Maggie didn't remember the storyline as well as she had for the other book. This was a novel written by Fyodor Dostoevsky in 1869. Maggie thought that Belle probably had read this one. Turning the pages, Maggie recalled the main character whose name was Prince Lyov Mushkin, a Christ-like figure of a man, who although deeply human, brings disaster to everyone he meets. Because he is divine, he lives in and produces states of constant conflict for himself and others, because they are not like him. He sees everyone around him obsessed with money, power and sexual conquest. Because of his anxieties, the man is seen by everyone as the title describes him, *The Idiot.*

Not long after, Maggie was deciding that the perfect world was probably somewhere between the animals who ran the farm with an iron fist, and the fanciful place the idiot was trying to create, when she was interrupted by a presence in the room. It was John.

"Any good?" he asked her, with a decided amount of charm.

"Yes it is. His powers of description are amazing." Maggie was yawning, and excused herself, handing John the book.

He put it back on the shelf after looking at the title and the name of the writer. "Don't apologize. We're being thrown out, anyway. It's time for them to lock up." John did not come down just to tell Maggie that, but to ask her something else. Being honorable, he preceded it with another question.

"Are you married or attached?" he asked.

Maggie was not used to being asked. Most everyone she had met on the road didn't care. "I was, my husband died some time ago. I guess I'm called a widow." She hated the name, and knew where he was going with the question.

Taken aback, John responded, "I'm sorry about your husband. Now I feel awful." He really did feel terrible; he hadn't taken her for a widow. John thought how sad that must be for her, and decided not to press her with questions about how he died, though it was his nature to be inquisitive.

Seeing John's surprise, Maggie asked, "What were you going to ask me?" Not wanting him to feel awkward anymore.

"Will you be in town long?" The question was proper, and old-fashioned.

"A couple of days. Why?" Maggie responded in kind.

"Can I take you to dinner?" John asked as he helped her on with her coat, and they began to walk down the hallway together. He was nervous, asking the question, being a little rusty. John was still reeling from the awful way his last relationship had ended.

For a moment, she said nothing. Now was the time Maggie usually said, *no*, just *no*. Looking into John's eyes, she could see that he was sensitive, and did feel bad for her loss. "That would be lovely," she said, surprising herself. "When?"

"How about tomorrow night? I know this great little Italian place. Is Italian OK?" John was being courteous, that was just how he was.

"Fine. I'm staying at the Holiday Inn by the Holyoke Mall. Seven o'clock?" Maggie was not really asking, but setting the time for them.

"Perfect." John was happy she had said *"yes."* He suspected she didn't often. John sensed Maggie's pain when she had called herself a widow. He was good at this, feeling someone else's sadness. It was perhaps by attrition. Besides Belle Skinner, he was sure they would have a lot to talk about. Suspecting Maggie was hurting, he aimed to not merely listen to her words, lending no opinions unless asked, he would *hear* what she was saying. John knew that sometimes, just talking about something that was hurtful, made it better.

TEN

The next evening, John was at the hotel waiting in the lobby when Maggie came down from her room. He was trying not to look as nervous as he was. She had taken a little more time than usual getting ready. The light blue dress she had on was stunning. Maggie didn't have to try hard to be gorgeous. In forty-five minutes they were sitting in the little Italian restaurant in Springfield that John had told her about. After ordering drinks, they began talking, getting to know each other a little better.

John began their conversation with a curious statement. "Rumor has it that Tom Terrific is from Holyoke."

"Tom who?" Not knowing what he was talking about, Maggie just looked at him with a funny stare.

The cartoon character called Tom Terrific. It's been said that he got his 'mighty strength' from the *energies* of Holyoke."

Laughing, Maggie pressed him for more details. "What does Tom Terrific do, John?"

"He saves the world," John knew he had peaked her interest.

"How?" she asked, shaking her head, playing along.

"By being mightier and more powerful that the villains he encounters." John had a habit of talking too loudly when he was trying to be funny. Knowing this he tried to be quieter.

"Does he always win his battles?" Maggie was enjoying this.

"Always, because he's from Holyoke." John smirked. Maggie smirked too. It was the perfect way to start talking, letting the humor begin the conversation. The waiter brought their drinks, took their order, and then left them to continue their conversation.

"Tell me what it was like growing up in Holyoke, John," Maggie said, leaning forward.

"You don't want me to bore you with old childhood memories," John replied in a self-deprecating manner.

Maggie leaned back. "Who better to give me some background on a subject that intrigues me, than someone who grew up in Holyoke." Leaning forward again, she put her arms on the table. "I do, *really*. I am interested." Maggie's body language confirmed for John that she wasn't just being polite, but really did want to hear about his life.

"OK." John spoke up, raring to go. "What do you want to know about: the physical Holyoke, the psychological Holyoke or the spiritual Holyoke?" He wasn't sure where to begin.

"Surprise me," Maggie answered. "What do you remember about what it was all like back then?" She was encouraging him to take his time and think back.

"Well, I guess I remember that it was slower and a lot cleaner. Holyoke was a nice place to grow up in. Mostly, because of the people who lived there. My father and mother's generation produced some real characters." He thought about how he missed them all.

Maggie stopped him. "What did your father do?"

"He manufactured medical products, disposables. Following in his footsteps, I became involved in the business of medical electronic devices when I was about thirty. I sold them all over the world, and made a bit of money doing it. He was a good father and my mother was only interested in making sure everyone had enough to eat, and our clothes were clean and pressed. All of the parents in our neighborhood were good parents, or so it seemed. They all went to work, mowed their lawns neatly, and we saw them at the ball games or at church. They loved watching their kids play sports." He took a drink of water. "You want the short version or the long one?"

Maggie smiled. "The long one."

He'd thought so, but he didn't want to be presumptuous, just in case. "Holyoke was prosperous back in the 1950s, in many ways. Our parents were products of the depression and World War II. They knew what it was like to be hungry, and to dive into a trench to stay alive. They had done what they had to survive it all. So, when they began to raise their families they wanted to give their kids the things they didn't have themselves when they were growing up. They wished for none of us to have to experience what they did with the depression. So, they probably gave us too much, trying to make up for their own losses. But, their real strengths were moral and spiritual. They had been well trained by the old school Holyoke people who built the city, and the priests, rabbis, ministers and nuns. Hell, I think they all had some type of manual they never showed us about God's laws, what we should and should not know and do." He was kidding and stopped to see her response. Maggie's interest was evident, through a genuine smile.

John continued, "They passed on those values to us by the way they lived their lives. There was a strong sense of community in Holyoke back then. It didn't matter if you were English, Irish, Black, Jewish, Polish, or whatever, we were all Holyokers. That was one of the city's greatest assets. There were very few divisions or prejudices. It was sink or swim together. We all played together at the 'Y' or on the league teams, went to the same schools and all knew one another. Our parents and teachers made sure that we all knew the same rules. If we didn't respect them, they had easy solutions. When someone did something wrong, everyone knew about it. It was hard to misbehave in Holyoke back then. You would get your ass kicked, because it reflected on everyone." He stopped, making sure he hadn't offended her.

Maggie knew what he was talking about. He wasn't much older than she, and the rules were the rules. She gave him a look that told him she wasn't offended. He went on, "The industrialists built Holyoke into the business giant is was in 1900. They were incredible men and women. But our fathers and mothers and our grandparents built the city up in other ways, by being the people they were. They were the second wave of, what shall I call them, the survivors. The Skinners and people like them set the examples, but those who followed, learning from them and experiencing the things they did in the wars and the depression, fine-tuned the Holyoke value system. Financially, there was still a lot of activity in Holyoke in the 1950s and 1960s. In the late 1940s, after the Second World War, many of the men came back here to where they left from, to their own families and to the women they left behind, the lovely ladies that waited for them to come home. Many got married and began their families in the neighborhoods they grew up in. We were the famous war babies. The city was full of us. Most families had six or seven kids. It was the Ozzie and Harriet generation, Maggie. There were Ozzie and Harriets everywhere." John stopped, expecting Maggie to say something.

Her face was burgeoning with inquisitiveness, "You said the town was prosperous. How?"

"When the mills ran and the money flowed from them, the city's economy was fueled by them. When the 1950s came, many of them had shut down or curtailed production. Remember those tags on everything, made in Japan. Well, by the 1960s those tags were on a lot of things in the United States, not just in Holyoke. So, the strength of the city's economy shifted into a merchant based economy, maintained by the banks lending money to the people who invested in businesses and bought houses, and of course the doctors, the lawyers and the other professionals who located here, because they wanted to. Remember, we were beginning a 'new society.' When Hitler was defeated, the United States was viewed as the new leader in the world, and our fathers and mothers were the country's conscience, so they did what they thought was right. They bought houses and cars, and raised their children with values. That was enough for them. They wanted to see their kids happy and safe. They were much more centered and balanced than people are today. But, let's not forget, they had good teachers and role models." He took another break, eating some of his dinner.

Maggie was enjoying the conversation and the veal she had ordered. She decided it was time to let John take a break. She motioned for him to pour a little more wine for her and began talking. "I remember growing up in the 60s, when the great men and women of America and the world were focusing on changing it, to make it a better place. I don't remember, who did you call them, the Ozzie and Harriets, but I remember the Kennedys, Martin Luther King, the Beatles, and the rest of them. You're right, it was slower back then, even though the world was changing fast, and the cold war was keeping us terrified of a nuclear attack, the pace was different."

"And, so was Holyoke changing." Swallowing, John went on, "There was a big difference in Holyoke in the 1950s and 60s. Our parents were able to hold it together for 15 years or so, after the war, but then the city began having social and economic problems they weren't prepared for. Maybe it was our generation bringing in new ideas, or people questioning the choices our parents had made. It got complicated. You know the old saying, 'you always think you know a better way.' Many of us left to go to college, to learn our trades. Of course, they paid for it. Like I said before, they just wanted us to have what they never did. Most of them couldn't afford to go to college, or if they did they worked their way through." He was thinking about his mother, telling him about what it was like to work 12 hours a day in the mills, and then go to night classes.

Maggie was almost done with her dinner, and was feeling guilty about

John's food getting cold. So, she told him to eat and started talking. But, not before asking him one question, "Who are Ozzie and Harriet?"

John almost choked, chuckling. He had seen, the previous day, how Maggie could make anyone respond to her quick wit.

"You must be kidding me. Don't tell me they were before your time." John was enjoying Maggie's company. He explained, "They were television personalities of the 1950s. They were supposed to be the 'ideal' of what everyone's Mom and Dad were. Their family was what all our lives should be. They never did anything wrong. Christ, they were perfect. Or so we thought." He smirked. "They were just distortions of *reality* and, *'yes',* I just said *the word*. But, no one knew it back then. We all thought they were *'normal'*."

Signaling for the waiter to bring her more water, Maggie began. "So, Holyoke grows to be a giant industrial community with strong moral values, and then feels the pains of the wars and the depression. It struggles through all of this, and maintains its basic honorable character. It then produces people like your Mom and Dad who weathered the storms and produced sons and daughters who they pass the memories onto, and fairly reasonable value belief systems that are only slightly abnormal, because of Ozzie and Harriet." Maggie took a breath and smiled. "Your generation accepts most of these, but looked for a better way to fine tune everything. What's wrong with that?" Maggie thought she had gotten a pretty good picture of where John came from, this place called Holyoke.

John responded, "Nothing is wrong with this. Questioning the way things are done is healthy. We didn't lose our way. But, in some ways we went in the wrong direction. A lot of us sold out, buying the crap about the more toys you have, the happier you are. As I get older, I look back and think, if I had to change anything I did, I would move a few pieces around a bit, maybe be more like them. That's why I came back, to see what I left behind." John looked closer at Maggie, thinking, comparing the chaotic world of today with the slower speed of the Ozzie and Harriets.

He was trying to be sincere. "The greatest gift the Skinners and the other great industrialists in Holyoke of the early 1900s left us, was a model of how to be innovative and how to create. They showed us how to build productive companies and how to construct a beautiful city with wonderful things in it for everyone to enjoy. Using the same value system of their predecessors, my parents and grandparents taught us how to live and work within the confines of rules of conscience." He paused. "This is the *energy* of Holyoke, Maggie. It's not the dam, it's the caliber of people it produces, they're everywhere now." John smiled, knowing how successful many people from Holyoke had become.

Maggie was impressed. She had finally met a man who would rather think about meaningful things, than sit in a bar and watch a bunch of people injure themselves on a football field or fight to death in a mindless movie. There still might be a chance that television programs hadn't captured all of them.

John finished talking about the city he loved. "Physically, the city has gone through the same changes many inner cities have. And, we ship our business overseas, instead of creating jobs here. The tags read 'made in China' now. We didn't protect our industries by supporting them and our workers by not keeping the business here. It's a national disgrace, a phenomenon not just isolated to Holyoke."

John suddenly switched gears. In a tender, subdued tone he asked, "What happened to your husband?" Wanting to know, he had completely changed the conversation.

Maggie didn't expect the question and sipping her wine, she almost spit it out. "He had a stroke. One day he was here, the next day he was gone." Maggie felt the emotions running all through her body. It was as if her system suddenly sped up on its own adrenaline.

"Want to talk about it?" John's earnestness was evident.

"Yes. I think I'd like to. But, not now, OK?" Maggie was not capable of talking about Bill right now. She felt uncomfortable.

"Can I get you anything else, Sir?" The waiter was doing his job. Asking Maggie with his eyes if she wanted anything, she shook her head, *"no."*

John could see tears in the corners of her eyes. He had struck a nerve. Not wanting to upset Maggie, he changed the subject. "The next thing we need to understand is how Belle Skinner fits into all of this."

Understanding John's intentions, Maggie took her handkerchief from her purse and dabbed at her tears. "What have you found?" Maggie was intrigued, although what she really wanted to do was flee and be alone. Sensing this, John gave just a brief reply. "She was born in 1866 in Williamsburg and died of pneumonia in Paris in 1928. But, it's time I take you back to the hotel. I've upset you, I'm sorry." Helping Maggie on with her coat, John felt awful. Walking to the car, he was angry with himself for disturbing her. John decided that he was not going to mention Maggie's husband again, not until she decided it was time to talk about him. Guilty, John was thinking it was a hell of a way to end a date. They didn't talk much on the short ride up to Holyoke, to the hotel. The silence said it all, but before John let her go to her room, he stopped her. Gently he said, "Tomorrow, I want you to read some letters that Belle wrote that are significant. Once you do, we can discuss what I think she was trying to tell us."

Watching Maggie walk away from him, John couldn't help but think that he had finally met someone nice who had a good idea about what mattered. It was a shame that she had to go through what she did.

ELEVEN

The next morning, Maggie went to Wistariahurst to meet John, and see the letters he had mentioned the night before. She arrived at 10:15 A.M. When Maggie got there, she accessed the museum using the same service entrance she had the other day, and went upstairs to the room where she had first met John. He was there waiting, and Maggie was happy to see him.

John stood when he saw her. "Maggie, about last night, I'm sorry if I upset you. I wasn't trying to pry." The look on his face was so endearing, Maggie could tell he was truly feeling bad about what he'd said. They both sat and faced each other.

"It's not you, John. I haven't talked about Bill with anyone. It was my fault last night. I overreacted. I know you were just trying to be kind. Let's just forget it." Maggie's response was warm, and the compassion she extended back toward John was sincere. He could tell she was not holding it against him, and he was relieved.

Glancing down at the table Maggie saw a stack of letters. She assumed they were the ones John had told her about. "These are them," John said proudly, motioning at the stack of papers. "Want to look at the letters?"

"Yes, I do." Maggie paused. "John, it is OK to mention Bill. We can talk about him later if you want. I was just a little uptight last night, first date nerves, that's all."

He pushed the first letter towards her. "Belle wrote these on the typewriter that's out in the hallway on display."

Maggie was just taking the letter out of its envelope when someone spoke to them. It was Tracey. "Looks like you guys decided to team up. Anything you need?" She asked them, smiling.

Seeing Tracey, John picked up where he had left off the day before. "How about some biscuits and a little jam?" He loved teasing her.

"He's going to start on me again Maggie. You better watch it Mr. Merrick, I'm in a mood." She was being her playful self.

John got up and went over to where Tracey was. "Some coffee will do then, and I'll be a good boy. Maggie would you like some?"

"Is there any tea? My stomach is a little upset. I think I'll stay away from coffee today." Maggie wasn't feeling all that well.

"I'm sure we can find some, if not, I'll go out." John was being a gentleman.

Maggie began reading one of the letters as the other two left the room, still kidding with each other as they went down the stairs to the kitchen.

It was a letter Belle had written to her brother Joseph, dated September 30, 1918:

Dear Joseph,

It was a long train ride home from New York, Joseph. You know how I dread the experience. There was an accident with one of the trains on the line. We were delayed for hours. It was wonderful to finally see the Holyoke Station sign. To know I was finally home. When I reached the house I was exhausted. It took the whole day to make the trip.

It was wonderful being with you in New York. We always have such a pleasant time together. I was reluctant to leave this time. But, the heat in the apartment was too much. It is much cooler here in the country. I am sitting out on the porch now, where Father used to. The gardens are looking lovely but I am thinking of making improvements. I want to make our home as nice as I can, for all of us.

Love, Belle

John came back in as Maggie finished reading the letter for the third time; not wanting to miss anything, she read every word over and over.

"Here's your tea." He put the cup down in front of her.

"Thank you. Did Belle spend a lot of time in New York?" Maggie asked him, picking up her cup.

"Yes, a lot—they had apartments there, and a house in Paris, and the Skinner offices weren't far from where they lived in New York City." John was to the point.

"Why New York City? Why not Boston?" Maggie asked, sipping the tea.

"The Skinners' products were world famous by the time Belle wrote that letter, and I suppose they loved New York, like so many people do, maybe because of the excitement and liveliness there, and the culture and art, and because it's such a beautiful city. But there were business considerations too, probably. Satin and silk brought in a lot of money from the hundreds, thousands, of clothing manufacturing companies in the garment district there. The bridal gown companies alone did an enormous business. They had customers from all over the world coming to them, looking at their fabrics, the famous Skinner label. Being the largest port on the East Coast, New York also had far more ships coming and going to Europe, England, the Far East, everywhere. It was highly accessible by the standards of the day, so it made more sense for them to be there than Boston."

"And Belle worked there?" Maggie asked.

"No, she lived there. Her brothers ran the business, and she looked after them, by taking care of the house and the charity work," he said, smiling.

"What else is here?" Maggie pointed to the other papers on the table.

"Lots. Besides the letters, all of the men and ladies of Wistariahurst left journals. There are also cables they sent each other." John handed her one left by Katherine Skinner Kilborne. "It's quite informative. Some letters from Belle to Joseph and William have obviously been returned to the archives."

Maggie began leafing through an old book labeled "William's Journal." John pushed three letters towards Maggie that he had set aside for her. "These were deliberately separated by Tracey from the registered letters of the archives. They are from Belle to William, sent a month after that first one you read. They are all much different than the one she sent to Joseph. Why don't you take your time, and study them. I have a few errands to run. I'll be back in an hour." The look in John's eyes underscored his words. Maggie could tell that he wanted her to read the letters very carefully.

As Maggie watched John leave the room, she was determined to do just that. Picking up the letter on the top of the pile, she looked at the outside of the envelope. It was just as John had said, this time it was from Belle to her brother William. The letter was addressed to a different apartment in New York than the one Belle had sent to Joseph. The typeset on the envelope was the same as on the other. So Belle must have been here when she typed it.

Once Maggie took the letter out, she could see that is was also written on more expensive stationery than the other. It was sent to William,

Second Summit House Courtesy of Harry Craven

on October 8, 1918:

My Dearest William,

I'm sure Joseph told you about the wretched train experience I endured on the way back. It was dreadful. But, that is not why I am writing to you, to complain. Rather, I want to tell you about something that happened to me that is truly remarkable.

In the past few days, I had regained my strength after resting and working in the gardens. I awoke yesterday feeling heat early in the morning. It was unusual for this time of year. On a whim, I decided to go to the mountain. To where there would be cooler air. I know you and Joseph think I am silly to do these things, alone. But, it gives me pleasure to have my little adventures.

Do you remember when we all used to go to the mountain, the fun we had.

I did not take the coach up this time. It has been a long time since I rode the trolleys downtown. So I decided in haste that it would be nice if I went up in that fashion. The carriage dropped me in front of the City Hall where the Mt. Tom trains pick up passengers for the journey up. It was wonderful to see the people of Holyoke downtown. They all seem so happy. The town is busy. It is because of the war being over. I know it. We are all glad to see everyone home. Wars are insanity, come to life.

The slow train, which was full, reached the lower station of Mt. Tom, one hour later. I could hear the music from the amusement park when I arrived. I know you must recall the ride up the steep hills, on those open coach trains, how noisy they are. Do you recall the names of the two that take you up and down, the Elizur Holyoke and the Rowland Thomas.

Boarding the Elizur Holyoke, I met Mrs. Beth Smith, the nice lady who used to work in the house for us. She is such a lovely person. We rode up together talking about how much she loved father and mother. I do so miss them. She said everyone in our mills is talking about how wonderful the Coffee House and the health clinic we set up are working. It is nice to know they appreciate our efforts.

The ride up was jarring. I hate those seats that are mounted at an angle to keep you in. They hurt your back. We reached the Upper Station just as the sun broke through the clouds to light up the valley and wash away the morning's mist.

Mt. Tom is a grand place in the fall. Looking out over the surrounding mountains from the boardwalk up the top is breathtaking. It is as they describe it up there, the autumn colors are unlike any others on this earth.

The Summit House was repainted recently. It is a deeper yellow than before. Do you remember how lovely this hotel is? It is so ornate, with its three separate square floors, all the rooms wonderfully decorated and tastefully furnished. The dining room is my favorite with its shiny pine floors and ivy covered walls. The room is so elegant it reminds me of the best New York restaurants. I went in trying to get a table. Many of our friends were there. I walked around the room and was gracious. Not being in a social mood, I did not stay to sit with any of them. I was courteous, but I left to be by myself.

Wanting to see the radiant colors of the trees, I went to the third floor landing where the small lounge is. I wanted to stand on the porch just to enjoy the views. I found a spot just below the gold dome to my liking and remained there. In an hour feeling chilled, the cool air coming in from the north, I went inside to get a warm drink. There was no place to sit, the room being fully occupied.

A man was sitting by himself at a corner table. It overlooked the west side of the mountain at the entrance I came in through. I noticed him because he was sitting next to a birdcage with two rare white African Parrots in it. He was drawing them. When he became aware of my circumstance, he asked me to join him. It was the only proper thing for a gentleman to do.

He was from France, here for a respite from the war. Hearing of Holyoke's beauty, he had come to the mountain to paint pictures of the remarkable views. He wanted to capture the brilliant red and orange colors of our valleys. You know how I love paintings. It was not long before we were talking about the value of beautiful things. We spoke for hours about what is worthwhile.

When it was time to leave, to go to the train down, he walked me to the Upper Station. It was cold and even with my coat I was uncomfortable so he loaned me his until the train arrived to keep warm. As the train descended the mountain, I thought about what he had told me. When I did, I felt more chilled. He himself had been badly injured in the fighting, and he had gone home to find out that he had lost everyone he loved during a raid on his village. All of his family was dead.

I cannot imagine losing you, Joseph and everyone else I love. And, like him, still be able to paint beauty on a canvas.

Love, Belle

Putting the letter back in the envelope, Maggie picked up the second one, again sent to William at the same address. It was a shorter letter, and the date on it was October 9, 1918:

My Dearest William,

Don't think me silly for writing you again so soon after my last letter. But, I have been exposed to a most marvelous set of circumstances. I could not get the thought of the man I met on the mountain out of my head the next day. Not knowing why, I walked to the train at the city hall station not wanting anyone to know my destination. I went back up to the mountain house.

This time it was the Rowland Thomas train that took me to the top. I cannot tell you how surprised Mr. Clancy the conductor was when he saw me board his train a second time in as many days. I told him I was going up to see a friend visiting.

When I reached the top I went straight to the lounge where I had met the stranger. It was almost the same time of day as when we last met and I was hoping he was a man of patterns. Not being there I inquired about him at the desk. I was told he was out on the mountain, painting.

It took me only a short while to find him. When I did, he was surprised, but glad to see me. I could not take my eyes off of what he was painting, the style being one I have never seen before. It took my breath away. I watched for hours as he created on his canvas what we both saw in the valley. We spent the day talking while he painted the most beautiful picture of the Mt. Tom Range I have ever seen.

I did not leave until the last train at dark. We had a most pleasant day.

Love, Belle

Maggie put that one away and took out the third. It was dated October 11, 1918:

My Dearest William,

You must think I am losing my mind writing you so much within such a short time. I went up to the Summit House a third time yesterday. I could not help myself. I am enchanted with this man, with his painting and his goodness. He is unlike anyone I have ever met in my life. He is leaving soon to go back to Europe. I don't know how I feel about his going.

We talked about my being trapped in France in 1914 during the war. I told him about my driving on the roads in Verdun, seeing all the dead bodies there and the poor children screaming, some of them with arms and legs blown off. He cried when I described this to him, saying they could have been his children. His tears mixed with his paints and as he painted his thoughts of the horrors of the war became enmeshed with the colors of his wonderful painting, frozen in time, forever.

I felt so awful seeing his anguish, William. I must go back to France to help. Tell me what to do.

Love, Belle

That was it. There was no more.

John had said there were a few interesting letters separated out from the others, and he had not been exaggerating. Each one became more intense than the other as Belle continued to write to her brother about the man she had met on the top of Mt. Tom. Wondering whatever happened to the painter, Maggie decided to ask John if he knew when he returned. She put the letters back in their proper sequence and placed them next to her. Maggie picked up Katherine's journal and began to read it. It wasn't long before John came in. He was holding something in his hand. It was one red rose.

"Call me old fashioned, but it is Wistariahurst, and they all did love roses. I'm really sorry about the way things ended last night." He stood there like a little kid, waiting for Maggie to say something.

She thought his gesture was sweet. "My favorite color too. You didn't have to do this. You didn't do anything, John."

Wanting to start over, John asked her a question. "What do you think about Belle's letters?"

"I think Belle met a man on the mountain, and he was a brilliant painter. That's what she told her brother. She apparently was enchanted by him." Maggie thought the same thing.

"But she was in her late forties when she wrote these letters, Maggie," John said.

Thinking she was almost that age, Maggie sat up in her chair. "So what. What does age have to do with a woman's feelings?" Her demeanor changed slightly.

Realizing he had struck a nerve, John spoke quickly, "Oh God, Maggie, I'm sorry. I did it again, didn't I? Jesus, I think I have to go get another flower." They both laughed, knowing that like it or not, they enjoyed each other's company.

Letting the air settle, John asked Maggie a more complicated question. "What do you read between the lines?"

"She was trying to tell her brother that she was having strong feelings for someone she just met." Maggie was guessing.

"*Yes,* and what else?" John agreed.

"That she didn't know what to do about them. She was confused by her feelings." Maggie knew she was right.

"Do you think it ended there, with her being in conflict and the painter going back to France?" John was leading her.

"Probably not," Maggie's reply was quick.

"Neither do I," he agreed.

"What do you think then?" Maggie was becoming intrigued.

"I think she must have written more than just three letters about him. I think Belle sent William and other family members more than just these." John had no proof, but it did seem likely. "I wonder if any of them mentioned the painter again, in any correspondence."

"Where would they be?" Maggie asked. She suspected he was right.

"I have no idea. They're not here in the open for viewing as part of the collection." He had already checked, so was sure of it.

"Do you think someone destroyed or is hiding them?" Maggie was intrigued

"I don't know. Neither does anyone here," John responded.

"You asked them?" Maggie thought it was curious that John had been as diligent as he had about tracking down the whereabouts of these potential love letters.

"Of course. How else could I find out, than to rule out other possibilities?" If someone knew about other letters they would tell him, he thought, unless there were reasons not to. "But I haven't got an answer. The ladies are discussing the possibilities."

"If there are other letters, John, what's the worst that could be in them?" Maggie's suspicions were mounting.

"I don't know. Maybe Belle had suddenly decided to give away a lot of their money. She was writing William to ask him if it was OK." John had turned serious. "Well then, are you ready to take the next step?"

"What did you have in mind?" Maggie knew he was speaking about Belle, but allowed herself to smile in only a slightly flirtatious way.

"If you want to understand a person, what's the best way to get to know them?" John was leading her.

"Would you please get to the point?" she said in a frustrated tone, as if talking to a kid brother.

"You talk to them. What better way to get to know Belle Skinner than to have a conversation with her?"

"Are you nuts?" Maggie interjected. "She's been dead for seventy-five years." Maggie paused, and smirked at John. "Did you have a séance in mind?"

"Not exactly." John held Maggie's coat out for her. "But I have a little surprise for you. Last week I asked Candice for a favor. I think it will help me get more insight into the family, what made them the way they were. She said *'yes'* and made some special arrangements." John was being mysterious. "I asked her this morning if you could come. She said it was fine. But it doesn't take place until seven o'clock tonight. Since we have a few hours, why don't we take a little ride, and I'll show you the mountain where those two people met. There's a reservation there now. Even though you can't take a counter-weight train up to the top, you can drive up, and it's still just as beautiful at the summit."

TWELVE

John took Maggie up to the Mount Tom State Reservation, the park that was "the mountain" they read about in the letters. He showed her approximately where the Summit House was before it had burned down. Then he took her to the other side, to the place where Belle had boarded the train at the amusement park called Mountain Park, which was no longer there. After this, they took a ride around the city. John showed Maggie the magnificent homes that had been build in Holyoke's prosperous years, those that were still there, in the nice neighborhoods.

Maggie had wanted to see the dam and the river, so John took her there. After that, since they were on the bridge already, he took Maggie over to South Hadley. John wanted to show her Mount Holyoke College and the golf course that Joseph Skinner had built for his daughter, Elizabeth. This was the golf course called "The Orchards" that the family had given to the college, where the U.S. Women's Open was played this year.

Then they drove to the Joseph Allen Skinner State Park, the reservation on Route 47 in Hadley. On the top of Mount Holyoke there had been another grand hotel built in the middle and late 1800s. Other trains had brought guests to the top to meet the woman who ran it for years whose name was Frances French. Joseph Skinner bought the property and built a mountain house on the site of the old hotel for his family to use as a summer retreat. He donated the house and over 300 acres of land to the state in 1940 for the residents of the community to use as a recreational facility.

After seeing that, John and Maggie went to have a late lunch at a small, comfortable restaurant on the side of Mount Tom back in Holyoke. It was next to another old city landmark, the Log Cabin. John had asked for a table that looked out over the hills and valleys with the Berkshires in the distance. Sitting by the window, looking out, the two saw the same views Belle and the painter had seen, minus the foliage. They had a lovely lunch and more importantly, a long talk. This time, Maggie wanted to talk about her husband, Bill and her son, Tom. She wanted to share with John the hell she had lived, going through what she did. As Maggie disclosed to him how she could not have made it without her son, John began to realize how hard it had all been for her. As she spoke, he could feel her emotions. Losing someone you love is always an awful experience.

A little later, looking at his watch, John saw they had been talking for two hours. It was almost 6:30 P.M., and the event that he and Candice had planned was going to take place in thirty minutes. So, he asked the waiter for their check and paid the bill. They left to go back down to Wistariahurst, where Candice and the others were waiting for them with his "little surprise." He didn't want to be late for the show.

THIRTEEN

Maggie and John didn't enter through the servants' entrance this time; guests of the Skinner family always entered through the front doors of Wistariahurst. The first thing Maggie noticed was that the hall and rooms were beautifully lit up for a party. The huge chandelier in the Great Hall was fully illuminated, its light almost blinding Maggie when she turned the corner. Harpsichord music emanating from the Music Hall resonated throughout the house, just as Belle had envisioned. Spotlights made the paintings and objects d'art stand out—gold vases, antique clocks, Tiffany leaded glass pieces and glimmering Baccarat crystal pieces that seemed to be everywhere—that Belle had brought back from France. Irving Ramsey Wiles's portraits of the Skinner family members graced every wall, the women painted in blues, red and greens, and the men in darker browns and blacks.

In the middle of the Great Hall, Maggie stood before the portrait of William Skinner, observing his stern face. She thought about his values that had aided him in amassing his fortune. It was not only the mills' work and his thriving business that had made him successful. Every day, he had taught everyone around him by the way he lived, and that made him different. When he lost everything in the Williamsburg flood, he had gone in one day from being on top of the world to being almost penniless. The flood had taught him many lessons, especially the importance of a community of good people, and a strong faith in God. Without God's grace and the help of his friends in Holyoke, he would have given up. Looking at his portrait and those of Belle and Katherine, Maggie concluded that his values were his greatest gift to his children. The Utopian ideas that were put into practice in Holyoke, where everyone benefited from the success of the company proportionate to the work they did, reminded her of a piece of wisdom her own father, a loving but no-nonsense man with a solid belief system, had bequeathed to her when she was young; it was, in a way, an updated version of William Skinner's point of view.

"Don't let the low lifes bring you down with them. Rise above the lies, and do it the right way."

The Dining Room was as bright as the Great Hall, with its chandelier giving off so much light that it was not hard, even from a distance, for Maggie to see that the oval dining table in the center of the room had been set for a dinner party. It was all as it must have looked one hundred years ago.

Turning to John, Maggie raised her eyebrows quizzically, and he replied, "What better way to learn about the Skinners, than to have one of their famous dinner parties, complete with us as the guests," he laughed, "and all of the trimmings included!"

"You guys are crazy," she said cheerfully, and allowed herself to be led into the room.

As Maggie admired the elegant plates, water glasses, wine glasses, silverware, pitchers and candlesticks on the table, the door to the butler's room and kitchen swung open and a man in a stiff, formal outfit appeared. "Good evening, Sir and Madame. My name is Pierre, and I will be serving you with the rest of the staff this evening. May I take your coats?" He was quite proper. He helped Maggie out of her coat, then John, and was carrying the outerwear away when a new figure came through the butler's door. It was Candice, with Tracey not far behind.

Candice solemnly looked at the two standing on the opposite end of the table from her, and said, "When Belle and William had guests, everyone was seated formally. They always sat opposite each other in the center, not at the ends of the table. I entreat you to please look at the place cards, and find your seats." John smiled at Candice and found his place card, then motioned to Maggie to stand next to him, in front of hers.

Tracey was the next to speak. "Belle thought you would enjoy facing the Conservatory and Music Hall, because it is a delightful way to hear the music clearly." As John and Maggie stood at their places, uncertain of what to do next, Maggie heard steps descending the wooden staircase behind her. She turned around, fully expecting to see the old woman, Katherine, coming to join them. But it was not Katherine. It was a somewhat younger woman. She had light red hair, pulled back in a tight bun, and white fair skin, and she was wearing red lipstick. She looked to be about fifty years old and was unmistakably stunning. Her dress was made of elegant red silk, and matching red shoes kept her feet warm. Maggie immediately recognized the outfit. An extra-long strand of white pearls swayed left and right across her bosom as she elegantly strode towards the Dining Room. Just behind her were the two Wiles portraits, painted in 1928. One showed Katherine Skinner, and the other, the lady in the red dress, her sister Belle.

"Good evening," said Belle. "It's wonderful to see you all. Pierre, would you please see that everyone is here, and that dinner is on time. Would

Belle Skinner

you care for some claret? I know I would like a glass!" She was immediately in control of the Fête, as she called her festive occasions.

John whispered into Maggie's ear, as Belle welcomed Candice and Tracey, "She's an actress. She has studied everything about Belle's life, and performs whenever they have events or concerts here." John was trying to be quiet.

"What is that you said, Sir? Please, talk louder. You know it's not proper to keep us ladies wondering what it is that you are saying," Belle told him. Her look was subtle and suggested that he should watch his manners when she is around. "I don't believe I have had the pleasure?" The pitch of her voice varied pleasantly as Belle walked over to Maggie.

"Maggie O'Reilly, Miss Skinner," Maggie answered, turning to her, not knowing quite what to say.

"Are you from Holyoke, Maggie?" Belle asked.

"No, Miss Skinner. I'm from Salem. I came for a holiday, a visit." Maggie was still trying to decide how to respond to Belle graciously.

"My name is Belle, Maggie. Call me Belle, as everyone does. And don't be nervous, dear. Soon we will all know everything about each other." She turned to John. "And you, Sir?" Belle asked with a cordial smile. How could I not know such a handsome man?" Maggie was tempted to giggle at Belle's innocent flirting, but didn't think it would go over well.

"John Merrick, Belle. I'm a friend of Candice's." He was calmer than Maggie, and had not minded Belle's comment about his whispering.

"We're lucky to have our curator, Candice and her assistant, Tracey. They do organize us so nicely," Belle remarked. "It's lovely that you two are friends. Please make yourself comfortable, Mr. Merrick. Is there anything you need?"

"No, I'm fine," John answered her respectfully.

"Good. Then let's sit down and have a nice dinner," she directed, lowering her palms towards the table and taking her seat. It was essential that the seating be proper for her to feel comfortable. Belle insisted on decorum and order, and became agitated, nervous, when it was threatened. Abruptly, Belle got up and did what any good hostess would do. She walked towards the butler's room and kitchen to make sure that her guests had something to drink. "Pierre, Pierre, where is that wine?" Turning around, she looked at Maggie and said, "Good help is hard to find these days," before disappearing into the kitchen.

Five minutes later everyone was sitting at their assigned seats, with

Belle occupying one of the main spots at the center of the table. No one sat at either end of the table, ever. "I am sorry that William could not be here. He was so much looking forward to being here tonight. But, business is pressing, and I'm sure he tried his best to get free." Belle's older brother loved to be at the parties.

John played along and continued the conversation. "We love your home, Miss Skinner!"

She chastised him gently, saying, "Belle, please. Call me Belle if you would."

"*Yes,* Belle, of course. We had a tour of your house, and it was wonderful and very informative. But, I'm wondering if it would be possible for you to tell us, yourself, more about you and your family." He waited for her to respond.

"What is it that you would like to know?" Belle asked.

"Everything!" Maggie interjected.

Warming up to the opportunity before her, Belle began slowly, yet with confidence. "Well, then, let me start at the beginning. That would be when I became part of all of this. I was born in Williamsburg on April 30, 1866, the daughter of William and Sarah Skinner. I have two brothers, William and Joseph, and two sisters, Katherine and Elizabeth. I don't remember very much about growing up in Williamsburg, except that it was out in the countryside, and not at all like our Holyoke here. I do remember the terrible rainy Saturday in May of 1974, the 16th day it was, when the awful flood hit. I'll never forget it. How could I? My father came running into the house to get us, to rush us out the door to high ground, to safety. William was seventeen, Elizabeth fifteen and Joseph was twelve so they could get out on their own. But, I was a child and Katherine was a baby, a year old. She had to be carried out.

We lost our three silk mills, but not our friends. My father was down by the stream and when he saw what was happening, he ran into every one of those mills and got everyone out, and then came to get us up at the house where we were waiting, frightened. He was white as a ghost when I saw him run in. He kept yelling that we all had to hurry and leave everything behind. The next day we went back, and the only remains were the battered rooms of our just finished house. Everything else was destroyed, or washed away. Financially, we were completely ruined." Belle signaled that Pierre should begin serving the first course, a consommé with sherry and thinly sliced scallions. "Mr. James Newton could not have been kinder to my father. But he had great confidence in him, seeing what he had accomplished in Williamsburg. He relocated us to Holyoke, and helped father start over. It was not easy for him, beginning again. And he was never the same man again. After losing everything and seeing so many in the community die, and so many others lose everything, he apparently realized how delicate life is. One minute you can have all the possessions and money in the world, and the next minute it's gone. But, you can always recover what you have lost and more, with the help of good friends. It puts life into perspective, and he raised us to never forget this life lesson. Character, he always told us, is the most important thing in life. It is more valuable than silk."

"That must have been awful, Belle, for you and your family. How old were you?" Maggie asked, thinking how terrifying it must have been for such a young child to see everything perish.

"Eight years old. I can still remember picking up my little sister Katherine and carrying her out of the house, with the water chasing us. Fortunately, I was strong. Most of my memories of that time, the flood, the losses, and our move to Holyoke, are foggy…it was a terrible time for my family. But things slowly became better. Once the pieces of the house were put back together, and father began to build his mills with the help of the moneymen in Holyoke, our lives settled down once again. But, as I said dear, we all appreciated what we had much more the second time around." Belle stopped to taste her soup.

John took the opportunity and asked, "How far back do you remember about what Holyoke was like?"

"Grade school, I guess, John. We all went to the public schools here. I can recall being in grade school with the other children, the sons and daughters of the other mill owners and those of the workers. I remember learning never to feel sorry for myself, seeing how some of them had to live. A number of the girls came to school dressed in the same dress every day. Many of the girls only had one dress. And their shoes were in terrible shape, which was especially bad in the winters when there was freezing rain, and the dampness from the river and canals seeped into our very bones. Then father set out with the other business owners to change things. They built their companies strong, but not just for their own fortunes, but so that everyone could have a better life. I remember him coming home one night in tears. A tragedy had occurred. A child of three, a boy whose father worked in his office, had been playing near one of the canals and had fallen in. No adults were nearby and the child drowned. Father could not help thinking that it could have been one of us. He cried for hours." By now, the soup bowls had been taken away and the salad served.

"What did Holyoke look like back then, Belle? Can you describe it for us?" John asked, not realizing that his questions were preventing her from eating.

Looking at him calmly, Belle smiled, said nothing for a moment, seemingly lost in recollections. Then she looked around the room at the heirlooms on the walls and in the cabinets, and began to speak. "It was noisy, John, because of all the new construction going on, and everywhere you looked there was work being done. Every time I went downtown it seemed as if there was a new building. Everyone was busy. The laborers were everywhere. Whenever I went to visit Father, it seemed as if he was busy seeing to a new piece of machinery. Our mills began to grow faster and faster, and before I knew it we were shipping Skinner products all over the world. My brothers were in the business with father, and we had an office in New York City, but Holyoke was always like heaven, a noisy, somewhat dirty, and very busy place for us. Before I knew it, we were more than prosperous. We were very rich. Our employees struggled for us and us for them. None of us will ever forget what the wonderful people of Holyoke did for our family." Belle thought of the thousands that had worked for her family.

John implored her, "But what did downtown look like?"

"It was remarkable, John. The lower wards of the city, where Father's mills were, and where the merchants did their buying and selling, were constantly growing. I sometimes walked down there with my sisters after school. There were also many public and private buildings being constructed there, mostly along the canals, and on Main and High Streets. Extra tracks were being laid down by the railroads; machines and materials were being hauled into the city on carts pulled by huge workhorses and oxen, or coming in on the trains. Sometimes Father would get angry when he saw us come to the mill, knowing we had walked there unattended. It was improper, but safe, it was certainly safe. No one ever bothered us, nor did they bother anyone else. If they did, I'm sure a few of Father's employees would have made sure they never did again. Everyone was working to build the city up, not to cause problems. People were excited, because they knew their lives were improving. We all lived together, right here in Holyoke, and it was a common thought that the more prosperous the mills were, the better for everyone." Belled paused. "I have wonderful memories of my childhood here. My goodness, looking back on it, I was the luckiest girl in the world! I remember fondly the night we all went to the Opera House downtown to see Sarah Bernhardt perform. That was a majestic theatre and very similar to the old opera houses that one still sees in Paris. Backstage, afterwards, Miss Bernhardt thanked my father and Mr. Whiting for being so nice to her, in bringing her here. I will never forget how beautiful that woman was, and so gracious. She asked me my name and told me that I was a lovely girl for bringing her flowers. Can you imagine her having time for me, a little girl? She wanted to know if I had ever been to Paris. She told me that was where she was born. At the time, I had not yet been there. Miss Bernhardt told me it was the most wonderful city in the world. I believed her, and told her I would make sure to go there someday." Thinking about how respectful the great actress had been, her eyes lit up. "When the *Theatre Sarah Bernhardt* opened in Paris in 1899, I made sure that I went to see her again. I sat in the first row to be able to see everything. Half way through the performance she looked straight at me. She actually recognized me. I don't know how! I was so young when she last saw me. When the show was over, she invited me backstage to talk. I had an aura around me, she said, and I was destined to make something eventful happen. I wasn't sure what she meant by that. She said she saw strengths in me that I was unaware of, and one day I would understand. It made me realize afterwards that like her, I could do wonderful things in my life, meaningful things, if like Father and Mother taught me, I kept the true values of life in their proper order. Then she started to talk about our city and how pleasant it was, even though it was so 'far out of the way.' The Opera House was one of the nicest theatres she had ever performed in, without a doubt, she said. When I left I couldn't have been more proud of my city, to impress a lady of such stature. Imagine, John, all the way from Europe, the best in the world came here to entertain us!"

And then Belle dropped her voice in patriotic respect. "Then there was the time President and Mrs. McKinley came to stay at the first Summit House up on Mount Tom. The whole city turned out for his visit. The streets were lined with people wanting to get a glimpse of him and his wife. I was introduced to them at the dinner held in their honor up on the mountain. I also met President Calvin Coolidge on another oc-

Skinner Mills Courtesy of Marcus Printing

casion, at the City Hall, the impressive stone building like a fortress on High and Dwight Streets that Father and the other Holyoke business owners helped build to conduct Holyoke's civic business." Belle was delighted to talk about the glorious past.

"Of course there were trips to Father's mills when we were old enough to go there by ourselves. I am so proud of what he did, and the way he respected everyone no matter who they were or where they came from. And, oh, how he loved the children of the men and women who worked for him, as if they were his own. After he died, we built a coffee house for the women and younger girls to take their time-offs, in honor of his memory. There were always children in there with their mothers. Father would have wanted his people taken care of."

Pausing briefly, she motioned for Pierre to remove the salad plates, then Belle continued. "Once I finished my schooling here in Holyoke, I went to Vassar College to study. I was President of my class and earned two degrees, one in Music and a minor in French History. I loved to read the creations of the great writers and poets too. Balzac was my favorite. I even wrote some of my own poetry and gave several readings at the college. In addition, I performed numerous times on the piano and the violin in Poughkeepsie and in Holyoke. After I graduated, as was customary, I went on 'The Grand Tour' with some of my schoolmates."

"What was the Grand Tour, Belle?" Maggie asked.

"We saw the world, Maggie!" Her eyes were shining. "We went everywhere. By boat, we traveled to China, Japan, the Far East and Europe. Truly, we went all over the world. Egypt was my favorite place. The Pyramids are indescribable. I was away for more than a year. It was during this trip that I first saw Paris. I fell in love with it, and consider it now to be one of my homes, along with New York City, and Holyoke, of course. One's roots are in the city one grew up in. That's why I could never leave our home at Wistariahurst, and Holyoke. There are so many memories for me here. My Father died in 1902 here, and Mother in 1908. So much of our family's history is in Holyoke. I can't imagine ever not being here. And it is so lovely and so safe."

"It was. I don't think you could walk the streets and be safe now, Belle," Maggie answered quietly. "You'd be lucky to make it to High Street before you were mugged, I'm told." Maggie was not thinking about the effect her words would have on Belle.

Belle drew back. "My goodness, what are you talking about, dear?"

"It's dangerous here now. Holyoke is full of thugs and drug addicts now." Maggie answered insensitively.

"What, criminals? Here? No, I don't believe it! You clearly have the wrong place in mind or perhaps you have had just a bit too much wine." Belle's manner toward Maggie changed perceptibly.

"Yes, because of all the drugs and crime here. It's a filthy, dangerous place." Maggie remembered how she had felt the first time she had walked from the street into the public library.

"There is very little crime here in Holyoke, dear. You must be thinking of somewhere else." Belle was talking about her hometown, the city she grew up in. Maggie was describing a different place entirely. And what had she meant by "drugs?" "Holyoke is guarded by its laws, Maggie. It is clean, spic and span. We have a beautifully trained, very decent police force that keeps it free of undesirables who want to bring their corruptions, violence and new gimmicks here. We all know they want to be here. But the elders of the city will never allow the city to become crime-ridden. I don't know what you are seeing, dear. It must be your imagination." Belle maintained her composure.

Belle went on to explain patiently, "Holyoke is a growing and a well-respected community. As I said, prominent stage people, Presidents, and other dignitaries visit us here. They come to Holyoke to see its beauty, and how well ordered it is. It is marvelous. We all go to bed, every night, thankful that we live here. It is this way, because its people respect the laws, the rules of the city, which includes dressing properly and being courteous. If they break the laws, they will not be allowed to stay. Our men are strong and brave, and they have moral character. They know what corrupt influences can do to a place, and so, put people like this on the next train out of town." Belle was describing the men who were like her father, brothers, and everyone else who lived and worked in Holyoke.

John was the next to speak. "I think what Maggie is trying to say is that Holyoke has changed a little, lately. Maybe you haven't been downtown recently. Have you, Belle?" he asked her, gently.

"I have been abroad. No, I haven't been downtown recently. Actually, I've been away for quite some time now, and have just returned," Belle answered.

"When you go away, sometimes things are different than when you left," Maggie added, realizing that Belle would be devastated if she learned the truth about Holyoke's demise since she last saw it.

"How could Holyoke change so much in the few short years I have been away? When I left, business was booming, the smoke was bellowing out of all of the factories' chimneys twenty-four hours a day, showing very high levels of production. The streets are kept spotless by a veritable army of sweepers whom the city employs, and who wash the streets down every night just like in most great cities. The homes are all kept neat and tidy. From Main Street to the Highlands, we respect what we own, and we respect our neighbors, storekeepers, teachers, workers and civic employees. We take pride in our community and our heritage. Our children are lovely, and we set a high priority on having something to hand down to them. The measure of our success in life, in fact, is what we leave behind for the children, and for them to leave to their own children. Everyone in Holyoke knows this and lives by it. It is impossible to believe that all this has been lost."

The main course was served and when it ended, the conversation changed to other topics. After Pierre and two maids picked up the dinner dishes from Belle first and then her guests, the elegant lady stood and led them in the direction of the Music Room. Turning to John and Maggie, she said, "Please join me for some music, to calm us. I cannot imagine what you described, a Holyoke that is sordid, beastly. I don't want to even think about such a disgraceful development. So let us enjoy what my family and the good citizens of Holyoke have created, and speak no more of matters that don't exist. My music is here. My instruments are here, beautiful musical creations for everyone to enjoy. We have frequent concerts on Sunday afternoons, as you perhaps are aware. We raise money for many charities, by asking our friends to help us. Pablo Casals performed for us here. When the famous pianist and composer Maciej Paderowski came here, he said my collection of instruments was the finest he had ever seen. Please come and listen to the angelic music they create. It will make you feel better. It will calm my frazzled nerves."

In the Music Room, Pierre served dessert and coffee. Belle told him to have Prudence, Belle's companion, join them, as Belle needed Prudence's settling influence. Belle appeared as gracious as she had been when she first walked down the stairs, but internally she was jittery, an affliction Belle often experienced when faced with stressful information or situations. Belle hid it well, but she was becoming disoriented. She could feel an uncomfortable sensation growing, thinking about the city her father and the other great men and women had built. Was it possible that it had all been lost? Belle was becoming physically sick just thinking about it.

One hour later, Pierre whispered to Belle that Prudence had gone out unexpectedly, and had not yet returned. So, Belle, John, Maggie and Tracey spent hours talking about myriad subjects. Candice had excused herself earlier and left for the night, leaving Tracey to close and lock up. The four people left from dinner conversed about Belle's schooling, what exactly she had learned in the Holyoke schools, and about her favorite school chums.

Belle was proud of her Vassar education, and had never stopped adoring music and French. Over the years, she had collected a multitude of valuable musical instruments, mostly antiques, and built one of the finest collections of its type in the world. "The early virginals and spinets are my favorites. But the harpsichords, guitars and French bugles are exquisite as well. When I die I want everything kept together. The collection is too valuable to be separated."

Then, Belle told them about her family, William, Joseph, Katherine (Kitty) and Elizabeth. Despite their differences, they were all Skinners. Belle was very close to Kitty and her mother Sarah, and had a close relationship to William, mostly because he was the first-born, the heir to his father's responsibilities, and she looked up to him as she looked up to her father. Joseph was more her friend.

John was more interested in hearing more about the times she had spent in New York and Paris, and Belle obligingly described how overwhelmed she had been the first time she went to New York with her father and William. The size of the city and the number of people there made Holyoke, previously the center of her universe, seem small, and caused her to change her perspective. Besides the well-appointed theatres, it was the shops that interested her most. Belle loved to look in the store windows and had so many choices of where to shop. There were too many to frequent them all. Belle said that New York's offerings, while no higher in quality to Holyoke's, were certainly greater in quantity and variety.

"But it was Paris that stole my heart, dear. Once I saw that city, I knew I had to be there, live there, feel it. It wasn't just the city's age, or the depth of its museums, or the incredible architecture of its buildings, or the lay-out of its streets, but its history. Paris has a history unlike any other in the world. And it's all there to be seen and lived. It excites you. It begs you to stay and be part of it. So I did. The feelings and emotions I experienced in Paris are unlike any I felt in New York or Holyoke. Have either of you lived in Paris?"

Maggie and John both answered, "No," in unison.

"Well then, it's hard to explain. When Miss Bernhardt told me about Paris, it was as if she was calling me there. Although, I was more interested in learning how I could be more like her than experiencing the city she had described. She was so beautiful, and incredibly captivating. Everyone in the Opera House that night wanted to get close to her, near her, to feel her warmth. I wanted to be just like her, worldly and confident. I was going to become that type of person, someone who takes people's breath away just by being herself."

"From what I understand, you became that person," Maggie offered.

"Oh, my dear, you flatter me too much! I enjoyed the limelight; it's the fast pace, it thrilled me. But, something else was moving me, a force. It's hard to explain. I felt like I was born to be helpful, to make a statement. I am a very complex person I suspect, but down deep, truly thankful for the opportunities I was given."

Belle was grateful, and laughed. "I don't deserve such a generous compliment!" After a moment, she rose from her chair and said, "Now I am rather tired, and must respectfully retire. Although, I would far prefer to stay up and continue with this most interesting evening. Please carry on and enjoy yourselves, however you wish. Pierre will see to your needs. And perhaps after all the New Year celebrations are over, you can come back, and we can continue our discussions. I have so enjoyed your company. You are both delightful. And when you do come back, I want to show you a little film I had made when I was in France." She walked into the Grand Hall, with Maggie and John following. They all said goodnight.

Watching her ascend the stairs with difficulty, Maggie and John realized that *Belle* was more than tired. She was exhausted. Reliving Belle's life experiences was draining for her. She needed to rest.

After thanking Tracey, Maggie and John left together. They were standing in the driveway by their cars, talking about their individual plans for New Years, and agreeing to return to Holyoke the following week to continue their explorations into the past. They exchanged phone numbers, and were about to say goodbye when a figure emerged, walking quickly, too fast for comfort, from the darkened street. They both tensed.

"Are you John and Maggie?" the stranger asked, with a French accent.

"Yes," they answered together.

Unveiling herself, by pushing the hood of her black cloak back, she said, "Forgive me, please, for not joining you this evening. An emergency came up, and I had to leave. I'm Prudence Lagogue, Belle's friend." She excused herself, opened the front door of Wistariahurst, went in, and shut the door quietly behind her.

John figured it out first. Knowing how real Tracey had wanted to make the dinner party, he said, "It's Tracey. She just got us with one of her practical jokes. I should have expected this."

A light from a second floor window suddenly shone down on them, and when the curtains were pulled back, they saw Tracey's figure. She was looking out at them, waving her fingers whimsically, in a fan like motion, to say goodnight. With light hearts, Maggie and John got into their cars, and drove slowly out the driveway of Wistariahurst. As the sign cautioned, they were mindful not to harm the dinosaur tracks in the slates of stone. Maggie and John had both enjoyed the evening. It was a good way for everyone to start the New Year.

FOURTEEN

The holidays can bring up myriad subterranean emotions, and the second day of January usually brings a sigh of relief. It is a shame, but this is so common. Family issues, past and present, in the case of Maggie and John respectively, were a concern. Although they did speak on the phone, Maggie steered the conversation away from personal matters, especially her husband. It was all she could do to get through New Year's Day without thinking about Bill, as the turning of the year had always been a special occasion for them. Each year was more difficult than the one before. But this year, Maggie's son was coming home, and she would be able to spend an entire week with him before the hectic pace of this "American" life banished their repose.

John, dealing with his own baggage, decided that a quiet night with a few friends was the best way to ring in the New Year. He and Maggie had agreed that they both wanted to know more about Belle Skinner, and that working together on their quest made sense: a reporter and a writer would be able to gather and evaluate masses of information and write a compelling story. While one was strong in gathering details, the other had imagination and literary skills. But it wasn't until Monday, the 10th of January, that they were able to make plans to see each other and further inspect the archives. They set a date with Tracey for Wednesday at 10:00 A.M. to look at old letters that were in storage at the Skinner house. John made Tracey promise to refrain from melodrama and teasing, as he was temporarily not up for it. "Not until I get warmed up," he told her. Her promise, however, had been unconvincing.

For Maggie, Tracey's sense of humor was a welcome relief from the flatness of her own life. Tracey was idiosyncratic, a little out of place at Wistariahurst. Or, maybe she was in the right place. After all, leprechauns might be anywhere, even in a historical museum.

At the appointed time, the three gathered at the mansion. After some small talk about the dinner party and the holidays, the threesome went to the conference room. "Where do you want to begin?" Tracey asked.

"When last we met," John started, "Belle brought us somewhat up to date about her early life to the time of her father's death in 1902. I think we're clear about her schooling and getting her feet wet in the big world, outside of Holyoke. By the time her father died, she was a woman of status with apartments, or houses in Holyoke, New York and Paris. We know she spent a great deal of time traveling. But, can we look at some of her letters from the time between her mother's death in 1908, and the first or second year of World War I? I've seen only a few files… you must be hiding some of the best letters," John said, giving in to the urge to tease her.

"Mr. Merrick, I thought you wanted me to behave!" Tracey teased back.

Shutting *Pandora's Box,* he apologized. "All right, but how's this? May I please see more of Belle's letters?"

"You certainly may, Mr. Merrick," Tracey answered, winking at Maggie, drawing her in.

In ten minutes, Tracey returned with five file boxes, each neatly labeled and numbered. "Remember the rules, please," she said, an archivist at heart. "Wear the cotton gloves when you handle documents, and put everything back into the folders in the same order they were in before. I also brought a number of journals for you."

"OK, we will." Maggie answered for them both.

It didn't take long before they were immersed in the letters, some with newspaper clippings attached. Some were from Belle to William, others to Katherine. A few were addressed to Joseph, Elizabeth and various friends.

"Find anything compelling?" John asked.

"There's one here dated November 15, 1902 that talks about the girls opening the coffee house in memory of their father on what would have been his seventy-eighth birthday. It says, *'The shop is located on Main Street opposite the Holyoke Machine shop, in the store formerly occupied by the Lemeul Sears and Company.'* But, I thought the coffee shop was in the Skinner mill," Maggie said.

"From what Belle told us, I think the idea got its start, but it expanded quickly, and eventually evolved into a sort of Girls' Club, with the help of local women, complete with a library, games and other activities suitable for children," John said.

Maggie looked up from a letter she was reading to tell him, "It says that 150 girls came to the opening to thank Belle and Katherine for their kind efforts."

"It was a nice thing to do for everyone," John added, "and a wonderful tribute to their father that they named it the *William Skinner Coffee House*."

"Here's a letter dated April 25, 1904 from Belle to Katherine, who is apparently on her honeymoon." Maggie handed the paper to John. "She says Katherine is an old married woman while she is still clinging to the parent stem. Belle must have been thinking about her future, whether she would ever be married. Belle is wondering if she was going to be an old maid and all that nonsense."

John gave Maggie a journal and pointed to an entry in it. "They built a monument in Forestdale cemetery and had an angel monument erected. There's an entry in Katherine's journal about it."

Reading on, the two were concentrating, turning pages, moving from one letter to a journal to another letter, and absorbing the contents in each. "This one is from Belle to Katherine dated March 29, 1912. She's traveling in Sicily, seeing the ruins, studying Greek history, and compares the wisteria there with the blossoms at Wistariahurst. She writes, *'There's nothing to compare with Mother's wonderful vine.'* She was proud of her mother."

John smiled, "She was quite devoted, wasn't she."

"Yes, Katherine, too. And the letters to William show how close they all were." Maggie thought it nice to see such a close-knit family staying in touch with each other through their letters. "It's as if they were picking up the telephone, back then."

"They knew someone on the Titanic. It was written from Belle, who was in Paris, to Katherine in Holyoke…" John carefully handed Maggie the crumbling letter.

Maggie continued where he had left off, "… dated April 13, 1912. She wrote, '*I have just read of the terrible disaster to the Titanic. I noticed Steve Blackwell was on the ship. Poor M.*'" M's name was not spelled out. "'*It will be the end of her, if Steve is lost.*'"

Another dated April 18, 1912 from Belle to Katherine read:

> *I can think of nothing but the terrible catastrophe. Think of that great Boat actually sinking, and all of those good people gone to their deaths like rats in a trap, or freezing in the water*

> *hoping for Rescue. It frightens me. I think I shall choose smaller Boats and slow ones in the future. I wrote to Clara today. It will really kill her Mother, I think, to lose Steve in this shocking Manner. The Question on everyone's lips is, 'How is that Ismay, the President of the Line, was saved?' I don't believe he will ever be able to give a satisfactory Reason for not going down by his Captain's side. I have very little news of myself…I have ordered three pretty Gowns at Worth's… (R.C.) wants me to see her house. She talked in 'Millions', as usual, telling me that Mr. Marks of Chicago (he had as much as adopted her brother Charlie), left Charlie $7, 000,000 and Charlie now Lives in a Palace on Michigan Avenue, has five automobiles and Nothing to do.*

John said. "It looks as if someone was suggesting a suitor for Belle."

Maggie thought John had a surmise. She asked, "How much was $7 million worth back then?"

"Jesus, I don't know Maggie, a lot. I guess you just have to add more zeroes. These guys were the billionaires of today, and there were fewer of them."

"Here's another letter where Belle is concerned about being on the White Star line after the Titanic sank." John passed the letter to Maggie. It was dated April 23, 1912. Belle wrote from Paris:

> *People can still Think and Talk of Nothing but the loss of the Titanic. I do hope the Senate Committee will probe this to the bottom…The Chases will not travel by the White Star again as long as Ismay remains President. Speaking of the Chases, I Dined with them at the Ritz Sunday evening. Daisy Gordon was also Dining there. She was gorgeously dressed and looks like she never had a care in the world. When she heard of the Titanic disaster, she is 'said' to have said, 'Oh dear, and not even one of my three husbands went down with her.' I can't believe she really said it.*

"She certainly did move in one of the top echelons of the world," Maggie said, raising her eyebrows. "They all knew each other, the rich ones."

"It seems so," he agreed.

Not long after, just before noon, Tracey carried a tray with coffee and biscuits into the room where Maggie and John were. "Can't let you guys get tired," she said, setting the tray on the table. "Find anything interesting?"

"She knew a lot of important people," Maggie stated in a way that would lead Tracey to give her opinion.

"Oh, yeah, Belle traveled in the fast lane. She knew everyone. When she was in Holyoke, she dined with the wealthy here, and the same was true in New York, Paris, or wherever else she was. Belle had made the big time."

"Thanks for the refreshments, Tracey." John said.

"You are very welcome, Mr. Merrick." Tracey curtsied and began to leave. "OK, I have a student coming in for an interview, so I'm going to leave you two alone again." But, before exiting Tracey turned and asked, "Did you get to the part yet, where she gets trapped in France when the First World War begins? You'll like that one."

"Not yet," John answered.

"She was amazing, truly amazing," Tracey commented, as she walked out. She knew she had intrigued them further.

Maggie took a cup of coffee from the tray and decided that now was a good time to ask John about something she'd been thinking lately. It had nothing to do with the Skinners and their letters. She launched in with, "John, you haven't told me about your relationship, the one you're so sad about."

John was taken aback, he put down the letter he was reading and looked away. He thought for a second about what to say. Then John summed it up, saying in a quiet voice, "We were assaulted, she never recovered." The turmoil his last love affair had caused him was readily apparent.

"Did she die?" Maggie asked, thinking about her own loss.

"No, she just… went away. Tragedies change people. Sometimes they're just never the same again. That's why it is so hard. *You know* they could still be that person, but they're just not. It's why we call them tragedies."

Not wanting him to feel worse than he already did, Maggie said, "Maybe someday you can talk to me about it. For now, let's stay on the subject of Belle. I'm sorry for your trouble, I know how it feels." She was, and she did. Maggie handed John a letter from Belle to Katherine that was written in June 1914. Maggie let John know by the way she handed it to him and looked at him that she sympathized with his loss.

"Things are not good there," Belle had written, *"but we're going to Paris anyway."*

Belle had included a tear-out from a French journalist's report that said: *With Serbia already agonized by the two Balkan wars (1912–1913) Serbian Nationalists have returned their attention to liberating the South Slavs of Austria-Hungary. Col. Dragutin Dimitrijevic, head of Serbia's military intelligence believes the cause of their Secret Society Union of Death would be served by the death of the Austrian Archduke Francis Ferdinand, Heir to the throne of Austria.*

A news brief clipped to the report said, *"June 28, 1914, 11:30 a.m.—In the Bosnian capital city of Sarajevo, Francis Ferdinand and his wife Sophie, Duchess of Hohenberg, were shot to death by a Bosnian Serb, Gavrilo Princip."* Two headlines were attached, one from July 28—*"War declared against Serbia"*—and one reading, *"Germany declares war against Russia."*

Maggie noted that Belle had apparently made her bookings in advance. "She wasn't going to let anything stop her from going. Belle wrote to Katherine on July 11, '*It's time to leave for Europe.*' She sailed out of New York, and sent Katherine a cable from the ship: *'I arrived at noon with Prudence, ready to sail at noon on the SS George Washington. It finally left at one a.m. I will cable you when I arrive.'*"

She handed John a book, William's Journal, and pointed out an entry penned in New York on July 19:

> *Telegram received, Belle has arrived in Paris—she says it was a beautiful voyage, but where is she now? I want to go there, but the N.Y. Stock Exchange has closed (First Time in 41 years). All the Stock Exchanges in the world are closed. Prices for securities have gone to smash-awful prices. Cabled Belle to find out where she is. I am dreadfully worried about her, for her safety.*

"William knew the devastating effects wars have on the world's stock markets. It would appear that he was interested in diversifications, and had expanded the Skinners' financial interests into many markets," John speculated. "He also, apparently, thought Belle was foolish to go to Paris, seeing bad things developing, but couldn't talk her out of it."

"The prices of stocks are driven down low, and financial panic comes with most wars, just like now, with the war in Iraq. The only ones who benefit are those making the moves." Maggie finished John's thoughts for him.

"Anything else?" John asked, motioning to the letters and journals in front of Maggie.

"Yes, quite a bit." She handed him another letter, and gave him a summary. "It's a letter from William to Katherine, dated July 21. He says, *'I'm worried sick about Belle. No more cables.'*" Then Maggie showed John a letter William had sent to Katherine on July 31. "He wrote that *'There is still no word from Belle.'* William told Katherine he'd sent a letter to a Senator Weeks to have the State Department look Belle up." Maggie hesitated. "By August 4, according to another letter William sent Katherine, no one knew where Belle was. William wrote, *'I am nearly crazy with worry. Germany has declared war on England. It is awful... it is too colossal.'*"

Maggie kept going. As she did, she handed the slips of stationery to John. "On August 5, William had a courier deliver a letter to Katherine saying that he had finally received three cables from Belle, all very much delayed. *'In all she says she is comfortable and will go to London once the railroads are running again.'* What does she mean, *'once the trains are running again?' Things are critical in Europe now, Katherine. Belle is in danger.'*"

Maggie indicated that the order the letters were written in was important. "On August 7, William sent a cable to Katherine, *'No recent word from Belle.'*" Maggie paused, thinking how worried he must have been. "On August 11, he wrote a letter informing Kitty of a wire he'd just received, *'a fine cable from Belle from the Divonne-les-Bains,'* the secluded place where Belle went to find tranquility. From the tone of these letters, and his choice of words, he was more than a little concerned for Belle's safety."

Commenting on the solitude Belle apparently found at the baths, Maggie said, "Not this time. She didn't find tranquility. What she found was what she wrote in this cable to William: *'War is awful.'* The war must have been closing in on her there." She took up the journal again, and an entry caught her attention. "William writes in his journal, *'I cabled her back immediately, I advised her to go to Geneva. I told her that the war is raging everywhere in Europe now. The Kaiser is certainly crazy. Get out of there.'*"

She pushed another piece of paper towards John. "It's a cable from Belle received by William on August 12."

It read: *"Will leave for Paris when I can, thanks for gold."*

"It seems William found a way to cable her money, or at least something of value to use to get her out," Maggie commented.

"Here's another letter from William to Katherine on August 21," said John. Reading aloud, "*'Still no cable from Belle, I am anxious. Germans have captured Brussels and the Belgians have made Antwerp the Capital. About 12,000,000 are fighting.'*"

Maggie produced a cable from Belle to William. "This is dated August 25."

It read: *"Having a hard time, no food—no hot water."*

John rested his hand gently on Maggie's shoulder. He wanted to rest and evaluate the letters and their dates before going further. "Things were out of control by then for Belle, and they all knew it, do you agree?"

"Absolutely," she answered.

John passed her another piece of correspondence, between William and Kitty. "William thinks Belle is badly *'on edge'* according to a cable he sent Kitty on August 31, after receiving one from Belle. He writes, *'Belle appears to be used up nervously. She sailed from Liverpool to Philadelphia on August 28th 1914.'* He's frightened that Belle won't make it back."

The table was covered with papers, mostly in neat piles, but some of them scattered all over. Maggie picked up another cable. "Here is one where Kitty tells William of Belle's hasty return home to the safety of Holyoke on September 7. *'She did not stop in New York to see you because she was not feeling well enough. She had to get home.'* And another," Maggie continued reading:

She looks pretty well now, but still 'very nervous'. She has seen so many wounded soldiers and ordinary people dead and mangled, it is 'on her nerves, she says.' REPUBLICAN and UNION newspapers both have fine articles on Belle's experiences. All Holyoke has called up Belle on the telephone as they had read the accounts of her being caught in the middle of everything happening there.

Maggie was getting tired. John got up from his chair and looked at the odd assortment of papers before him, their edges curling and frayed, some of them ripped and worn through at the faded creases. Some of the dates didn't match up, but a clear picture of what happened to Belle was beginning to form. Going to her favorite retreat, Divonne-les-Bains in France near Geneva, to settle her nerves, Belle had gotten herself caught up in the fighting when the war began, and had been detained for three weeks. As the English were capturing German gunboats, the Germans were driving themselves into Belgium. The Belgians were repulsing them at Liege, and Russia was gathering its forces for a major strike on Germany. Although Germany did not declare war on Russia until the first of August 1914, and on France on August 3, the intense hostilities had begun a month earlier, in July. Meanwhile, France and England were active at a number of fronts. Europe was becoming a vast battlefield.

And once released by her captives, Belle was trying to get out of France to Liverpool, where she could hopefully buy a place on a ship to America. Once she was on the ship, she would pray that it would not be sunk by a German submarine. But unfortunately for her, along the way, there must have been thousands of corpses and injured soldiers, as well as civilians, even children. She must have witnessed villages in ruin and breathed the smell of fire all along her route. On the roads, at the train stations, outside her window and in the distance, she had witnessed the results of warfare, the aerial bombings from the large artillery guns, and the mortars and machine guns from the trenches. The once peaceful countryside became alive with the sounds of death. It hadn't been long before northern and eastern France were the scenes of intense fighting, with constant bombings and Big Bertha shelling attacks on cities and villages. Hostile occupations and slaughters were taking place everywhere. And Belle was in its midst. Because of no other reason than bad timing, she had become a first-hand witness to a bloody horror show.

"How are we doing?" Tracey's voice suddenly broke the silence.

"Have you read these?" John asked. "These accounts of what she saw?"

Tracey looked down at the piles of letters and newspaper clippings on the table and said, "They're all out of order now, guys. Why don't I help you put them back in the proper files, so we all don't get into trouble, and, *Yes John*, I've read all of them, and what Belle saw must have been awful. My guess is that she was never the same person afterwards. Seeing things like those described in the letters has to horrify you. It would me. Did you read the letters Belle wrote on August 9 to William, where she tells him the trains are not running, and that she'll cable him when they are? She was trapped without a way out. Or, William's Journal entries dated in August, where he writes that he is concerned that Belle is used-up nervously. He's worried she may never be the same. The exposure to the world of war changed Belle's luxurious life forever. It's why she did what she did at Hattonchatel years later."

"What's Hattonchatel?" Maggie asked.

"Not, what Maggie. Where," John answered, having come upon a few letters that mentioned it. "Hattonchatel is a small village in the Lorraine region of France, not far from the Belgian border. The town was destroyed during the war. Belle and her family rebuilt it later."

"How does a family rebuild an entire village?" Maggie asked him.

This time it was Tracey who answered her, "It's a long tale, Maggie. We have to go now. But if you two are here tomorrow I'll tell you all about it. There are more files and letters that explain what they did there. Why don't you go get something to eat? Talk about what you read today and when you come back in the morning you'll probably have some questions I can answer for you. We can also discuss the subject of Apremont, France—it's another little jewel of Holyoke history we can explore."

Picking up the now organized file boxes, the three of them went to the top landing. Tracey had to put them back in the archives room. "Show yourselves out," Tracey said. "I have some work to do in here, and will see you in the morning. How about the same time as today? Oh, and John, why don't you take Maggie to a nice place tonight. How about dinner at the Yankee Pedlar? It's as much a part of Holyoke history as anywhere. She'll love the atmosphere. It's lovely." She loved bringing people together, and, when possible, teasing and causing a bit of mischief. She knew John wouldn't get out of the Yankee Pedlar for under a hundred bucks. Playing one of her practical jokes, she had just gotten Mr. Merrick again. Watching him go out, she could see that he knew it.

FIFTEEN

The Yankee Pedlar was an old New England Inn that had been converted to a restaurant. Dinner there was fine. But it was the conversation that Maggie and John had that was great. John opened up about many things, mostly about what he was finding unsatisfactory in his life. After John's love life, it was the nation's leaders wanting him to chase around after money and buy lottery tickets, along with their penchant for thinking up more investment schemes that irritated him the most. Money mania was everywhere in America. It was getting to John. He was tired of it, having spent thirty years looking for something that was an illusion. The regime running the country had stolen enough of his mind, money, and time as far as he was concerned. John had come to the conclusion that if he was for sale, they couldn't afford him anymore. John wanted to spend the rest of his life deciding for himself what was worth living for. He had come back to Holyoke to find out what it was here that he had missed.

Maggie, too, knew what John meant about chasing elusive rainbows, but, she really hadn't done it. Maggie was grounded, and her responsibilities had kept her busy. Maggie's tragedy was that she'd had what she wanted, only to watch death take it away. Then she was alone. Maggie thanked God every day for her son, though. Now, she lived for him. Unlike John, Maggie didn't know why she was in Holyoke. In a sense, she was just chasing an interesting story that had crossed her path. Maybe it was out of habit, a return to Maggie's old patterns as a reporter. It could be here or maybe not. She liked searching for something that was concealed. The chase was a high for her. Maggie just didn't feel right unless she was looking for something.

The next morning, all three arrived on time at the museum. Tracey could see that the intrigue she and Candice had set up for them was having its effect: that the writer and the reporter were caught up in the bits and pieces they had uncovered of the Skinner story. Now it was time to hook them good. Tracey didn't want Maggie and John fishing around idly anymore. They might miss something, or they might not, but she wanted to make sure they found it. Tracey directed Maggie and John to a specific place this time, the precise file boxes that had just what she wanted them to see. Those were the ones they should look at. Would Maggie and John confirm Tracey's suspicions about the French village? Sounding more like a schoolteacher than an archives director, Tracey tried to explain the relationship between Belle Skinner and the French village of Hattonchâtel.

"Why call it a relationship? That's an odd way to talk about this." Maggie asked a reasonable question.

"Belle called the village 'her baby,' and she had that kind of relationship with it. In that she never married and didn't have any children, it was what Belle did in her life that she considered worthwhile. You and I have children, and that's what we love the most, being mothers. For Belle this did it, it made her life meaningful." Tracey picked up where they'd left off the previous night.

Sitting in the same room as the day before, in different chairs this time, Maggie and John listened to Tracey's backgrounder. "OK, this is kind of boilerplate, so please bear with me. This kind of thing is not my forte, and I'm not a writer, but I've been able to collect some information from the Internet. This is what they responded with when I sent a written request for information to the village." Tracey took out a typed sheet of paper and began reading her synopsis:

> *The Château is one of the most picturesque in France, situated on a high point of a mountain, it overlooks the plain of the Pleine de Woevre, near the Belgian border. Its history revolves around the invasions of the Huns, the Hungarians, the Swedes, the Russians and of course, the Germans. The old Romans were probably the founders of the village, although some say it was occupied before they arrived. In any event, they undoubtedly were the first ones to fortify it, and they made it one of their principal trading centers.*
>
> *The French King Charlemagne came there in 800 A.D. and became the proprietor of the village with the consent of the Bishop of Verdun, whose name was Hatton. Chatel is the old French word for Château. Put the two together and you have the name of the village.*
>
> *At the time of the Thirty Years War, which lasted from 1618*

to 1648, the Swedes captured the village and tortured its inhabitants, trying to make them reveal the hiding place where they suspected the Romans had kept their money. This happened between the years 1630 and 1634. They seemed to think a treasure was hidden somewhere in the village. They left, finding nothing.

In the late 1600s, the village was looted and burned by Richelieu in a religious war. It took at least two hundred years to recover, and by the late 1800s, it was rebuilt and back to being a fairly seCuré place.

By the beginning of the First World War, Hattonchâtel had become a tourist stop, mostly because of the beautiful Château, the Abbey, many ancient homes, the old market, and the tomb of the Bishop of Verdun, who died in 1500, in the church there. When the Germans invaded France it became one of their strongholds: they occupied the Château for almost four years, and when they were driven out by the French and American troops, they left nothing standing, destroying the Château, the Church and Abbey, many of the houses, and most of the other village buildings. They also poisoned the town's water supply and fields. By the time the war was over, the once beautiful village that sat atop the mountain, overlooking the hills and valleys was uninhabitable.

There is a wide range of speculation as to why Belle chose this village to devote her efforts and money to. Some claim they heard her say that it was because it reminded her of Mt. Tom and the Holyoke Range. Others maintain that she was traveling around France in her Hispano-Suizi automobile, driven by her chauffeur, and they just stumbled upon the village while looking for a place to rest. Maybe she saw it when she was fleeing the country. It really has never been understood, why Belle chose Hattonchâtel as her project. What matters is that she did, and what she accomplished.

Tracey had come to the end of her written piece and handed Maggie and John maps of the northeastern region of France. "It's not like there is a main throughway from Paris straight to the village, although there are old Roman roads connecting some of the villages. One does have to take a few turns here and there, though. And, it is way up in the mountains—it was apparently quite hard to get to back then. And it was quite a distance from Paris. Back in 1920, it was a one-day journey, sometimes more than that. Anything could go wrong on the trip. They could run out of gas, and there was very little around to spare. They could have become lost or hit bad weather. The roads were almost impassible after the war. There were big holes in the roads, trenches everywhere. Perhaps a little leftover fighting by some disgruntled troops was possible? They could have been attacked. All sorts of problems lay on the road from Paris to the blown-up village of Hattonchâtel that Belle chose to restore."

"When did she return?" John asked.

Tracey went to a different box and took out a file. "Let's begin with when she went back to France. Remember the Treaty of Versailles wasn't signed until June 28, 1919, so most people were not traveling to Europe until then. Look at these entries in Belle's journal. The first one after the war is dated November 11, 1918. She wrote, *'Armistice document signed.'"* Tracey showed them the entry. "The next accounts in the journal are war costs, in her own handwriting. Where Belle got the numbers, we don't know, probably from newspapers or private sources. *'Cost of war: Allied and Associated Powers calculated to have mobilized more than 42,000,000 men and to have lost more than 5,000,000 lives.'"*

Maggie interrupted her, remarking, "That's a lot of zeroes!"

John immediately made the connection with their previous discussions of the investments made by the moneymen and the real losses in wars. Not understanding completely, Tracey continued:

> *Russia and France together: 3,000,000; the Central Powers, with Turkey and Bulgaria, mobilized nearly 23,000,000 & lost nearly 3,400,000. (Germany & Austria-Hungary together, nearly 3,000,000), wounded over 21,000,000. Indirect cost of the war: Nearly $30,000,000,000 for property losses on land, $6,888,000 for ships and cargoes lost, $45,000,000 for loss of production, $1,750,000 for losses to the Neutrals and $1,000,000,000 for War relief.*

"These are the numbers from her calculations in 1918 that she is listing. She is accounting for everything. The entry was duplicated in a letter she sent to her sister Katherine on May 16, 1919 from Paris," added Tracey.

"She went back to Paris before Versailles was signed?" Maggie couldn't believe it.

"They were still sinking ships in the Atlantic, for Christ's sake," asserted John. "We've all seen the movies about the U-boats that didn't realize the war was over."

"Belle was Belle. By now you both should know that when she made her mind up to do something, she did it." Having made her point, Tracey went on with her story. "So, Belle goes back to Paris. And we know she is there on May 15, 1919, because here is a letter she sent to Katherine on that date." Tracey set the letter down on the table by itself, away from all the other papers, and read what Belle wrote to Katherine:

> *Not to worry about the Villages Liberes & not to have its success or failure on your mind... except by talking it up when you have the chance... pretty soon I will be able to send some 'definite' data as to what indemnity the French government will really pay & how & when... if it is necessary to consolidate. I'm quite ready to do so—provided I don't have to follow anyone's ideas but my own. I heard through the Red Cross the other day that I had made an excellent impression at several different bureaus and that they are all in favor of 'Village Adoptions.'*

Tracey stopped, looking for comments from the other two.

John asked, "She was doing war totals? Calculations from Paris—but for whom?" He wondered whether Tracey knew, but realized that she didn't from her blank expression.

Maggie was next. "I'm still stuck on the zeroes. Both in the lives lost and the monies it cost. Belle was apparently concerned about this a great deal. She's asking Katherine who it is that really pays for wars?"

"Yes, she is," Tracey affirmed.

"And she wants to know how the wisteria is growing this spring at their home," John said to lighten up the conversation. "Look, here she writes that she wants Katherine to ask Joseph, the gardener, if much of it died during the winter, and to tell him to keep on the job of trimming up all the new vines that came in last summer. Hell, she's tabulating the war costs in Paris and giving orders to the gardener in Holyoke at the same time, telling Katherine to keep Joseph busy."

Tracey corrected, "What is evident is that Belle knew how to manage people, whether in Paris or Holyoke, and how to do things right, and make them a success. The Red Cross thought her version of the 'Village Adoptions' program was a good idea, because it was, and because it was Belle who presented it to them. She was working off ideas begun by people like Edith Wharton and her organization, American Hostels for Refugees, to provide shelter for the homeless. And a project underway by a Mrs. Crocker of California who, with the help of a committee in California, was using their own money to rebuild a village called Vitrimont, which had been damaged in the war. In contrast to Mrs. Crocker's program, Belle's idea relied on an adopter who would provide whatever sums of money that were necessary for the village reconstruction, with the government of France initially supplying 25% of the money, and the benefactor the rest. Once completed the adopter would be reimbursed for any money that was invested that the French government saw as reasonable, and not as being luxuries. All additional monies invested at the discretion of the adopter would be their own investments or donations. In exchange for the monies supplied to the people of the village by the adopter, the villagers would sign away their rights to an indemnity in favor of the adopter. By December of 1917, Belle, at fifty-one years old had founded the American Branch of the Villages Liberes, and not long later had picked out Hattonchâtel to be her own project. She had also involved the City of Holyoke in her mission, and its people had adopted a village nearby. As a result of Belle's work, and other caring women's involvement in creating publicity for helping the people of France rebuild their country, there were other projects begun. Anne Morgan raised millions of dollars in America for the cause, and the Rockefellers gave money to open up theatres in many villages in France to show films on tuberculosis." She paused, making sure they understood everything.

After observing Maggie and John's acknowledgement, Tracey began again, "OK, so we have Belle, being herself and going back to France in May 1919, while many people are still getting killed, to do an assessment of war casualties and costs. At the same time, she has become interested in the village restoration project, which she suggested to the Red Cross, and has picked the village of Hattonchâtel as her own target. First Belle gains the approval of her brother, William; that is the way the operation begins. Without his financial support the project isn't feasible. Having chosen the village and gained William's vote of confidence and support, Belle starts working on it at some point between the summer of 1919 and the spring of 1920. We can document that by a letter she wrote to Katherine from Paris on April 22, 1920, in which she says:

We are nicely settled now, my friend Regan is a daily visitor, & it seems as though I had never been away from France & 'the works.' Regan is as enthusiastic as I am over Hattonchâtel & so is my other friend Ford. The works there is going on famously & everything is rose colored. We are all going to the village on May 3rd, William, Regan, Ford, Prudence and I, to spend a few days with the Curé.... After my visit, I shall write to the V.L. Committee and enlarge upon 'Reconstructions.'

John asked, "I know Regan and Ford are Belle's friends from America who helped her begin the rebuilding of the village. But who is the Curé?"

"He was the priest of the village, a short, stocky man with a sour personality, somewhat meek, but two-faced. In the beginning he was pleasant. He became less cooperative as the project progressed and became an irritation at the end. The town was Catholic and Belle had to have his blessing; otherwise there would have been no reconstruction. The Bishop of Verdun also had to agree with what she wanted to do before she could start," Tracey clarified.

Maggie interjected, asking, "How long were they all at Hattonchâtel the first trip, the one Belle describes in that letter?"

"About a month, give or take a few days. William left to come back to New York on June 15th. What they did on the trip was to make plans for what was going to be done and get William's consent to supply what was required financially. Belle wrote this letter to Katherine from Paris on May 15, 1920:

The days at Hattonchâtel were so full & the evenings so short that I couldn't get in any writing. It was a wonderful experience. Like living a page of Balzac. The Curé, though born a peasant, has through education and experience gained a grace of mind that is perfectly delightful, & of course that made him a perfect host. And then this wonderful reception the village gave me. Do you remember the song, 'No half-in-half affair, I mean, But a right-down regular, Royal Queen'. Well, that's the way I felt.

"But you said he became irritating?" John questioned Tracey.

"Yes, later," Tracey responded. 'We'll get to it."

"It must have been amazing," Maggie said, quite impressed. "Can you imagine, after years of war, to have someone do something like this?"

Tracey read more of Belle's words:

It was thrilling, when the motor approached the village gates, to see the triumph arch in green (laurel leaves), & the way barred

> *by children holding garlands of white flowers, and all the ceremonies which followed were so simple, pretty & in perfect taste. But, I think the thing that pleased me most was when I walked about the streets, to have all the children say, 'Bonjour, Marianne' (fairy godmother), & the older ones, 'Bonjour, M'lle, Notre benefatrice,' it is quite touching, and makes me very happy I started this 'game.' Judging by what the Curé says 'I am running the Virgin Mary, a close second.' The village itself is really the prettiest in France, I wish the children (Katherine's) might have been with me the other day to see this, they would have entered into Everythink, as I did."*

"What's *'Everythink'?"* John asked.

"It's Belle's special world where anything is possible," Tracey explained.

"Like a magic land?" inquired John.

"Yes. After seeing the hell men can produce when they destroy everything, *Everythink* is a world where everyone works together to make a utopia. It's where her mind took her in her dreams of what could be, a way to imagine things that were possible. And once she saw that world, she worked to create it." Tracey spaced out for a second, which was unlike her, and imagined a perfect world. How lovely it must have been when Belle, William and their friends entered the village of Hattonchâtel for the first time, with the children happy, singing, and the fields blooming and wildflowers growing again. For a brief moment Tracey herself entered the world of *Everythink*.

Seeing her, Maggie too closed her eyes. She tried to think of what it had been like in that village on that day, after four years of deprivation and loss, to have the fairy godmother come to town bringing a ray of sunshine to the people, a promise to help put an end to some of their suffering and give them hope for better days to come.

John brought them back to the present, asking, "What did they do first? What was most important to them?"

"They bought a bell," Tracey answered sharply, after abruptly being pulled out of *Everythink*.

"What kind of bell?" John inquired.

"A big one, the kind that hangs in a belfry, in churches. But, they had a small problem, John." Tracey was short with John, being perturbed at the interruption of her reverie.

"And, what was that?" John was cautious now, thinking Tracey was going to be mischievous again, because of the odd way she eyed him.

"They had no belfry. Actually, they had no church. The Germans blew it to pieces. Only the walls and some remnants of the ancient church and the holy altar were left standing. There was no place to hang the bell; there was no belfry or ceiling." Tracey paused, and then continued. "They made an agreement with the Curé. In exchange for the Skinners providing the bell, the Curé would find a way to hang it. And he wanted to inscribe Belle's name on it. But, there was another problem." Tracey stopped, wanting them to beg for the rest.

Maggie took the cue. "What was that, Tracey?"

"There is no Saint Belle in the Catholic religion." Tracey smiled.

"So what?" Maggie asked her.

"So, they had to find a saint whose name was like Belle's, but not 'Belle,'" she said, "which took some time, days actually, to reach an agreement. Belle liked the idea of her name on the bell." Tracey took a letter from a different box. "This one Belle wrote to Katherine from Hattonchâtel on June 23, 1920." Tracey read:

> *All Christian names, (in France), are the names of Saints, & only Saints names may appear on the bell. So I had to give up Belle & have it written my full name Isabelle, there has to be at least two Christian names preceding Skinner, so I chose Sarah and the name will appear… 'Sarah Isabelle Skinner.' I thought that Mother would probably be able to stand the strain of appearing in my company on a Roman bell. The Curé is busy arranging the ceremony for the christening of the bell with this name.*

"Belle was being facetious. She and her mother got along famously." Tracey clarified the note.

"Should I ask what happened to the original bell of the church?" John was curious.

"The Germans melted it down to make bullets," Tracey responded with a sigh.

"Nice," was all John said.

Getting back to the bell named Sarah Isabelle, Tracey continued reading the letter:

> *A ceremony will take place at the end of July. I wish William might have stayed for the ceremony. I am also going to have a cinema reel made of the event so Stewart can show it on his*

> *screen. I spent the morning at Apremont. The peasants are counting the days till the gay event there.*

She finished and waited for a comment.

"What is Apremont, another French village?" Maggie answered her own question.

"Precisely, the one adopted by Holyoke. Belle involved the entire city in sponsoring this village. There is even a highway here in Holyoke named after the village. Let's see, somewhere here there's a news article." Tracey pulled it out of a box and handed it over to Maggie and John:

> *Belle Skinner the President of the American branch of the 'Villages Liberes' movement, spoke in Holyoke in October 1919 about how her city had become the first one in the United States to 'adopt' a French town under this organization. The amount required to accomplish this was $30,000. Holyoke adopted Apremont-LaForet where so many Massachusetts men had fought and were killed. A plaque was placed near the restored waterworks, on it was inscribed, in French, 'These waterworks are dedicated to the sacred memory of our boys who fought and fell here, as a gift to you, people of Apremont, from us, the people of Holyoke, Massachusetts, U.S.A. 1922.'*

"But let's stay focused on Hattonchâtel." Taking the article, Tracey returned it to its proper place in a folder and then began to talk again about Belle's project. "Any questions about what Belle did in Hattonchâtel?" she asked.

"Yes, quite a few, actually. Let me see if I'm hearing you right. Belle decides to reconstruct an entire village, after it is almost totally destroyed by the Germans, and the first thing they can think about is a bell?" John asked the obvious question concerning the priorities of villagers.

"Yea, a bell. Not only a bell, but a bell that they couldn't name Belle," Tracey laughed, enjoying a respite from the seriousness of the morning, as did Maggie and John, thinking of the absurdity of it all. It took a moment before they regained their composure and could talk again.

"Why?" Maggie asked her, wiping tears of laughter from her eyes.

Calming down, Tracey finished her saga of the Curé and the bell, "To ward off demons. The superstition goes back centuries in the Christian religion. When the bell is rung, the bad angels are forced out and the saints are called. Heck, if it's that easy, why not do it! Ring a bell, and get rid of the devils." Tracey was finding it hard not to start laughing again. It was getting contagious, that hysteria, so Tracey made a well-timed suggestion to take a break.

They all knew that when you're in a museum, you're supposed to be quiet and well mannered, and they were not being respectful. Agreeing with Tracey, the three headed downstairs, trying not too successfully to stop laughing, and still a little out of control with the idea of the bell that couldn't be called Belle.

SIXTEEN

Back in the room, twenty minutes later, they had all regained their composure. It was time to get back to business. Tracey continued telling them what she wanted them to know. "Belle was back in Paris by July 1, because she wrote to her sister again:

> *'Katherine, I am enclosing a clipping from the* Paris Herald*… it really makes me quite famous, & now people are beginning to meet me. I hope my head won't get turned. I keep saying to myself that there is nothing 'personal' in my success… If William hadn't put up the money, I couldn't have done it.'*

And she wrote her again from Paris on July 20 that

> *'my friend Prudence has been angelic since her mother's visit, & I have not had an unhappy moment because of her.'"*

So, Belle was in Paris and according to another letter, had secured a house for herself and Prudence to live in. She could hardly wait to move in. She had plans to live in Paris most of the time, and once the Château in Hattonchâtel was restored, to stay there some of the time. It's all documented in letters to Katherine." Tracey looked at Maggie and John to make sure they were keeping up with her. Both nodded to show they were following her as she passed them the relevant letters.

"Let's get on to the big event, the *Christening of the Bell,* Sarah Isabelle Skinner. And, you two, behave this time," Tracey cajoled, knowing it was she who had begun the last uproar. John and Maggie waited for her to go on, both conscious of the fact that she was the comedian in the room.

Tracey felt it was important to tell them what took place at the *Ceremony of the Bell,* which galvanized the whole restoration project by formalizing the support of the Curé and the villagers alike. It also coordinated the efforts of a number of high-level French officials, the Bishop of Verdun and diplomats from the American embassy in Paris. It was not a small undertaking that Belle was embarking on, and if everything was to go smoothly, it augured well to begin with a ceremony. It took place on September 13. Tracey read them a letter dictated by Belle from the Hotel Maurice in Paris and sent to William on September 15. Belle had apologized at the top of the letter in a handwritten sentence saying that she was too tired to type it herself. Tracey told them, "Belle was staying at one of her favorite hotels, unwinding from the exhausting event at Hattonchâtel. It wasn't the ceremony and the reception that tired her out so much. It was the complicated preparations required to produce it that were so draining. She wrote William:

> *I want you to know what a wonderful success the Fete was. It was wonderful in every detail. To begin with, the day was ideal, a cloudless sky, no wind, and just cool enough to be comfortable. It was the loveliest day of the summer. Then, everyone was in the mood for the celebration and it went off with a gusto and charm that was astonishing. When I woke up in the morning at 8 o'clock and looked out of my window, the hill was covered with people walking up. They came from all over that part of the country, twelve hundred strong, and it was a very well behaved crowd.*
>
> *At half past nine when I went out of the Curé's house, I could make no progress in the street so eager was everyone to salute the 'Marraine' of Hattonchâtel, and by the time the distinguished guests began to arrive, at 10 o'clock, the excitement was all on. All the gentry were there and all frightfully jealous that their town had not been adopted, as was Hattonchâtel. Those who came from Paris were the Seegers, the Harpers, the Duke and Duchess of Taillerand, the Cotchetts, the Eddys, Sadie Williams, the Walmouths, Winifred Schroeder and Joseph and William.*
>
> *The Fete began at half past ten with a mass for the dead. We had repaired the church temporarily so there was not danger of the stones falling and the setting was most picturesque. The church altar was placed in from of all that greenery that has grown up under the part where the roof was destroyed, and the shrubs made a lovely background. The service was conducted by the Bishop of Verdun assisted by six priests all in full regalia and was most impressive. Of course the whole service was chanted and the two priests who did most of it had beautiful voices.*
>
> *Part of the service consisted of the Memorial tablet that I bought with the money Robert gave me. The priests sprinkled*

it with holy water while the choir and the priests chanted. During the ceremony there was a fanfare of trumpets announcing the arrival of the General Berthelot who was a little late. I went out to meet him. He came in with his whole staff and you can imagine how stunning their uniforms were in that ruined church just packed with peasants. From the church we all went outside for the blessing of the bell that took place in front of the cloister. The Bishop conducted the ceremony while the General took his place on the Tribune. It was a wonderful setting. The blue sky overhead, that exquisite ruined cloister, the Bishop in his red robes, the General in his blue uniform, the Military and the peasants all about and my friends properly arrayed for the occasion. Before the christening of the bell, the Bishop made a patriotic speech, one of the finest I have ever heard. A speech about France of course, and the American help in that section during which he made reference to the bell. He paid a perfectly lovely tribute to me. It was not overdone and was in excellent taste.

After this, assisted by two priests he christened the bell and then the tongue was placed inside it. A blue ribbon was attached to it and the Bishop sounded the bell three times. Then it was my turn. The Curé had told me in advance that as a Protestant, I could not take the ribbon from the Bishop's hands so it was arranged that Prudence should take the ribbon and pass it to me, and then I would strike the bell. But, when the moment arrived the Bishop changed all that, he motioned for me to come forward and he himself put the ribbon in my hand and I rang the bell three times, to be heard a thousand miles away. After that the mayor and the Curé rang it three times.

That ended the ceremony and we all went in a procession to the Tribune where the civil exercises began. The General made a speech, followed by a speech by the Prefect of the Muse, and the playing of the Marseillaise and the Star Spangled Banner. Then we all went to the restaurant for a lunch, marching to the music of the Marche-Lorraine. The 'restaurant' had been arranged in the shape of a 'T,' it was the property used as a stable before the destruction. We had built a roof over it in case of rain and we looked out at the same wonderful view that I have from my window in the Curé's house.

After this we went to the Monument at Vigneulles that marks the junction of the French-American troops, and placed a wreath upon it. The French musicians played The Star Spangled Banner. The wreath was carried by a French and an American soldier, while two American officers and I stood at attention. The bishop said a few words for the dead. After that the French troops went back to Metz, the Americans to Thiaucourt and all my friends started off for Paris. I of course went back to Hattonchâtel to help straighten things out. I had a flag pole put on the site of the old windmill and raised the Stars and Stripes which could be seen for miles around. The American boys told me they could see it in Thiaucourt, miles away.

I left for Paris at three o'clock on Tuesday and arrived at half past eleven. Today, I am resting, having dinner with the Seegers tonight. I will sail on the 24th. My boat is due Sunday, October 2nd, and I will be glad to see you at the dock. Please bring a lot of currency as I have ordered more dresses.'"

John spoke first, "Belle was amazing to do all of this by herself. No other woman in the world was doing anything quite like this during this time."

"No one had the money and the ambition. You needed both," Tracey answered him. "Look at what she did downstairs in the Music Room. It's a tribute to her intelligence and her creativity."

"Where did they hang the bell?" Maggie was not trying to be funny.

The Dedication of the Peasant Woman Statue during the Fete

"They made a makeshift belfry in the church. It was the first thing they did to restore the village. Then they set to work on rebuilding the physical structures of the Church, Abbey, Château, Chalet and everything else that had been destroyed." Tracey knew how they did it, the sequence of events. "A few of the men hung it up while Belle, the Curé, and the rest of the town watched."

"So, if I read these letters correctly, Belle came back to the States not long after this to visit her family for a time. When did she go back to France again?" John wanted to know.

"It appears that she went back in January 1921. She was back and forth a number of times that year and the next to inspect the work being done, and to make any decisions with the Curé and her architect that were necessary."

"What were the time frames and the expenses involved?" Maggie asked.

"About five years and $1 million, give or take a few hundred thousand and some months. William was very generous, and the contractors and villagers just kept on building," Tracey answered, raising her eyebrows in a question to John, the mathematician of the three.

Understanding what Tracey was implying, John answered, "In today's monies, $1 million was worth between $50 million and $100 million in buying power."

"Wow," Maggie said, "that's a lot of village."

"Belle probably had plans to live there once the job was finished and wanted everything done right," Tracey said. "She was rebuilding the Château or at least part of it to live in. The rest of the village, including houses, the school and various other houses were being rebuilt for the villagers. The 14th and 15th century Church and Abbey were beautiful, and reconstructed meticulously for the Curé. Other buildings and residential areas were made to look like they did before the war. We are not talking about a small effort here. Everything needed to be set, one stone at a time. It was a fortress and an entire village. Let's not forget, the Germans left nothing behind but destruction. The water wasn't fit to drink, so they had to clean up the streams and flow systems. Food was a problem; there wasn't much. They had to till the soil and plant crops. The vineyards needed to be re-established—it's hard to grow anything on shrapnel, and the ground was still full of metal. They needed to replace their domestic animals and their herds. These people literally started from

French President Raymond Poincare at the Celebration of the Bell in Hattonchâtel

scratch to rebuilding a medieval village to look like it did three hundred years ago. Want to see some before and after pictures? It will give you a better idea of the obstacles they faced."

Tracey produced two sets of pictures. One showed the bombed-out town after the Germans had been driven away. It was a shell. Most of the walls meant to keep out invaders had been leveled. There were holes in the sides of all of the buildings, and not a roof was to be seen, anywhere. It was a scene of total wreckage. There was not much to look at, just rubble. What once had been a famous, beautiful, countryside village was destroyed, almost lost forever.

"Looks like parts of Holyoke." John was being sarcastic.

Tracey looked at him. "Don't start."

"OK, but it's quite a mess. Which buildings are what?" he asked, unable to distinguish one from another.

The second set of photographs, which Tracey put side by side with the first ones, somewhat clarified the town's layout. The photographs of the village under reconstruction were astonishing. Tracey also placed a postcard from 1910, showing what looked like a medieval walled village in the 1600s. The 10th century Château, after restoration, looked almost identical to the older one, except of course for the quality of the stonework. The new Château looked more polished, the stones probably of better quality. The villagers rebuilt their village from nothing, because of the project begun by Belle Skinner.

"It's like looking at a miniature version of a castle in one of those pictures you see of the great walled cities of Europe, belonging to the kings and queens who ruled the empires," Maggie commented.

The postcard read, "Château de Miss Skinner, Bienfaitrice d'Hattonchâtel." The lettering, renaming the village in Belle's honor, was etched around the top of the largest of the three towers.

Tracey explained what she read about the restoration. "As was usual with most fortress villages in France, the main wall of the Château was made to face the open plains, so that it would be easy for the townspeople to defend against an attack. They rebuilt that wall first, and it served as one of the main support walls for the Château that was separated from the rest of the town by a drawbridge. The Château was L-shaped with the main living quarters at one end. The Church and Abbey were down the street from the Château. The Chalet was at the other end of the village. The inside and outside walls of all of the buildings were made of fine stone blocks fitted meticulously together by the townspeople. The towers at the ends of the Château were coned, and there were a number of gated archways used for entrances into the village and between buildings inside. The main section of the building that was to be the Château had two floors and two large towers at the end of the long great wall. The center sections were square, with a slanted roof of slate. The Chalet had only one tower, and looked like it was of German design. There were a number of small barred windows in the towers of the Château and a series of windows on the second floor. The pictures of the interior of the main part of the Château show it to be plain, not fancy. It was broken up into about three different sections downstairs, with what we would call the living room being the largest. The upper floor was where the bedrooms and chambers were. The inside ceilings, walls and floors of the entire Château were made of cut stone, similar to the outer walls. All of it had to be pieced together perfectly. One stone at a time was carted in, cut, and put into place. There was a dining area in one part of the Château for entertaining, and a long table with many chairs was set there, but the rest of the main section was almost bare, except for a few sparse tables with nothing on them or around them. The inside rooms were heated by immense fireplaces. In addition to the reconstruction of the Château, the Abbey, Church, Chalet and about twenty houses and a school were built for the townspeople. Belle also had electricity brought to the village," she sighed.

Belle and her American architect, John Sanford, had used what was there as a base to build upon. Even after months of work, the Château looked rustic. But, there was no doubt about their intention. What they were doing was restoring the village to look like it did in 1900 or for that matter, three hundred years before. In restoring the village, Belle was recreating what had existed in the French historical descriptions of it.

Tracey continued, "The Château, with all of its separate sections, was transformed back into a medieval masterpiece. Everything in the fortress looked original, almost. There were upgrades in the plumbing systems to make it more livable. All it took was the wisdom and imagination of the brilliant, compassionate woman from Holyoke, and an enormous amount of money from the Skinner family."

"And the sweat and toil of all of the villagers and hired laborers," Maggie said.

"That goes without saying. But, Belle provided the other necessary ingredients too, the ones that really pulled the place out of the proverbial ashes, and I don't mean money."

"What do you mean?" John asked her.

"She brought them faith, hope, and showed them by her example, courage. These were the three necessary tools for success. Without these, the little village would still be in ruins." Tracey pointed to the before pictures. "Look at this, can you imagine the pride with which they rebuilt their village? Now look at the town before its occupation and destruction." She handed them another postcard. The difference was remarkable.

Beginning to understand Belle's grandeur and vision, and knowing how strict Catholic rules are, Maggie said, "The bishop must have broken a long tradition when he gave her the blue ribbon. It must have been a violation of church protocol, and could have caused him to be censured. But, standing in front of him was a real life angel of mercy." She paused. "These wonderful creatures don't come along that often in life. So, when they do, you make your best effort to show them that you know who they really are."

SEVENTEEN

For the rest of the afternoon, the three went through other letters Belle had written to her brothers and sisters between the years 1921 and 1923. Most of the letters were progress reports on the reconstruction at Hattonchâtel and related to the funding by William. One brief note stuck out like a red light though, showing the respect Belle Skinner's project garnered in France. Written on January 26, 1921, and sent to everyone in her family, it mentioned offhandedly that she had been awarded the Cross of French Legion of Honor by President Raymond Poincare of France, and that William would be receiving the same honor soon for his efforts. After the three commented on the significance of this honor being bestowed upon a woman in the 1920s, they returned to the piles of letters.

It was exhausting to do what they were trying to do. Tracey had already read the letters several times, but was afraid she had missed something or drawn erroneous conclusions, and wanted Maggie and John's fresh observations. Indeed, Maggie next said, "Did you know Belle had scarlet fever as a child, and complained of being tired, fatigued a lot?" She was reading a clip from a Holyoke news article.

"I knew she'd been quite ill as a child. Like most children, I assumed it was something minor though," Tracey answered.

Remembering his father talking about it, John added, "That might be why she complained of 'ups and downs' in a few of her letters. As I recall, scarlet fever, at that time, often caused long-term conditions, nervous disorders and heart problems. She makes mention of how she enjoys going to retreats to relax and rejuvenate herself. Of course, if any of us did what she did we would be a little weary too. I'm tired just reading about it. The travel back and forth to Europe, not to mention the events she planned and pulled off, would be exhausting. It says in this article that once the project in the village was running full speed, she was asked to be a guest at many parties and political events in Paris, too."

Maggie added, "She sometimes had a case of 'nerves' and suffered from 'fatigue.' When she was up, she could do anything, when down, she needed the retreats. In a letter to Katherine, she complained about having to satisfy her 'socialite obligations,' finding them exhausting. In another, she seems to enjoy them—she writes, *'Now that I have arrived, so to speak in Paris, I am dying to attack London. There is much climbing to be done here.'*"

It was Tracey's turn. "Maybe. I think what she was doing in Hattonchâtel was satisfying some of her needs, but she was very social, and at least sometimes enjoyed being the center of attention. But, realistically, it couldn't have been easy to be her. Everything she did was dramatic and eventful, captivating. It was just her personality or destiny. That's why we are engrossed in reading about her now."

"Did she move to Hattonchâtel?" Maggie asked.

"No, never full time. She had wanted to wait until the project was completed. She went back and forth between the village and Paris, and stayed in the Curé's house for a while at first. When the project didn't go as fast as she'd hoped, she moved into a smaller house that was somewhere in the village. We have a film of her and William entertaining friends on the patio of the house, overlooking the hills and valleys of the Woevre."

Tracey thought it might be a good time to show the video she had made from Belle's original silent movie of events that took place at Hattonchâtel, including the *Ceremony of the Bell.* Excusing herself, she went to get the video and the television monitor. Warning them that although she had Belle's recording enhanced, it was still low quality. Tracey had Maggie and John set their chairs close to the monitor and darkened the room. A number of clips showing various occasions had been spliced together to make the movie. The first part was the *Christening of the Bell.* It showed the people gathering in the streets, the dignitaries arriving, the priests saying Mass and the General with his entourage, then the ceremony itself, the banquet and finally everyone leaving. The village was just as Belle had described it: a mess.

The next cut was the one Tracey had described of Belle entertaining friends on the patio of a house overlooking the Seine. The poor quality of the film made it hard to make out the faces, but Tracey pointed out who some of the people were. The Curé and William were easy to distinguish; the Curé with his long black robe and beads, and William dressed impeccably, as always, with a plain colored tie; he had favored

red ties, Tracey said. The last segment showed Belle near a car, then taking some friends back to Paris, and pulling out of a garage. Then there was footage of a family gathering at the Skinner's Holyoke mansion, with several adults in the yard of Wistariahurst; the rose gardens, the ones with the 365 different types of roses from all over the world that Belle had planted, were visible.

"I understand everything was done by Belle in France, because she was—how did they put it in the articles—a benefactress, but there were other motives, too, I suspect," John smiled.

"Do you know something I don't, Mr. Merrick?" Tracey smile.

"Maybe, maybe not. Is there any mention in any of the other letters, giving reasons for her generosity? She would have shared her feelings and thoughts with Katherine if there were." John knew how close the sisters were.

Tracey pulled out a pile from the last box. "These are the last ones. They may be the last words Belle wrote to anyone. You decide. Take a look, and see if you can find something I missed. I'm going to put this equipment away, and check my messages. I'll be back in about an hour." She left them to read the last thoughts Belle had shared with her family and friends before she had died.

For the next hour Maggie and John swapped letters and discussed items of possible interest.

"Find anything?" Tracey asked when she returned.

"Quite a bit," John replied. "She spent five to six months a year in the village between 1921 and 1927. The official rededication was in 1923, and was quite an event. The President of France presided again. And although she stayed in a small restored house when she was in the village, she mentions another house as well."

"John Sanford's house?" Tracey asked.

"Maybe. Belle describes it as hers," Maggie replied.

"A few houses were restored first, so that there were living quarters on site during the bulk of the reconstruction. Sanford stayed in one, and Belle in another. But, it was officially Belle's. Technically the whole village was hers, until the repayments were made. Sanford wanted one of them badly. He seems to have been odd, possessive, controlling, and resented anyone interfering with anything he did, according to some of Belle's letters. Did you find any other reasons Belle might have had for doing the reconstruction?"

John turned it around. "What do you think?"

"I have a number of theories on the subject."

"Can we hear them?" Maggie asked.

"OK. First, there is Theory 1. I think that Belle saw what her father and the rest of the great men and women of Holyoke had accomplished here, starting with nothing and making a prosperous, well-run, progressive city. They made history. I believe that part of the reason Belle did what she did was because of this example. She too wanted to build something wonderful. There was a bit of ego here, and I think she wanted to make the village into a monument both to herself and to the villagers."

John replied, "There's no question that she loved the fame. I'm glad you mentioned it. It's in many of her letters, where she is clearly proud of being known all over Europe for her work. '*It has put me on the map*,' she wrote Katherine. But I'm curious about something. She wrote that she hoped the village didn't become a 'resort,' and seemed to have concerns that it might. Also, she seemed to have some serious disagreement with the Curé and the architect over what she refers to as 'matters,' in 1926. I'd like to know more about that."

"You mentioned reading a description or list of work done by the time of the rededication in 1923. Where is that?" Tracey asked.

"Most of it is in here." Maggie handed her a NEW YORK TIMES article, which Tracey read aloud.

> *Sunday September 16, 1923—Under the leadership of President Raymond Poincare, assisted by Sheldon Whitehouse, Counselor of the American Embassy, this tiny but famous fortress town today celebrated the fifth anniversary of its liberation and at the same time feted its restoration by its American benefactress, Miss Belle Skinner of New York and Holyoke, Massachusetts. At the ceremony President Poincare said, 'A second bell has been donated by the Skinner family to commemorate this occasion. It is named 'Elizabeth Katherine,' after Belle Skinner's two nieces. To date there are 40 houses built, the church and abbey have been restored, the school is operating and the children are back learning their lessons and now have a future thanks to the lady they call their fairy godmother. Shower baths and a new water system have been installed. The town hall is redone and other civic buildings are restored. The fields are planted. The vineyards are growing and a great piece of French history has been*

salvaged by this remarkable woman.

She put the paper on the desk for them to read the last part along with her.

> *He then thanked a Colonel Winship, the first man to enter the town driving out the Germans with his troops, Sheldon Whitehouse, counselor to the American Embassy, William Skinner, Belle's sister and brother-in-law, Robert and Katherine Kilborne and their children, Belle's sister Miss Elizabeth Skinner, Miss Julie Chapin, Prescott Childs, and Belle's companion Prudence Lagogue for attending these ceremonies, along with the clergy and the townspeople to make this such a historical day for the country of France. In recognition of Miss Skinner's bounty and personal efforts, the townspeople have placed in their new Town Hall a bronze plaque of her unveiled by the Mayor in the presence of Miss Skinner, M. and Mme. Poincare and the Prefect of the Meuse. The Prefect gave a speech thanking Miss Skinner and her family for their generosity, and then he received from her, the key to the Marie. At the end of a lunch that followed this, the President conferred upon her brother, William Skinner of New York and Holyoke, the Cross of the French Legion of Honor.*

"What's not to be proud of? It gives me the shivers. Isn't it amazing that so few people in Holyoke today know anything about the Skinners, Belle, and Hattonchâtel?" Tracey said, putting the article back into the folder.

"What about your other theories? You said you had more than one." John asked.

"Help me out here, guys. You read all the letters the same as I did. What moves people to do things that are almost impossible? What stands out among all of the letters that makes a significant impression on you?" Tracey entreated.

"The painter!" Maggie exclaimed. "The man at the Summit House on Mt. Tom, who had such a tremendous effect on her in such a very short time."

"Theory 2 is the painter. Let's talk about it." Tracey pulled up a chair, and the three began to discuss the one thing that moves people to move mountains or build villages in a far away country, something called love.

"Do you think she went looking for him?" Maggie asked.

Tracey explained her thoughts about the possibility that the painter was more than a passing fancy for Belle. "The dates between the time she met him and the time she left to start up the restoration program in France are compelling. But *no,* I don't believe that she was love-struck and went searching for him. There's nothing in any letters after those she wrote from Holyoke that mentions him. I think he had a remarkable effect on her, he mesmerized her, but I don't think it was the man, specifically, that she went to find. I could be wrong, but I think he solely inspired her."

"In what way?" John asked her.

"The powerful word, 'love,' means many different things. Personal, emotional, passionate, 'love' is the most compelling, but not necessarily the most enduring. I believe the painter touched Belle's soul. He showed her, by the way he converted the pain he felt from the loss of his family to the beauty he was able to paint on his canvas, that life has unlimited possibilities. It was his masterpiece. I think in some ways that Hattonchâtel was Belle's canvas. It was her work of art. She was taking something in pain, and making it beautiful. Just like the painter did with his brush and paints," Tracey stopped.

Maggie thought about it and then spoke, "Then he was a teacher, a mentor, one of those people who come into our lives from out of nowhere and change it." She glanced over at John.

"Precisely," Tracey agreed.

"And the fact that he was from France was immaterial," John said, not convinced that Belle hadn't fallen in love.

"No, I think it's very material," Tracey retorted. "I think she was in her own way giving back the gift he gave her, hoping it would ease some of his pain." She had done a lot of thinking about this.

Maggie agreed. "John, do you really think that Belle hopped on a boat and traveled all over France looking for one man? She was beautiful, elegant and rich, and surely had many suitors to choose from. A few had proposed marriage. Do you think she was like a schoolgirl in love?"

John was unsure. People do crazy things when they are in love, or think they are. "I see no reason not to think Belle fell in love with him, and didn't want to let it get away. If it meant motoring all over France to find him in his little village, I can imagine her doing it. Why wouldn't she?"

"But there's no mention of him being anywhere near Hattonchâtel," Tracey said.

"None that you've seen," John pointed out.

"You're right." Tracey agreed. "I've often thought there could be other letters that weren't collected by the archives, or that Belle kept to herself, or shared with only Prudence, or a diary."

"The painter could have been in the village or close by," John pointed out. "We don't know that he wasn't."

"We will never know, unless other letters surface," Tracey responded frankly. "But, why would they have been kept separate? Belle wasn't secretive." They all pondered this for a moment.

Maggie had a thought, "Maybe she felt William wouldn't approve, or it would lower her social standing with the Bishop, and others, and interfere with the project. Remember the fuss here at Wistariahurst when Stewart got married, and was asked to leave Yale, and Belle took them in? To me, that points up Belle's romantic side."

"They could have just been friends, too," John added. "Happens all the time, a relationship doesn't have to be sensual to be valuable. Sometimes it's better without so many complications. Perhaps they just enjoyed each other's company, and kept seeing each other. But, you're right. Unless a bit of evidence surfaces that links them in France, I think this particular theory is not provable. I agree with you, Tracey, that maybe they met on Mt. Tom, he painted a picture there that inspired her, she learned from the experience about the transformation of pain into a masterpiece, and took what he showed her to the village restoration project. She created her own masterpiece there, out of her own pain at seeing the devastation and deaths of World War I."

Maggie looked sad. "It's the romantic in me, wanting the happy romantic ending," she said. "You know, girl meets boy on mountain, they fall in love looking out over the beautiful valley of the Connecticut River painting a picture together, then they go to France to a small village where he grew up, and together they make it beautiful again. It's a place where everyone is happy, and they call it *Everythink*." Maggie realized it had been a long time since she had felt so sentimental.

"Sounds like a romance novel or a movie, although it's too old-fashioned, and wouldn't do well at the box office. No one's getting their head blown off, so Hollywood isn't interested."

"So, what else? What is Theory 3, now that we ruled out Theory 2?" John pushed on.

"Not completely," Maggie corrected him. "Let's leave Theory 2 open."

"OK, not completely," John conceded. "But, where do we go next?

What really motivated Belle to spend the last eight years of her life, and tons of money, restoring Hattonchâtel?"

"I'm still working on it. Theory 3 is still in the works," Tracey said, that mischievous gleam back in her eye.

Maggie saw it too, and began to laugh, knowing Tracey was ready to tease John.

"What do you mean, it's in the works?" John asked, taking the hook. "You said you had another theory."

"I think I can prove this one. I am 90 percent sure that I know why Belle did what she did at Hattonchâtel. But, a few items need to be put in order to prove Theory 3 conclusively, and I can't do what is necessary to do it."

"What would that be?" John inquired skeptically.

"Someone needs to go to Hattonchâtel." Tracey answered. "We need to check out a few details, and get some answers to questions I have about a few people, and what they did during the restoration."

Maggie interjected. "Do you think there's more involved than Belle being a fairy godmother for the village?"

"Yep." Tracey was sure of it.

"What?" Maggie implored.

"Can't tell you, yet. Unless, of course, one or both of you want to help out."

"You want us to go to France to check out your 'suspicions'?" John was amused.

Without saying it, *yes*, Tracey wanted them to go to Hattonchâtel, because she needed them to check out some details to prove or disprove her Theory 3. Her look said it all.

Maggie was more than a little taken aback. "That's asking quite a bit, Tracey. Why doesn't someone from the museum go? Why not you? Call it a research project, which it is."

"It's a conflict of interest. We work for the City of Holyoke. No one in the government is interested in any of this city history, and because we work for the city, we can't do anything they don't approve of or fund. I have my husband and children to think about. I might lose my job. When someone from Apremont called in the 1970s to get information from the mayor's office on Holyoke's investment in their village, the city officials brushed him off, and said they didn't know where Apremont was, and couldn't tell them anything. Do you think they'd appropriate funding for me to go to France? Not likely. It has to be someone not on the city payroll, or linked to the Skinner family, like one of you or both. I hear the weather this time of year in France is somewhat pleasant, and the drive up to the village from Paris is delightful. Belle says so in the letters. You'd both enjoy the trip. It would be like reliving a part of Belle Skinner's life just to go there."

What Tracey was suggesting was intriguing, yet inconvenient as far as John was concerned. Maggie, too, was hesitant. Tracey was suggesting they spend their own money and time on a project Tracey was unsure of, and that had no future for her. Besides, Maggie was at a time in her life when there were hundreds of commitments she could make. Why this one?

"Think about it?" Tracey asked, wanting them to keep an open mind. "We have plenty of time. This issue has been lingering for eighty years, so there's no need to rush in making any decisions." Having planted the seeds, Tracey was comfortable waiting. "But I'd like you to do something for me, a little closer to home, first." Tracey saw that it was three o'clock, which would give them time to go to the cemetery, and be back before dark. "At the top of this hill on Cabot Street is Forestdale Cemetery where the Skinners, and other great people of Holyoke are buried. If you would be kind enough to go there, and look at the Skinner gravesites, I believe you'll get a little closer to making up your minds about going to France. Belle is buried there. I find it inspiring to visit her grave, and I think you will too."

EIGHTEEN

John didn't need directions to Forestdale Cemetery; he knew exactly where it was, having friends buried there. But he'd never noticed the Skinner graves. He and Maggie drove through the Cabot Street entrance and began looking for the name "Skinner." Maggie found she recognized many of the names from her readings of the men and women who had helped build the city, those in the Whiting family plots, the Metcalf, Fay and Warren families, as well as names like James Newton and Benjamin Lincoln.

"What's that over there?" John pointed to a stone with a figure holding a trumpet. He drove to the large, twelve feet high, but otherwise relatively plain monument and stopped the motor. The figure was an angel blowing a horn with its arm around a woman who looked sad, perhaps in mourning. Across its face was the name "Skinner." Maggie and John walked the short distance from the roadway to the monument. It had snowed the night before, and there was a dusting of white powder on four small, dark monuments in front of the Skinner stone, as well as a number of other stones with the names Kilborne, Warner and Hubbard on them.

Maggie walked to the first one. "Katherine is buried here with her husband Robert Stewart Kilborne," she said, "and this is Elizabeth and her husband, the Reverend William H. Hubbard."

John brushed the snow from the first of the small gravestones. It read, "William Skinner, 1857–1947;" the next was that of his father, "William Skinner, 1824–1902;" and the third was his wife, "Sarah Skinner, 1834–1908." Maggie stepped carefully around the stones, and they looked at the last small stone together. Maggie and John were inexplicably moved as they read the inscription, "Belle Skinner, 1866–1928."

"It isn't what I expected," Maggie said. "Look over in that direction, at the huge mausoleums. They're everywhere. This is so plain and ordinary. With the Skinners' money they could have bought the whole cemetery, but instead they have such simple stones."

"When all was said and done, glamour wasn't their style, was it? They didn't need that type of recognition. They played around with it, but in the end they knew who they were. Even in death, they were a part of the community. They knew a lot about life," John said respectfully.

Walking a few steps to her left Maggie noticed a small stone next to the others. Looking down, she read, "'Hattie Riley – Born in Harrowgate, England, March 2, 1848 – Died in Holyoke, Massachusetts, December 14, 1926 – In Remembrance of 47 Years of Faithful Service.'"

Turning to John, Maggie said, "They buried their housekeeper with them. That's a touch of class." Maggie shivered, it was cold out with a strong breeze blowing in from the north of Mt. Tom.

"Let's go. We'll catch pneumonia if we stay here." John hadn't said the word intentionally, pneumonia, but he knew it was what Belle had died of in Paris on Easter Sunday in 1928.

When they returned to the Cabot Street museum, Tracey was sitting in the kitchen, on a stool, having cereal with milk.

"That was fast," she said. "Want something to eat?"

"No thanks," John said, mildly surprised she was eating cereal so late in the day.

"It's supposed to get colder tonight, below zero. That's why I wanted you to get up there before the sun went down. John, put on some water, and I'll make us some tea. Looks like Maggie could use a little warming up." Tracey pointed to the kettle on the stove.

Ten minutes later, John and Maggie were back up in the second floor conference room. It was warmer up here, and they were waiting for Tracey to join them. When Tracey walked into the room, without hesitation she asked her first question, "Well, what did you think of the Skinners' plots?"

"I expected them to be different," Maggie confessed.

"How so?"

"Maybe a small cathedral, certainly something impressive."

"There's actually a wonderful chapel down at the Second Congregational Church on Appleton and Maple that the Skinners built for everyone to worship at. As far as their final resting places, they apparently didn't feel the need for impressive tributes to themselves. If you're satisfied with the way you live your life, I suppose that's your monument."

"The graves all face to the north, towards Mt. Tom," John said. "Any reason you know of?"

"They must have had divine foresight," Maggie interjected. "They don't have to see what's become of the city. It would make them turn over in their graves."

"Let's get back to the business at hand, Belle's life," Tracey said. "Did you both finish reading all of the letters and cables?"

"Everything in the pile you gave us," John answered.

"Then you know Belle spent a good deal of time traveling back and forth between Holyoke, Paris and Hattonchâtel, from 1925 until 1927. You are undoubtedly aware that most of the major restoration work at the village was completed by 1927, and that Belle planned on having William and other members of the family see it in the summer of 1928. She especially wanted the children to visit her there. She wrote a number of letters to William, Katherine, and some of her nieces and nephews in 1927, telling them how beautiful 'her village' was, asking them to make plans to vacation there the following summer."

Maggie responded in the affirmative. "She was very pleased, and said in a number of letters that every time she went there she received a fine welcome."

"Almost every time," Tracey corrected her. She put two copies of a letter before them. She had not included this letter with the others, but had saved it for the right time, which was now. "Read this. It will explain it somewhat."

The letter was written on July 27, 1926. It was from Belle to Katherine.

> *Our trip to Hatton has been a great success... glorious weather... they gave us a fine welcome... 'Sanford's' house was barred to me, so we stayed in Nancy as planned...—But I've decided now definitely that I really want to build the Château, it doesn't mean that I'll be away from home any more than I am now—only that I'll have a pretty place at Hatton."*

Maggie was confused, "What does she mean by 'barred' from Sanford's house? Wasn't it her house? Sanford worked for her. They restored over twenty houses. Couldn't he have stayed in another house? Couldn't Belle have any house she wanted to?"

"Exactly my thoughts, and that was where Belle liked to stay when she went to Hattonchâtel," Tracey responded.

"The architect wouldn't let her into the house?" Maggie was outraged. "What kind of nonsense is that?"

"Good question. Perhaps there was some unhappiness involving that particular house." Tracey didn't elaborate.

"What?" Maggie asked her.

"That's what I don't know. I think Belle was preparing to make some changes, too. Maybe it was involved with that particular house, but it's only a guess."

"Do you think something was going wrong at Hattonchâtel?" Maggie was curious. "Is that what Belle was doing, correcting some problem? Few of her other correspondence talk about anything but the good progress there."

"You be the judge," answered Tracey, "but it looks that way to me. Belle was not the type to put up with things she didn't like. And, I'll tell you something else. Sanford had apparently changed houses without her permission."

John pursued the logic. "At the end of July, she was being 'barred,' as she put it, from entering the house Sanford stayed in. Belle also referred to problems with the Curé in letters. Something wasn't right. In retrospect, you can feel it in the later letters. Her mood is different, more intense. It also appears that she was well on her way to addressing some issues. She talks in many letters of having more than a few troubles with the Curé and Sanford."

Tracey confirmed that Belle had written to Katherine about needing to be aggressive to keep the Curé in line. It appeared that Sanford, too, was giving her trouble. John was stalled now in his logical analysis. His information was not complete. It was inconclusive.

Maggie brought them both back to today. "What does all this have to do with our going to Hattonchâtel?"

"Maggie, whatever problem there was in Hattonchâtel was probably never resolved. Belle died before she dealt with whatever the issues were. I think it would be nice to close the book on this, maybe find out what it was. Go for a few days, ask some questions of people there, look around. You can say '*no,*' and then I'll put the letters back in the archives, we close the door on it and go home or maybe you use what is already known in a book or article. It's your call. I'm doing what I think is best. There's a puzzle here, as far as I'm concerned, and whether or not we help solve it now is your choice." John did not want to force Maggie's hand one way or the other.

Neither Maggie nor John said anything for a few minutes. "Choices, life is full of them," Tracey said, breaking the silence. "I will await your phone calls. I put my cell number on the top of the first letter. Take your time. Maggie is right—this all happened eighty years ago. But I'm wondering, before you go, if you would do me another little favor," she coaxed. Maggie and John were tiring of her manipulative approach and requests for favors.

"What is it this time?" John asked.

"Answer for me a few simple questions, while you're considering," Tracey said in a surprisingly quiet voice. Coming a bit closer she said, "Why do you think you're here now, eighty years later? And, who is it that's reaching out to you here? It isn't the actress."

Nineteen

Sunday, January 16th 2005

An Air France jet left Boston's Logan Airport bound for Paris. On board were two Americans on holiday to France at the request of a friend a few weeks earlier. They were going to Hattonchâtel. Maggie and John had each decided the lure of adventure was not something they wanted to put aside, and the unanswered questions regarding Belle and the village were sufficiently intriguing to merit the trip.

John had decided first; he had been having strange feelings about the material in the archives for several days. Maggie took longer. She thought that the final letters Tracey had brought out raised interesting questions, but being a reporter, Maggie was accustomed to loose ends that weren't necessarily going to tie up neatly. It took a little prodding from John to convince Maggie to go. In the end, her curiosity had won her over, and her son, who had said, "It'll be the trip of a lifetime, Mom, and it's only five days. Nothing will go wrong at home, and you have no reason not to go. If you don't go, it's because you've lost all your sense of curiosity. It's time, Mom, to get it back." His only concern was that she had known John for less than a month, and suggested that she find out more about him before traveling together.

Taking her son's advice, Maggie had asked around. It is convenient to have friends who work as reporters, and can run background checks easily. John Merrick turned out to be authentic, and she liked him. So, Maggie took her son's advice, and gave in to her curiosity about Belle's project and possible complications with it.

Their departure from the International terminal had not been without the unexpected, though. John and Maggie had arranged to meet at the Air France ticket counter at six. They thought they'd go over their itinerary, grab a bite to eat, and be at the gate in plenty of time for their

8:10 P.M. flight. What they hadn't expected was that someone would be waiting for them when they came into the terminal. It was Tracey, smiling and waving to them. They had seen each other outside and were walking in together.

"Hi," was all Tracey said. She had been waiting there for an hour, not wanting to miss them.

"What are you doing here?" Maggie asked, wondering whether there was a problem.

"Hello Tracey," John greeted her.

"Just a little going away present, that's all. Let's find a bar and have a drink." Wheeling their luggage, Tracey led them in the direction of the food court. When they found a suitable place, and were served wine, Tracey smiled, running her finger around the top of the glass. The look on her face was not the elfish smile they'd seen whenever she asked them to do her "a favor." It was a different look, one that made her look caring, motherly. "I couldn't let you go without giving you two more things. You're going to need them." She took out of her oversize pocketbook two cell phones. Taped seCurély on the back of each phone was the international telephone number, as well as her cell number. "This one's on me. I want you two to be safe while traveling. I know you both have cell phones, but these are set and ready to go for international calls. It will save you a little money. They're both the same number, so if I call you'll each get a ring. It's the least I can do." Tracey said the words and raised her glass in a toast.

"It isn't necessary, but it's nice of you," John responded.

"Thanks," Maggie said, "I'll call my son at school and tell him what a wonderful time I'm having." She toasted Tracey back, signaling to John that he should be more grateful for the thoughtful gesture.

Putting the Motorola in his jacket pocket, John asked, "What's next? You didn't drive all the way here to just give us these." He knew her well.

Tracey looked at both of them and said, "You know, working in a museum can make you a little nuts."

"I've noticed." John couldn't resist the temptation. Maggie gave him a look that told him to behave.

Tracey accepted his comment gracefully, "Thank you, John."

They relaxed and were feeling like a team, when reaching into a large bag, Tracey said, "You're right, I didn't come only to keep you in touch with the world. I want you to take these with you, and read them on the plane. It's not like I could give them to you at the museum, before you made the decision to go, and I haven't seen you since then. But, I can't let you go without them." She paused, took a breath, and said, "The last letters I showed you in Holyoke weren't really the last ones Belle wrote. Read these on the flight over. Once you understand what's in here, you'll know why I'm a little concerned about what happened in the village when the project was almost finished." Tracey stuck out her tongue at John, and then broke out into a fit of laughter. The other patrons in the bar looked at her as she did this, wondering what the commotion was, but no one said anything. It was usual behavior for an airport refreshment center. Everyone behaves a little strangely in airports.

"Oh, God," John said when Tracey handed him the manila envelope.

"Why not two sets this time, one for each of us?" Maggie's question was legitimate.

"Because you're traveling as one now, Maggie, so let's get our heads together as one. When you 'think' with someone, you get more done. At least that's what my husband tells me." Tracey sipped her wine.

Knowing Tracey's husband, and appreciating how intelligent Tracey was, John replied, "Being married to a psychologist has its merits, huh?" He was being serious.

"He keeps me on my toes," she replied with an Irish lilt.

This time it was Maggie who couldn't resist the opening, "That can't be easy for him," she said in jest, realizing it was the first time she'd entered the fray.

"Cheers!" John said in appreciation.

"Cheers!" Tracey repeated, loving it and patting Maggie on the back.

They all laughed crazily one more time. No one bothered to turn or notice them this time. It was just three friends having a few drinks and a good time before two of them boarded a plane that would take them to Europe for a holiday.

Airborne for an hour, sitting next to each other, Maggie looked at John after they had each accustomed themselves to the plane and the flight information had been dispensed. Not having traveled together before, they both wanted to get comfortable before they brought up the subject of the letters.

"We land at 9:00 tomorrow morning, Paris time. It's a six-hour difference in time zones. Have you done much overseas travel?" John who was an experienced traveler, asked.

"None," Maggie said.

"Never?"

"It's my first time to Europe," she smiled.

"It's beautiful there. It's much different than the States. But, you can make up your own mind about it." He was enjoying her company in a different way than at the museum. He felt comfortable. "We have to adjust to the jet lag. I'll show you how, it's easy." He paused and said, "Well, do you want to open it or shall I?" Maggie had taken possession of the envelope at the terminal gate, but didn't say anything. "Go ahead, your turn," he continued. They were intensely curious about what was important enough for Tracey to hand deliver the envelope; it was five hours round trip between Holyoke and the airport. Maggie took the papers from the manila envelope.

"Looks like more of Belle's letters," she said. "I thought Tracey said she showed us all of them, the ones she thought were important."

"Yes, but at the airport she said there were others."

They began to look at the papers and found that as Tracey had suggested they were looking with one mind. It was different from what they had done in Holyoke, where they had each formed their own opinions, then shared their ideas. Now, they built on what they already knew, and evaluated the materials together one line at a time.

Belle had indeed written more letters, and these had not been included in the regular archive boxes. As usual, Tracey had put them into sequence for them, and this time she had numbered them. Maggie picked up the top letter.

Letter number 1 was dated June 11, 1922. It was a letter that Belle wrote to Katherine from Hattonchâtel, and said:

> *... Two or three days ago, while cleaning out the cellar, Sanford's workmen came upon an earthen pot buried in what they call a "cachete." Accidentally the workmen broke the pot & out rushed several hundred pieces of ancient money—gold and silver. Some go back to the 10th Century. The most modern date is 1517. The coins are beautiful. There was a general scramble for them among the workmen, but Sanford was there himself, & stopped the looting. The State expects me to give them one third. The other two thirds are mine. I'll probably give most of them to the Commune to be exposed to the new nuns, the Mairies. I think though I'll keep one or two.*

Closer than they'd ever been before, because of the seating on the plane, John and Maggie looked into one another's eyes, and could almost feel each other's heartbeats quicken, reading the words "gold" and "silver." Maggie went to the next letter numbered 2. It was again written to Katherine by Belle, the date of the second letter was soon after the first, June 19, 1922.

> *... All Paris is agog over my finding a pot of gold at Hatton. The French paper,* Le Matin *has asked to publish the story first, and I have promised to let them have the tale tomorrow. The keeper of the coins at the Louvre says these of mine are of great value. They are all from the 14th and 15th centuries. I think I told you in my last letter that the State has a right to a third of the 'find' but I think they will waive that right when they are assured that I will use the coins to start a museum at Hatton. Anyway, it's frightfully exciting and don't you think it's romantic that I (from far away America) should have been the one to unearth the treasure that was burried [sic] long before Columbus set out on his venturesome voyage! Everybody in Hatton is sitting up nights now to dig.*

"They found the Romans' hiding place, the ones the Swedes were looking for. You remember, it was mentioned somewhere in the archival material. They tortured the villagers in the 30 Years War, looking for the treasure they thought was there. But, they left with nothing."

John and Maggie were dumbfounded. Maggie reread the part of the letter in which Belle found a "pot of gold," while John reasoned, "It must have been the bombings, the assaults by the Germans during the war that unearthed the treasure. The holes made by the bombs must have been deep enough to uncover the place where the Romans kept the coins." He was speculating as to why they had finally been discovered in 1922.

"It's possible. Belle wrote that the entire village was full of metal, shrapnel and remnants from the bombs. The village was devastated, but maybe in the destruction a little treasure was exposed," Maggie mused.

Belle Skinner, being benevolent, had chosen to restore an obsCuré French village that she knew nothing about, except that it was in the northeastern part of France. By what seemed like an incredible stroke of luck, she had chosen a town on the top of a mountain that might be full of gold.

The only thing Maggie and John could do was shake their heads in wonder. They were thankful that no one was sitting in the aisle seat to hear what they were talking about. Maggie reached under the seat in front of her and took out her bag, again. Maggie wanted a pen. Being a reporter, she was going to take some notes. The first thing she did was to list the dates of the letters, next, jot down a few thoughts about what was written, and then the surmises.

Letter number 3 was the one Tracey had "committed to memory," as she had said. It was written two months after the coins were found. On August 17, Belle wrote to Katherine, *"That personage (the Curé), by the way, is returning to his Jesuitical methods, so I have been obliged to 'show him my claws,' on several occasions."*

On a post-it, stuck to the letter was a note from Tracey, "I'm including this letter for two reasons, first to document what I said, and second, please note the date of this letter and compare it to the dates of the first two. It looks like things were beginning to change more than just a little bit, after the 'pot of gold' was discovered." It was signed, "Good Luck, Tracey."

Maggie took notes in her daily organizer, looking to John first to make sure it was OK with him. He agreed completely. From this minute on, they needed to start documenting everything. The next piece of paper was a newspaper headline, numbered 4 by Tracey, dateline August 18, 1922:

> *The publication 'The World'— Miss Belle Skinner of New York, Godmother of Hattonchâtel, in rebuilding French village, finds buried treasure. Over four hundred gold and silver coins from the fifteenth century unearthed by a blow or by a pickman's pick. Some were unique and all will go to museums....*

Letter number 5 was a short note Belle had written to William on June 24, 1925, in which she said:

> *I do not notice the 'coolness' that Sanford prepared me for, so I think the change in feeling 'among the villagers' exists only in his imagination. Certoux, however is a regular 'crook,' but Harper will make him give back 'all' (I think) that he has stolen from me. (Monument Commission wants to buy Château, property).*

Next came letter number 6, dated June 29 and from Belle to Katherine from Hattonchâtel. It was on the same paper of letter 5 to William:

> *I am still 'after Certoux.' He has been robbing me right and*

left, but I expect to get him… everything was peaceful at Hatton. I let them know that the 'bonne marraine' is dead and buried, & a fury has taken her place. It's better so. They respect me more. Am invited out constantly. That does not prevent my thinking of you all, however, & hoping all is pulpit-extra.

"Robbing her blind?" Maggie wasn't sure what Belle meant. "And, who is Certoux?"

"I don't know. Let's finish reading them, then maybe everything will make sense." John looked at her, being as curious as she was by what they were learning. Letter number 7 was a copy of the one Belle sent to Katherine on July 27, 1926, in which she told of the reception she received at Hattonchâtel, and the trouble she had with John Sanford.

They gave us a fine welcome –'Sanford's house was barred to me so we stayed at Nancy as… planned'.

Knowing they had read this one, Tracey had added a post-it note here also. "The same reason, for documentation, and for you to begin to keep a time frame of the dates of the letters and the events, Tracey."

"There are only a few more in here," Maggie said as she pulled out a letter 8. On it were two notes that had been copied. One was from Hattonchâtel dated August 6, 1926 from Belle to Katherine, just seven months before she died. After describing the beauty of the flowers and the village, she said more Roman ruins had been found in the town. Then asked Katherine to tell the children to come to the village next year—*"they will adore the spectacle of Jeanne d' Arc at Nancy."* The second to last letter was dated August 16, 1926 and was also to Katherine, this time from Biarritz. On the letter in pencil, Tracey had written, "to be kept." Belle wrote:

We have had thrills. Providence is wonderfully interesting. The Roman ruins everywhere are in a wonderful state of preservation. But the high spot of the trip was Lourdes. It is an unforgettable sight. The setting of the scene, the hundreds of sick on stretchers, the procession of peoples—all the nations of the earth, led by the Bishops & priests, the voice of the leader and the answers of the believers, 'all' makes an impression that goes frightfully deep. There is nothing tawdry about it, no claptrap, 'just faith.' There was no miracle performed that day & some of the sick looked very sad, but somehow it all fit in. Then in the morning there was a torch light procession, 6000-7000

> *people (of all nations) each carrying a torch and all singing, 'Ave Maria'—it was a marvelous experience. I can't begin to write out the details, but you, Kitten must someday visit Lourdes. It is a 'soaring' experience.*

The final enclosure, number 9, was a copy of a letter Belle wrote to a woman whose name was Justina. Belle wrote it while she was on board the SS PARIS on September 7, 1927, more than a year later. John and Maggie read it together, comparing the date to the other letters in the package. It was probably one of the last letters Belle wrote to anyone:

> *Thank you again, for putting me in touch with the Abbe. It really is a wonderful favor you have done me, & I am very grateful...I went to Epernay, called on the young de Azalao, told them my story & promised to lunch with them on my return to Paris. Mr. de Azalao was thoroughly interested and very enthusiastic, but in spite of his enthusiasm and mine, we agreed that it would be better not to do any sounding until I can be 'on the spot.' In other words, I'd like to have for myself the thrill off... [??]waters, so to speak in the will. Therefore nothing will be done until I return to France next spring. In the meantime I have several books on the subject to read this winter & Mr. de Azalao will lash the Abbe into a proper state of excitement.*

There were no notes on the letter from Tracey, who apparently wanted Maggie and John to reach their own conclusions. "This is what Tracey was talking about when she said Belle was doing something about some disturbing matters months before she died," John said.

"Who's Justina?" Maggie asked.

"No idea. Not a Skinner family member. Maybe a friend of Belle's in France or someone Prudence knew."

"That's all that's in here, John," Maggie said as she put each of the numbered letters, notes, and clippings back into the manila envelope, making sure first that nothing else was inside.

Thinking aloud again, John said quietly, "Belle was moved by what she saw in Lourdes, just like she was when she saw all of the dead bodies on the roads when she was trapped and running in France at the beginning of the war in 1914. The tone in her writing shows her emotions and moods."

"The people she talks about in Hattonchâtel, those in the other letters, might be a lot more interested in more Roman coins that could be underneath them than the restoration of the village." This was Maggie's first guess. John's expression told her that he agreed.

"In the year between the time she wrote about ongoing problems with the Curé, and Sanford 'barring' her from entering her own house, and her visit to Lourdes, something happened that moved Belle to seek the assistance of the Abbe, and a man from Epernay named de Azalao, at the advice of someone named Justina," he said bringing it all together in a way.

"What do you think she wanted him to do?" Maggie asked John.

Putting his head back against the headrest, and looking into her blue eyes, John answered, "I think that's why we're going to France, Maggie. What was so unacceptable to Belle? What was going on in the village? Why did the trip to Lourdes affect her so much? And why did she want these men to help her change whatever was happening in Hattonchâtel that was so upsetting? I think these are the pieces of the puzzle that Tracey doesn't have the answers to, to prove Theory 3 is correct."

Maggie looked down at the envelope lying in her lap that held Belle's last letters. Thinking about the wonderful things Belle had done, Maggie felt that Tracey was smart to ask them to check out these missing links. Maggie and John needed to find out who Certoux was, and why Sanford and the Curé had begun to be "bothersome." The questions had to be answered.

John shared Maggie's impressions: It seemed as if a few people were more interested in what was under the ground in Hattonchâtel than in the reconstruction above it. And, it began around the time Belle's workmen discovered the coins.

TWENTY

Monday, January 17th, 2005

The plane landed smoothly and almost on time at the Charles de Gaulle airport in Paris. After clearing themselves and their luggage through immigration and customs, John and Maggie went to the car rental agency where they had reservations. After signing the Europcar contracts and getting directions, they walked to the terminal parking area to their car.

Having received reasonable information, but no map from the agent, Maggie and John found their way out of the airport. After that they took a few wrong turns, and ended up in the center of Paris, instead of the superhighway north. It took three hours from the time they landed for the two to find Route A4 to Verdun. After a brief stop for something to eat at a roadside Auto Grill, they double-checked their directions with a man they found there that spoke some English, and continued on. Not trusting anyone with directions, Maggie had the good sense to buy a map. Following it, they headed towards Nancy, and then they took a series of connector routes that in four hours brought them onto Route 908 that took them around a rotary into the village of Fresnes. Five minutes later, traveling on the same road, they entered the village of Heudicourt, and saw the sign Rue de Charles de Gaulle. Driving down only a short distance, they saw the hotel on their right where they had made reservations, the Hotel du Lac de Madine. It was a crème colored building with periwinkle framed windows and doors. There was a small parking area to the side of the front entrance where John and Maggie parked the car and got out. They were greeted by a gust of cold air blowing at them from the direction of the lake nearby, the Lac de Madine. Taking their bags, the two checked in and went to their adjoining rooms to drop off their luggage. Once they did, they went down to the front desk to inquire as to what direction the village of Hattonchâtel was. The pleasant young woman there told them the way, and they returned to

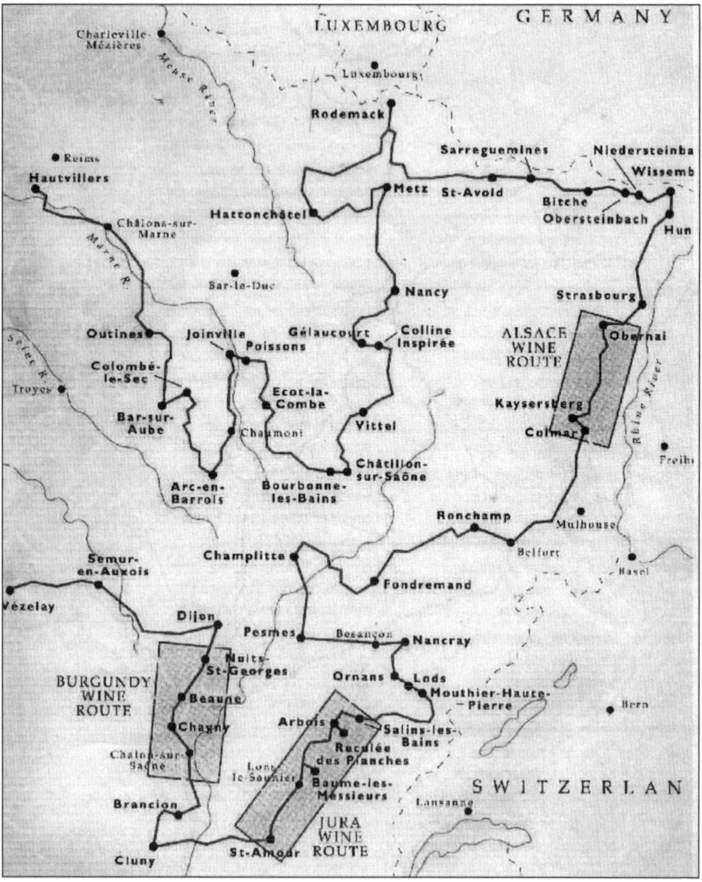

the car and headed out.

"The hotel is lovely. I noticed the dining room in the back is set for dinner. Don't most French people have their main meal in the middle of the day?" Maggie asked John.

"The people who live here do, then they rest. But, we Americans are used to eating dinner late. So, they accommodate us."

Traveling back on the same road, they took it north this time. Seeing the sign the girl had told them to look out for at the rotary, they followed Route D179. It directed them to Hattonchâtel. The distance from where they were was listed as 2 kilometers. Noticing the orchards all around them, Maggie asked John if he knew what they were.

"Mirabelle plums mostly, and apple trees. The fruit from the trees is a well known product of the Lorraine region according to the descriptions I read in the lobby while you were getting directions."

A few minutes later they both saw it at the same time. It was like looking up into the sky and seeing a vision. The Château and the buildings of the village of Hattochatel were above them not far in the distance. It was a sight to behold. Finding the road to the village was easy. The signs were clearly marked. Driving up the paved road that led to the top of the mountain, the two became silent. Knowing that in minutes they would be in Belle's village, they each began to prepare themselves for a memorable experience.

At the bottom of the hill, a few hundred feet underneath the Château, John pulled the car over to the side of the road so they could get a good view of the Château on the top of the mountain above them, and the hills and valleys all around them. He was attentive, because the paved road was slippery, and the drop off was significant. They had lucked out, and there was not a lot of snow on the mountain or the road, but he was cautious, realizing that a slide could cause a catastrophe.

"How in God's name did she find this place in 1920? It's way out of the way. It must have taken her days to get here back then," Maggie said, looking around. "Look at this place, it's a fairytale."

John was looking up, "That's unbelievable. Where's King Arthur?"

Hattonchâtel Village Entrance

"That's England, John. This is France. But, it is definitely like something you'd read about in a knight's tale from any European country." She remembered reading about these kingdoms as a child.

"No boarded up buildings here. Looks like they are taking better care of the Skinner investments," John said, referring to the abandonment of Holyoke by some people. "How do you say Skinnerville in French?" he joked.

Putting the car back into gear, John steered it onto the road carefully. In a matter of minutes, they were passing by the first houses of the village. There appeared to be a few new houses being built on the outskirts of the village that were styled like those that lined the road leading into the village. Passing by a number of them, John saw the sign, Rue Miss Skinner. To their left, they saw a statue, the one they read about that Belle has donated to the village, *The Peasant Woman.* It paid respect to the women in the village who had lost sons in the war.

John parked on the side of road near the first large building that had to be the Saint Maur, because of the steeple on it. John and Maggie began to walk around the village to get their bearings. It was chilly, but not intolerably cold. The sun was setting and dark shadows were hiding some of the buildings on the far side of the village. But, at the end of the long street, on the far side of what looked like a village green, they saw the Château. Even in dim light, it was something to behold.

It was while they were walking towards the Château that they heard the noise, the ringing of the bell. Both of them stopped when they heard it, but it was Maggie who made the comment. "It's her bell," she said respectfully.

"I think we've arrived. Someone is greeting us," John answered her.

The village seemed deserted. There was no one walking around, anywhere. Most of the houses that lined the street were obviously inhabited, because there were lights on. But no one was to be seen anywhere.

"Do you think the Church is open?" Maggie asked, turning right and walking towards it.

"I doubt it. It doesn't look like anything is," John said.

As John approached the Church, he reached to open the side door, finding it locked, he turned to Maggie and said, "Maybe it's too late in the day. It looks like everyone has gone home already."

Walking back down the Rue de Château that led to the Château, John was thinking that it might be a good idea to come back in the morning.

As they approached the front entrance of the Château that was separated from the rest of the village, a man appeared from the inside of a small house to the left that was marked 'Guard House.'

"Bonjour," he said.

"Hello," John replied.

Realizing that they were not French the man spoke to them in English. "Can I help you?"

"We have come to see the village. We are from America, and have heard the stories about Miss Skinner." John was brief. "Actually, I am from the same city she was."

The man's eyes lit up when he heard the name. "Miss Skinner was our savior. You are from Holyoke."

"Yes. " John answered him.

Smiling, Maggie said, "We have come to look at what she did here. We might write a story about her."

The man replied, "Very few people come to the village this time of year. It is off-season. I am the guide who shows people around in the summer. If you come back tomorrow, I think I can find time to give you a tour. It is late now, and everyone is gone."

"What time?" John asked him.

"Ten o'clock." The man began to close the door.

Before he did, Maggie asked him a final question, not knowing what was acceptable for them to do. "Is the Château open now?"

"It's a private residence," the man answered. "I'll ask if we can go in the morning." Shutting the door, he said no more.

Walking back to the car, Maggie felt a chill. It wasn't the cold air circulating around them. Looking around, she was excited to be here.

Noticing a few more of the buildings from the descriptions they had been given by Tracey, they both began to take notes on what they saw. Writing everything down would make it easier for them to remember where everything was when they came back. After thirty minutes, they had decided it would be a good idea to head back to the hotel. They were both tired and hungry. Not having gotten much sleep on the plane ride over, it was essential that they rest and eat so that they would be sharp for the next day. So, the two finished up with their notes and threw their backpacks into the back seat of the car. Then, they drove out of the village the same way they came in.

Driving back down the mountain, John stopped the car when he saw the village cemetery to his left. "Want to take a look?"

"Tomorrow, John," Maggie said, "I feel awful."

Realizing the travel and time difference were getting to Maggie, and deciding that he didn't feel so good himself, he continued on. Hearing the bell, faint in the distance, John pushed the button to lower the window. As they drove away, he decided he wanted to hear the sound one last time. It was part of the reason he came here. Behind them, Belle's bell was ringing.

Twenty One

Tuesday, January 18, 2005

The following morning, John and Maggie met in the breakfast room of the hotel at nine o'clock. John had heard her just getting up as he was leaving his room, and waited for her to come down before eating. Drinking only coffee, he smiled when he saw her come in. John couldn't help but notice how beautiful Maggie looked in the early morning light.

"Can I get you a cup?" John said, standing to help her with her chair.

"Please," Maggie answered, "why don't you make it two while you're at it. I feel like I have a hangover, John. Is that normal?"

"It's jet lag. Have something to eat and you'll feel better." He was quick to get her coffee and some water. They both needed to drink a lot of fluids if they were to feel better. "Maybe we should have had dinner last night. How did you sleep?"

"Fine. Don't apologize for last night. I couldn't eat anything. I went right to bed. It's a very comfortable hotel, and quiet. I don't remember my head hitting the pillow." Drinking her coffee, she noticed her hand shake.

Seeing it John said, "It's not easy making the crossing. People don't realize what it does to your sense of balance."

"Did you try anything?" Maggie asked him looking at the breakfast table with an assortment of foods and fruit on it.

"No, I was waiting for you. The croissants look marvelous. Remember we're in France. Everything tastes good here." He went to the automatic machine that dispensed the coffee to freshen up their cups.

As he did, Maggie noticed the pleasant music playing through the hotel's speaker system. It was coming from a French radio station. The song she was hearing had melody, beat and composition. She thought how nice it was in comparison to some of the chaotic songs being played in America that had no structure. It was a sign of the times. Music was supposed to soothe the savage beast, Maggie recalled the old saying, not create one.

John returned to the table. "A couple who came from Wales is traveling to their home in Greece and just left. They both spoke good English and told me they visited Hattonchâtel a few days ago. They said we shouldn't miss the sculpture in the old part of the Church, done by a man named Ligier Richier. It seems he did many in France, and people come from all over the world just to see his works." John was still waiting for the machine to finish dispensing more coffee.

"Really. I never heard of him," Maggie replied.

After sampling everything on the table, and having many more cups of coffee, the two walked out of the hotel towards their car. Dressed for the cold, they headed towards the parking lot where the car was. Walking on the road, Maggie noticed a statue of a soldier with a gun in his arms and an outstretched hand across the street. Curious, she crossed the road, making sure that no cars were coming, and took a closer look at it. The inscription on it read, "*Hommage Et Reconnaissance a Nos Enfants Morts Pour La France – 1914-1918.*"

"Anything interesting?" John shouted from the other side of the street.

Walking back over to him, she tried as best she could to translate the writing. "Literally it says, '*In memory of our dead children who died for France, 1914-1918.*'" Maggie then added, smiling, "I think it's all going to be interesting."

At precisely ten o'clock, John and Maggie rang the bell on the guardhouse door at the end of the Rue de Château in Hattonchâtel where they had met the pleasant grey-haired man the night before. As they did, they heard the sound of construction not far away, and saw a number of workers walking around some of the houses close to where they were. There was a lot of activity in the village this morning.

A few seconds later, the middle aged man appeared dressed in heavy corduroy pants and a black wool turtleneck sweater. He was putting on a parka and hat as he came out from the inside of the small house. "Good Morning," he said, remembering John and Maggie had spoken English to him the night before.

Noticing that he was carrying a tape recorder, John said, "We didn't have a chance to tell you our names last night. I am John, and this is Maggie."

"I am Bernard, the caretaker of the Château and the village. It is nice to meet you."

Walking beside Bernard they told him some of the reasons they had come to the village. "We read a great deal about what Belle Skinner did here in the 1920s but we have only the American version of the story. We want the French one, too." John was direct and to the point.

"That is simple, John," Bernard answered. "What she did was save our village. In French or English, I believe it is said the same. She was dynamic." He stopped after they walked over the walkway where the drawbridge used to be over the moat below them, and reached the tall, heavy metal gate that was locked. It was the main entrance to the Château. Unlocking it with his key, he pulled it open with some effort and smiling, said, "Come inside, and look at what her genius created. Cast your eyes on a sight only a few get to see."

Passing by him, Maggie and John entered the courtyard of the Château. The first thing they noticed was the large rectangular water pool set in the middle of a long circular driveway. The water in it was frozen, but it was obviously meant to display floral or plant arrangements in the warmer months of the year. Walking a bit further, the main building of the Château became entirely visible to them. It was breathtaking. It appeared as it had in the pictures they had both seen, only more impres-

The Château at Hattonchâtel

sive in person. It absolutely looked like it belonged in a knight's tale.

As he began the tour, Bernard turned on a tape recorder that gave descriptions of the Château and the village history. "We are at the terrace of the Château. It was built in the year 859 for Bishop Hatton who was the 29th Bishop of Verdun. He received this village and several castles from Lothaire II in thanks for services he rendered. In this era, the Bishops of Verdun were both Bishops and Lords. They lived in Verdun as Bishops and in Hattonchâtel as Lords. It is here in Hattonchâtel that the Bishops of Verdun minted their coins and rendered justice." Bernard switched off the tape, and looked at them expecting questions.

Maggie did a double take, not prepared for this part about the mint so quickly. She just looked at John when she heard this. He put his arm around her shoulder, directing Maggie to follow Bernard to the end of the terraced gardens. As John did, he whispered in her ear to not say or ask him anything. Smiling at Bernard, John motioned with his head that they did not have questions and for Bernard to continue.

The tape played on, "Prestigious and authentic, the building reflects the Gothic style architecture of the 16th century. The entire Château was rebuilt in the 1920s by an American lady whose name was Belle Skinner. The facade is polished stone, and the woods used are of the finest materials. You will notice that the main part of the building, where the front entranceway to the inside is located, has a balcony that extends from one end of the structure to the other. There are two cone shaped towers at the far end, one in the middle, and another at the far end adjacent to the front gate. Most of the Château had to be completely rebuilt after the First World War. The only parts of the original building are the first floor rooms, and the set of stairs that lead up to the second floor to the left of where you entered the courtyard. The entire second floor of the Château had been destroyed, and only the walls of the fortress remained. The building is L-shaped; with the longer middle section being the living areas. If you would be kind enough to continue walking, we will now go to the far side of the terraced courtyard to look at the view from the small sitting area that is there." Bernard turned off the tape. "Any questions, now?"

John spoke up, "The polished stone that was used in the reconstruction was from where?"

"There are several quarries in the area. It all had to be brought in by carts. Most of what was left here after the war was useless. As you can see, the stone used was also of different colors, light and dark. Some were from one quarry, the others from another. It must have been difficult to position the stones in place. They are heavy, and as you can see, it took a large number of them to rebuild the Château."

"What is that outbuilding over there?" Maggie pointed to the far left of the entrance.

"It is the old marketplace."

Reaching the sitting area, and looking out over the large valley below, Maggie asked, "It's called the Lorraine Region, but what is the valley called, and what is the name of that lake?" She pointed to it in the distance.

"It is the Woevre valley. The lake is the Lac de Madine. The Lorraine region is between the Champagne and the Alsace regions of France." Bernard's descriptions were brief. "It is much more beautiful in the summer when the fruit trees are full, the lilies of the valley are in bloom and the grass is green," he added, looking down at the white snow that covered parts of the valley. "Let's get out of the cold for a time, and go inside."

As they walked to the terrace, Bernard switched on the player again, "The Bishops of Verdun remained owners of the Château for 700 years, until at least 1546 and perhaps later. The Bishop of Verdun, being a member of the family of the Duke of Lorraine, wished the Château to remain in the hands of the Lorraine's, and gave the entire village, along with 18 others, to them: properties from Esternach to Luxembourg. The Bishops made many improvements and beautifications to the Château. You see the front door with the trefoil tympanum. All the mullioned windows are ground level, typical of 14th century styles. The Dukes of Verdun did some work before the Bishops of Verdun arrived. The Dukes set up a Marquisate for themselves, and had it legally preserved for centuries. But, in 1623 Richelieu, in order to weaken their power, destroyed the defense towers of Hattonchâtel. There were towers all around the village then, but unfortunately none but 2 remain, one that is found at the entrance of the terrace, and one joined to the village Church. After the departure of the Dukes of Lorraine, the Château passed into the hands of different Lords up to the war of 1914-1918, the Great War. The Germans who occupied the entire region used the Château as an observation post, and the French who tried to take back the village, bombed and caused severe damage to all of the buildings of the ancient village."

John asked Bernard about this, "The French bombed their own village?"

The guide answered, "Yes. Between the Germans and the French fighting for it, not much of Hattonchâtel was left after the war."

Once Bernard was finished explaining the destruction he turned on the recording again. "After the war, an American woman who visited the battlefields had been attracted by the site of Hattonchâtel. For some reason, she decided to restore the Château and the village. Unfortunately, she did not benefit from her restoration, since she died coming to its inauguration. The old Château was therefore, not entirely completed, and her heirs, knowing that the Château had belonged to the Bishop of Verdun for over 700 years, returned it to the Diocese of Verdun. Observe the wall surrounding the Château; the wall encircled the entire village, and there was one tower every 100-150 meters around it. This was a fortified village, and there were 14 of them. From here, when the weather is clear, we enjoy a most beautiful view of the Lorraine. On the right, we see the American memorial that is at Montsec. To the left of it, we see Lake Madine, the largest lake in Lorraine. To its left, we catch a glimpse of Mount St. Michel where Toul is, and further to the left is the road to Nancy." The tape stopped, Bernard removed it from the player, and turned it over. Standing in front of the entrance to the Château, Bernard turned the recording back on to play the second part.

"After the bombings, nothing was left of the Château, but the ground floor. You will see the other stones of the building are different from those on the first floor. All the rest of the Château was reconstructed between 1922-1928, financed by Miss Belle Skinner and her family. At the extreme left, you see a Norman stairway that the American woman had brought from Normandy, and rebuilt here. At this site in the 9th century, there was a stronghold (castle keep), called the town of Amace."

Stopping the tape for a moment, Bernard asked John and Maggie if they knew anything about the history being explained to them by the man talking on the tape recording. *"No,"* John answered for them. "This is all very informative." Looking at the guide and then at the sights around them John and Maggie smiled and walked closer to the entrance door, wanting to go in.

Seeing this, Bernard went with them, and turned on the recorder to let the man on the tape describe the front of the building to them. Walking quickly, they climbed up the stone steps at the end of the terrace that led to the front door of the Château. They passed by a series of rose bushes, and as they did Maggie noticed the elaborate carvings on the balcony above them, and the large glass windows that lined the second floor of the Château from one end to the other. There was a walkway at the top of the stairs that went from one end of the building to the other. It looked like it might be used for a sitting area when the weather permitted it, to look out on the gardens.

The tape described the carvings: "You will notice a beautiful frieze of sculptured stone that follows the balcony. If you look carefully at it, you will see at the bottom of the frieze, slightly around the middle of the window, a small sculpture in stone, a meter to the right, a mouse, and at the left, the branches of the rose bush, a butterfly, and a bird. The frieze was crafted by an artist, not an artisan, and dates from the 14th century."

Entering the Château, looking at what was being described, John and Maggie both had the same reaction to what was inside. It was spectacular. Looking at one another, they remained silent, listening to the voice on the tape describe the beautiful, spacious rooms they were now in.

When they looked comfortable, Bernard moved their attention to the main room of the first floor. It was to their left. Once he led them in, the only thing Maggie could say was, "You have got to be kidding me." Listening to what was being described on the machine, John thought her remark was more than accurate.

"We are here in the Burgraves Room. Burgraves is the name the Bishops used while they were Lords and warriors. It is in this large room that the Bishops rendered justice. Notice the immense fireplace on the other side of the large center table, and chairs that are well proportioned for the grandeur of the room. You will see on the mantle the coat of arms of the Haraucourt family who were the Bishops of Verdun in the 15th century [1432] in the family of the Dukes of Lorraine. To the left, you have 3 eagles that represent the coat of arms of the Dukes of Lorraine, and on the right the coat of arms of the Bishops of Verdun. On the floor are red ceramic tiles, and black marble slate. You see, there, the Lion who signifies the coat of arms of the Dukes of Lorraine, and the Imperial eagle of the Dioceses of Metz. Toul and Verdun were under the protection of the German empire until 1552. This paving is from the 15th century. The windows all around are of radiant, Gothic style. To the back of the Château, you will see the location of the original chapel. What you see is not the chapel of the old Château. That was destroyed entirely by the bombings. Nothing original remains, except for the superb support beam sculptured in oak overhead that is more than 400 years old, and the arch of the cove of the cage that is above the great metal door in the portal. It is one of the original pieces of the first Château fort, and was put in place more than 1100 years ago." Bernard turned off the recorder.

The room was huge, and just as described had an immense fireplace at the end of it that had to be twenty feet high with a fire burning in it. There were a number of archways that went from the front of the room to the back. They were all fitted stones, and the bottoms were columned with squared bases. The huge floor was a combination of black marble and tile. The expensive looking materials were colored red and black. There were several cast iron chandeliers hanging down from the ceiling that had to be thirty or forty feet high. In the middle of the room there was a long formal looking table with eight large chairs around it. All around the room were antique tables, desks, more chairs and a large number of old clocks, and pictures decorated the walls.

Noticing their expressions, Bernard turned on the tape recorder again. It further described the room in detail, and gave a brief history of the Château, village, those who had lived here in the past and what had happened here. "The village dates back to Roman times. In the 9th century, it has been documented that several distinguished members of the Royal Family of France lived here. Legend has it that a mint was built in the Château around this time. In the 10th century, the Bishops of Verdun, Metz and Toul used it as a retreat, and monks came here. In the centuries that followed, the village was fortified with high walls to keep out invaders. The Church built a Gothic style chapel with an Abbey attached to it, and a palace where the Bishops lived. Houses were built for the clergy, and the villagers who farmed and worked for them. For over a century, the village was used mostly as a monastery. In the 11th century the Countess Mathilde of Flanders took possession of the village, and made it into a palace again. In the next few centuries, the fortress was inhabited by the Huns, Spaniards, Russians, Swedes, Hungarians and the Germans. They all valued the fortress for its beauty and its easily defendable location on the top of a mountain. It has been said that many groups of knights and squires stayed here. In the 14th century, the major buildings of the village were destroyed, including the Château, Chalet, Church and Abbey. The peasants of the valley built homes in the village, and not much was done to rebuild what was destroyed, except for the Church.

The Church of St. Maur was rebuilt. It was used only as a place of worship for the villagers. A school was constructed for the children to be taught their lessons. For several hundred years, Hattonchâtel existed only as a simple farming village. The villagers lived a quiet life with the men and boys tending the fields, and the women bringing up the water from the old Roman well that was 1000 yards down the hill from the village. In the 14th and 15th centuries, realizing its historical significance, the Château was rebuilt and occupied by several Dukes, Duchesses and other nobles. It was destroyed in the 16th century and rebuilt in the century that followed. In the 19th century, monks came here to live in the Abbey, meditate and write in the old 14th century Church. For a time, Prince Rupprecht of Bavaria had his headquarters in a crypt under the village. When the Germans invaded the village in 1914, most of the buildings had been rebuilt, and looked like they did in medieval times. The bombardments during the German invasion destroyed most of the structures, but parts of the Château remained intact, mostly at ground level. The Germans used what was left as a base of operations. When they left, they destroyed everything, and by 1918 little remained. After the war, the Château and all of the major buildings of the village were reconstructed by a benevolent woman from Holyoke, Massachusetts named Belle Skinner."

"There is an underground crypt here?" John asked Bernard as he turned off the tape.

"Yes. In the old days, there were underground passageways that connected most of the houses and buildings of the village to the Château. I know of a number of them that exist now. But they are all blocked. The bombings sealed them up. One leads out of the village to Hattonville, one to the Church, and at least two go in the direction of Miss Skinner's house."

Both John and Maggie stopped in their tracks. "Miss Skinner's house?" John asked.

Bernard turned to them, realizing he had not pointed it out. "It's the one next to mine. Forgive me. I should have shown it to you before we began the tour. When we leave, I'll make sure I point it out to you." He turned and walked back towards the entrance to the Château. "The living area is this way, as is the Library, Office, the old Chapel Room and two of the five bathrooms in the house. There is also another fireplace at the end of the building that is the same size as the one in the main room that is set between the two towers." John and Maggie followed him trying to appreciate what they were seeing.

Looking back, John began to compare the pictures he had seen of Belle's restoration of the Château with what he saw now. He remembered the photos of the huge stone room with the marble floors with the one long table in the middle of the room, and maybe a few other tables scattered around. That was all that had been pictured. The six black wrought-iron ceiling lights were the same as in the photos, except they had been candle fixtures before. The bright light they now provided to the room was more than adequate, and John thought it was an intelligent improvement over the dim light the candles must have provided.

"The fireplace looks the same as the pictures," Maggie said.

"The wall cuttings, too. I recognize the one of the crucifixion of Christ, over there." John pointed to an intricate carving on the wall as they walked. The morning sun was shining through crystal-clear glass above him, and its rays were beaming in all directions throughout the building. The amount of light coming in from the small glass openings was amazing. It was like a giant prism. The reflections brightened up the whole building, but just in the morning when the sun was high on this side of the Château. What John saw when he shielded his eyes enough to avoid the blinding light flashes were the iron-barred circular windows on the second floor of the tower. He knew it was why they built Gothic buildings this way, to allow the light to come in.

Bernard led them closer to the towers. As he did he turned the tape recorder back on. It described the objects of value that were in the Château and their histories. The stone tower was round with a cone shaped top just like the second one that was about twenty feet away from it. They were about sixty feet high, and made completely of stone. The windows in them, from which the light was shining in, had been cut small to prevent uninvited guests from entering. The towers, the short wall, and the exterior supports, called flying buttresses, served as one solid end of the L-shaped fortress.

As Maggie listened to the tape, she quietly spoke to John, "Look at all of the antiques and the art. It's amazing," Maggie said, interrupting his thoughts. "Do you think Belle paid for some of the furnishings too?"

John began to notice what she was talking about. All around them were what looked like old period pieces and wall art that certainly looked medieval. If the artwork were reproductions, they were expensive ones.

"There's maybe a small fortune in furniture and paintings here," he said.

"Kind of reminds me of a Royal Palace," John said to Maggie. He did not remember anything like this in the photos.

Giving them adequate time to take everything they were seeing in, Bernard said, "This is a private home now, and the first floor is all that I can show you. Use your imagination though. There are ten bedrooms, three bathrooms and a large attic. I wish I could show you the bedrooms upstairs. They are all exquisite. Did I mention the Château is for sale?"

John answered him, "No, you didn't. I thought the Skinner family turned the property over to the Bishop of Verdun?"

"They did. It was back in the 1930s," Bernard said. "But, the Bishop sold the Château in the 1970s. I actually work as the caretaker for the present owner."

"How much is it selling for?" Maggie asked him as they walked out the front door.

"$1,677,000 Euros, that includes all of the property and the house I am living in." Bernard was exact.

Figuring out the exchange rate, because the American dollar was losing its value everywhere, John said, "About two million dollars. Seems like a steal for all of this."

Bernard concluded his tour of the inside of the Château with, "That's a bit of the Château's history. The tape ends here. Again, most of what you see was not here until Miss Skinner rebuilt it. The second floor is off limits as are the tunnels." Bernard began walking towards the front entrance to show them out.

Maggie wanted to know more about what was underground. She was just about to question the guide about what exactly was below the Château when John said, "Bernard, we are interested in knowing everything about Miss Skinner, and what she did here. There is a lot of information on the tape to remember. Is it possible to get a copy? It would be helpful to us when we get home." Hearing his request, Maggie did not ask her questions about the underground caverns.

Looking at John, Bernard said, "I don't see why not. I have copies. You can have this one." Bernard smiled, leading them out. As he did, he popped out the tape from the player, and handed it to John.

Seeing this, Maggie whispered to John, "They tell everyone about the underground tunnels and mint."

John took the tape and put it in his pack. Once outside, he quietly responded to what Maggie had said as they walked carefully on the cold ground to the front gate. "Without reading Belle's letters, no one would suspect what might be down there. Like the tape says, it's just legend."

Thinking there could be more than just the Château that went with the property, Maggie said nothing. They still had to prove that Theory 3 had merit, and something besides the beautiful buildings was here.

In five minutes the three people were standing on the walkway that led to the front door of the house. Bernard told them about in the Château; the one Belle Skinner lived in where the coins were found. "It's owned by a teacher and his wife; they have two children, and are away on holiday. I expect them back tonight. Look around the outside of the house. I'm sure they won't mind. Perhaps in the morning, I can get them to show you the inside. I have opened up the Church and the Museums for you. The Abbey is undergoing repairs, and is not accessible. The Chalet is private, and the owners are away, so it must be kept locked. Please be careful in the Church to not disturb anything. There are old sculptures in it. The Museum is full of paintings of Louise Cottin. She lived here and painted in the 1930s and 1940s. Her works are collected throughout Europe. I don't usually let anyone into the buildings, but being from Holyoke buys you some favors. My mother would like to meet you, too. Perhaps, after you visit Miss Skinner's house tomorrow. She is interested in everyone who asks about Miss Skinner, and told me to make

Belle Skinner's french cottage in Hattonchâtel where the coins were found

sure you come to see her."

Shaking their hands politely, Bernard walked away, leaving John and Maggie in the front yard of Belle Skinner's house next to a garage. It was not large in size in comparison to the Château or the Chalet, but it appeared to be a comfortable one. It was a small two-storied house. It was crème colored with white trim and a brown roof. There was a brick walkway that led from the Rue de Château to the front door. To its right in the center of the yard was an area that was gated by a square, six foot, iron fence. Peering down, it looked like they saw seven stairs that led to a door. Whatever was behind the door appeared to go under the ground. Turning their attention back to the house, and looking in through the windows, the main room seemed to be a living area that overlooked the other side of the mountain with a huge fireplace on the left side of the room. Walking to the side of the house that was on the Rue des Arcades, they saw a café across the street that was not open. When they reached the back of Belle's house, they saw it had a small kitchen, and what looked like a family room beside it. The bedrooms on the second floor were impossible to see from street level, but looking at the number of windows John guessed there were three of them. Returning to the front where the pathway was, they noticed a patio to the right. There was only a small amount of snow on the ground, so the path was clear, and the clay colored patio could be distinguished from it.

Looking down, John saw it first, and said to Maggie, "Isn't that a garden down there?" He pointed to an icy area about thirty feet away from them.

Seeing it, Maggie knew what he meant. "It sure looks like one. I wonder if that's where the coins were found?"

"My thoughts exactly," John said. "Let's take a look." Walking down the stairs that led to a lower patio, Maggie stopped when she heard it again. John turned around to see what the matter was. "Something wrong?" he asked her.

"It rings every 15 minutes. I've been counting" Maggie said, listening to the loud ringing of the bell. "Can I ask you something John?"

"Sure, anything." He smiled up at her, wondering what it was she was thinking.

"Two weeks ago, did you ever think you would be standing with me outside a Royal Palace in the north of France, in a village called Hattonchâtel, in Belle Skinner's yard, walking down to the place where she found a stash of old Roman coins, hearing a bell ring that is called Sarah Isabelle Skinner?" Maggie smiled.

John appreciated what she was saying. "No Maggie, I didn't. But lately, I've had a change of heart. I think Belle has had something to do with it. Now I believe that anything is possible."

TWENTY TWO

After looking in the frozen gardens for any evidence of recent diggings, and finding none, as they expected, the two headed across the street to the Church. The front door was unlocked just as Bernard had told them it would be. Walking inside, the first thing they noticed was the dirty floor. Unlike the Château where the floors were polished marble and tile, the floor of the Church was dingy. There was an odor in the air that was not pleasant to smell. The Church looked unused. The 20 pews in the middle section were dusty, and the walls were crusted. The stained glass windows in all of the walls had not been wiped and were clouded. Looking at the large standing candleholder in the back of the Church, John saw that the burned candles had not been replaced. Thinking about the stories he read about the Curé, John thought that whoever it was that was the Curé now, was not taking care of the Church.

"Look's like it's not very busy around here," Maggie's words reinforced John's thoughts.

"We should ask Bernard if the villagers are still using it. Maybe there are not enough people here to say Mass regularly." John was confused. He expected the Church to look differently than it did. Walking up to the marble altar, he noticed that there was not a cross hanging over it. There was an iron light fixture, lowered, hanging loosely in the air. It used candles, not bulbs. Like the candleholders in the front, those in it were burned up. Looking at the coverings on the altar, John saw that they were not pressed. Holding back the holy linens of the tabernacle to get a better look at it, he saw stains on the cloth. The tabernacle was old, and made entirely of gold. It was locked. John was about to make a comment about it, when he turned to see Maggie kneeling in one of the pews, praying.

Not wanting to disturb Maggie, John walked into the back section of the Church, expecting it to be a sacristy. It was not. He remembered that one part of the Church had been built in the 15th century and the other in the 14th century. What he was looking at was obviously the older

Church. It was amazing to see the difference. Unlike the Church he first walked into, this one had an atmosphere that was entirely different. It was cleaner and looked like someone was taking care of it. By today's standards, its physical condition was not at all what one would expect to find in a famous monastery. But, being a chapel more than a Church, John guessed that it had been the monks who held their services here. Therefore, it most likely had not been used in over a century. Then, out of nowhere, it hit him. Seeing and feeling what was in there, he realized where he actually was. He was in a shrine. It was incredible. It was timeless. Not being a member of the religious organization, Belle had preserved a sacred Catholic shrine from the middle ages.

John went to the front of the chapel to look at the altar. Unlike the one in the first Church, this one was made of stone, and was built into the wall behind it. Moving the coverings as he had with the first one, he found that this tabernacle was not gold, but stone, and was built in as part of the altar. There were elaborate carvings on it, and it looked to be very old. Looking up, John saw that there was a small cross above it, resting on the top of the tabernacle.

Walking to the back of the Church where John had come in, he saw it. The statue by Ligier Richier, the one the people from Wales had told him was there. It had been partially blocked by the door when he came in, and so he didn't notice it. Even though the lighting was bad in the chapel, even from a distance, John could see that it was magnificent. Walking back to it, he noticed a wall switch to turn the light on. Turning it, a series of dim lights went on that provided the chapel with a small amount of light. When he reached the ropes surrounding the sculpture he saw that there was a chair there. On it were information cards with descriptions of the famous sculptor's creation in several different languages. John picked them up, and finding the one in English, he read it.

"Take time to contemplate the Triptych carved in 1523, and reputed to be the work of Ligier Richier. The flight lines sculptured by the held-out arms of the characters in the central part attract ones eye toward the crucified body of Christ. Not less than three houses take place in a confined space, and the stateliness and the hauntedness of their look form a contrast with the most mournful mark of the scene. Jesus Christ's mother, her body broken by the pain, who is collapsing in the lower left corner. The left compartment describes the suffering man in the Calvary. We will recall the legend of Veronique wiping Jesus Christ's face as he was kneeling down and the print of his face remaining on the linen. The right panel evokes the bringing down into the grave. As we watch this scene, we must look down with our feelings toward the body that is going to disappear."

Holding the laminated card in his hand, John went closer to the carving, and began to match up the descriptions with what he saw. The triptych seemed to come alive as he did this. It was eerie. As he was doing this, Maggie came into the chapel and startled John. His back was to the door, and not seeing her, his body tensed sharply as he felt her next to him.

Seeing John's reaction, Maggie asked, "What's the matter, why so jumpy?"

Not answering her directly, he said, "This is the statue the people from Wales were talking about." He held out the card for her to read about it. Looking at him strangely, she read it. As Maggie did, John sat down on the chair that was next to him where the cards had been.

When Maggie finished reading she asked, "Are you OK?" As she said the words she began to feel the energy, too. Even though there was no one else in the chapel, there was something there that felt alive. The powerful sensations were unmistakable.

"It feels like there is something or someone in here," Maggie said, as she sat down next to him at the base of the large block of granite that the sculpture was set upon.

"Something is," John said, as he looked around the chapel, seeing nothing. "Let's get some air. I feel a little queasy, and it's definitely not due to jet lag and time zone changes."

Once outside the two of them discussed what had just happened in the chapel. They both had sensed the same presence. "Have you ever felt that before, the energy that is in there?" John asked Maggie.

"No. Sometimes when I pray and meditate on something in church, I feel different sensations. But, it's different in there. Someone holy has been here, and left their mark upon this place." Thinking about her readings about those sacred people who were canonized, Maggie thought that it might have been a saint or saints.

Letting their emotions settle back to normal Maggie and John sat for minutes on a wall outside the Churches, saying nothing more. A cold wind blew at them from the end of the street where the rows of the village houses were. Deciding that they needed to get on, they got up and headed to the town hall where the museums were. It was a short walk up the Rue Miss Skinner to the town hall she had restored. Finding it easily, John and Maggie stopped at the first archway of the building in an alcove.

They saw the bronze plaque immediately, and recognized it, because Belle's face was on it. It was the one the people of the village dedicated to her. It was set into the inside wall that led to the long courtyard that was on the other side where the museums were. The writing on it said *"Hattonchâtel Reconnaissant A Bienfaitrice Miss Belle Skinner De Holyoke Massachusetts Etats Unis."*

Maggie translated it, "Hattonchâtel, in remembrance of our Benefactor, Miss Belle Skinner of Holyoke, Massachusetts, United States."

Opposite it, on the left outside wall, carved into it, they read *"To the Lamented Miss Belle Skinner, Their Magnificent Benefactress, The Inhabitants of Hattonchâtel Vow Unending Gratitude."*

"This is thrilling," Maggie said, as they finished reading the words together. "It's one thing to see pictures of it, but another to actually see it."

"Let's see what's in the museums," John said, as he took Maggie's arm

The Museum at Hattonchâtel

and led her into the courtyard. "Maybe they have some of the coins."

The Museum on their right had the lights turned on. Set against the building was a metal sign that was obviously used to direct people to the place where the artist's paintings were. It read, "Muse Louise Cottin."

Going in, the first thing they noticed was the difference in lighting between the building they were in now and the old Church. The Church's lighting system was antiquated. The lighting here was modern and bright. Bernard had been kind enough to turn the heat on, too. Unlike the Church where it was cold, the Museum was quite warm. It was like a pleasant greeting to them from the caretaker.

The Museum was divided into two separate rooms. The outer one was a reception area with a counter on the right with a cash register on it, and a number of different brochures describing the works of Louise Cottin. There were many tables in the room. Other pamphlets set out on the tables, described the art collections in the other villages and cities of the region. Being the scavenger she was, Maggie began picking up all of the literature, and reading some of it. John was more interested in looking at the second room, the gallery with the refinished shiny floors where the artist's work was displayed.

Moving from one painting to another, he saw the reason the villagers were so proud of the woman who came to live and paint in their village. Most of the paintings were landscapes. Louise Cottin captured the different seasons of France by her brilliant use of colors. One particular painting caught his attention. It was a scene looking down from Hattonchâtel to the lake below in the springtime. The Mirabelle trees were in full bloom, and the grass in the valley was plush and green. The contrast she painted, between the bright trees and the dark grass, was wonderful.

Maggie came into the room, and walked over to John to enjoy the painting with him. "It's nice, isn't it," she said.

"Just think Maggie, if Belle hadn't restored the village, Louise Cottin might never have painted these." He looked around the room, counting nineteen paintings.

"One creation produces another. The reverse is also true, John. Destruction produces disasters. It's an unwritten natural law. If Belle didn't make Hattonchâtel beautiful, none of these would be here."

John appreciated Maggie's insight and wanted to learn more about Belle's restoration. " I'm going to see what's in the other Museum."

"OK," Maggie responded. "I'll look around in here, and read some of the information in the pamphlets. My high school French is getting a good workout," she was being facetious. Maggie had been trying to read and speak the language of France since they had arrived, like everyone else.

Maggie was doing a pretty good job remembering, John thought, as he saw her take out the small dictionary she had been using to translate the words she didn't know. Understanding little French, John kidded himself, "better than mine," he said aloud, as he walked towards the second Museum that was about thirty feet away on the other side of the courtyard.

Entering the Museum, John found that unlike the building he just left, the heat was not on, and the one room Museum was cold. The lights were just as bright, but there was not much to see. A large table was in the middle of the room, but nothing was on it. Looking at the eight or so paintings hanging on the walls, John was not impressed. He expected something entirely different to be here. He thought he would find memorabilia that related to the village's restoration, but there was none.

Seeing a small locked glass case set in the corner of the room, John's heart skipped a beat. He thought that maybe there was one of the coins in it. Why would it be locked? After all, Belle's letters told them that she was the one who was paying for the Museum out of the money she expected to get from selling some of the coins. It seemed logical that at least one would be on display, somewhere. As John walked over, he could see that it was empty. Disappointed, he was about to leave and report to Maggie that there was nothing much to see here when he noticed a door ajar in the back of the room. John wondered if Bernard had left it this way on purpose.

Pushing open the door, John went in. It was a storage room filled with boxes and chairs. Moving the ones aside that blocked his way, John looked for a light switch on the wall, but there was none. Finally seeing a hanging string that was attached to an overhead light fixture, he pulled on the light. One small light from above provided only minimal light in the room. Looking around, he saw nothing but packed up crates and dusty, unused furniture. John was about to turn the light off and leave when he saw the picture above the fireplace. It was a photograph of Belle Skinner.

Moving closer to the picture, John saw another frame next to it that was covered. He took the picture of Belle down and put it next to the door. After he did this, he went back and took the other one down and then brought both of them into the Museum where there was better light. Taking off the covering of the second picture, John saw it was actually a collage of pictures showing several events commemorating the restoration of the village. He was looking at them when Maggie came in.

"What did you find?" she asked him, walking towards him.

"These were tucked away in the storage room. It seems that a few people have forgotten what was done here." John looked up at her not believing where he found them.

"What do you mean they were in a storage room?" Maggie said, looking around. "Where is the Museum Belle paid for? Where are all her things? This is supposed to be her Museum." Maggie wasn't sure what to make of it.

"It appears that this is all there is." John was flabbergasted. He stood up. "Where's the camera you've been taking all those pictures with?"

Maggie took it out from her pack. "Let me guess. You want me to take a few pictures of what you found in the back room."

"Yea. I think we need to document this one. When we get back to Holyoke, perhaps we can send the Mayor of the village some copies with a letter asking him why Belle's Museum is a storage closet."

After John put the pictures back where he found them, the two walked to their car. As they did, Maggie was thinking how unfairly the people of the village were treating the memories of what Belle had done here. It reminded her of the way some people were behaving in Holyoke and America. She recalled the one word Katherine had used when Maggie had asked her why she stayed in Holyoke, *respect.* It was haunting. By paying no respect now for the sacrifices made by others who came before them, the ones who made the city and the country strong, those in the present become weak.

TWENTY THREE

After taking their pictures, John and Maggie left the Museum that wasn't one, and went to their car. Having seen enough of the village for one day, they decided to break up the trip by heading off to one of the larger cities nearby. It was Maggie who suggested it. In reading through the information in the first Museum, she found that around 1920 the town of Nancy was the art center for northern France. A movement known as the Beaux Arts movement had its major activity in this city and there were a number of art museums there with all kinds of art from the period.

In that Belle liked art and the Beaux Arts style, and the painter she met on Mount Tom was possibly from this area, perhaps the painting he did at the Summit House might be in one of the collections. If they were lucky enough to find it, they could prove Tracey's Theory 2 as being more plausible.

So, at just about two o'clock, they set off on Route D 907 for the one-hour drive to Nancy, wanting to make one short stop, which was on the way. John thought it was important that they drive through the village of Foret d'Apremont to see what Holyoke adopted. There was supposed to be a water works building with Holyoke's name written on it. He wanted to see if it was still there. The trip would prove to be both successful and disheartening.

Driving into the village that Holyoke had adopted proved to be a good idea. It was a pleasant sight to see the name, *Place D' Holyoke,* written in blue and white on the side of a building in France. There was also a monument directly across from it that paid homage to the sacrifices made by French and American boys in the First World War. It was worth the effort to go there.

Nancy, on the other hand, had proved to be not as satisfying. After reading the materials in the brochures Maggie had picked up in Hattonchâtel, she was sure that they would find the elusive painting that

was done of the Connecticut Valley in one of the Beaux Arts museums there. It would have been so simple if they had. It was the romantic side in her that moved her to think this way. It would in some way prove that it was love that moved Belle Skinner to do what she did in France. So, they spent hours searching for it. First, they went to Le Musée Des Beaux-Arts a Nancy, and then to a number of the art galleries in and around the main square in the city, the famous Stanislas Square. After hours of looking through them, they found nothing. What they did discover though, was that some of the best confection shops in Lorraine were in Nancy. Making the best of the situation and visiting quite a few of them, both John and Maggie were going home with a good sampling of the finest chocolates made in France.

It was after nine o'clock by the time they got back to their hotel. After having a lovely dinner in the restaurant, they returned to John's room to talk. Sampling another valued product of the Lorraine region, a bottle of Cotes de Toul wine that John had bought in the hotel, the two discussed what they had learned so far to make sure they agreed upon, and shared everything. They were just about to begin their discussion when their cell phones rang simultaneously.

"I wonder who that could be." John said in jest, as Maggie flipped her phone open.

"Hi Maggie. How are you guys doing? I just wanted to make sure these things worked, and to check and make sure you made it to France safely." Tracey's voice was clear from across the ocean.

"We're fine," Maggie responded. "The flight was smooth, and we found our way to Hattonchâtel with only a few obstacles, only a couple wrong turns. The Château is amazing. It's much more impressive than the postcards or the images we downloaded. The place is a whole bloody castle. It's incredible."

"Have you had a chance to look around for anything specific yet, you know, the letters I gave you?" Tracey was fishing.

"Kind of, but we're not through yet," Maggie said. John interrupted her politely by asking for her phone to say hello.

When Tracey heard his voice she asked, "Do you agree with me about what's in her letters?" Tracey didn't have to tell him what she meant.

"Yes." John was short.

"Good, then let's see what you can find out. If either of you needs anything, call me. I have the number at the hotel in case the cell phones don't work. I'll call you back tomorrow or call me if you need or find out anything." Tracey was trying to be helpful.

"Maggie or I will call you if we find anything," John said, sensing her excitement and her motherly tendency to worry about her friends. They both hung up after saying a quick bye.

John told Maggie, "She said to have a good time, and to tell you that you have to buy dinner tomorrow night."

"She did not, did she? She wasn't serious, was she? She knows better." Maggie kidded with him, the wine taking effect.

"Did you know what Tracey was doing when she had me take you to the Yankee Pedlar that night?" John was curious.

"Not at first, but it wasn't hard to figure out once I thought about it."

"That's what I'm afraid of," John said. He decided that he was never going to come out on the up side, with both of them working together.

Sitting up quickly, Maggie stared at John. "Tunnels underground and between the buildings, like the ones described in the knight's tales, from the master's bedroom to the queen's quarters. I would imagine there are a whole series of passages running underneath the village like Bernard described. Hell, it was on the tape he played that they are there. You've read about them in books. The tunnels and catacombs were everywhere, under most castles in the event they had to escape from the attackers or in this case hide something. By now, you must believe there are some passages underneath Hattonchâtel?" Maggie accepted this as reasonable and took a sip of wine, waiting to see what John thought. Though he did not answer her verbally, his expression told her everything. Maggie put her head back down on the pillow. Thinking some more, she asked, "Do we know any more now than we did before about the coins?"

John didn't have to think much about this one. He had already gotten the information for them, "Yes, we do, quite a bit more." He went on to explain, "I had a short sleep last night, some things that didn't make sense kept me up. So, I went online and pulled down some information about what it was that bothered me. Belle's letter's refer to Roman coins that she found in the village that according to her date back to the 900s, correct?" John was asking Maggie to remember exactly what the letters said.

Maggie answered him, impressed that he would do this, wondering what he had found out. "That's right. At least that's what she wrote in her letters. Belle said that the oldest coins she discovered were from the 10th century. The others were from the 14th and 15th centuries. The most recent ones were dated 1517."

John was impressed with her memory. He went on to tell her what he had read, "Well Maggie, what I found out was that we are not dealing with Ancient Rome, because its history dates back roughly from 700 years B.C. to the time of Christ. We are therefore talking about what is called Imperial and Medieval Rome when we look at the dates of the coins that Belle found and their origins." He stopped, letting her mind begin to grasp the dates and the different cultures.

Nodding to John, Maggie was with him so far. He continued with what he had read about, "In the years 790-810, in what we now call France, the Frankish King Charles the Great, known as Charlemagne, had unified a good part of Western Europe, including parts of Germany, Switzerland, most of Italy and northern Spain. When he did, he attempted to revive many of the concepts of the Great Roman Empire. These included Roman political structure, Greek culture that placed high emphasis on understanding man's place in nature and democracy, and the Christian Religion that was fighting to maintain the influences of the Christian Pope in Rome."

Knowing the capacities of John's mind by now, confident that he would know the answer, Maggie asked, "Where did all of this begin?"

"History records the Imperial Roman Era and its Caesars as dating back many centuries before Christ's birth. But, it became severely fragmented after his death. A revitalized Imperial Roman Empire began with the foundation of Constantinople in 300 A.D., and lasted, in parts, until the 15th century. The Empire really took hold with the Emperor Justinian I who ruled it with the help of his bewitching Cleopatra-type Empress, Theodora, beginning around 500. Their armies conquered many of the countries that comprised the former Imperial Roman Empire by this time. They were in power until his death in 565, and were supposed to have been amassed an incredible fortune, because of their conquests. Some say it was all because of Theodora. Owing to their strong control over the world, they were able to bring back many of the cultures, ideas and opulence of the Roman Empire's past. This period of history is known as the Byzantine era, because of the name of the city that occupied the site before Constantinople was built, Byzantium."

Maggie interrupted, "Where was Constantinople?"

"Istanbul, Turkey," John replied, waiting for her to ask another question. When she didn't he continued, "Constantinople was the center of the Byzantine Empire. The Pope in Rome and his Christian kings had little influence over the countries of Europe during this time." Maggie nodded that she understood and he went on, "After their deaths, lesser men governed the empire, and it became fragmented again. While Byzantine armies held off the attacks of the Germanic kings in North Africa, Italy and parts of Spain, the rise of Islam tore away the rich provinces of Egypt and Syria. There was not much affection between the Frankish emperors in the west and the Greek emperors in the east. From the 5th through the 8th centuries, even though the eastern part of the Byzantine Empire fought off the barbarian attacks, the Germanic kings and chieftains overwhelmed most of the western part of the Roman Empire. The lands from beyond the Rhine river and the Alpine passes, Britain, Gaul, Spain, North Africa and Italy, were occupied by the Germanic Angels, Saxons, Franks, Vandals, and Goths. In these former Roman provinces they set up loosely organized kingdoms. It became a time of constant warfare and upheavals between the kings. The Germanic kings and chiefs fought constantly. In their wake, a great deal of culture and civility in the lands of the former Roman Empire were lost. The only stronghold that tied these lands together was Christianity. The process of reconverting the kingdoms to the vanished Greco-Roman classical past began and ended in the 8th century. It culminated with the victories of King Charles, known as Charlemagne, and the restoration of the Pope's influences in much of the world in 800. By this time, Charlemagne was well on his way to conquering most of Europe. With the rise of Charlemagne, a rival to Constantinople's dominance arose. When Pope Leo III named Charlemagne, Roman Emperor, the world changed. Charlemagne was a modern thinker who embraced the concepts of the Greek and Roman cultures. He surrounded himself with only the most prudent and wise men, and made them his archbishops and bishops. Together, with his abbots and advisers, he sent them out throughout his kingdom to establish laws, God's laws, under which the lands were to be governed. Under his rule, Western Europe was unified to a greater extent than it would be again, until our day. What we now call France was the heart of his empire. But his armies dominated most of Europe by 810. The Carolingian Europe, as it was called, was vast forests. Towns that the Romans had built had been reduced almost to ruins. Only merchants with guards ventured into the forests to trade their salts, furs, animal hides and slaves. Monasteries were scattered, but substantial, and the monks who lived there were the only ones left in the territories that could read or write. The warriors and the bishops and abbots were kinsmen by necessity, and they shared everything in order to survive. By ceaseless wars, Charlemagne brought these peoples together, and brought the vast wildernesses into his kingdom, exposing his ideas. The abbots and the strong laymen were his ministers. They made sure the laws written by Charlemagne were known and obeyed throughout the empire. His kingdom was ruled with a sense of fairness, but with a strong hand by his armies. He issued, and his emissaries enforced, his directives, those that were approved by the Pope in Rome. As in the old days, tributes were collected by his collectors, those men he sent out to keep order in his kingdom. All of the valuables were brought back to him in France. It appears he amassed a tidy sum from his subjects, and no one knows what he did with it. His reign lasted from 771 A.D. until 814 A.D. When he died there were many upheavals and changes in the territories he ruled. When the Pope first proclaimed Charlemagne, the Roman Emperor, those belonging to the Byzantium sects who were not controlled by either Charlemagne or Christianity, challenged his Imperial authority over much of Europe and the rest of the Byzantine territory. As a result of this, in the centuries that followed the downfall of Charlemagne's empire, wars broke out incessantly, and up until 1346 the countries of Europe existed in states of constant conflicts. It appears that some believed Charlemagne left a treasury full of gold somewhere, and this in part contributed to the wars. They all wanted it." John stopped for Maggie to comprehend the history leading up to the fall of Charlemagne.

"What happened in 1346?" Maggie asked him, ready for more.

"Give me a minute, and I'll tell you. First, let's discuss the coins. The age Belle describes in her letters gives us a lot of information about them. One of the most significant things Charlemagne may have done in unifying his kingdom was to begin to replace the old barter systems that existed in all of the countries for trading goods, with the initial concepts of a money based system. He collected gold, silver and jewelry from his subjects. He melted the metals down to make money, mostly coins. The jewels were kept separate. Charlemagne's empire really collapsed because of internal conflicts; the rulers of his territories sought his treasures. Added to the domestic problems, there were outside assaults from Vikings, Hungarians and the Arabs. None of them ever found his treasure. Other warriors fought off the Arabs and by the year 1000, the Vikings and Hungarians had conquered most of Charlemagne's kingdom as Christian Europeans. Around this year, Europe experienced a remarkable surge of growth and economic development, and this lasted until the 1300s. Owing to Charlemagne's idea, money and credit increasingly replaced barter as a form of trade, and the merchants and landowners used coins to buy and sell goods and other properties. You're correct, Belle describes her coins as being mostly from the 14th and 15th centuries, but she does also say that the oldest are from the 10th century. That means that someone had set up mints somewhere, maybe Charlemagne. That would make those coins precious. Finding the mints, well, who knows what's there?" John just looked at Maggie, telling her what they could be sitting on top of.

"What happened in 1346, John?" Maggie was more interested in this than the money.

Understanding her need to know he told her. "It has been dated as happening between 1346 through 1348, Maggie. It was the epidemics of the Black Death, the Bubonic Plague that killed about one-third of the population of Europe. In Italy and some other more populated areas and cities, the death tolls were much higher. Losses in China were comparable to those in Europe. It has been called the single worst disaster in human history. This documented catastrophe was only the first of a series of outbreaks that would ravage Eurasia, until late in the 18th century." John's description of the worldwide epidemic was brief, but he added one last thought after reading about it, "It's hard to continue treasure hunting when you're burning up with fever. So, the gold in the mints was safe from pillagers for a couple of hundred years while the disease claimed all of those lives." Maggie had gotten her answer that was so important to her.

"So much for the value of Charlemagne's money system," she said, agreeing with him. "If you have the plague, money doesn't seem to matter. Even though it appears someone continued to run the mints while the epidemic was raging throughout Europe." Maggie wondered who it was.

"Don't try to explain human nature Maggie. It's impossible. But we don't have the disease and neither did Belle. So, we can concern ourselves with the gold and silver coins that were probably minted somewhere around here. The coins that Belle describes in her letters have to be some of the earliest made by the successors of Charlemagne's 'Roman Empire.' In that the major conquests of Charlemagne's territories and possessions were in and around France, it makes sense that the mints, and the vaults of his successors were here, too." John was assuming that this was the way it happened.

"So, it wasn't necessarily money minted by the Romans. It was the coins of the successors to the Romans, those who conquered the territories of Charlemagne's empire?" Maggie wanted to see if this was accurate according to what John had read and believed.

"If we stay with the dates of history, and the dates documented by Belle Skinner's writings, that is what I come up with. Don't forget these coins are only the ones that were found on the surface. If someone did some serious excavating they might find older ones, maybe some from Charlemagne's time. If they did, you wouldn't be able to put a price on them. Everyone knew Charlemagne spent a great deal of time here at the Château. For thousands of years after he died, many came looking for the hidden treasury they thought might be here." John was speculating, based upon recorded history, the accuracy of Belle's letters, and the newspaper documentation they had read that the coins were authentic.

Maggie sat up again, thinking about what John was saying. She agreed with him that if Belle found coins dating back to the 10th century, it seemed reasonable there might be older ones here. She also thought he was correct, that those who made the ones found in the 11th, 14th and 15th centuries probably did find a mint after taking over the Château, and used its presses to make their own coins. Why move it? They took advantage of it. They brought their own gold and silver here and turned it into money the same way others had. Looking at John who was imagining what could be under their village, Maggie asked him something else, "Do you think Belle knew about all of this, before she came here?" Her question was a good one.

Trying to decide how to answer her, John finally said, "Before she found the coins, *no*. But, I do think she was aware that she was restoring a historic, medieval village. After she found the coins, absolutely, *yes*. Belle was a student of French history. She took many courses at Vassar on the subject, and could speak and read the language like a citizen. You remember how she wrote Katherine that she was going to correct her nephew's letters, the ones he wrote to her in French, so he could learn from his mistakes. She had to know about Charlemagne, about his battles for the kingdoms. When she saw the coins, Belle was smart enough to make the connection between those that conquered him, and the coins she found here in Hattonchâtel. Belle could trace the dates and history almost as easily as I did. We both know how smart she was. For her, this was an easy task." What John was saying was true.

"Do you think we should call Tracey?" Maggie asked him. "Or someone else."

"I'll email her at her house to read up on Charlemagne, to study European history for a few hundred years after he died. She'll get the message. But besides doing that, all we have for sure is a priest in the 1920s who was looking out for his diocese's interests, and a museum that is missing a lot of Roman coins that are supposed to be there, according to Belle's letters. I think we have to be careful about what we send over the net. As far as the proof of the coins, we really don't have much that is concrete, except what's in Belles letters, and the news accounts that Tracey gave us. We haven't uncovered anything here that is news. Until we do, I think we just have to keep searching, cautiously." John was right in thinking this way. They had to have evidence to prove what they were thinking.

Listening to what he was saying, Maggie was thinking about how excited Belle must have been when she looked at the Roman coins for the first time, knowing that she had perhaps uncovered a treasure that dated back many centuries. Wondering what Belle felt, Maggie looked at John and smiled, appreciating his amazing evaluations, and being mindful of the need to document everything.

Who would have thought the winds of change that blew her into the doorway at Yale would have brought her here, where Belle had changed so much? Belle's antique collection of fine musical instruments was the beginning of a treasure of discoveries. Maggie thought about how interesting life is and so unexpected, anything can happen.

Twenty Four

Wednesday, January 19th, 2005

The following morning John and Maggie went back to Hattonchâtel to meet with Bernard and the teacher to see the house Belle Skinner lived in. Driving down the Rue du Château they saw the two men waiting for them outside the guardhouse where Bernard and his mother lived. Parking next to it on the dirt, they got out of their car and went to join them.

Speaking English with his pleasant French accent, Bernard greeted them. "Good Morning, Bonjour," he said. "How are you both this morning?" Not waiting for a reply he said, "This is Andre Marie, the man I told you about, who owns Miss Skinner's house."

Holding out his hand, Andre Marie showed proper manners by greeting Maggie first, "Bonjour. Welcome to our village." She could tell by the way he talked that he spoke fluent English.

"Bonjour," Maggie replied, noticing that the man was only a few years younger than Bernard. He had light brown hair, not gray, and was very neatly dressed. "I'm Maggie O'Reilly."

Stepping in and shaking Andre's hand, John was courteous, "Hello, My name is John Merrick. It's nice of you to do this."

"I understand you want to see my house," Andre said, making sure they still did.

"We would appreciate it. We have come a long way to learn more about what Miss Skinner did here. Seeing where she lived would be most helpful," John said.

"No problem. I don't usually like to let people in, but Bernard tells me you are from Holyoke, the city of Miss Skinner."

"I live there. Maggie is fast becoming a new member of the community." John said smiling.

"Come with me, then. We will start inside. After that, I will show you the grounds. The warmth of the house will make you more comfortable.

It is chilly out." Andre started to walk with them to his front gate, passing by his garage. Turning around he told Bernard, "I'll bring them back to you in about an hour or two."

As they walked the fifty steps to the gate, a part of the film they had seen at Wistariahurst shot into John's mind. There was a clip in it that showed Belle opening the doors of a garage to let a car out. The one they were walking by. Opening the gate, Andre began to explain how he came to own the house, "In 1973; the Bishop of Verdun put a lot of property up for sale in the village. I was looking with my wife for a house, and seeing this, we had to have it. It was perfect for us, and the price was low. I began to learn of its history after I put down a payment on it. The real estate people were quite informative. Knowing that Miss Skinner lived here made it more valuable to us."

Andre directed them to the front of the house, briefly explaining what he had planted in the flower garden along the path. "It's beautiful here when everything is in bloom." He briefly explained the front of the house to them as he opened the door. "It was designed to be a short-term home for Miss Skinner, and looks more like a cottage than a house. That's why it has the shutters all around it. There are six rooms in it. The main room is on the right side, overlooking the backside of the village.

Entering the house, being the gentleman he was, Andre helped Maggie off with her coat, and took John's to hang up on the hooks that were on the wall. "Please, make yourselves at home. Can I get you anything to drink, coffee or tea?"

"No, thank you," they both replied, having had many cups of coffee before they came.

Thinking she had too much, Maggie said. "Could I use the bathroom?"

"Certainly, Maggie. It's down the hall to the left. The light switch is on the wall." As Maggie walked away the two men began to talk.

"You teach what?" John asked him, trying to be friendly.

"Agriculture, at several of the schools in Lorraine. I teach the children how to farm. I am looking to retire in a few years. This will be the perfect place to do it. My wife and I have two children that are almost ready to graduate from college. Once they do, I want to concentrate on my passion."

"What's that?" John asked him.

"Woodworking. I am a fine furniture maker. I became interested in this when I saw some of the pieces that were left here in the house. Of course the Bishop sold most of the others at auction, but a few items that belonged to Miss Skinner were left behind. They are in the living room." Maggie came back to them as he was finishing his sentence. "Let's go there, it's the highlight of the house." Opening a door to their right, Andre led them into a brightly colored room with expensive looking oak floors that shined brightly up at them.

For some reason the floorboards caught John's attention. It was because of the way they were pieced together. "I've never seen floors cut like this," John said. "What are they, one foot boards?"

"Yes, very different, isn't it. Someone had imagination. They are angled to match one another. It is quite unique. As is the fireplace." He moved them into the center of the room to look at it. "It is a smaller duplicate of the ones that are in the Château. All were made in Germany." John and Maggie looked closer to see the intricate work of the huge fireplace. "There is of course a modern heating system in the house, but we use this on occasion. There is nothing like a fire to make a house more pleasant."

"Look at the view," Maggie said, looking out the windows at the valley.

"It's quite a sight, isn't it? It's why Miss Skinner had so many windows put into this room. She wanted the light and the sight to come in. Like us, she must have enjoyed looking out them with a fire blazing in the fireplace."

"This buffet is one of the pieces that was left, as was that tall hutch. Whoever moved the furniture out apparently decided that they would not fit through the front door. They were smart in not trying to move them. They would have been damaged. The furniture had to have been made in the house. The way the pieces are constructed is unique. Someone who made only fine furniture made these," Andre said, looking at John. "Seeing the quality of the craftsmanship stimulated me to try to make others like them."

The room was not made to be formal, as one would expect in the living room of a house Belle Skinner lived in. Even though it had been remodeled, and the rest of the furniture in the room was somewhat modern, the original design was elegant, but not overly impressive. The living room was made to be enjoyed and not to be a showpiece. Looking up, John saw the mahogany beams that lined the ceiling. Then he noticed the woodwork which, like the furniture was crafted by an expert.

Seeing John look around, Andre said, "She used only the finest materials in rebuilding this house. Everything in it is top caliber." Pausing for a minute to let them get a good feel for the room, he added, "The kitchen and family rooms are in the back of the house."

Showing them the simple kitchen and the family rooms with the wide screen television in it, the teacher began to explain what he knew about Belle living here. "She apparently was rebuilding the Château for herself, but needed a place to stay while the work was being done. This house was more than adequate for her to live in temporarily. Since moving here, I have had several discussions with the older people in the village whose parents were here when she was. They say her architect lived here for a time when she was away. But Miss Skinner and her friend inhabited the house most of the time when she came to the village to check on the work being done here.

Andre directed them to the hallway that led to the second floor. Passing by the bathroom, he made a cute comment looking at Maggie, "What can you say about a bathroom, other than, we are planning on remodeling it in the spring?" John had something to say about it. He needed to use it.

When John rejoined them, they all walked to the spiral staircase that led up to the second floor. It was not an ordinary one, it was smaller. There was just enough room for one person at a time to walk up. It was tight.

Maggie pictured Belle, walking up the staircase each night to go to bed, and compared it to the sight of the actress who played Belle for them, walking up the elaborate staircase in the Skinner mansion in Holyoke. Maggie almost laughed out loud, thinking that the real Belle must have had quite a light side to her to put up with this.

The three bedrooms on the second floor were all about the same size and were small. There was just about enough room in each of them for a bed and dresser. There were built-in closets in all of them that looked like they were add-ons and not part of the original house. In five minutes, the three people were sitting in the living room discussing the history of the house and what Andre knew about Belle Skinner.

"I have no family that lived here when she did. I guess I'm an outsider. Slowly they are accepting my family as being villagers. But the ones that have been here forever value their heritage. Not interrupting Andre, John thought about the previous day at the Museum. "What

Miss Skinner did here was historic," Andre continued. "She is a legend to not only the people of Hattonchâtel, but to many in the Lorraine Valley. They all know what she did here. They have but to look up at the Château and see its beauty to appreciate what she did for France. She captured a piece of history back for them."

Finishing the sentence, Andre walked over to the buffet and took out a picture book. Andre handed it to John, and he and Maggie began to look at the photos inside. They were of the events that took place during the time of the reconstruction. Some showed the work being done on the various buildings, and others the celebrations held to honor Belle Skinner. After they reached the last page, Maggie asked Andre, "Where did you get this?"

"I found it in an old trunk that was left in one of the bedrooms with the tape."

"What tape?" John asked quickly.

"The one the government of France had made of the events that took place here in the village. President Poincare wanted to have historical documentation of the celebrations that took place here, so he hired a photographer to make a film. Apparently, a few copies were made of it, and I have one." Andre didn't think it was extraordinary for him to have it. John and Maggie did.

"Can we see it?" Maggie asked him, just a split second before John's mouth opened to ask the same question.

"Of course. It's in the family room."

Minutes later, after having some trouble finding it among the many VHS tapes in the closet, Andre put the tape he thought was the right one into the player. He was happy to see he had the right one when the first sequences appeared on the screen. He didn't want to disappoint Maggie and John by not being able to find it. The tape they watched was not the same one that they had seen at Wistariahurst, the one Belle had brought back. This film was made to be of much better quality, the pictures clearer and the people more easily distinguishable from one another. It showed many things that were not on the one in Holyoke. There were sequences of the celebrations that were similar but the ones on this film were longer and more detailed. There were also many sections showing the entire village reconstruction project that were not on Belle's film. The last part of the film showed an old woman, the grandmother of the village, bringing up a load of clothes from the old water laundry, down at the bottom of the mountain where the women had to do their wash, before Belle built the one that was at the entrance to the village. Once the film was over, Andre asked if they had any questions. They didn't, and thanked him for showing it to them.

John made a mental note to ask him for a copy of it when the time was right. He didn't want Andre to think he was too aggressive. The teacher was a very pleasant man, and was doing everything he could to be helpful. The last thing John wanted to do was offend him. John would write down the exact spelling of his name and address to write to Andre when they got back to the States.

Maggie had a question, but it did not relate to the film. "What do you know about the underground passages?"

"The ones that lead from the Château to the Church and this house?" Andre answered her with a question."

"Yes," she said.

"They have been sealed off, a result of the bombings of the First World War. Parts of them are accessible, but not for any lengths of distance. Would you like to see some of them?" John and Maggie looked at each other in amazement. Like the film, the passages were not a big thing to the teacher. To them all of this was astonishing.

"Please," John answered him.

Smiling, the teacher got up and said, "Then lets get our coats on. The entrance is outside, in the front yard."

The back, iron gated area, that Maggie and John had seen the day before, was the entrance to the underground caves. Andre explained to them as he unlocked the gate that he kept it locked so none of the children of the village would get in. He also kept the light green doors at the bottom fastened for the same reason.

What they saw when they entered the tunnel-like cave was that it was being used as a wine cellar. There was a rustic looking table there with an empty bottle of wine on it, and empty wood crates were being used to sit on. "Me and the boys like to come down here on the weekends and play cards. It's quiet and we don't bother the wife and kids with our drinking. There's not a lot to do here in the bad weather, so a few toasts are made." He was telling them about how the village men spent some of their nights together. Looking around, by pointing the beams of the flashlights Andre had given them, they saw a number of racks filled with what appeared to be different wines.

"I'm a bit of a connoisseur," Andre said, explaining the bottles of wine. "It makes a wonderful wine cellar. I've been stashing these away for years. The passages start over there." He pointed his own flashlight to one of the corners of the tunnel. "It's blocked up like I told you. There are two or three of them. Without clearing them out, it's hard to tell how many are there."

"Have you ever tried to dig it out?" John asked him.

"No reason to. Besides, if as everyone in the village says, the passages run to the Château, if I started to move the dirt, it could cause a cave in, anywhere between here and there. The last thing I need is to have to repair damages. I'm a teacher, and make only enough money to get by. I don't go looking for expensive troubles. The passages have been closed off since the Germans bombed this place. Better to leave well enough alone." He directed his beam to another side of the cave. "I think there is another one over there."

John and Maggie's eyes followed his light. In the other corner there was a deep hole in the ground. Walking over to it, John asked him, "How deep is it?"

"About twenty feet. I was curious enough when I first saw it to send a line down to measure it."

"This is remarkable. The tape recording that Bernard played for us yesterday said that there were several passages. Some lead here, some to the Church, and he said there is a crypt somewhere under the Château." Maggie was asking him if he knew any more about them.

"We all have heard the legends. When I moved into the village, and saw these tunnels, I did some asking around. Everyone here knows there are real possibilities, but no one in the village had the money to open them up. The consensus was that it was best to leave well enough alone. Like I said, the last thing anyone in the village needs is to have to repair caved in streets or grounds because of useless diggings."

Walking back up the stone steps that led down to the cave, John said, "Do you know about the coins being found here?"

"The ones Miss Skinner found, of course I do," Andre answered him. "Some were found in the cellar of the house, which might be connected to this cave, and some in the gardens out back. But, the ones she found were the only ones uncovered. From what I have been told, there were not many of them, only a few pots. Come with me, I'll show you where the gardens are." Andre walked them to the right side of the house that looked out over the fortress wall that guarded the village. "Be careful, it's icy" he said, as they began to go down the twelve steps to the lower patio and gardens.

Once down safely, he pointed to an area that was in front of the cellar of the garage. You two are the first people to come here in decades that know about them. The discovery was made somewhere in this area. As you can see, it's below street level, so, yes, we have all thought there could be more, that the passages might lead somewhere. But, like I said, no, we have not dug for them. The coins were uncovered a long time ago. Most people have forgotten that they were ever found. So, there is little interest in the subject. It's old news. Like I said, the dangers far outweigh the prospects of finding another pot or two that is full of them."

Looking at his watch Andre said, "I think it is time to return you to Bernard. He said something about his mother wanting to meet with you. We can't keep her waiting. It's impolite. After all, she is the grandmother of the village now." Waving goodbye, after thanking him for being such a congenial host, Maggie and John latched the front gate behind them and turned towards Bernard's house and started walking.

Maggie stopped, looked at John, and said, "Another pot or two? That's all the villagers think might still be here?"

"Apparently." John had heard what Andre said as clearly as Maggie did. Snickering, John added in a childlike voice, "Let's go to see what's in Grandma's house."

Appreciating the humor of his storybook comment, Maggie joined in. She began skipping down the street like a schoolgirl, and didn't stop until she reached the walkway of the guardhouse. Knocking on the door while trying his best to stop laughing, John waited for someone to open it, so he and Maggie could go in.

A voice from behind them caught their attention. It was Bernard, and he was locking up the door next to the large front gate of the Château.

"The work never ends around here." He hurried to join them. "Mother is anxious to meet you," he said as he let them in. "I hope she is through with her cleaning. She's always cleaning." Saying something in French to himself that they couldn't understand, Bernard let them in. John thought Bernard was acting strangely. He seemed quite nervous and was very dirty.

An old lady was sitting in a high backed chair in a small sitting room not far from the door, holding a cup of tea. She smiled when she saw them come in. She had to be at least ninety years old, with a wonderfully sculptured type of face that was very beautiful. Her white hair flowed down gracefully to her shoulders and was obviously combed out sometime this morning to be very neat looking. The woman looked like she was going somewhere special. She was dressed in an elegant beige suit, a white silk blouse and was wearing shoes that complemented her outfit. Expecting guests, she had dressed up. Seeing them come closer, she put her cup of tea down on a table and looked to be preparing herself to meet them.

"Hello," she said, as they stood in front of her. The smile on her face told them she had been waiting for them.

"Hello." Maggie returned the greeting, not knowing what else to say.

"You are from Holyoke?" the old woman knew they were. Passing by her, Bernard handed his mother something, and then went to the bathroom to get cleaned up.

"Yes," John answered for them, not qualifying his answer this time. "I'm John Merrick, and this is Maggie O'Reilly."

The smile on the old woman's face was peaceful. "You came here, because of Miss Skinner."

"Yes." John didn't know exactly what to say, so he said no more.

"I'm sorry, John. My name is Michelle Dubois. Tell me why you are here, please?" Her clear hazel green eyes were captivating.

"Michelle, I'm sorry, but I don't understand." John and Maggie just stood in front of the woman, waiting for her to explain what she was asking them. Maggie looked at John wondering what they should say.

"What's to think about?" Seeing their dilemma, Michelle made the decision for them. "Hell, I'm just an old lady wanting to talk about my Aunt Prudence." The words Michelle said sent a shock wave through Maggie and John.

"Prudence Lagogue was your Aunt?" John asked Michelle.

"Well kind of. I'll let Bernard explain some of the details, children. We have a lot to talk about," the old woman started to get up. It was an effort for her to do so. She was obviously hurting as she did. John helped Michelle get out of the chair and stand up. Taking a few steps to get her balance, favoring one hip, it was obvious the woman had a hard time walking. But, once she got going, she moved quickly.

"Please sit." Michelle motioned to the chairs in the room. "I'll get you both a cup of tea," she said, not asking them if they wanted one. "It may be sunny out, but the cold could come back with a vengeance. It's best if you keep warm tea in you," she said, being the caring person she was.

John smiled at Maggie. His look told Maggie that he thought the old woman was nice. Maggie had the same feelings as John did about the reception Michelle gave them. Maggie liked her already.

Bernard had freshened up and was helping his mother in the kitchen. Thinking they couldn't hear her, Maggie asked John, "Do you think Prudence was really her aunt?" She whispered the words, wondering.

"There's only one way to find out," John answered. "We listen to what she has to say."

"It usually never gets bitter cold at this time of the year, but you never know what to expect when you live on a mountain. It's best to keep your body temperature up by drinking hot liquids." Michelle reinforced what she said before as they came in with the tea.

Maggie noticed the strong physical similarities between Michelle and Bernard. The facial features between the mother and son were almost identical. Bernard, seeing Maggie look at him and then his mother, comparing them, said, "She's cuter," he kidded, looking at his mother, fondly. He started to serve the tea from a silver tray.

"Not here, Bernard," the old woman shouted at him. It was because her hearing was not so keen that she said her words loudly. "Guests are served in the living room." Michelle said nothing more. She just shuffled herself into the sitting area where a fire was burning, motioning with her fingers for Maggie and John to follow her in. Once in the room, they saw the picture of Belle Skinner hanging over the fireplace. Next to it was one of Prudence Lagogue.

Ten minutes later, sipping warm tea, the four people began to get down to business. Bernard started their discussions by telling them why he wanted them to talk with his mother. "It's because you told me you were from Holyoke. You're the first people to come here in ages from there." Bernard knew where to begin.

John corrected him this time, "I'm from Holyoke. Maggie is not." He ignored the second part of his statement for the moment letting Bernard go on.

"You came to Hattonchâtel, because of the coins, the ones found by Belle Skinner." Bernard got right to the point. "It's why you were asking me about the passages under the village and the Château."

"The Roman coins are of some interest to us, but the main reason we came is because we wanted to see what Belle Skinner did here." Maggie was being somewhat truthful.

Michelle spoke next, "I'm almost a hundred years old. I think I have very little time left here on this earth. So, I don't play games like the others do. I don't waste my time. I asked you to visit, because I would like to tell you a little story. It's about things that happened a long time ago. It involves me, my family, Belle Skinner and our Aunt Prudence. Miss Skinner told me one day that someone from Holyoke would come here asking questions. May I continue?" She leaned forward getting herself more comfortable waiting for them to answer.

"Yes, please do," John said, liking the old woman's straightforward approach. But, he did not understand the part about what Belle had told her.

"I would like to hear about it," Maggie said, also appreciating Michelle's character.

"Before I do, what do you think of our village?" Michelle asked, being curious.

John just sat in his chair, saying nothing, letting Maggie answer. "It's beautiful, Michelle. We feel like we're in another world up here." Maggie gave her a quick response, anxious to hear what Michelle had to share.

After hearing this, the old lady began to tell her tale, the one that would explain why they were living in Belle Skinner's village, and why they called Prudence their aunt. "It was quite a sight, to see the great lady walking in the village for the first time. We had heard she was coming, but many of us thought she was a wish that may not come true. We had been told that our village was to be rebuilt. That it would look exactly like it did before it was destroyed. It wasn't that we didn't believe the promises of the grown-ups, it's just that we had never known anything different than the horror of war. I was born just before the occupation here, so I had no idea what the Château looked like before they blew it to pieces. Once they did, the Germans had let some of the villagers live, mostly the women, for amusement, only a few of the men, for slaves. The week they were driven out, my mother and father joined the fighting, trying to reclaim our home, hating the Germans for what they did here. I was kept in hiding with the other children in a barn down in the valley. Once the fighting stopped, I found my Father and Mother, dead. After a few weeks of scraping, trying to stay alive, I was taken in by one of the nurses who was sent in to take care of the wounded. When she left, I stayed with a small group of other orphans in the school, and one of the woman villagers returned from the lowlands, and took care of us. There was little to eat, dirty water to drink, no way to keep clean. All of the fields and streams were contaminated or poisoned. It all changed the day she finally arrived, the woman we called the fairy godmother. I was shy, used to hiding. I had never known anything different. When Miss Skinner was through speaking with the Curé, she demanded an accounting of the children. Not knowing what she was going to do with us, some of us hid. Finding us in the school, too afraid to talk, she did what she did best. She issued orders. With regards to us, a temporary shelter was constructed where we could be kept safe. Food was to be brought in daily and fresh water and medicines were provided. I don't think you people from Holyoke know what she really did for Hattonchâtel. It wasn't just that she reconstructed the buildings of our village that were destroyed. She saved our lives. She gave us hope." The old woman stopped, tears in her eyes, remembering all that happened.

"I never thought of it that way," Maggie said. "You're right. All we know about is the money spent and the beautiful buildings being put back up."

Michelle spoke up, "Once the reconstruction began, we all tried to help. We did anything we could to make things better. The children were not frightened so much, once she was here. Belle Skinner became our salvation, we trusted in her, and she never let us down." She paused and took a deep breath. "Why do we call the woman Aunt Prudence? Well, that's another part of the story."

Cheering up, the old woman went on with her tale. "The day of the *Celebration of the Bell* was a big event for us in the village. It wasn't just the bell coming, or the important people that were arriving, it was a sign of the new life that was beginning for us. To think the people that came here were doing this for us was incredible. But we were only children, so everything seemed special, especially after the way we were treated by the Germans. I was one of the girls chosen to help with the beginning ceremonies. After the speeches, I watched the men hoist the bell onto a makeshift wooden support they made to hold it, until the Church could be rebuilt, and a belfry put up to hang it in. The first sounds it made were music to everyone's ears. Miss Skinner was the center of attention of course, but being who she was she wanted everyone to be included. We all were part of the festivities afterwards that she arranged. After the speeches were finished the children cleaned up while the adults went to the shrines to pay their respects. By the time everyone came back, we had almost finished tidying up. We were all exhausted from the day. When Miss Skinner came back, she found a place on a makeshift patio of the town hall overlooking the valley to sit down and rest. The regalia had caught up with her, and she was tired. Out of nowhere, a little girl appeared. It was me. I was only twelve years old at the time. I had in my little hand a bouquet of wild flowers that I had carefully picked from the fields. There was nothing special about the flowers, except the effort I had taken to get them to her, the famous American. Looking at me, Miss Skinner sat up in her chair, and realizing the courage I had in coming to her, she hugged me. Not knowing how to speak English at the time, I told her in French that before she came I could not sleep, being afraid of the dark. Now that God had given me a new mother, I could. Not knowing what to say, Miss Skinner started to weep. It was the crowning touch of the day for her. It made everything she did complete."

"Mother made a big impression on Miss Skinner that day," Bernard said. "It wasn't just the fact that she did what none of the other children were capable of doing, approaching her and thanking her, without being told to by the older people. It's the way she is, how she does everything. No one has to tell her what is the right thing to do, she just knows." Looking over to his mother, Bernard began to tear up.

Michelle continued, "The following morning, Aunt Prudence came for me. Miss Skinner had begun to prepare a room in the small house she was staying at, the first one they worked on. Picking up the few possessions I had left in the world, I went with Aunt Prudence. Meeting us at the door, the '*bonne marraine*' told me I would live with them for a while, and that Aunt Prudence would take care of me when she was not there. Missing her own daughter terribly, Aunt Prudence thought it was a wonderful idea." The old woman was about to begin another sentence when Maggie stopped her.

"Prudence had a daughter?" Maggie didn't know this.

"Her name was Cecile," Michelle answered Maggie. "She was born in 1907. You don't know about Aunt Prudence, and how she came to work for Miss Skinner?"

"No, it has never been explained to us." Maggie turned her attention back to Michelle.

"Miss Skinner hired her as a maid in Holyoke. They became friends. The two traveled the world together. Before working for the Skinners,

Aunt Prudence was engaged to be married, became pregnant and was disowned by her parents. Miss Skinner knew about this, and she became the baby's godmother. Once she did this, her grandparents accepted the girl, and she went to live with them. Miss Skinner supported her financially. Cecile came here for a time with her husband many years after Miss Skinner died." Michelle was through, for the moment.

"Can you imagine the effect she had on a child who was not hers, the one she took in and treated like she was," Bernard reinforced his mother's statements.

"This was in Belle Skinner's house, the one we just visited?" John asked them.

"Yes, once the disputes between her and Sanford were finished up," Bernard answered him, wondering what they knew.

"Can you tell us more about what happened?" Maggie asked him.

"Certainly, but first tell me what you know about these men so I know where to begin." Michelle's request was reasonable.

John answered for them, deciding that it was time to take a risk. "We have been through the archive's letters, journals and cables of the Skinners. Sanford is described as being Belle's young architect, the man she hired to direct the project to restore Hattonchâtel. She describes him in the first series of her letters to her brother, William, and her sister, Katherine, as a likable and capable person. It seems though, that troubles developed between them a few years before Belle died. She said a man named Certoux was overcharging her. Belle complained in her letters that she is sick of his stealing from her and plans to take matters into her own hands to recover her losses. That is all we know. She isn't specific about who the man is. We don't know who Certoux was."

"He was the French contractor Miss Skinner employed to do the construction work. He was charging her too much," Bernard paused. "You obviously know about the age of the coins found here. How?" Bernard asked another interesting question to try to understand more of what they knew.

"Letters, newspaper articles, clippings that are in the archives. The finding of the pot of gold, as the writers called it, captured world attention," Maggie answered him this time.

Michelle was listening carefully, to every word, content to let her son do most of the talking. "You mentioned the fact that these letters you read talked about troubles between Belle and Sanford. Do you know what the trouble was?" Bernard decided to be direct.

"The letters say that he barred her from entering her own house, the one he was in." John spoke about the letter Belle had written on July 27, 1926 to her sister Katherine.

John said the magic word, "barred." Both Bernard and Michelle heard it loud and clear. Michelle had heard Miss Skinner talk about the specific letter and her use of the word. The word that convinced Bernard and Michelle that these were the people from Holyoke, who the great lady said would come after reading her letters, motivated by the same forces that brought Belle here.

"To the house you were just in," Bernard clarified things a little expecting a reaction.

He got one. "You're sure it was that house she was talking about, it was that one where the coins were found?" Maggie asked him, wanting to be sure.

It was Michelle who answered Maggie's question. "Yes my dear. The other house she talks about is down the street next to the Chalet. It's the one with the number 1 on it. Let me explain. In the beginning neither house was really what you would call finished or comfortable. The one the teacher lives in was larger and a bit more livable. So we stayed there. When Miss Skinner wasn't using it, Sanford came up and lived and worked on it, and we would go back to the one by the Chalet. We used to trade off when Miss Skinner came back to the village. Back then, no one in the village had permanent quarters. We all moved around a lot. After the coins were found, it was the house next door Sanford refused to leave when Miss Skinner and Aunt Prudence came back to the village. He was like a man possessed in his not letting her in. He was relentless in his objections. It wasn't until much later that Miss Skinner finally forced him out." Changing the flow of the conversation she said, "Maggie, why don't you and I warm our tea up, and we will come back and talk with John and Bernard about the rest of it."

Ten minutes later, after Maggie and Michelle had heated up the water in the kitchen, and John helped Bernard get more wood for the fireplace, they all returned to the sitting room and began where they left off.

"The chair you're sitting in was Aunt Prudence's favorite. It wasn't in Belle's house, then. It was in the house down the street," Michelle continued, explaining about the village living arrangements.

John interrupted her. "Belle owned both houses, right?"

"Yes, in fact, she owned all of them. But, not caring, Sanford took the cottage over completely in her absence. Only his workers came in and out. You know that Miss Skinner was barred, as she put it, from her house by Sanford, from reading her letter, the one written in 1926. When this happened, she first went to Nancy without Aunt Prudence, and then came back a short time later, and stayed with us briefly in the smaller house. It had been her intention when she came back to move us back up to the one next door, because it was bigger and close to being finished. Sanford didn't want to hear about it, and refused to let her in, telling her it was unsafe. He insisted he was protecting her from thieves who might break in looking for more coins. That was a lie." Michelle answered their questions, and then looked to her son to take over.

"In the beginning, he had planned to renovate a third house in the village for himself, and Miss Skinner wanted to live in the teacher's house until the Château was ready. But, finding the coins changed everything. Some were found in the ground outside, but most of them were dug up in the cellar of the house, especially the older ones. There were not many of them discovered, only about four hundred coins. They were definitely of interest to Miss Skinner. But the rebuilding of the Château was her first priority. She didn't want anything interfering with it." Bernard remembered everything his mother had told him.

"The first batch of coins was dug up on June 8, 1922, and the looting began soon after." Michelle embellished her son's story with a few more details.

"What looting?" John asked.

"The townspeople thought they had found a goldmine. There were holes dug everywhere, around the houses and the village. They even tried to get into this house. Like I said, Miss Skinner was more interested in the restoration project than the coins, but the workers and the villagers were focused on the prospects of finding more gold. It became a fiasco. So much so that Miss Skinner left and went back to Paris, content to let the people make fools of themselves. After they found nothing, everyone went back to work on the buildings. Then she came back." Michelle thought how mindless they had been. Miss Skinner had almost given up on the project when she saw them act like they did, so disrespectful.

"After that, the restoration resumed? There were no more delays?" John asked.

"For a time," Bernard answered. "The Château was the first building to be worked on. The Church and Abbey were next. The school and town hall followed. Then, one at a time, all of the houses in the village were rebuilt. By 1925, everything was looking pretty good. But a great deal of finish work was still left to be done."

"What was the problem with Certoux?" Maggie asked them.

Knowing they had read Belle's other letters that told them about the terrible problems Miss Skinner had with the three men in 1927, Bernard answered, "He was hired by her and the Bishop to do the rebuilding according to Sanford's plans. He was billing Miss Skinner too much for his work, taking advantage of her good nature and her absence from seeing that everything was done. He was no match for her, though. She saw through him, and became angry. She went to the Bishop to report him. But, he didn't pay much attention to her complaints, and didn't do anything. When the problems continued, Miss Skinner went to see the Abbe and the lawyer in Epernay. She had enough of what was going on and was going to put an end to it one way or another. Of course, you know about the disagreements she was having with the Curé? He was just as much of an irritation as were the other two men. But, let's stay focused on why John Sanford wouldn't let Miss Skinner into her own house. It started in early December in 1925. It has to do with the importance of the Roman coins found in the cellar of the house. That's the real reason you're here, isn't it?"

TWENTY FIVE

Being fairly good judges of character, and deciding John and Maggie had come to the village with honorable intentions, Bernard and Michelle spent the next few hours telling them why John Sanford and the other men had acted the way they did. "The architect didn't want Belle Skinner in the house, because he was digging in the cellar, again. He had been since she left. By the time he refused Belle's entrance, he had the cellar completely torn up," Michelle informed them.

"It seemed that someone or something convinced him that there were more coins to be found," Bernard told them. "It was most likely Certoux tempted him to look for more coins. He was a sly dog, always looking for angles and chances to make a big score. Look at the way he tried to defraud Miss Skinner with his bills."

"Did they find any more coins?" John asked Bernard.

"Yes, quite a few. So, someone was right suspecting they might be there. The cellar was full of coins dating back to the 11th century. We think they made quite a haul before they were stopped." Bernard confirmed what they thought.

"The Curé? Was he involved?" Maggie asked.

"We don't believe that he actively participated. He certainly knew what they were doing here. We all did. They kept us up nights with their incessant banging. But it's doubtful that he benefited directly from their looting," Bernard answered.

"What did Belle do?" Maggie asked them.

"After talking it over with her friend in Nancy, she decided to not act in haste. When she came back, she knew more coins had been found. But the village project was still her main objective and she wanted it finished. She needed Sanford to at least complete the part of the project he had in progress. She let him know though, that she was aware of what he was doing, and his time was short. He backed off, frightened he would be let go without getting his payment. He backed down, and we moved back in. So the restoration proceeded without further incidents." Bernard shared with them what had actually happened, and Maggie and John were thrilled to finally have the information.

"Miss Skinner had a trip to Nimes and Lourdes planned the following week. Not wanting to have her schedule fouled up, she went. But, not before warning Sanford to behave himself." Michelle added, "Certoux did not show his face in the village while she was there. He was a coward."

"When did she return from the trip?" John asked them.

"She came back to the village in late August, and sailed for America in September. She had a concert in Holyoke scheduled for October that she had to get back for. She stayed only a short time before going to Paris to prepare for the voyage." Michelle had a wonderful memory.

"All of this happened in 1926?" John asked, trying to get his dates straight.

"That's right." Bernard confirmed it.

"And, she came back from America to the village, when?" Maggie asked.

"The following spring. That would be in 1927. She was here only a few days when the troubles began again. Sanford had not obeyed her. He was still digging behind the house. We knew it. We heard them." Michelle added the year of the date, trying to help them keep the timeframes straight.

"Did she go to see her friend again in Nancy?" Maggie asked.

"No. There had been a problem in the winter, poor health. The man died a few weeks before Miss Skinner came back. She was devastated by his death. He was a close friend, a confidant. When she learned of his sickness, Miss Skinner booked the next available boat back to France to be with him. But she arrived too late. That's why she went to the people in Epernay, because he was not around to help her anymore. She needed their opinions and confidence." Michelle didn't elaborate. "She spent the summer here, and made Sanford finish up his work before she paid him anything. She kept telling him that he would not get a penny until he did. In July, she went to see the Abbe and the lawyer. Sanford and Certoux had caused her enough problems. In her mind, they were both finished. If the Bishop wouldn't do it, she would. She was going to make sure of it." The old woman offered the explanations.

"We read the letter she wrote to her friend Justina, while she was on the S.S. Paris on September 7, 1927, on her way back to the States. It's all in there, what you're talking about. Belle said that she was pleased with the progress at Hattonchâtel, and that she was looking forward to the thrill of dealing with the scoundrels when she returned the following spring," John said.

Not having read what he was describing, Michelle and Bernard just accepted what John said as being true. Michelle added, "The next six months were exciting times here in the village, that is the fall of 1927 and the winter of 1928." Michelle was still trying to make things easy for them.

Following her dates, Maggie asked her, "How so?"

"Aunt Prudence went back with Miss Skinner to America, but when they came back to France, she came here after staying only a few days with Miss Skinner in Paris. While they were away, the village people forced the Curé to make sure that Sanford did what he was told this time." Michelle remembered it all like it was yesterday. "The architect hated the last few months he was here, because they had made it so hard on him, and because the fountains of coins he found in the cellar had dried up. There were no more found. Finishing his contract work on the Château, and aware of Miss Skinner's trip to the lawyer, he accepted her payment, and left quickly in December. Certoux just disappeared into thin air never to be seen again. We began working on this house shortly after Sanford vacated it. Miss Skinner planned on moving in here the following spring." The old woman still remembered the condition of the house when they began to work on it, after Sanford dug it all up.

"Who completed the restoration of the house?" John prompted her.

"The whole village," Michelle answered. "Everyone helped. They were feeling guilty after the debacle of the coins. She had done so much for us, it was the least they could do for her, to make her home beautiful, to try to make up for their stupidity. Miss Skinner had decided not to move into the Château immediately. Instead, she was to become one of the villagers by living in one of the village houses, the one she had wanted all along, the cottage next door. We brought up the few personal things she had here, once she cabled us she was returning. We were planning a 'Fete' as she used to call them, a celebration for her return to the village. It was to be held when she came up from Paris the second week of April in 1928." Michelle was the one to begin to cry this time, thinking how Belle Skinner never got to live full time in her own house at Hattonchâtel.

"She never made it back," John said, realizing the time frame.

"Aunt Prudence received the message late one night, and left immediately. She and Miss Skinner had arrived in Paris from New York on the ship, the Ile-de-France on the 23rd of March. Aunt Prudence came here to check on things and Miss Skinner stayed in Paris. While Miss Skinner was there, she complained to friends of not feeling well. Her sickness lasted only weeks. On the eve of her departure to come here, she became very ill. It was that night Aunt Prudence got the message. She was with Miss Skinner when she died of pneumonia on Easter Sunday, the 9th of April, 1928. Aunt Prudence accompanied her body back to Holyoke for the burial. Until the very end, Aunt Prudence was Miss Skinner's dearest friend."

"God," was all Maggie could manage to say.

"... loves her for all she did for everyone," Michelle added the words, without thinking about them. Her expression told them how much she cared for Belle.

Bernard thought they all talked enough about the final years of Belle Skinner's life, and wanted to put everything in perspective, saying, "Look at the village now. See everything she accomplished here. It is a treasure for us all, forever." Walking to a cabinet next to his mother, he took out a bottle of rare, aged French brandy. "In Miss Skinner's honor, I would like to offer a toast." Bernard waited for his mother to get the snifters, then poured the brandy, and handed them around. Raising his glass to the portrait of the lady that Prudence had hung up next to hers, he said, "To whatever code of honor they taught her in Holyoke that inspired this woman to do everything she did in her fabulous life." Drinking, everyone looked up at the picture, knowing how remarkable Belle Skinner truly was.

TWENTY SIX

*I*t was customary in the home of Prudence Lagogue never to allow guests to leave without something to eat. Continuing the tradition, Michelle and Bernard invited Maggie and John to an early dinner, knowing they were leaving the following day. John and Maggie accepted the offer graciously, but only if they could help with the cooking or cleaning up.

"How long have you actually lived here?" John asked Bernard, while the ladies cut vegetables.

"Like I said, we all came back to Miss Skinner's house with Aunt Prudence after Sanford moved out. We stayed there after the donation."

"What donation?" Maggie asked.

Michelle answered her, motioning for her to put the vegetables in the pot boiling next to them, "The Skinner Family donation of the Château, and the rest of the village to the Bishop of Verdun. You don't know what happened after Belle died, do you?" It was her turn to ask a question.

"No," Maggie said, being careful not to burn herself on the stove. Ever since she had done so as a child, she watched herself around things that were hot.

"William came here in 1934 to settle up legal matters. Belle had expressed in her papers her desire to keep financing the continued restorations and the other affairs of the village. A new water system was needed for instance, and a request was sent to William to provide the money to put it in. Not having the same passion for the village, and tired of paying its bills, he came here to get rid of the Château and everything else for whatever he could get for it. The Skinners had paid for everything, and had not been repaid, so technically, they owned it all. Therefore, by rights he could sell it or give it away. There were no buyers. In the end, he gave up their investments, giving everything away to the Church, wanting to be rid of the ongoing financial burdens. The house was excluded from the agreements. Belle had wanted Aunt Prudence taken care of. So, it was agreed that she could live in Miss Skinner's house, until she died. We lived there, until she died in 1967, and actually, for some years afterwards, until the legal matters were taken care of. When the Bishop sold it in 1973, Bernard and I moved here. He took the job as caretaker for the people who bought the Château." Michelle remembered how hard it was for her to leave the house. There were so many good memories there.

"He didn't even want to talk about the cable when he was here. William was a lovely man, but he was tired, worn out. He missed Belle terribly, and wanted just to get on with his life in New York and Holyoke," Michelle added to her statements.

"What cable?" John asked.

"The one Aunt Prudence sent to William two nights after Miss Skinner died," Michelle replied.

"We've never seen it," John said.

"We wondered about that," Michelle said. "Whether he ever saw it, if it was anywhere in the Skinner collections. When he was here he didn't want to talk about anything other than settling matters up. He left without us knowing if he ever received it." Michelle remembered every word of the cable Belle had directed Prudence to send.

"There's nothing in the archives that we read. There's no cable from Prudence to William after Belle died that we have seen," John said, and Maggie shook her head in agreement.

Putting the plates down, and beginning to serve everyone, Michelle said, "Enough of this old business, let's have a nice peaceful dinner, and enjoy each other's company. After we're done eating, I'll go and get it, and you can read what she sent to him. In the meantime, I would like to know more about the two of you. Maggie do you have any children?"

After a delightful meal, and a pleasant conversation, Michelle did what she said she would. She showed them a copy of the cable that they thought William Skinner might have never seen, because he never talked about it. Sitting back in the living room, they were given the worn out piece of paper, "It was Miss Skinner's last request. Besides, of course, what she had already written into her will, that Aunt Prudence be taken care of according to her wishes as stipulated in the bequeaths." Michelle handed them what Prudence had sent to William on April 11, 1928. It read: *"Miss Skinner wanted to continue finding the treasure which tradition says lies hidden in the village, but why now?"*

"What does she mean, 'but why now'?" John asked them.

"Aunt Prudence was grieving. We think those are her words. Before she died, Miss Skinner, saying the rest, asked Aunt Prudence to cable her request to her brother, William. She did, and that was the last anyone talked about it." Michelle was certain that her aunt had sent the cable, and respectfully said no more about it.

Looking at the old paper cable, Maggie and John were speechless. This was why they came here, to find something just like this. Theory 3 had just, maybe, been proven for Tracey by Belle's own words as written in Prudence's handwriting, dated and documented by the French cable wire service.

Michelle wasn't through. "There's one other item that we have. A letter sent to Mrs. Tina Hollister from the lawyer in Epernay whose name was Eddie de Azalao. Have you read any letters regarding this man? Aunt Prudence was sent a copy of the original letter, and said a second copy of it was sent to William Skinner in 1928?"

Maggie answered her question. "We read one that Belle wrote to a woman named Justina on September 7, 1927. At this woman's advice, Belle went to see this man regarding some problems she was having in the village. She wrote to thank her for putting her in touch with this man and the Abbe. She was sure they would help her solve the disagreements she was having with the Curé and the architect. If I remember her words correctly she said:

> *"It really is a wonderful favor you have done me, and I am very grateful. I went to Epernay, called on the young de Azalao, told them my story and promised to lunch with them on my return to Paris. Mr. Azalao was thoroughly interested and very enthusiastic, but in spite of his enthusiasm and mine, we agreed that it would be better not to do any sounding until I can be 'on the spot'."*

Those were her exact words. Belle promised to lunch with him when she returned to France the next spring.

Having an investigator's memory and a gift for details, Maggie had memorized everything she had read.

Michelle handed Maggie the letter she was holding. "If that is all you know, then I guess you haven't seen this one either."

As Maggie took the letter from Michelle, she did not recognize it. She held it close to John so he could read it with her. It was dated as being sent to William Skinner on 6/18/28, months after Belle died. The letter told about Eddie de Azalao's intentions to visit Belle in Paris in the spring to further discuss the business they had spoken about when she went to see him. It was a meeting that never took place because of Belle's death. The lawyer wrote to Mrs. Hollister:

> *The phone call came through, poor Miss Skinner died at four o'clock in the morning... Prudence has lunched here twice and on behalf of Miss Skinner has asked me to continue with the Sourcier etc... but I can assure you, I just feel I cannot. Poor Miss Skinner, for her, it would have been my greatest joy in being instrumental in her finding the treasure, which tradition says, lies hidden.*

"Who's Mrs. Hollister?" John asked.

"One of Miss Skinner's friends." The old woman's explanation was short.

"What's the matter?" Bernard asked them, smiling, seeing their expressions.

"Belle knew there was more treasure here," Maggie said.

"Of course, we all suspected it," Michelle was enjoying this.

"What's a Sourcier?" Maggie asked her.

"A waterfinder, also known as a pendulum or rod. I'm sure you both have seen pictures of them,"

Michelle answered. "They have been used all over the world for centuries. The word can also refer to the person who has been chosen to use the instrument to find the water."

"What does finding water have to do with any of this," John asked her.

"The rods are also used to find metals underground, like in tunnels, crypts and chambers. To seek treasures. During the reign of King Louis XIII, the Baron de Beausoleil and his wife discovered 150 mines in France with the aid of divining rods." Michelle was telling them what the lawyer's letter actually said.

"Wow," John said, looking at the letter, realizing the real reason Belle went to see the lawyer.

"She wanted the lawyer to be her Sourcier?" Maggie asked her.

"It would seem so," Michelle smiled.

"Why haven't you gone after it?" Maggie asked her the obvious question.

"The message, and the directions in the cable, and in the letter have a double meaning. Miss Skinner thought the treasure of the Romans should be looked for, but not at the expense of losing what she created in the village. She didn't want anyone from here to do it. What she wanted was the Château, and life in and around it to be the focus of everyone's life, a peaceful existence with meaning. She had seen what happened when the villagers rushed after the gold, how crazed they became. She didn't ever want to let this happen again. For her, serenity and peace were more valuable than the treasure. I think she was asking for the lawyer, and maybe her brother to search silently for Charlemagne's fortune, without disrupting the calmness here. The lawyer withdrew. William either never knew exactly what Belle found out, or wasn't interested in chasing after something that might not be here. Like I said, he was tired of it all. When there was no response to Belle's requests, Aunt Prudence never mentioned it again. That's about it!" Michelle was very sure about what she was saying.

"So, what happens now?" Maggie asked.

"You enjoy your last night in our lovely little village, you get in your car tomorrow, and drive back to Paris. The day after tomorrow, you take your flight back home, remembering that you are always welcome to come back here."

Being the delightful person she was, Michelle asked them, "Would you like to see the upstairs bedrooms before you leave?" Some of Miss Skinner's and Aunt Prudence's things are up there."

Nodding *yes*, they followed her to the stairs. Making apologies, Bernard didn't go with them.

"There are three bedrooms on the second floor. Bernard and I both have our own, and the largest one is for guests," Michelle was giving them a description of the upstairs as they slowly reached the top landing. "This is the guest room. The one with the big bed, and the picture that belonged to Miss Skinner in it."

They both saw it at the same time, and knew exactly what it was by Belle's descriptions. It was not the large bed in the center that caught their attention. It was the picture depicting the valley Holyoke was in that was hanging directly over the bed that did. It was the painting that the painter had done from Mt. Tom when Belle was with him, up at the Summit House. Seeing their expressions, Michelle was taken aback, "Is there something wrong?" she asked confused.

Looking at Michelle, guessing that she had no clue about the letters

Belle had written to William, Maggie asked her, "Did Miss Skinner ever tell you about the man who painted this?" She couldn't take her eyes off the painting. It was mesmerizing. The combination of red and orange colors made it magnificent to look at.

"It was painted by her good friend from Nancy, the one she trusted. When he died, he left this to her. She kept it wrapped in paper, wanting to hang it in her house. We thought she would like it in her bedroom, so that she could wake up to Holyoke every morning. It was going to be our surprise for her when she came back. When we moved, I made sure I took it. It's one of the few things I have of hers that reminds me of her." Michelle had no idea what the real surprise was.

Thinking about what Belle had said in the letters to William about the man, John said, "I think we had better go back downstairs, and have another shot of your brother's fine brandy, Michelle. This time it's our turn to tell you both a little story."

Twenty Seven

Thursday, January 20th, 2005

John and Maggie got up early the next morning: early, because they wanted to do something before they left, besides stopping at Michelle and Bernard's house to say goodbye. Having heard it ring on several occasions, Maggie had asked John if they could go to the Church, walk up the stairs, and see Belle's bell.

Looking at it proved to be a thrill, seeing the view of the countryside from the belfry was too. Seeing what Belle and the painter might have, they both agreed, it reminded them a lot of the Holyoke range.

Not long later, they were standing outside the opened front door of the guardhouse, thanking Michelle for a lovely evening. They left the car running, not wanting to take up too much of Michelle's time. "Where's Bernard," John asked her.

"At the Château. A broken pipe needed to be fixed. He's been working underneath the castle for a few days now," Michelle told them. "He said for me to say goodbye, if he isn't back by the time you leave." Knowing they were coming, Michelle was wearing a white suit this time with a flowered blouse, and had put on a cashmere coat, because it was brisk out. "Miss Skinner taught me that if you're going to feel right, you have to look good. She was very kind with buying us all nice clothes to wear when we were young. It's a habit now. Are you sure you won't come in for a minute?"

"No, we have bothered you enough," Maggie smiled. "We'll get on our way. But, don't worry, you haven't seen the last of us." Two young girls and a boy walked by and said hello, smiling to Michelle as they passed by. "The children are so pleasant," Maggie made the observation. "I know it's a small village, but do all the children treat their elders with such manners?"

"It's how we bring them up, to be considerate of everyone. It's a Belle

Skinner rule," Michelle said. "Besides, they have to be nice to me, I'm the Grandmother of the village. What I say goes." She gave them a sharp grin that told them she wasn't just a little old lady living out in the country. Not realizing Michelle was in some ways in charge of the village, Maggie and John just looked at her, thinking she knew how to enforce the codes of behavior.

"Miss Skinner showed me many things besides how to dress, even though we weren't together long. Aunt Prudence finished the job. They taught me what was important, the rules to be followed, how to think and behave. Now it is my turn to pass these lessons along to our children. I do it by keeping things in order in the village, showing them that acting right and sharing life, not owning it, is what makes people happy."

"But that's not why I wanted you two to say goodbye." Michelle smiled. "I want you to bring something back to Holyoke for me."

"What?" Maggie was enjoying every moment of being with her.

"I want you to help me do something I could never do myself. Visit the grave of Miss Skinner, and pay my respects for me," Michelle said.

"How can we do this for you?" John was standing next to them, thinking what a nice lady Michelle really was.

"I have a little something that I want you to give to Miss Skinner." She took a small box out of her pocket, and held it out for them to see. It was sealed up." A token of my gratitude for all she did for me, for all of us. I want you to carve out a small hole at her gravesite, and bury this with her."

Taking the box, Maggie said, "Yes, of course we will." She didn't ask what was in it, but was understandably curious.

"Open it when you are on your plane ride home if you wish to see what it is before you get to Holyoke." Michelle was giving them her instructions. Buttoning up her coat, she told them that they had a good day to travel. Walking with them to the car, Michelle asked them, "Is there anything else you need to know before you leave us?"

"No. I think we found what we came here looking for. Thank you for everything." Maggie wasn't just talking about the copies of the cable, and the letter from the lawyer Michelle had made for them on her fax machine last night, knowing how valuable they were. Michelle looked to John to see if he wanted to know anything else.

"No, thank you for everything. I will not forget you," said John. He began to realize, as they stood there in the beautiful restored village, that he had pieced together for himself a better idea of what "reality" was. Knowing this, he didn't want anything more than the moment.

Hugging them both as a goodbye gesture, Michelle watched as they drove down the Rue Miss Skinner. When she could see them no more, she left to attend the meeting at the town hall she had scheduled with the Mayor the night before, to discuss the Museums. Maggie and John were right. Some things needed to be moved around. Michelle was going to make sure it was done.

Driving out, they passed by the old Church. Remembering the overpowering sensations they felt there, Maggie wondered which monk's spirits were still in there. Thinking this, she asked John, "Can we stop at the cemetery on the way out. I want to see who is buried there." Being certain who wasn't, Maggie thought about the Curé, the man who had given Belle such a hard time. Wondering what happened to him, Maggie had asked Michelle the previous night. She had replied, that causing no further problems for anyone, the Curé just passed away into the everlasting life on a summer day, years after Belle died. Michelle had no idea where he was buried.

Watching the village disappear in the rear view mirror, John stopped

Château from a distance

the car half way down where the cemetery was. Looking at the stones and markers and not seeing any familiar names, they were about to leave when John turned around and looked up. From the graveyard, they could see the Château from a totally different angle. It looked different. Doing so, he said, "Well what does it look like to you, now that you know a little more about it? When we arrived you said it was a fairyland castle in the sky."

"It looks like something that was created from someone's special imagination," Maggie replied. Knowing exactly what she meant, they got into the car and drove away. They were off to Paris.

TWENTY EIGHT

John and Maggie were driving on the A4 superhighway an hour later, talking about everything that had happened in the last month. Maggie was looking through a guidebook as they did. It was one of the fifty or so pieces of literature she had picked up in their travels. Seeing that one of her favorite artists had worked in the city of Reims, she asked John if they could stop. Telling her it was something he would like to do too, they arrived in the famous French city not long later.

The Cathedrale De Reims, where the renowned Jewish painter and glass-work artist, Marc Chagall had crafted a masterpiece, was not hard to find. It was huge, and they could see it from the highway. Once they exited off the ramp, they drove only a few blocks, and found it easily in the middle of the city. Parking on one of the streets, not far away, it took them only a few minutes to reach it.

When they entered the immense cathedral, they realized why several French coronations had taken place there. It was huge. There was room for thousands inside. Looking at the many different stained glass windows that were there, they found the one they were looking for easily, in the back of the church behind a number of prayer stations of those there who had been canonized.

Standing in front of it, they read from a brochure about the way the Russian born Chagall used 14th century techniques to make and design his stained glass. The colors he selected for these windows were unlike any they had ever seen. The deep blues of his creation were a sharp contrast to the other stained glass windows of the basilica. Watching the sunlight from the outside filter in through them, they became alive with other shades of blue that only appeared when the light passed through them. It was what the artist himself saw when he made them. He created colors that did not exist without the proper light.

Stopping briefly at the souvenir desk at the entrance to buy a few gifts to take home, Maggie told John about her love of churches, how they made her feel. She thought her son would like a silver medal of the Madonna from here to wear. She had noticed the last time he was home that his looked worn. It was time for a new one. So, thinking about how much she missed her son, Maggie bought it for him and an identical one for herself. Seeing this, John thought that it was a good idea. So, he purchased a third, and had Maggie help him put it on.

They made only a few other stops in Reims. Walking leisurely through the old district, they shopped in some of the stores to buy a few more remembrances of the trip. Maggie always went a little overboard when she went somewhere, in bringing things back for her son and some friends. John had brothers and sisters that he didn't want to forget. He also bought Maggie a fancy hat. She loved them, and when she tried a particular one on it looked so nice on her, he couldn't resist getting it for her.

Walking out of the last shop and turning a corner, they saw an open square not far from where they were. In the middle of it was a wonderful old two-tiered carousel. Once she saw it, Maggie had to have a ride. So, she and John each climbed up on one of the brightly colored horses, and for a few moments forgot about the troubles of the world, doing something childish. It was a good way to begin to end their trip.

John decided, once they were back on the highway that instead of going directly into Paris to find a hotel, it was a good idea to find one out at the airport. Since it was late afternoon already, it seemed like a good idea to stay around the Charles de Gaulle terminals, turn in the rental car, and take a shuttle in the morning to catch their plane. He had many bad experiences with rental car companies, and didn't want to have another in the morning, and miss their flight. If he brought the car back tonight, he could deal with whatever problems there were now, and they would not be delayed tomorrow. Being experienced, John was well aware that one never knows what might go wrong in returning rental cars.

Thinking it was smart, Maggie began looking in her collection of booklets for a list of airport hotels. Finding the name of one, she jotted down the address. In three hours, they pulled into the parking area of the hotel, and went inside to see if they had rooms available. Finding that they had plenty, they checked in. After he put his bag in his room, John suggested that Maggie go to hers, and stay there. Being the considerate person he was, he would bring the rental car back to the parking garage by himself. There was no need for both of them to go. She could take a bath or rest until he got back.

It took two hours for him to do drive there and turn it in. Having the foresight to think there could be problems with the rental agency was in order. There was a discrepancy in the charges. The conversion of the dollar to the Euro was the sticking point. The rental company had guaranteed his rate in dollars, and then charged him in Euros. It took over an hour to fix the mistake, and it was almost eight o'clock by the time he returned by taxi to the hotel.

John knocked on Maggie's door. As she let him in, he said, "It just cost me almost a hundred dollars to fill up that little car. It seems the oil barons are not just overcharging everyone in America. They're doing it everywhere. So much for world economic globalization being a good idea. It's not. It produces too much paper work and exchange transactions. This makes some people a lot of money. We need another Belle Skinner to put the crooks in their places, just like she did with the contractor who was billing her and the villagers too much." He was agitated.

Seeing this, Maggie suggested they have a nice quiet dinner downstairs. "Don't let them get to you John. Things will change. People have had enough of the dishonesty. And I agree with you, another Belle will show up to make them back off."

After a pleasant buffet dinner together in the modest restaurant, Maggie and John went to bed, both calling the front desk to ask for an eight o'clock wake up call. They had a one o'clock flight, and wanted to allow plenty of time to check in, go through security, and be at the gate an hour before the plane boarded.

TWENTY NINE

Friday, January 21st, 2005

The following morning, after paying their hotel bill and having two cups of coffee each from the vending machine in the lobby, they took the shuttle bus to the Air France terminal for their flight home. Even though the airport was only fifteen minutes away, it was 9:30 A.M. by the time they got there, because the bus stopped at several hotels along the way.

They had cleared Immigration and Customs twenty minutes prior, and were presently sitting in a lounge at the gate area, waiting to board their 1:15 P.M. flight back to Boston that would land at three in the afternoon, because of the time difference. Looking at her watch, Maggie saw that it was 12:20 P.M. The departure screen across from where they were told them that their plane would leave on time, in just about an hour.

"What are you thinking about?" Maggie asked John. He had been silent for minutes now.

"About reality," he smiled at her, thinking about their first conversation.

She laughed, knowing what he was saying. "What about it?"

"I'm still trying to decide what it is, exactly? Was it what we saw in the village?" John wasn't sure. He wanted Maggie's opinion.

"Nothing good was happening there, until Belle came to town. Before that, Hell was there. She was the catalyst that made things happen." Maggie was talking about the awful effects of wars. Trying to relate it to reality, she went on, "Once she went to her special place, to let her mind be free to see what could be there, Belle saw what it was that she could create. Then she set out to do it, to make it real. In part, that's reality, John." Maggie thought about Belle's mental abilities, and how her creations related to his question.

John was thinking as Maggie talked about their findings of what Belle's gift made, what Belle could imagine. Then, he shared, "I think then, that reality is maybe somewhere between Ozzie and Harriet, and the world of the landlords that want everything for themselves. For a time, some of it existed in Holyoke, and in America. Then, the bad guys took over, and destroyed it. What's going on now in America isn't reality. It's a distortion of it. I agree with you. Belle saw in *Everythink* what was possible. I think other visionaries, knowing it exists, have seen the same things. To get there we need to fight off the invaders who are destroying our dreams, rebuild the village, and recreate what was once there. It's a place where everyone matters. Those who want to live in it have to behave responsibly for the good of the community. Those that don't, can't stay. Just like Belle rebuilt Hattonchâtel, looking to make her visions a reality for everyone, and cast out those whose greed threatened them, we have to do the same. *Everythink* is not an illusion. It is an objective. This is 'The Belle Skinner Legacy.'" John looked at Maggie with kind eyes, as he told her what he had sorted out.

"Anything can happen, John, and usually does." Maggie shared her thoughts about how dramatically her life had changed since a windy day in New Haven. "It's all about vision, understanding, and doing what's right and fair for everyone. For me, it sure isn't what's going on back home." She was referring back to John's evaluations, the first time they met, about what reality was not. "The violence, the drugs, the devil's songs and violent movies are false realities, perversions. I agree with you, none of it is normal. They can have that world. You're right! I like what I saw up in the mountains better. And the air is cleaner." Maggie summed up her own feelings.

"I agree, all that is the antithesis of what made Holyoke and America great. It's all turned upside down." John knew why the Republic was failing.

"It's just as Michelle said, Belle taught her the rules of life. She obeys them and tries to make sure everyone else does by setting an example. Everyone's happy if they treat each other respectfully. If she didn't, they wouldn't. Our guys don't think this way. They want it all for themselves, and don't really give a damn about the rest of us." Maggie was making a comparison between good and bad villagers.

Settling herself, Maggie reached for her bag, "Speaking of Michelle, do you think she would care if I open this before we got on the plane?" Maggie's curiosity was getting the best of her as she looked at the neatly wrapped package. Just as she said this, the ringer and the vibrating mechanism on her cell phone went off. It was directly under the package Maggie was about to take out. It unnerved her. She thought it was something in the box. Realizing what and who it was, Maggie answered the call and said, "Hello."

Hearing the ringing sound, John didn't react the same way. Knowing it must be Tracey, he took out his own phone to hear what she was going to say.

"It's Tracey." The voice on the other end said. "Are you at the airport?" she asked Maggie.

"Yes, our flight leaves soon. You're up early," Maggie said calculating the time difference.

"Any good news?" Tracey asked her, not knowing John was listening in on the conversation.

"Lots. Theory 3 is most likely a go, Tracey. It's proven on paper, and we're bringing it home with us. There is a lot to this." Being excited, Maggie repeated herself.

John let Tracey know he was there by saying, "Hello."

"What did you find there, John?" Tracey asked him, hearing his voice.

Thinking, and not wanting to play childish games with her anymore, John answered her by saying exactly what he felt, "*Everthink*."

There was a short pause. Tracey thought she knew what he meant. It was what she was hoping for. "I'll pick you guys up at Logan, like we planned. You can tell me what it looks like. Have a safe flight. I'll see you in about eight hours if your plane doesn't crash." Once she said the words, the phone went dead.

Listening to what Tracey said, Maggie put her phone and the package back into her carry-on pack. She looked at John somewhat amused by Tracey's offbeat comment.

"Aren't you going to open it?" John asked her, watching her put it away. He was shaking his head about what Tracey said.

"When we get on the plane," she smiled. Thinking about when Michelle told her to open it, she said, "The rules are the rules, for everyone. If people make up their own as they go along, that's when they start boarding up the buildings." Understanding what she meant, John sat back thinking about everything they had seen and heard, and waited for the gate attendant to announce their flight's boarding call. He decided as he did that it had been a good decision to go to Belle's village. He had learned and seen a lot.

Two hours later, after a slight delay, they were airborne at 35,000 feet. The pilot had turned off the seat belt light, and as is repeated hundreds of times a day around the world, they were free to move around the cabin. Maggie didn't want to. She wanted to open the package Michelle had given them. Looking at John, Maggie made a facial expression to make sure it was OK, then she reached for the bag that was stored under the seat in front of her.

Smiling at her, and proud that she had waited, John said, "I wonder what Michelle thinks is so important that it should be buried with Belle Skinner in Forestdale Cemetery." Being as curious as Maggie was, he couldn't wait to see what was in the box Michelle had given them. As Maggie carefully unwrapped the package, she found a note. Underneath it was a little jewelry box.

Maggie and John read the note together, "They didn't know where to look." John and Maggie looked at each other after they read it. Both of their hearts began to beat quicker. They each had the same suspicion about what could be in the box. Opening it up, Maggie took out a round object. It was a coin, similar to the ones described in Belle's letters that the workers had unearthed at the house. Just like the ones found in 1922, this one had cut edges, was gold, and had a figure on it. The lettering was scratched, and the coin was tarnished. But, when she held it up to the light, they both could make out the date. It was not blurred. The year was 846.

Maggie's fingers began to twitch. Then her hands began to shake slightly. Her nerves were reacting to what she was holding. "It's older than the ones Belle found." It was all she could manage to say.

Taking it from her, John held it up closer to the light. The inscriptions were so worn that he could not be sure if the writing was French, Latin or another language. But, he agreed with Maggie, the date was what was important, and it was clear. "They dug deeper," he said the words, and just looked at her, knowing the value of the coin in his hand. Understanding what John was saying, Maggie was thinking about the expression on Michelle's face two days ago when she told them that Bernard had been fixing a broken pipe under the Château. She decided that Bernard had taken the job as custodian of the Château so they would have access to it. They knew what might be under it.

Maggie and John, realizing they were in possession of a small piece of the world's history, both stopped to think about its possible significance.

Wondering why Bernard and Michelle were sharing this with them, Maggie thought about how Sarah Bernhardt had recognized Belle in her theater in Paris, after not seeing her since she was a little girl. Why people are drawn to each other for no apparent reason? They just are. Maggie thought it must have something to do with energies. At certain times, forces bring people together to produce changes. This apparently was one of those times.

"Would you like a soft drink or maybe something else?" The stewardess was standing next to them, asking the routine questions.

"No, thank you, maybe later," John said, covering the coin with his fingers.

When the stewardess reached the next aisle, John put the coin back in the jewelry box, and gave it to Maggie. "Michelle wants us to bury it with Belle, so she knows what is there."

Thinking about it, Maggie responded, "The mountain is probably full of these. God knows what else. They found more of the treasure." She stopped for a second to consider the level of confidence Michelle and Bernard had just placed in them.

"Someone from Holyoke will come one day," John said.

"Huh," Maggie was thinking about the worth of Charlemagne's treasure that might be buried under the Château.

"That's what Michelle said when we walked into their house." John remembered the woman's words exactly, the ones she said Belle had said to her. Bernard and Michelle knew this would happen one day. Someone would come to bring something back to Holyoke.

Holding onto the box tightly, Maggie said, "You're right. Belle knew someone, someday, would figure this all out."

Considering what Belle probably thought, Maggie asked John, "Do you think all of this was troubling to her? Is this why she was so unnerved before she died?"

"Who wouldn't be upset by suspecting this? Her whole life was full of conflicts, drama and earth changing choices. This was another one. Belle lived two different lives. At night she was dancing at the Ritz, the next morning she was feeding starving children and taking care of many others who needed help. In the process, she was finding rare coins, maybe even a treasure that belonged to a king who ruled a good part of the world. She knew someone would find Charlemagne's gold someday," John added.

"And then, everyone would have to make a choice. Just like Belle had to decide. What's of more value, a pot full of gold, or keeping the village uncorrupted to make it wonderful for everyone?" Maggie summed up Belle's decision to stay focused and to try to create her dream.

"Unbelievable." John said the one word that described it all. Changing the subject a bit, by thinking about their discussions of Holyoke, John asked Maggie a question unrelated to the worth of the coin, "As an outsider looking in, what made Holyoke great?"

"Cheap power and little interference in private business by the city's government. In addition, the people living in the city cared about each other. They weren't in it just for the money." Maggie was quick to answer, because she had already thought about it.

"Why is America failing?" John asked her for a comparison between the fall of the historic city, and a great nation.

First pausing, because this was something else to consider, she then answered, "Overpriced energies that result in expensive living costs, and too much corporate involvement in the state and federal governments, special interest groups. People's individual priorities are much more selfish. They care more about money than anything else. But it's being screamed at them every day by the televisions. They've been brainwashed. It's a trick." Maggie sounded like a newspaper reporter again.

"What era do you choose," John asked, "Belle's or ours?" He was trying to shift their attention away from the valuable object they had been given.

Looking at his face, Maggie didn't answer his question for a moment. She was thinking about how it related to what she wanted to do with the rest of her life. Taking in John's expression, Maggie had made up her mind about a lot of this. She knew exactly where she was going to when she got home, besides Holyoke. Maggie had already decided that she wasn't going back to work at the city desk of the Globe. She was tired of wasting her time writing about the corrupt politicians and construction companies in Boston who were creating a state of financial ruin. The only way things could be fixed was to get rid of them, and that wasn't likely to happen. The people of the Commonwealth were doing nothing about it, content to buy more lottery tickets to support them. With stories like Belle's to focus her attention on, Maggie began to realize that there were many worthwhile projects in the world that she could spend her time and energies on.

"Belle's." Maggie finally said.

Thinking about the black nun in Connecticut, giving her the pamphlet of the Catholic Church's mandates on *Just Wars*, Maggie added, "Belle didn't run away through the battlefields, she looked around them. It's in the letters. She saw the innocents being slaughtered. Before it was over she went back to try and help." Then out of nowhere, Maggie added, "You have to write your book." She did not pay any attention to his expression. "You need to start writing immediately when you get to Holyoke."

"Excuse me?" John didn't know what she was talking about, where she was coming from. He hadn't made up his mind to do anything yet.

"When we met at Wistariahurst, you told me you were looking through the materials to see if there was anything in the archives that was worth writing a story about." Maggie returned his look.

"I remember saying something like that." John wasn't sure he wanted to move in this direction any further.

"Well, besides proving Theory 3 correct for Tracey, we have a little tale to tell together." Maggie had already decided this for the both of them. That they were going to do it.

"We do?" John asked her, wondering what she was thinking now.

"It's going to be about a little girl from Williamsburg who grows up in a great city in Massachusetts and has mighty strength, just like your friend Tom Terrific," Maggie said. "She travels out into the world and does amazing things. She rebuilds a castle in the mountains of France that maybe has a king's treasure hidden underneath it, and saves all of the people of the village who live there from disasters."

John recalled his descriptions of the cartoon character that fought off villains and always won, because of the powers he possessed by being from Holyoke. "No one would buy it. It's too incredible to be believable." John was amused by her comparisons.

"While you're writing your descriptions, I'm going to the Forestdale Cemetery. There is something I have to do there. I made a promise to someone special that I intend to keep." Maggie looked at John, and on impulse, she did something she had never done with him before. She kissed him. It felt good. For the first time in a long time, Maggie felt the heaviness in her heart lighten. She felt like life was worth living again. "After we finish with all of it, I think we should take a trip back to the village, bring a copy of the book, and tell Bernard and Michelle that Belle was right."

"About what part?" John was enjoying this.

"About us honoring their trust, and Belle's decisions. I think very few people in life are called upon to make the types of choices she was. Most of us will never have the chance to give away things of such value, or have the opportunity to recreate famous villages because we want to do something that is meaningful for everyone. Those who have the money or the possessions almost never do anything like this. Not caring, they hoard their money or buy things that have no value. Making the right decisions is what made Belle unique. Look at her motives. They were genuine. Along her path she chose to give up what she had to help those who were suffering, or in the case of the musical instruments, she wanted to put them in a safe place for everyone to enjoy. Leaving all of this behind, she entered into eternity with a joyful soul." Maggie couldn't imagine dealing with the kind of power Belle had been given to rebuild the entire village.

Continuing to talk like a changed woman, Maggie said, "The world of imagination and the world of those who lust in search of gold treasures that might be in the mountain are opposing forces that ultimately collide to produce chaos for everyone. We all know that, read the books, the endings are always the same. The gold diggers and the corrupt landlords never get to see what is valuable in the land of *Everythink*. Belle chose the world of positive things, of creations, not destructions or deceits. It's why she gave her priceless collection of musical instruments to Yale. It's why she rebuilt Wistariahurst in Holyoke. It's why she restored the village, the Churches, and the Château in Hattonchâtel. She wanted to create something valuable, and then give it all away for everyone to enjoy. Belle wanted the world to see what she saw as worthwhile when her mind took her to her special place. It's about all of the parts, all of her decisions, John, not just any one of them." Maggie sat back, waiting for him to think about what she was saying.

John understood what she meant clearly, and he didn't need to say anything. Maggie had summed it up perfectly. He sat in his uncomfortable airplane seat, agreeing with her, thinking that he would have to make some changes in his own life if he wanted to find a legitimate reality for himself. It did seem as if he had been chosen to write a book to do it. Feeling hopeful that he was getting closer to finally figuring some things out and letting others go, John realized that a strong part of what it would be was sitting right next to him.

Just as Maggie was going to do what she knew in her heart to be right, bury the coin in the grand lady's grave, John was going to tell everyone everything that he had learned about the fabulous lady named Miss Belle Skinner. And Maggie was going to help him do it. By telling her story, they would share with the world the power of the values Belle learned in Holyoke and America, that made her so special and strong that she was able to change a part of the world. Once they did, maybe it would make a difference. Realizing what Belle did, someone else might do the same thing.

Who knows, John thought, maybe all the church bells of Holyoke might start ringing again as they did in the past to drive the devils out of the city. When they did, the saints would come back in.

The End

Coin of Louis The Pious, Son of Charlemagne.
Mint Unknown
Oxford, Ashmolean Museum

Epilogue

*I*n writing this book, one of my editors asked me to document the histories of some of the founders and developers of Holyoke who I name here. Thinking about it, I told her that it would be a challenge for anyone to do this. My own recollections of the city I grew up in were what convinced me of this. You see, for many of us who were raised in Holyoke, we are simply, from Holyoke. Even though all of us can trace our ancestry back to Ireland, England, Poland, Canada, Russia, Africa, Italy, Puerto Rico and many other countries, we are all from Holyoke. From well before 1800 until now, the city was a melting pot, just like America has been for many ethnic groups and cultures. For 150 years, immigrants have come to Holyoke from all over the world and left their marks. They became integral parts of the city's history. In some ways Holyoke became an island unto itself, a new homeland. People did not identify only with their former countries, they created a new community that in some ways produced a more powerful heritage than what they had left behind. They were all proud to be from Holyoke. They cast their lots with each other, sharing the good times and the bad, and built a wonderful city with a marvelous history. That's why so many of them are buried here. They're still together. Belle Skinner was one of them. She rests with those others who made Holyoke great. Writing this book has put this into perspective for me.

Jack Dunn